WHEN WE WERE STRANGERS

When We Were

Strangers

PAMELA SCHOENEWALDT

HARPER

NEW YORK · LONDON · TORONTO · SYDNEY

HARPER

WHEN WE WERE STRANGERS. Copyright © 2011 by Pamela Schoenewaldt. All rights reserved. Printed in the United States of America. No part of this book may be used or reproduced in any manner whatsoever without written permission except in the case of brief quotations embodied in critical articles and reviews. For information address HarperCollins Publishers, 10 East 53rd Street, New York, NY 10022.

HarperCollins books may be purchased for educational, business, or sales promotional use. For information please write: Special Markets Department, HarperCollins Publishers, 10 East 53rd Street, New York, NY 10022.

FIRST EDITION

Designed by Janet M . Evans

Library of Congress Cataloging-in-Publication Data
Schoenewaldt, Pamela.
    When we were strangers / Pamela Schoenewaldt. — 1st ed.
        p. cm.
    ISBN 978-0-06-200399-7 (pbk.)
        1. Italians—United States—Fiction. 2. Immigrants—United States—
Fiction. 3. Women immigrants—Fiction. 4. Women dressmakers—Fiction. 5.
Chicago (Ill.)—Fiction. I. Title.
PS3619.C4497W47 2011
813'.6—dc22

                                                                    2010018085

11 12 13 14 15   OV/BVG   10 9 8 7 6 5 4

For Maurizio,
whose presence in my life
is a constant coming home

Contents

One

Threads on the Mountain

I come from the village of Opi in Abruzzo, perched on the spine of Italy. As long as anyone remembers, our family kept sheep. We lived and died in Opi and those who left the mountain always came to ruin. "They died with strangers, Irma," my mother said over and over in her last illness, gasping between bouts of bloody coughing that soaked our rags as fast as I could clean them. "Your great-grandfather died in the snow with Frenchmen. Why?"

"Mamma, please. Try to rest."

All Opi knew how Luigi Vitale had left his land, his sheep, his sons and his house with three rooms and a stable to walk north out of Abruzzo and up through Italy to invade Russia with the Grand Army of Napoleon. On the long retreat from Moscow, a Russian peasant pinned Luigi's feet to the earth with a pitchfork and left him there to bleed and freeze to death. *"With Frenchmen, Irma. Why?"*

"Shh, Mamma. It doesn't matter now," I said, although I had always wondered why Luigi went to Russia even for a mercenary's pay if winters in Opi were cold enough to freeze a man to stone if that's the end he wanted.

The next to leave was my grandfather. Clever and ambitious, he said he'd find work in Milan's new factories, send for his wife and son and they would all live well in the North. Months later, news drifted home that brigands had robbed and killed him two days out of Abruzzo. I cooled my mother's brow with rosemary water. "Ernesto was different before that," she insisted. "He sang and told stories."

"Yes, Mamma." She must have been delirious, for I never once heard my father sing. Perhaps he told stories in the tavern, but at home he rarely spoke.

In 1860 her brother Emilio left Opi to enlist with General Giuseppe Garibaldi, but he died on the beach in Sicily. "His patriot blood nobly spilled so our country might live united and free," Father Anselmo read to my mother in a telegram signed by Garibaldi himself. From that day on, she called Sicily "that place, that cursed place that killed Emilio and threw him in a pit with strangers."

In 1871, when I was ten, all Opi was summoned to the church piazza, where Father Anselmo read a proclamation from Rome that said we must stand tall for we were now citizens of the glorious and invincible unified Kingdom of Italy. But unification changed nothing in our lives. We were still poor, we never saw the king and my mother still hated Sicily.

That year brought her sickness. At first the bright, dry summers and wild herbs I picked with Carlo eased the coughing, but then came that cruel mild winter. A wool merchant from Naples pressed for early shearing, pointing to the swelling buds on all the trees as signs of a marvelously forward spring. Old women pleaded with the men to wait, swearing that the stars, the birds, their very bones foretold a terrible coming cold. But the sheep were sheared and a good price paid for the wool. That night as men crowded our tavern to celebrate, a blizzard roared down the Alps. We pulled our breeding ewes from the fold and brought them home in the blinding snow, where for three days and nights there was only the stench of sheep to warm us. The rest of our naked flocks froze to death. Beasts ate their flesh. Two days later an avalanche covered the grain fields with rubble. And so began a hunger year, not Opi's worst, the old ones swore, but terrible enough. I washed clothes for the mayor's wife, who paid me the few centesimi her husband allowed. Carlo took day labor in the next valley, dragging himself home with barely strength to gnaw the bits of bread and onion that were our constant fare.

Slowly we rebuilt our flock and cleared the fields but my mother's cough dug deeper in her chest where no teas could help her. Fevers came in waves, and she coughed up threads of blood. My father sold our crucifix to pay for a city doctor who listened to her heart through a gleaming brass tube, wrapped clean white fingers around her wasted wrist and backed away from the bed. "Tell me what to do, sir," I pleaded.

"Sit with her, talk to her," he said quietly, refusing my father's coins. "No one can save her now." He gave us a vial of laudanum for the pain, put on his fine coat and gloves and left us.

On the morning of her last day, my mother whispered, "Irma, don't die with strangers."

"I won't, Mamma."

The soft fog of our breath hovered over the bed. My brother Carlo was there, my father and our aunt, old Zia Carmela, who had come to live with us. Neighbors filled our room, standing against the walls, the women crying softly. When Father Anselmo closed my mother's eyes, three women silently came forward to wash and dress her.

Walking home after the funeral, my father cleared his throat and said, "Irma, you must cook and clean for me now as Rosa did."

"Yes, Papà."

"And you will sing her songs and wear her clothes. You will do this for respect. You are an Opi woman now."

Barely sixteen, I felt as old and shabby as my mother's brown shawl, melting into Opi and the place carved out for me. As I knew my own plain face in our tin mirror, I knew each stone in the four walls and floor of our house. I knew the narrow streets draped across the mountain crest like threads for lacework never finished, unraveling into shepherds' trails. These threads caught and held me like a web. I knew which families had carved wooden doors and which had rough nailed planks. I knew the voices and shapes of our people. By the sound of their footsteps I knew which of them walked behind me. I knew the old women's coughs, the old men's stories, the good husbands and those who came home stinking drunk from wine on market day. I knew why the mayor's wife covered her bruises with a fine silk shawl. In a tapestry of Opi you'd see me in the shade of the olive trees with my dull brown hair and face turned away.

Opi was mine, but after my mother died, I grew anxious. If I didn't wed soon, how could I live? It was not for love that poor girls sought husbands. We yearned for daily bread and a tight roof, firewood in winter and with luck a man who wouldn't beat us, who would talk with us in the long evenings and comfort us when children died. We hoped, above all, for a man who was healthy and did not drink, who worked each day and helped us bear the hunger years.

Single women rarely had claim to a house in Opi. Zia Carmela lived with my father, who kept his aging sister out of charity. She hoped to die before he did, for who would take her then? And who would keep me? Carlo was good to us in his own rough way, but not a man to keep a sister or an old blind aunt. If by chance he married, it might be to a jealous wife who did not care to share her home. Father Anselmo said I had a neat enough hand to sew for fine ladies, but where were the fine ladies? Three of our pretty girls had found good husbands in Pescasseroli. But I was not pretty, had no light foot for dancing and my dowry of 120 lire would not tempt any decent man.

"Our wool fetched a good price at market," Carlo told my father that spring. "Let Irma buy some cloth for a new dress. She doesn't have to look like she's from Opi, this lump on the miserable spine of Italy."

"Silence!" my father ordered. "A man who scorns his birthplace is worse than a gypsy."

So I would have no new dress. Slipping out to the well in the damp, windy evening, I let Carlo's words turn in my mind. Yes, there was truth in them. Even our name, *Opi*, was a bitten-off, rag-end of a name, nothing next to *Pescasseroli*, a morning's walk from Opi and the biggest city I'd ever seen. What pushed our ancestors up this mountain and kept them here with our sheep and tight little dialect? We tried to talk like city people, but keen ears caught the drag in our words. I told Zia Carmela, "I don't even have to open my mouth. People just look at me and know where I'm from." I turned so the shadows hid my high Vitale nose.

Half blind from lace-making, Zia traced my profile with her finger and said, "You must be proud, Irma. Our ancestors sailed from Greece before Rome was ever built." I put down my needlework and stared into the fire until the licking flames became high-prowed ships bearing warriors with our noses west to Opi.

Carlo spat at the hearth and muttered, "Greece is a rock, old woman. What fool leaves one rock for another? You think these ancestors had worms in the head, like our idiot sheep? Before there was Rome we lived here in caves, like beasts." My father smoked his pipe and was silent. He had never once considered his nose or told me to be proud.

"There's always the church," old women told girls with no beauty or too many sisters. We knew what they meant: if a man won't marry you, the Lord always will. They sent my pockmarked cousin Filomena to the convent of San Salvatore in Naples. A year later her father went to visit and found her gone. "To the streets," the nuns hinted darkly. He stormed back to Opi, tore apart everything that Filomena had ever sewn or knitted and threw the pieces out the door. It was the week of high winds. Soon we found shreds of Filomena's work everywhere: bits of cloth on the bench near the baker's shop and by the village well, a scrap of red in a crevice by the church stairs. When I carried lunch to my father in the fields, a bright thread snagged on a rock might be hers. But Filomena herself would still be in Opi if there had been men enough for all of us.

In those years, we had five men my age. The two best ones had already spoken for the baker's beautiful daughters. The next two were imbeciles, twins born early and barely able to dress themselves. Gabriele, the fifth, beat his sheep and bitch dog so hard that she lost her pups, beat his crippled mother and beat the earth when he had nothing better.

My father said, "Don't worry, Irma. It won't be Gabriele." But who?

"Sell the north field and give her a better dowry," Carlo suggested, but my father refused. The mayor's price was an insult, he said, and that field had been Vitale land for generations. "Then you watch," said Carlo. "He'll get you back." Carlo was right. We lost our water rights to the field and then no one else would buy it. Still my father would not sell to the mayor. Soon after, men from Pescasseroli claimed my father had broken into their fold on a dark night and bred his ewes on their prize rams.

"Liars," my father swore. "The Good Shepherd himself couldn't move ewes in heat through that stinking town at night and nobody hear them."

When even Father Anselmo could not bring peace, men in Pescasseroli spoke harshly to me on market day and my father said I must never go down to the city again. In truth I was glad, for once they heard about Filomena, even women whispered at my back: "Look, there goes another Opi mountain whore."

So Carlo took our goods to Pescasseroli and brought back what we needed. One market day he came home late and elated. "Listen," he demanded as I spooned out lentils and onions and my father silently cut our bread. "Alfredo the blacksmith is in America. He sent a letter home and the schoolmaster read it out loud in the piazza."

My father's spoon knocked the wooden trencher. "Well," said Zia finally, "what did this letter say?"

Carlo's eyes glittered in the firelight. "Alfredo found work making steel in a place called Pittsburgh. Everyone there is lucky, everyone. A day laborer from Naples has his own grocery now. Two orphan sisters from Calabria have a dry goods store and rent out rooms above it. Alfredo rides streetcars. He has two good suits and lives in a big wooden boardinghouse. On a regular night, not even a feast day, they have beef, potatoes, tomatoes, beer, soft white bread and pie with apples," Carlo finished triumphantly, tearing at his crust.

"Soft bread?" my father snorted. "Did that boy lose his teeth in America? And tomatoes? My grandfather never ate tomatoes and not my father either."

Carlo exploded. "In Rome, in Pescasseroli, in Opi, you old fool, people eat tomatoes now. Only here in this hovel, we eat like a hundred years ago: dry bread, lentils, onions, watered wine and whatever cheese we can't sell. I bet pigs eat better in America."

My father pushed away from the table, walked to the fire and kicked a log so hard that the wood splintered and blazed. "Alfredo lives in a wooden house. What will he do when it burns?"

"Find another one," Carlo snapped. "At least he won't die on a rock."

A week later, Carlo threw his sheepskin cloak on our table and told my father, "Here, take it, sell it, give it to the beggar. I don't want to walk around dressed like a sheep anymore, following sheep, eating sheep cheese, smelling sheep shit all day. You know what we are up here? God's drool on the mountain."

"Hush," Zia Carmela scolded. "The Lord will punish you."

"Not likely, old woman. He doesn't even know we're here."

"Don't be an *idiota*, Carlo. You're a shepherd and *basta*," my father shouted as Carlo stormed out to the tavern. Nobody touched the cloak all evening, and at night I used it to cover myself and Zia in bed.

Early the next morning Carlo followed me to the well. "I'm going to America," he whispered. I kept walking. "Say something, Irma. Don't you believe me?"

"Remember what Mamma said? If you leave Opi, you'll die with strangers."

"What did Mamma know? She never saw the other side of Pescasseroli. Listen, I met a man with an uncle in Naples who runs merchant ships to Tripoli, in Africa."

"Africa isn't America."

"I know that, but listen. We work six months for this uncle and then he buys us passage to America. Second class, in cabins."

"He says that, but he won't."

"He will. And my friend has a cousin who'll find us work in Cleveland."

"What's Cleveland?"

"A big city in America full of jobs."

"Suppose you get sick? Do you understand, Carlo, dying alone? No one to have a mass said for you or light a candle for your soul." The baker's cat had caught a pigeon and was eating it by the well. "You'll die like a beast. Like that," I said, pointing.

Carlo took our water bucket, set it down and gripped my shoulders. "Irma, believe me, it's better than working here like a beast. Better than living in one stone room with *him*. He's worse every year since Mamma died." Carlo stepped closer. "You can't stay here when I'm gone. Come with me."

"To work on a ship? No. And who'll care for Zia?"

"When I'm in Cleveland, I'll send for you, you'll get a job and then we can both send her money."

"I can't leave, Carlo, you know that."

He sighed and took his rucksack from a hollow in the chestnut tree. So it was not soon that he was going—or the next morning, which would have been hard enough—but right away, that afternoon. I gripped the linen shirt I'd made him. Carlo held my hands. "Listen, Irma, I'll write to you."

"You don't know how."

"I'll find a scribe. I'll write from Tripoli and then from America." He kissed me and touched my face. "God keep you, Irma. I have to go. They're meeting me at noon on the Naples road."

"Then *addio*," I whispered, go with God, and then more loudly, "Addio."

"Addio, Irma. Take care of yourself. I'll write." Then Carlo walked quickly down the narrow street we grandly called Via Italia. Not ten paces and his feet disappeared as the road dipped down. With each pace, more of his legs dropped from sight, then his back, straight shoulders and finally the peak of his red woolen cap. Soon our domed rock hid him. When I saw him again, he was a speck on the road to Pescasseroli.

Carlo never wrote. My father asked everywhere, but nobody had ever heard of an uncle with merchant ships to Tripoli. "Perhaps he met a traveler with an uncle," I suggested.

My father spat. "And believed a *traveler?*"

With Carlo gone, there was no more fighting in the house, but now silence filled the room, pressing on us everywhere like the smell of wet sheep. That summer the baker died and his widow Assunta took over the bakery. After three months of mourning, both her daughters married. My father drank himself sick at the wedding feast. Still, two good things happened that season. The ewes gave such rich milk that our cheese fetched well at market. And just before Christmas, Father Anselmo hired me to make an embroidered altar cloth for the church. He even brought us beeswax candles so we had light to work in the evening and Zia Carmela could see enough to knit thick sweaters we sold to farmers. But our silent evenings were longer now. We never spoke of Carlo and no one in Opi ever mentioned him again, as if he'd never lived.

The winter passed slowly. On days too cold for outside work, my father fed the sheep and then sat by the fire watching me sew. Sometimes he said, "Sing Rosa's song about the moon." When he called me

Rosa once, Zia Carmela snapped: "She's *Irma.* Don't go soft in the head, old man." Aside from these sudden sparks, the click of our needles and the crackle of fire, there was only the swish of my sweeping, the knock of our wooden bowls as I rinsed them, the crunch of raw onions at meals and the thud of the fresh loaves I brought from the bakery each week and set on the table. The end of each week brought new sounds: dry crusts rattling in our bread box.

When Father Anselmo came to inspect my work, he said he'd heard that Alfredo's three cousins would join him soon in America. Two families from the next valley were going as well. Giovanni, the shoemaker's son, had sent enough money from a place called Chicago to build a new house for his parents and buy back their fields. He said he'd be home in a year to court the landlord's widow.

"She wouldn't refuse him now," Zia muttered.

"Perhaps Carlo will write from Cleveland," I said. My father's jaw twitched but he said nothing. We sat in silence as the fire spat.

Father Anselmo watched me, my head bowed over the altar cloth. "Irma needs a husband." He sighed. "But there're hardly any young men left even in Pescasseroli with so many going to America. Did you hear? The mayor's daughter is marrying Old Tommaso." I gripped my needle. So what I heard at the well was true: no decent man wanted Anna now that her belly was swelling. If clubfooted Old Tommaso took her, the mayor would forgive his debts. Poor Anna, who was so beautiful that she might have had a doctor's son.

"Don't worry," said my father gruffly, "Irma's fine." Just then, I realized that since Carlo left, there had been no more talk of a husband for me. Could I *not* marry? Perhaps if the altar cloth was fine enough, Father Anselmo might recommend me to other priests in other towns. I pricked myself to keep from dreaming. What if my father died? I couldn't sew and also keep sheep, and no single woman I knew, even in Pescasseroli, lived by her needle alone. But if I didn't marry soon, who would want me when I was old and still wearing my mother's clothes?

"Keep sewing," said Zia. "We'll think of something."

I tried to imagine Carlo in America, but it was like searching out a sheep in a snowstorm. I could not picture my brother in a foreign land. Yet the word "America" tossed in my mind until it lost all sense and seemed merely strange, like the fruits that Father Anselmo said people ate far away: pineapple, coconuts and bananas.

The winter crept on silently, my needle flying. At least we had light, but now candle flames glittered in my father's eyes. When Carlo was with us, they both stared at the fire and smoked all evening. Now my father's gaze fixed on me as I moved around the little room, dragging at my skirts like wet ferns in a forest. Carlo's voice came drumming back: "You can't stay here when I'm gone."

One night after dinner, my father lurched from his seat, as I lit the beeswax candles. He grabbed my wrist and snapped, "Rosa, get me Carlo's wool shears."

"She's not Rosa, old man, and it's not shearing time," Zia snapped.

"Get them," my father repeated.

I went to our shelf. Carlo had been so proud of his shears, never trusting the journeyman knife sharpener, but honing them carefully and keeping them wrapped in soft wool. Carlo will come back—I had comforted myself all winter—if only for his shears. But I gave my father the woolen package and never saw the shears again. I heard he traded them at the tavern for half their worth in credit.

One evening early in Lent, I had finished a piece of the altar cloth and was pressing it on our board while Zia Carmela dozed in her chair. My father came in from the tavern and stepped behind me. With a grunt, he pulled the warm cloth from the board and wrapped it around my shoulders. His rough hands grazed my breasts, then cupped them. "No!" I shouted. "Stop!" but stone walls swallowed my voice. He grabbed my dress. When I pulled back, the sleeve ripped like lightning sheering mountain air.

"Come here, Rosa," my father whispered hoarsely. "Show yourself off like a rich merchant's wife." I gripped a chair, burning with shame.

Zia Carmela, groping, found the altar cloth and snatched it from my shoulders. "Ernesto! Go back in the tavern, you filthy goat. Leave Irma alone."

"Why can't I see her in lace? She's pretty."

"Stop it! The Lord's watching you," she shrieked.

"Let Him watch!" My father hit the board so hard the iron fell, ringing on the stone hearth. Lunging, he yanked the altar cloth from Zia's lap and wrapped it around me again, pushing into my breasts. He pulled me to our mirror hanging by the fire. "Look!" he commanded. "See? You're pretty now!" My face in the cracked glass was white as frost on stone.

"She's ugly, Ernesto! Leave her alone!" Zia shouted, hitting my father with her walking stick. I twisted away and the altar cloth fell at my feet. Kicking it aside and dodging my father's grasping hands, I shoved open our heavy plank door and stumbled into the street. Cold air burned my throat.

Through the door I heard coughing, wood splintering and my father crying out, "What do you want from me, Carmela? You think I'm not a man?"

"Irma!" Zia wailed, but I didn't stop.

I was running now, wood-soled shoes clattering on the stone streets: "Ugly, ugly," and then: "You think I'm not a man?" My chest ached, my breasts burned. I stumbled to the stone bench outside the bakery, panting. For a blessed minute I felt only the slow easing of my chest and the gathering cold. Then words came spinning out like knives: *Bread, how do I earn my bread? Ugly, how can I marry? Man, you think I'm not a man?*

Everyone in Opi knew of the woodcutter's daughter who had lived with her father and lame mother. When the girl's belly bulged and then flattened, people whispered that a babe had been smothered in birthing sheets and buried in secret, for it was an abomination. Why else was the girl found hanging from their roof beam, the weeping mother trying helplessly to pull her down and the father blind drunk, stumbling through the forest?

Cold closed around me tighter than my cloak. Where could I go? If I knocked on any door, people would know my voice and take me in, welcoming yet curious, for no decent woman walked outside at night. But what would I say, what would they think and how would they look at me tomorrow? What would become of us all after I ruined my family's name, and how could I face Zia if my own words tore bread from our mouths?

I started back, dragging my fear like chains. I thought of my great-grandfather freezing in an enemy land. Before that Russian pitchfork nailed him to his death, he must have dreamed of home. Where else can one go for comfort? In the empty streets, wooden shutters rattled in the wind. Sounds leaked out: children crying, singing from some few houses, from others came moans and grunts of pleasure. I knew what happened at night and why young couples met in the thick bushes or dark streets, even in shadows behind the church. No, I vowed, not for me, never.

Cold tore through my thin wool dress. If frostbite chewed my fingers, how could I sew? Outside our house I pressed my ear to the door. My father was snoring. I slipped into the house and then into the bed I shared with Zia. "Come close, Irma, you're so cold," she whispered, holding me like a child and stroking the ugly from my body.

My father rose long before dawn, pulled on his cloak and ate his bread standing, his face turned away from us. When he had left the house and his steps faded into wind, Zia pulled me out of bed. "He needs a wife," she announced.

"Like old Tommaso? A girl half his age?"

"No, not a girl, a woman. Assunta the baker's widow is lonely. She and Ernesto used to go walking together, but then the baker spoke for her and Ernesto took up with your mother." Nobody had ever told me this, not once in the long evenings. "Irma, you go buy some bread. I have to see Father Anselmo." When I tried to protest that this was not our bread-buying day, she pressed a coin in my hand and pushed me firmly out the door.

I went to the bakery. "Good morning, Signora Assunta," I said, watching her sweep out crumbs for the birds that flocked our door each morning. "I'll have one of your loaves with a light crust, please. My father says that with your fresh bread and his cheese, a prince himself could be content." The Lord forgive this lie, my father never spoke of princes.

"Ernesto said so? Here's a nice one, Irma, warm from the oven. Give your father my regards."

"Thank you, Signora. I will." Go on, I told myself. More. "He was saying just last night what a good man your husband was, how hard it must have been to lose him."

"Yes, Matteo was good to us, God rest his soul." We crossed ourselves.

"And your daughters are gone too, Signora Assunta. Your house must feel so empty." I gripped the loaf. "Ours too, since my mother died." We crossed ourselves again. Assunta was not a bad woman, not grasping or sharp. She fed cripples and beggars with day-old bread, not stale crusts like the baker in Pescasseroli. She would be good for my father and good to Zia perhaps, but would she want another woman in her house? I pulled Carlo's cloak around the loaf and held it to my chest. Customers were crowding in, calling impatiently for their loaves. I dropped my copper coin in the money box and slipped out the door.

"Signora Assunta sends her regards," I told my father at dinner. "She said she's lonely now with her daughters gone."

"And that's my affair?" my father snapped, but he chewed his bread more slowly. A week passed in silence. He still went to the tavern, but on Sunday afternoon he combed his hair, washed his face and hands, put on leather shoes and a good shirt and did not come home until evening. Our coins dwindled but at least we had peace.

Father Anselmo came to our house to ask for an embroidered medallion on the cloth that would show altar boys where to set the communion chalice. I worked hard to make the circle perfect for this holy purpose. Then I started the border of leafy vines. As the days crept past, a catechism looped through my mind.

Marry in Opi? No, for there are no men to wed.

Marry in Pescasseroli? Who? Even if there was a man to wed me, for all my life I'd hear women whisper: "Opi mountain slut."

Stay with my father? And if he came after me again, if Zia wasn't there?

Live in Opi alone, unwed? How could I earn my bread? Who would help me in a hunger year?

Call down death like the woodcutter's daughter? I stared at the cross on our wall. Father Anselmo would not bury the girl in the churchyard, for by taking her own life she had damned her soul. The folds of the altar cloth ran over my legs like the hills around Opi. How could I live in these hills?

Leave Opi? To die with strangers? The needle grooved a line in my thumb. "It is better to die alone than to live here like a beast," Carlo once said. What of the two sisters from Calabria in Alfredo's letter with the dry goods store and rooms to rent? But they had each other, they were not from Opi and did not bear the Vitale curse on those who leave our mountain.

On the eighth night my father stood over me as I sewed, blocking my light. I worked in darkness until he left for the tavern. Then I pulled out my last stitches, for they were all ragged and wild. On the ninth morning Zia made me stay in bed. "What's wrong with her?" my father demanded. "Why isn't she up?"

"Women's sickness," my Zia announced briskly. "You go buy the bread today." He looked at us sharply. Only women bought the bread in our village. Besides, I was never sick. "It's early, there's nobody there yet," Zia said quickly, handing my father his cloak.

His eyes grazed the mirror as he ran a rough hand through his hair. "I'll do it," he said gruffly, "this once."

When my father came back with our loaf, larger than usual and very light, he and Zia ate in silence as I lay turned away to the wall. When he left for the fields I got up and set my chair in the doorway to finish the last bit of fringe. Zia's knitting needles sat idle in her lap. "Are *you* sick, Zia?" I asked finally. "Do your eyes hurt?"

"No, they're just tired. Go on. You could finish today." Early that afternoon I did finish. Together we cleaned our table carefully and laid the altar cloth across it. Father Anselmo would be pleased, but it seemed that I had made my own shroud. Zia Carmela stroked the cloth, grazing the medallion, the border and silky fringe. "Irma," she said quietly, "light a candle, close the door and get me the iron box from under our bed."

"Why?"

"Just get it." She had never undressed in front of me, so I didn't know that a tiny brass key hung inside her skirts. She had me open the box. "Look inside. What do you see?"

"Nothing but old boots." They were frothed with mildew and nibbled by mice, stiff as wood. Not even a goatherd would wear such boots. Then I saw the holes, close together and piercing the soles.

"Is that—?"

"Yes. Your great-grandfather, remember, was stabbed to death in Russia. He must have fought bravely, for the captain honored his dying wish and sent the boots home to his widow. She cleaned them and bought this box to keep them. Give me the boots, Irma, and watch." I set them in her lap and pulled my stool beside her.

She felt both heels, then cradled one boot and gently twisted the sole from the heel. A small chamois bag fell out. Bent fingers teased it open and I gasped at the glint of gold coins. "This was Luigi's pay from Russia. It has been kept by the women in our family for the one who would truly need it."

"All this time? My mother said they sold their beds once in a hunger year. They ate boiled straw."

Zia Carmela closed the gold in my hand. "We knew those times would pass, but you must go to America, Irma. There's no life for you here. Father Anselmo says that in America even decent girls can earn their own bread. Perhaps you'll find Carlo in that place called Cleveland. If not, at least you can work. You can make beautiful things with your needle." Her hands trembled.

"But Zia, I can't leave you."

"You know that I love you like my own soul, Irma. But you must go. You know your father. What will happen if he drinks again and comes after you?"

"But to go so far. Why not an Italian city: Milan, Rome or Naples?" I suggested wildly.

"We have no family there. People would think—Irma, you know what they would think."

That I was a mountain slut. "We don't know that Carlo reached America. He never wrote," I reminded her.

"No, he didn't, but Alfredo did. He's content. You're clever and work hard. You'll go to Naples, find a good ship and cross the ocean. You'll find rich women in Cleveland and sew for them."

"Come with me, Zia."

"How? I can't even walk down the mountain." Her bent fingers stroked mine. "You go, make money, and come back like Giovanni the shoemaker's son."

"And buy us a house?" I said slowly.

She gripped my hand. "Perhaps. But first you must leave Opi. Father Anselmo has some papers for you. There's a cold wind today. Take Carlo's cloak." She felt for it on the nail by our door and wrapped it around my shoulders. I put on my wooden shoes and hurried to the church.

Father Anselmo was cleaning the communion chalice. He sat me near him as he worked. "Irma, you know I came to Opi from Milan," he said quietly. "Your own people came from Greece, Carmela says. The world is full of adventurers, more than you think."

"But that was long ago. My mother said—"

"Carmela told me what she said, that all who leave will die. But Irma, your mother died in her own bed and the baker died in his shop, kneading bread. Death finds us where it will, and every soul leaves this world alone. Is it the ship that frightens you?"

Yes, that too. I had never seen a ship, an ocean or even a great lake. My heart rocked inside my chest. Cold seeped through my wooden shoes. "I don't know anyone in America. And Carlo never wrote to us," I added, my voice cracking.

"Letters take a long time. Carmela told me what happened that night, what your father tried to do. If he marries Assunta, can you stay here even then, you *and* Carmela?" I said nothing. Assunta was kind, but perhaps not kind enough to keep two women in her small house. A mouse skimmed over the paving stones and disappeared beneath the baptismal font. "Irma, *can* you stay?" he repeated.

I stared at my hands laid open on my lap. "Perhaps not, but I'm afraid of leaving, Father."

"Of course. But what can we give you in Opi, we who love you? Many find happiness in America. And if we have another hunger year, you can send money to help your family. It's better that way, is it not, than to live here by charity? Or to marry a man who will use you badly?"

I closed my eyes. No other way appeared.

"The Lord will watch over you, my child, as the shepherd keeps his sheep. He will watch your going out and your coming forth," the warm, familiar voice continued. Tears dotted my hands. "Here." Father Anselmo pulled a soft cloth from his sleeve and dried my eyes. Outside the hour chimed. He cleared his throat. "Irma, look." He pulled out a sheaf of folded papers. My birth certificate, he explained, and a letter to the ship's captain and port officers in America that I was of good character from an honest family, skilled in fine needlecraft, that he had hired me himself and was pleased with my work. "And this is for you," he said, holding up a rosary of tiny coral beads. "It weighs nothing but will comfort you on your journey. If Carlo writes, I will tell him to find you in Cleveland. I'll have Ernesto release your dowry and see that he and Assunta keep Zia after they marry."

"Thank you, Father," I managed. So it had all been arranged without me. When we culled ewes for market or slaughter, the others went on grazing, barely noting their sisters' leaving. Once I was culled, Opi too would continue without me. My eyes ran over the windows and frescos of the church, the columns and oak pulpit I might never see again, and ended at Father Anselmo's patient face. "Will you give Zia the altar-cloth money so she won't go to Assunta a beggar?"

He promised and walked me to the church door. "Addio, Irma," he said, and kissed my two cheeks. "Write to us."

That afternoon I walked down every street in Opi. It seemed the wind had blown out word of my leaving as it once blew Filomena's threads through our town. The mayor's wife drew me behind a chestnut tree by the well. Her little daughter asked eagerly, "You're going to America, Irma?"

"Hush," said her mother and pressed twenty lire into my hand. "Buy something pretty in Naples." She stepped closer. "They say in America, women don't have to marry. It's a wonderful country."

"Will Irma come back?" the child whispered.

"No, never!" said her mother fiercely, her eyes blazing. I had never felt envy before. She kissed me and hurried away, pulling the child behind her.

I *would* come back, I told myself. But when? For now I must take Opi with me. I climbed to the high, flat rock where our pastures began, took out a scrap of cloth and sketched with needle and black thread the jagged line of our city wall, the mayor's house, our church and bell tower and finally the low jumble of the street where I lived— where I once lived. The sun was low by the time I went home. My father, who never returned before dark, had dragged his chair to the doorway, his lined face russet in the waning light.

"Your dowry's there on the table, one hundred twenty lire," he said gruffly. "Wherever you go, tell people that you are a Vitale from Opi. Here, take these too." He gave me a salami and small wheel of our cheese. "You can eat decent food until Naples, at least. Work hard in America and send money as soon as you can. You're a good girl. Don't dishonor us." I could not remember my father ever making a longer speech.

"Will you marry Assunta?" I asked. He shrugged. So yes, he would marry. "And Zia will live with you?"

My father glanced at Zia and nodded. Then he jerked his head toward the hearth where I kept my pressing irons. "And Irma," he added gruffly, "that night when . . . that night I was thinking of your mother, wanting her." He cleared his throat. "A man gets lonely, that's all." He stood up heavily as if these words had exhausted him. Then he pressed my shoulder, pulled his cloak from its peg and left us for the tavern. He did not speak to me again.

After my silent meal with Zia, I pressed the altar cloth and scented it with lavender oil, and then packed my sewing box, documents and rosary from Father Anselmo, my few clothes and apron, good shoes and a small stone pried from the wall of our house. I blew out our candle and climbed into bed beside Zia. When I tried to speak, she whispered, "Hush, rest." She cried in her sleep and I held her tightly. When I woke, my father had already gone to the fields.

At dawn, I drew water from the well for the last time. Assunta met me there with a small dense loaf, still warm. "It's good for traveling," she said. "And don't worry, I'll take good care of your Zia."

"Thank you, Assunta." Tears wet the loaf and I brushed them away with my shawl.

"Listen to me, Irma, your father is a good man."

I said nothing.

"When he was young," Assunta insisted, "he had a beautiful laugh. You know that he and your mother lost three babies before Carlo was born? He told me once that he was afraid of loving his children too much and then losing them." My father never spoke of this. Perhaps I would never have known this if I wasn't leaving Opi. "It's true. Here," said Assunta, pressing five pewter buttons into my hand. "They're very fine. You can sell them in America for a good price or use them yourself." I tried to thank her, but she hurried away. The buttons in my hand grew as warm as the bread as I made my way home. My last coming home. My last time mounting our worn stone step.

Morning sun cut through our window. "It's time," said Zia as I entered the room. "Now leave me Carlo's cloak and go." She sat in her chair without moving as the goat boy clattered down the street. I put my dowry and the gold in a chamois bag I hung between my breasts. Then I smoothed Carlo's cloak over our bed, lit a candle and knelt by Zia's chair. She touched my face, my nose, and kissed my two hands. "When you are safe in America," she said, clasping my hands so tightly that they ached, "write to me."

"Yes, Zia, I promise." When I tried to kiss her, she gently pushed me away.

"Go now, Irma. Be proud and God keep you."

I left, the bag beating against my heart as I hurried down our mountain and the birds cried, "Stranger, stranger passing."

Two

ATTILIO

By the time I reached Pescasseroli, my shadow had shrunk to a puddle. I took cover from the noonday sun in a slice of shade beneath the city gate while once-familiar streets gaped and taunted: "Mountain girl, if you're so afraid now, how will you get to America?" Working my rosary to calm myself, I realized one small blessing: the streets were nearly empty. Merchants' wives must be resting in the cool of their high-ceilinged, curtained rooms while husbands drowsed in shops and market stalls. Perhaps no one would point to my pack and ask with a smirk if I was bound for a convent, like *Sister* Filomena.

As I crossed the main piazza, only a pair of sleepy beggars watched me fill my water pouch at the fountain, not for thirst, but by habit. Once when we were young, Carlo had passed a mountain stream in summer without drinking. "Idiota," my father cried. "The next one could be dry." He didn't waste his breath to add: "Irma, you drink too."

Rinsing my face and arms, I looked up and saw Opi sitting like a brown-gray lid on the mountain. A jagged line of rock and trees seemed for a moment like a crowd of all my people: my father and Zia, Assunta, the mayor's wife, Father Anselmo, even Gabriele and the goat boy all there without me. "Irma embroidered this before she left," the women might say as my altar cloth was laid out next Sunday, but then talk would drift to wool prices, an ailing child or a marauding wolf the men must hunt. My father rarely spoke of my mother after her death and doubtless he would not speak of me after I left Opi. My shoulders shook until a beggar turned his bleary eyes at me. "Go," I told myself. "Move your legs." I gave the beggar a piece of my bread.

"God bless you," he murmured and added, "wherever you're bound, signorina."

Outside the city walls, the road curved south, drawing me from Opi as we drew weaning lambs from their ewes. To keep from looking back, I fixed on pine needles pressed in packed earth, on dragonflies and thorny humps of blackberry bushes that would bear fruit when I was gone. I watched the clouds, not the whole ones we saw from the mountaintop, but white bulges glimpsed through trees. The water pouch dug at my shoulder and the money bag beat at my breasts. I thought of embroidery stitches and catechisms, anything but home.

After perhaps an hour of walking I came upon a gray-haired peddler fixing his cartwheel, copper pots neatly stacked by a ruddy, broad-backed horse tethered to a tree. "Brace the spokes?" the man asked the horse thoughtfully. "Good idea, Rosso. Such a clever boy." My father never spoke so kindly to any man.

I offered the peddler a drink, for his brow gleamed with sweat. He swallowed, glanced at me, and when I nodded, drank again and then wiped the spout with a clean cloth. "Thank you kindly," he said. "I did need that." He had a long wedge of nose, waves of wrinkles ruffling his face, a wide smile and kind eyes. "My name is Attilio," he said. "And this is my companion, Rosso. We're bound for Naples to buy copper pots. And you, signorina?" he asked politely.

My throat went dry. To inquire of a name was surely common enough for city people and travelers, but at home we knew each other as we knew our own clothes. "Irma Vitale," I managed. "Daughter of Ernesto Vitale. Of Opi."

"Opi? Oh yes, just north of here, no? Too small for my trade. But," he added quickly, "I'm sure it's a fine town."

I nodded. Soon nobody would have heard of Pescasseroli. Strangers might stare at me as we once surrounded an African juggler who ventured into Opi. We children had dared each other to touch his sheep-thick hair and Carlo asked Mamma if his skin had been burned to make it so black. Father Anselmo overheard and whispered, "Hush, Carlo. Don't you see a child of God?"

"So Irma, are you bound for America perhaps?" Attilio asked. Was America written on my face? "I'm guessing," he added quickly. "We see more people going all the time, even whole families."

"Not from Opi. My brother left, but no one else."

Attilio bent over his work. "Well, some places are like that."

When I asked how far we were from Naples, Attilio scanned my shoes and bundle. "With good weather a man on foot might get there in five days. But a woman alone would do well to find a group to travel with or a family at least. Further on you can get a train." Carlo had described long iron boxes on iron wheels that ran faster than any horse. People rattled and slid inside the wagons unless they had lire for first-class salon cars. Attilio cleared his throat. "Signorina, you could ride with us. You hardly weigh much. Rosso's strong and I'd welcome the company."

It was true that peddlers often took travelers free for just this reason.

Even respectable women accepted rides on a public road. They sat in back and nobody gossiped. How else could they get to market without a horse? Attilio seemed honest. He was respectful to me and kind to Rosso. He worked steadily at the cartwheel, letting himself be studied. He was a good man; I knew this as surely as I knew how much wool a sheep might yield or how long a line of stitches a pull of thread could make. Still, surely it was better to pay for favors from a stranger. I saw rips in his shirt and vest.

"I'll mend those clothes if you get me to Naples safely."

"You needn't, signorina. Many peddlers gave me rides before I bought Rosso. It costs me nothing to return the favor."

"I can embroider as well if you'd like something made for your wife," I added, for there was an air of married man around him; the locket around his neck surely held a portrait. I took from my pack an apron I had made for my mother in her last sickness. Yellow poppies and wild roses bloomed across the linen. She had judged each flower sharply before her strength fell away. "What poppy droops like this?" she demanded. I remade the petals, cupping them to the sun. "How can it bloom?" she asked of my first rose bud. In her last days, she held the finished apron weakly in her hands and raised it to her face. "Smells of roses," she whispered, and slept with the apron in her arms.

Attilio studied the flowers gravely. "You have a gift, Irma. Your needle paints. Yes, perhaps you could help me." He plucked from his own pack a fringed shawl of fine blue muslin. "A present for my wife. She is not well." He chewed his lower lip for so long that I finally asked, "Would you like a design on the shawl?"

"Yes, a design." He stroked the muslin. "She took fever last winter. Afterwards, she was as gentle as ever but like a child." He looked up. "She still loves roses."

I traced a line where the blooms might go, and we agreed on three full-blown roses with tendrils and buds. I would mend his torn clothes as well. At the next market town Attilio would buy thread and English needles and help me choose a good ship in Naples, for he said it sometimes happened that people bought tickets for ships that had already sailed. A fair exchange, even Carlo would agree, but I was astonished how many steps lay between me and America and how easily one might slip.

When he'd fixed the broken spoke, Attilio cleared a place beside him, handed me his torn vest and we started south. Opi women would have plucked my sleeve and asked, "Irma, have you lost your wits to sit beside a stranger?" They might whisper at our well that mending leads easily to other "services" for a man whose wife has turned simple. But they hadn't seen how gently he held the muslin shawl or how when he offered me onion slices he held them by the edge so that not even his fingertips grazed mine.

Spring rains had left the road so lumpy that I pricked myself constantly as I sewed. "Here, Irma," said Attilio. "Use this." He held out a spongy spike of aloe leaf and showed how to squeeze the healing jelly on my bleeding fingers. "The road gets better soon. Just look around for a bit now. You've never been so far from home, I wager."

Never. So close to Opi and so much had changed, even in women's dresses, their skirt borders, the cut of bodices and puff of sleeves. The language, too, was changing. When a boy called out to a group of girls, making them laugh, Attilio had to explain the joke to me. In Naples, would I seem as foreign as the African in Opi? All afternoon the road thickened with travelers: merchants, friars, gypsies, shepherds and goatherds with their flocks, ragged soldiers wandering home and rich

signori whose coachmen shouted us aside. We passed families going
to America, one with a baby who would take its first steps there.

"Irma, who do you know in America?" Attilio asked.

"My brother Carlo left to work on a ship for Tripoli and earn his
passage to America. By now he could be in Cleveland."

"I see. So he might not meet you at the New York port?" I took a
stitch and shook my head. Attilio cleared his throat. "I've heard that
American police question single girls to make sure they won't be a—
problem." A "problem" like Filomena, did he mean?

I tugged at the thread. "My Zia said I could sew for rich women in
Cleveland. I thought I'd go to a shop or ask at churches for work while
I look for Carlo."

"I see."

I read doubt in Attilio's quiet face and now my stomach ached like
the night I ran from my father. Cast out of Opi, closed out of America,
would I be homeless as the wind?

"Don't worry, Irma, we'll stay with my sister's family tonight and
think how to help you." Bent over my work, I nodded and sewed, trying to think only of stitches. "See? The road is easier now," Attilio said
kindly. "You aren't pricking your fingers." It's true, I was learning to
move with the cart. Soothed by my needle's steady slip through cloth,
I remembered Giovanni's letter and his plans to marry the landlord's
widow. "Attilio, don't some people go to America and then return?"

"Some men, yes. They come back to marry." He ran a finger down
his long nose. "Perhaps some women as well."

"But no women you know?"

He shook his head. "I'm sorry, Irma. But you could be the first. Or
you could make a good life there." I had made dresses, altar cloths,

aprons, cheese and wine. But how to make a life? Tiny stitches crept across the cloth. Could I make a new life thus: one stitch at a time?

At the next town, as he promised, Attilio bought embroidery thread for the shawl, pinks and reds for the roses, greens for the leaves and stems, yellows for the centers and long-eyed needles made in England. I gasped at the price but Attilio only shrugged. "Good copper makes good pots," he said. "There's no other way."

In late afternoon, we stopped on the road to Isernia in a crowded farmhouse where his sister Lucia lived with her husband's family. A smile as wide as Attilio's warmed her plain face as she welcomed us.

"Come with me, Irma," she said. In walking to the well, drawing water, feeding chickens and gathering vegetables for the evening soup, Lucia's quiet listening and gentle questions teased out my hazy plans for America. Although I had determined to tell no one of the night my father touched me, I told her that as well.

"Help me cut the onions," Lucia said. As I cut and cried, she leaned close and whispered, "You did right to leave Opi." Heat swarmed up my neck as I confessed the secret shame that by my father's touch I was tainted like Filomena.

"You're blameless," Lucia insisted. "Did you tell your priest what happened?"

"My Zia did."

"And did he say you must confess? Did he set you any penance?"

"No."

"Well then," said Lucia briskly, "you see? You haven't sinned." She handed me the broom. "Sweep the floor. I'll be back."

I had swept, filled the kindling box and scrubbed the oak table by the time she returned. We ate quickly and in silence as at home, but while we scraped the trenchers clean, a stream of neighbors filled the house, standing along the walls and studying me, not unkindly but intent, as if I were a horse that they might buy.

Attilio led me to the table. "Irma, I said we'd help you get in America. Come close to the fire," he invited the neighbors. "Welcome." In the murmuring scuffle, I saw that many had brought their own chairs and stools, as we did at home for pageants in the church piazza. Now I was the pageant. He asked for my documents and I fished them from my pack. Someone ushered in the schoolteacher, who read Father Anselmo's letter aloud and shook his head. "I'm sorry, signorina, but you'll need a letter *from* America to prove you won't be alone."

"Here," said Lucia, handing me wine in a clay cup. Her child laid a warm hand on my sleeve.

"She has a brother," Attilio offered and explained Carlo's plan for Tripoli and Cleveland.

"He left six months ago?" the teacher asked. I nodded. "And you've heard nothing from him?" When I shook my head, the others whispered in dialect. "Carlo will write you now, Irma," the teacher declared loudly. "He'll invite you to America. You'll tell the police that there's no envelope because you lost it." As the teacher filled his pen, those around the table debated what work I could do in America. Factory work, some suggested, millwork or glove making. Others suggested I paint ceramics, cook, or be a nursemaid to the children of rich Italians.

"Not a lady's maid," one said, "she's not pretty enough."

"Baker!" cried Lucia.

"Needlework," I offered into the din.

"You know, she wouldn't need a trade if she married Carlo's friend," a rumbling voice announced. The teacher looked up, considered and nodded.

In the heat and close air, my head spun with wine. "What friend?"

"Your brother's in America, no?" the teacher prompted patiently. "And he will meet people there, no, men from Italy?" I nodded, although in truth Carlo rarely made friends. "So then, Irma, if such a man were single, might your brother not wish for him a good wife and think of you? So Carlo invites you to Cleveland and sends money for your passage." Now suggestions for my fiancé's name thickened the air like blackbirds: Giuseppe, Antonio, Carmine, Matteo, Paolo, Pietro, Salvatore, Luigi, Federico, Gabriele or Ernesto, like my father.

"Federico," I shouted. In the sudden silence the teacher inked his pen.

"And where does Federico work?"

I thought of Alfredo of Pescasseroli. "In a steel mill?"

A one-eyed man they called Salvo scoffed. "With all those Irish and Poles? Why not gold mining in California?"

"With all those brothels and bars?" demanded a woman.

"Sara, you think all America's a cesspool!" he snapped.

"Well, isn't it?" Sara huffed, but other voices covered theirs. As spring rain pours into valleys, stories poured into the room. Everyone knew someone in America. A cousin made glass; brothers or uncles worked in saw mills or breweries, packed fish, made bread and or drove spikes on the railroads. A sister kept a boardinghouse; an aunt cooked. A city's worth of people gone and I knew nothing of it. Their misfortunes came rolling out too: a man robbed on the boat to New York, others cheated at cards, sold false railway tickets, crushed in factories, buried in coal mines, dead of diseases or shot in taverns. "Listen, Irma," the people called out. "Listen to this."

The schoolteacher thumped the table. "Let's say Federico's a blacksmith in Cleveland. Yes, Irma?" I nodded, a little dazed.

"Why Cleveland?" Salvo demanded.

"Because my brother went there," I reminded him, but now everyone called out better places: Boston, New Haven, Philadelphia, Chicago, Saint Louis, Baltimore.

"In Dakota," someone announced, "they'll give her free land."

"Why? So she freezes to death?" Salvo demanded. "Dakota's worse than Russia." When the teacher suggested New Orleans, a blast of voices cried, "Malaria!"

"Malaria, malaria, malaria!" a small boy chanted gaily until his mother hushed him.

"There's lots of Italians in New York City," said a hook-nosed man. "Markets and shops and churches. You'll never have to speak English."

"And live in a tenement like my sister Anna Maria?" demanded a woman in a corner. "Noise, drunks, you boil in summer and freeze in winter. Bad water. One outhouse for seven families, children always sick, filth in the street. My sister works twelve hours a day trimming ladies' hats and now the boss says he'll give her work to Russian Jews. She's spitting blood. Three little ones, another on the way and a no-good American husband who beats her. He'll leave when she dies and they'll have nothing but the streets, poor babes. Go back to Opi, girl. At least you have family there and good air." Silence spread over the room until someone coughed and a rush of voices tumbled in speaking of money, good farmland, clean air in the country, a friend's cousin with his own tavern, two brothers with a dry goods store in Pittsburgh and a sister who married well and even kept an Irish girl for cleaning.

A sweet dream lifted my heart like a leaf: I was returning to Opi in a fine dress and feathered hat. I had bought Zia a house with three rooms and a carved wooden door, new pots, painted China plates and a tiled floor. Children born since I left tugged at their mother's skirts, whispering, "Who is that American lady?" Everywhere people would smile and welcome me and I would nestle home like a child.

"Once you cross the ocean," the hook-nosed man intoned, "you're always on the wrong side, even if you come home rich. Old friends will cheat away your American gold. It happened to my uncle. Now he's too poor to leave again. There's nothing left to sell and he's back to day labor for the landlord."

"Irma," said Attilio quietly, "do you still want Cleveland if Carlo—" he coughed. I know what he meant. If Carlo wasn't there. I closed my eyes. Names of American cities tangled together like skeins of bright thread on a merchant's table. True enough: if I wasn't sure to find Carlo I could go to any city. But Cleveland was woven through my mind now.

"Yes, I'd go there if it has mountains and work," I said.

"I think—" Attilio began.

"There are mountains," Salvo declared. When Lucia asked how he knew, he hit the table boards as my father did when Carlo challenged him. "Cleelan is built on mountains."

"Cleveland," the teacher corrected. As winter wind blows hard, changes course and blows again, talk around the table turned now to local matters, troubles with landlords, water rights and grain markets, while the teacher finished my letter, signing: "Your loving brother, Carlo Vitale." He gave it to me, carefully stopped his ink bottle and put on his cloak. I gave him two *lire*, which seemed to be the price for letters, since he took them without protest.

"Addio, Irma," he said gravely. "May the Lord be with you in America."

Neighbors drifted after him. Some pressed saints' tokens into my hand. Women grasped my arms and hands, telling of men who had gone to America and never written. "Look for Domenico DiPietro and tell him that we're worried. We pray for him every day." One man had a scar on his chin; one named Antonio had a lazy eye, I couldn't miss him. "Francesco's hair is just like mine," said a woman, pulling back her scarf to show dark chestnut curls. "He's in Boston. Make him write." I promised to try. But it would be hard enough to find Carlo.

When the women left at last, I saw that Lucia had filled a large linen sack with straw and laid it over the table boards. "You'll sleep here, Irma," she said. The others found or made their beds as Lucia banked the fire.

I whispered my prayers and stretched out on the sack, picking out the sleeping shapes of six people, three cats and a sheepdog pup. Attilio snored. In the darkness, I felt Zia's voice close by: *"At least you have a warm bed now. You've done well on your first night. And perhaps you will marry a Federico. Better than a Gabriele or Old Tommaso. Buona notte, Irma."* Her scent hovered briefly and then drifted away. The darkness filled with rustles and sighs. In the corner a cat killed a rat so neatly that its last squeak snapped like a dry twig. I groped for my embroidered sketch of Opi and fingered the thread lines. Here was the shoemaker's house, here the wall and hump of road where I last saw Carlo and here the slow rise to our house. I pressed the scrap to my face as sleep folded over me.

Lucia woke us before dawn. She set out bread, onions and watered wine for everyone and a package of cheese and dried figs for Attilio and me, refusing the coins I offered. "Keep them for America," she said, kissing me. From the cart, I waved until a long curve swallowed her.

"Do you have a sister, Irma?" Attilio asked.

"No."

"That's a pity."

"Can Lucia read?"

"No, but if you send a letter, the schoolteacher can read it to her." Of course I'd have to pay a scribe. In our few lessons with Father Anselmo we had learned only enough to piece out a few prayers and catechisms and slowly sign our names. I'd have to find a scribe in one of the American piazzas.

"What would we write about?" Carlo had demanded when I lamented our poor learning. "Every year is just like the next in Opi, and all our lives are the same. *We're* all the same."

That much wasn't true, I protested. "There are hunger years and good years. And you aren't like Gabriele or the mayor. I'm not like his wife—or Filomena." Surely not like Filomena.

Carlo sighed. "Irma, you think too much."

"Lucia would be proud to have your letter," Attilio was saying softly. "She would keep it always. Look, there's a fine day coming."

I followed his finger to a violet band glowing to the east. When there was light enough to sew, I mended Attilio's shirt and outlined the first rose at a village market. "What does America look like?" I asked as we moved through low hills covered with olive trees.

"They say it has everything: cities, towns, villages, rivers and huge lakes, plains, deserts, swamps, mountains and forests bigger than all Abruzzo."

"Where there aren't Italians, people speak English?"

"I think so."

Working the first petals, I remembered how we stared at the African juggler who could not speak our language. No, better to think of roses, how curled each petal must be and how thick the stems.

Attilio hummed and sang, sometimes asking Rosso, "What's the next verse, old friend?" On a flat stretch he said, "Irma, you might find a real Federico on the ship, you know. Or in Cleveland."

"The mayor's wife in Opi said that in America, women don't need to marry. They can find work."

"True. Still, you needn't be lonely."

But what about the bruises on the mayor's wife and Assunta's desperate wail at her husband's funeral? Or Attilio's own sorrow when fever made his wife a child again? Why risk such pain? "I don't need to marry," I insisted. He opened his mouth to speak, and then closed it.

We were silent through two shabby towns until he noted, "We aren't stopping at the next one. Malaria came through and no one's buying pots." I had seen malaria when deaf Eduardo's sons returned yellow and shaking from a summer of roadwork in Calabria. They died soon after, limp as rags although they had been ram-strong men before leaving Opi. "Don't worry, it won't touch us so early in spring," Attilio assured me. "But you'll see where it passed."

I did. We saw Death's trail in abandoned fields and the gaping door of a silent abbey. "Look, no bell in the tower. I bet you won't find a crucifix in the church either, or a silver chalice. Stealing from the Lord's house." Attilio shook his head.

Beyond the abbey we passed a village strung along a dusty road. Listless men and women sat in doorways weaving baskets. Children curled like cats in the shade, blankly watching us pass. From the houses came coughs so deep and ragged that my own chest ached. When a man cried out for blankets, the weavers sighed and crossed themselves.

"Can't they help him?" I asked.

Attilio shook his head and clicked to hurry Rosso. "In a few minutes he'll be freezing. The most they can do now is make some coins by weaving. They're too weak for fieldwork." A haggard priest came out of a dark doorway, passing a hunched, laboring woman as he made his way toward us. He raised his hand slowly in blessing, as if any movement pained him, and Attilio pulled Rosso to a halt.

"Father, take this," I said, holding out three lire from my pouch, but the priest ignored me, grasping the sides of our cart with hands as stiffly curved as a shepherd's crook.

"You're headed south?" he asked Attilio.

"Yes, to Naples."

"There's a little girl down the road who's still healthy. Her name is Rosanna." The priest's head shook like a weight in the wind. I glanced at Attilio. Why wasn't one child's health a joy in this den of sickness? "Her whole family's dead. These others," the priest waved behind him, "can barely care for themselves. The child can't stay alone."

Attilio chewed his lip. "I'm a peddler, Father, and Irma here is bound for America."

"Take the child to Naples, at least. She has an uncle near the port. Here's his address." The priest pulled a scrap of paper from his cassock and held it out, the gnarled hand wavering.

I knew why Attilio hesitated. The child might be infected. We might not find this uncle or he might not want her. Then what? "I'll do it," Attilio said finally, taking the paper scrap.

"God bless you both. Give the lire to Rosanna. She's in the last house on the left. Say that Father Martino sent you." A howl rose behind us. "Go," he whispered. "We'll bury her family when we can, but take her away." The weavers barely raised their eyes as Attilio clicked Rosso to trot. Father Martino shuffled towards a woman's shrill cry.

We found the girl sitting by the stone stoop of her house, rope thin and gray with dust. Death rot poured from the door, a sickening stench. "Rosanna," I said, "Father Martino sent us. We're going to see your uncle in Naples." Her dry lips barely wavered. Death had scoured her face with sadness, yet she gazed at me through lank, tangled hair like a child who had once been loved. She was as light as a gourd when I lifted her but the dark eyes never left mine.

From rustling squeaks within the house, we knew that rats had found the bodies. "Is there anything you want in there?" Attilio asked. When the child shook her head, I set her in the cart on a mound of packs and gave her a water pouch that she sucked dry and then devoured a fistful of my bread and cheese.

"Not too much at once," Attilio said. "Sleep now, Rosanna." She curled under his traveling cloak, still as a copper pot.

"Suppose we can't find the uncle?" I whispered to Attilio.

"Then she'll have to go to an orphanage." We were silent then, both knowing how children were used in those places. Rosanna slept steadily. I woke her from time to time for water and bread and bits of cheese. She would not speak, but each time she curled back to sleep I saw that she had edged closer to us.

With every town, the hills flattened slightly, as if a great hand was smoothing the land. Fields stretched wider and some had two ox teams plowing. The roads smoothed as well and I sewed more quickly, the bright sun sparkling on my needle as I finished the first rose. "Amazing," Attilio said. "It looks so real."

"The next one will be better."

Awake now, Rosanna propped herself against a copper soup pot and watched me work, following each stitch as if her eyes were threaded to my needle. "Can you sew?" I asked. She stared, unblinking as my father's sheep. I imagined what Carlo would say: *"Probably an idiota. Don't waste your time."*

"Watch," I told Rosanna. I threaded a basting needle with coarse thread and made running stitches in a scrap of cloth. "Now you," I said. Each stitch crawled, for she poised the needle over the cloth, held a long breath before easing it through and drew out the thread as carefully if it were spider spun. After a fair piece of road, she had made ten tiny stitches, precisely equal. She slept with the cloth that night in the tent we made beneath the cart.

The next day, in Caserta, while Attilio set up his goods in a market square that was larger than all Opi, Rosanna hunched over an old cloth sack I had found for her, working tiny stitches in an intricate tangle. Often she tore out an hour's work to make a new design that seemed as random as the first, but still with careful, even stitches. She never spoke, but smiled when I brought her a clutch of ripe tomatoes, my first. We ate them all, licking the sweet, seed-studded juice from our fingers.

Attilio was in good humor, for he was doing a brisk business in Caserta. Sewing steadily, I started the last rose and winding, leafy stem. It looked real; even my mother would have said so. Near noon, when Rosanna finally stopped stitching and uncurled her slender fingers, the dark eyes fixed on my needle working the shawl, watching avidly, as if I were spinning gold. Sometimes her mouth moved, but words melted in the dry air. "Here are the French knots," I said instead, "and here the satin, bullion, back, feather, running and couching stitches."

"They're beautiful," she finally breathed in a gauzy voice so unexpected that Attilio looked up from a haggle over flat-bottomed pots.

"You can make some stitches on the shawl, child," he said. "My wife won't mind."

A customer snapped, "I gave you a fair price, man. Will you take it?"

"Watch me, Rosanna," I said, taking up her sack. "You make a knot like this. They'll go inside each rose." When her practice knots came out as round as pearls I let her make one on the shawl. She gazed at it awestruck, one spindle-thin finger hovering over the flower. "In Naples you'll learn to sew better than I do."

She sat rigidly, staring at the shawl, slowly opening the thin, cracked lips. Her voice rasped like a rusty hinge—an aged voice, horrible in a child. "They all died. My grandmother. My father. My mother. My little brother." She pushed the shawl away. "I tried to take care of the baby but she died too. Everyone. One by one."

"The priest told us."

"I knew I'd be next."

"But you weren't, Rosanna. We're taking you to Naples and you'll be safe there."

"*Don't promise*," Carlo would say. Rosanna slowly stroked the sack as Attilio tried to explain what a fine city Naples was. She turned away, curling around a stack of pots with her head cushioned on my bag and slept all afternoon. She was still sleeping when we lifted her into the cart at dusk, for Attilio said that we must ride all night to reach Naples by daybreak.

"We'll try to find the uncle first, and then I'll take you to port," he said. "Look there, you've come a long way to see it." He pointed west to a long silver line, straight as a needle beneath the red-streaked sky.

"What is it?"

"That's the Tyrrhenian Sea, which joins the Mediterranean. Further west are the Straits of Gibraltar and then the Atlantic Ocean and then America." I stared at the line. I knew these names from Father Anselmo who had once showed us a map, but I had never imaged this silver line or the great width of water to cross. The line shimmered like glacier ice.

"Attilio, when someone dies on a ship, what happens to the body?"

"You won't die, Irma."

"But if someone does?"

Attilio slapped the reins although Rosso was moving steadily. "It's buried at sea."

"Buried?"

"Well, wrapped in a weighted shroud and dropped. With prayers," he added quickly.

"There's a priest?"

"Perhaps." So there was no priest, only a body falling like a stone beneath the waves with no one to know where it lay. Eaten by fishes. I pulled out my rosary. Yes I was healthy, but death could find us unaware, Father Anselmo said. The Lord may claim us in our strength for we are His. Perhaps He had already taken Carlo.

"Look at the sunset, Irma," urged Attilio, touching my shoulder and pointing to red-violet streaks over the silver line quickly turning black. Save me, Lord, from death at sea. Work, one must work. I turned the shawl over to clip thread ends in the dying light.

"Even the back side is lovely," Attilio observed. "If the road were longer, you could make a whole bouquet. You could make one in America, you know, with all the flowers you remember." Yes, I could do that, a year's flowers in the same bouquet, from the earliest snow crocus to the last yarrow my mother coaxed from her garden.

Attilio sighed. "My wife used to paint bowls and sell them. She could read and write. Catarina did so much—before the fever took her mind."

"And now?"

"She watches birds. She cleans copper. When I'm home, she's glad to see me, but if I leave for a morning or a month, it's the same for her." His eye fell on dark roses in the dim light. "She still loves beautiful things. She'll follow every thread of this shawl. Look there!" He pointed south and east.

The moon was blooming over Mount Vesuvius. Stars twinkled like sparks in a night fire as we ate bread and cheese and I tried not to think of the ocean. When Attilio grew drowsy, I took the reins but held them slack, for Rosso kept a steady pace, finding smooth tracks in the moonlit path. By dawn I would see Naples, a city that was already old, Father Anselmo said, before Rome was even founded.

A fox streaked across the road, startling Rosso. I sang him one of my mother's songs of a shepherd girl in the summer, her face all white and fair. "In summer?" Carlo always snorted. "Shepherd girls turn brown as nuts." I sang another song that Zia had taught me, of a girl whose lover goes off to sea and marries far away. I said my catechism, pictured the houses in Opi and all who lived in each, the names and habits of our sheep, and then it was dawn and time to wake Attilio.

He fixed blinders on Rosso and took the reins to lead us into Naples. The city was nothing I could have imagined, a maze of narrow streets wedged between stone palaces that cut the sky to ribbons. I saw marble fountains and streets made of stone that Attilio called basalt, sleek and black as a priest's silk vestments. Even windows towered, not like our square portals a child's head and shoulders might fill, but tall enough that a standing man could leap from them.

Rosanna was awake now, peeping through a wall she'd made of pots. "Irma, where are we?"

"In Naples, where your uncle lives."

"All these buildings?"

"And more," Attilio said. We saw women with goiters hanging like melons from their necks, hunchbacks, dwarves and legless beggars on tiny carts, their hands bound in leather globes to push themselves along. Bareheaded women with red flounced skirts slipped in and out of gentlemen's carriages. Street boys snatched fruit from carts. I saw two priests talking while a thief picked their pockets. We saw a church made of stone cut in diamond shapes, enough stone in that one church to build another in Opi. Peddlers sang out their wares. I saw balls of mozzarella bobbing in vats of milky water, boiled pig heads, onions and mountains of artichokes, barrels of olives and wine and carts piled with dimpled lemons as big as two fists.

In a clogged piazza we stopped behind a cart from which a friar hawked palm-sized replicas of body parts. Thin silver lungs, hearts, intestines, breasts, throats, eyes and kidneys dangled from posts, flickering in the breeze. A limping woman bought a little silver leg. "She'll give it to the church and perhaps be cured," Attilio explained.

"Which one cures malaria?" Rosanna asked.

"Don't worry," said Attilio. "The sea air protects you here." When she looked at him doubtfully, he stopped by a man with a pot of boiling oil. "Watch him, child," Attilio said. When the man tossed a handful of dough into the pot, it sank and then bounced up, brown and bubbling. He deftly scooped it in a wicker ladle, shook it dry, scattered it with sugar and tossed it up to Rosanna, flipping Attilio's coin in the air to catch it in his cap. Rosanna gave out a low, cramped "ha, ha" as she jiggled the hot ball in her hands. "Careful," Attilio warned, but she was already nibbling.

Men sold pasta from great pots, serving handfuls to men who threw back their heads and aimed the quivering strands at their throats. A grown man sang for coins, his voice as high as a boy's, his cheeks as hairless as mine. Attilio glanced at Rosanna and said briefly, "cut," making a gesture I knew from watching my father castrate rams.

Rosanna was wolfing her dough, licking each finger. "Why?" I mouthed.

"If a poor family has a boy with a good voice," Attilio whispered, "they might give him to the church, sell him really, for a sack full of lire. The boy will be cut in hopes he'll sing like an angel all his life, bringing glory to God. And his brothers can eat." A shiver ran through me, like the first cold of winter. "We're in Naples, Irma, not Opi."

We had come to Piazza Montesanto. Chickens swirled around our cart. Wheelbarrows, fine carriages and peddlers' carts jostled us. In every doorway someone worked: sewing, filling mattresses, carving wood, weaving cane, painting plates, braiding rope, nursing babies or shelling beans. There were Arabs in robes, Africans as black as the basalt they walked on and travelers from blond northern places. Naples was a city of foreigners, Attilio said. Some great palaces were owned by English and most of the nobles spoke French. When Attilio asked a peddler how to get to the fishermen's quarters, Rosanna gulped the last of her dough.

"We could go tomorrow," she ventured. "After we find Irma's ship."

I gathered her slight body close. "Let me comb your hair, Rosanna," I said, longing to promise that she could stay with me if the uncle didn't want her. But how could I keep a child in America or even buy her passage there? I combed her hair, smoothed her dress and wiped the damp, thin face.

We turned down Via Roma, a great street lined with stone palaces, each with a guard and carved doors broad enough for two carriages. Who knew there was such wealth in the world? We entered a warren of narrow dirt streets and turned south to the fishermen's quarters, where streets dissolved into twisting lanes and boys clustered around our cart, leaping and calling: "Guide, guide, you need a guide!" Attilio picked a high-jumping boy, gave him the uncle's name and showed a coin the boy would get if he took us straight to the house.

The boy darted through the crowd, shouting and pushing dogs and children from our path, leaping between puddles and calling, "Come, come," when Rosso balked. We stopped at a squat white-washed house between two scrub pines. "Arturo the fisherman lives here," the boy announced, seized his coin and scampered away. The house was small, but clean curtains fluttered in the window. A hand-some, strong-jawed woman sat in the doorway weaving fishnet and did not look up until Attilio stood at her side. His back was to me so I could not hear what he said, but the weaving never stopped. Rosanna peeped from her den.

At last Attilio came back to the cart. "Come," he said. "She wants you." I gave Attilio ten lire so the child would not go empty-handed to her new home.

Rosanna waded slowly through the pots. "Here, take your sew-ing," I said, pressing the cloth into her arms. She let me kiss her but the glittering eyes were fixed on the woman who was standing now in a swirl of fishnet. As Attilio lifted Rosanna from the cart and walked her to the house, she turned once to smile at me, a thin curve up like a crack in a clay plate, and raised a bone-thin arm to wave. Is this how

Zia felt, hearing my footsteps fade as I hurried down our street and out of Opi?

Attilio set Rosanna by the door and offered my lire to the woman, who first refused and then took them. As they spoke, her wide hand cupped Rosanna's shoulder. The child did not pull away, nor did she look back as the woman drew her into the house.

"Well?" I demanded as Attilio climbed back in the cart.

"Arturo's still at sea. Their only son drowned last month and she's past childbearing. They'll be happy to have Rosanna. The woman said she always wanted a daughter. So it went well, no?"

"It did, yes." Rosanna wasn't my blood and I had only known her two days, Carlo would remind me. Yet already I ached for the steady breathing as she made her wild designs, her famished eyes following my hands and the warmth of her body in the little time that I'd held her.

"Well, now let's find your ship," said Attilio. "The port's this way." I wished it were further, but the packed dirt street quickly became a paved road leading to a harbor thick with shabby fishing boats, elegant pleasure boats and iron-clad ships sprouting smokestacks between high masts. They burned coal to make steam, Attilio explained, and used sails on breezy days. Beyond the ships, the Bay of Naples stretched like a bolt of blue cloth stitched to the sky, beautiful, but the water seemed hardly strong enough to bear the crafts that skimmed so carelessly across it.

"How far is America?" I asked.

Attilio rubbed his long nose. "Two or three weeks."

Three weeks floating on water! In hard winters our world turned white for weeks, but at least we were on land in a house with our own people around us.

Attilio worked his cart through the crowds to a patch of shade by a water pump. "You stay here with Rosso and the cart. I'll find you a good ship." He was gone two hours by the church bells. To pass the time I brushed Rosso, cleaned out the cart and put my documents in order. I watched passing waves of merchants, porters, fishermen, fishmongers, and gaudy women calling to sailors.

At last Attilio returned. "The *Servia* is bound for New York in a few days. The stevedores say she's sound and there's a lodging house where you'll stay while they finish repairs."

"Repairs?"

"All ships need repairs. Look," he waved his hand at the port where nearly every ship swarmed with sailors, cleaning, pounding and hanging off ropes like long-legged bats. "But you must get your ticket now to be sure of your place."

"Yes." I couldn't move.

Attilio smoothed Rosso's flank. "You have to see the ship's doctor first."

"Why? I'm not sick."

"I know, but one of the ships last season carried a family with typhus. It swept through steerage and a week out of Naples reached the crew. They were shorthanded across the Atlantic." Attilio spoke quickly, stroking Rosso's neck. "So the *Servia*'s captain is having the steerage scrubbed and he hired a doctor to check the passengers. You see, he's prudent. You'll be safe."

"Did many die in steerage?"

Attilio shrugged. I saw wrapped bodies swallowed in waves. "They could have been weak already," he said, suddenly as cool and brisk as a stranger stopped for directions. What did I expect? He was just my passage to Naples and I was just a shawl maker for his imbecile wife.

Salt air burned my throat. "How much is the ticket?"

"Twenty lire, a good price. And don't worry about typhus, Irma," he said earnestly, the old Attilio again.

"We never had it in Opi," I admitted.

"So there's nothing to worry about." Attilio studied the cart. "The pots are in order and Rosso's brushed. Irma, you didn't have to do this."

"It was nothing." I would have gladly cleaned the cart again to put off the wrench of leaving. I nearly begged him not to leave, to take me with him back to Opi or even on his travels, endlessly winding through Italy, but not leaving, not cast off and alone. I tried to speak and Attilio too opened his mouth, but then his brusque busyness returned. He helped me into the cart, loosened and then tightened Rosso's harness and silently eased us through the crowd to the ragged ticket line, where travelers bunched together, shepherding trunks, crates or simple bags like mine.

"There's the shawl," I said, pointing to it folded on his seat, the roses framed on top.

Attilio touched each flower gently. "It's beautiful. Catarina will be so pleased." He grasped my arm. "Irma, remember, don't pay more than twenty lire for the ticket."

"I won't."

"Remember to buy enough food for the passage, things that keep. You have money?"

"Yes."

"And tell the officers that Carlo will meet you. Say he sent you to come marry his friend. If they ask. They might not."

"Yes."

"Don't worry about the doctor. You're healthy, you'll be fine. In America you'll sew for rich women just like your Zia said."

"Are you putting that cart on a ship or not?" a man behind us snapped. "If not, get out of the way."

I jumped down with my bag. A sea breeze puffed across us. "Thank you, Attilio," I whispered. My eyes burned. Attilio kissed his hand and gently pressed it to my cheek. "God keep you, Irma, and take you safe to America."

"Out of the way, peddler!" someone shouted.

Attilio sat up and clicked Rosso's reins. A water cart pushed behind him, then a fisherman hauling nets and a cart piled high with wine barrels.

"Get in line, signorina, if you want the *Servia*," said a woman with a child gripping her skirt. The woman's almond eyes studied me, searching the crowd. "Was that your father?" I shook my head. "Husband? Brother?"

"He's a—peddler who gave me a ride to Naples."

"Oh. Well anyway, look after your bags. This port is full of thieves."

I pulled my bags behind hers, watching the gray-blue patch of Attilio's shirt disappear in the crowd.

"Mamma, why is the lady crying?" the child whispered.

"Leave her alone, Gabriella."

Three

On the Servia

The ticket line snaked languidly across the piazza, bunching and stretching over basalt paving hot under our feet.

"My name is Teresa," the woman announced.

"Mine is Irma," I said. Why give a family name if nobody knows your family? Travelers called to each other up and down the line, words skimming overhead.

"Greek," said Teresa pointing. "And Albanian over there. Those two women are from Serbia."

"How do you know?"

"I live—lived near the port in Bari. Merchants came to trade from everywhere. Weren't there foreigners in your town?"

"Not often." Once a drunken Swiss mercenary wandered up to Opi, slept awhile in our piazza and then left in heavy fog. Days later, shepherds found him in a crevasse, half-eaten by wolves.

"My father's working in America," Gabriella announced. "He'll have his own store soon. Isn't that right, Mamma?"

"Yes."

"And he's waiting for us, waiting for us, waiting every day," chirped Gabriella, nudging a pebble around a paving block. From the way Teresa plucked at her faded skirt, I suspected that not all husbands waited. In the next days, I learned my suspicions were true. Some men were bewitched by American shopgirls with soft hands, bright hair and no dust of the old country. Some women found nobody waiting in New York. One Sicilian retrieved his wife at the port, hauled her like baggage to a rented room, stayed long enough to get her with child and then slipped west on a train.

Yet wives stood in lines like this. "I had to leave Bari," Teresa told me. "Everyone knew I was married. They whispered if I spoke one word to another man. Gabriella was growing up half orphan. Enzo had taken my dowry money to America so Papà sold a field to buy our passage. I wrote Enzo that we're coming and he telegraphed back, but he's been gone five years. Perhaps he's changed." She glanced at her daughter. "Stand up straight, Gabriella. Don't kick rocks like a country girl."

Men behind us boasted of the fortunes they would make in America and how they'd return to Calabria, buy the land their fathers had toiled for day wages, buy vineyards, pay their sisters' dowries and spend their long afternoons like gentlemen in the fine cafés where once they were not welcome. A large family finished its dealings and the line lurched forward. When sea breezes caught a creaking sign that said TICKETS TO AMERICA, talk fell away as if the same thought ran through us all: leaving was real enough, but what of our airy dreams? Suppose we who were poor and whose fathers and grandfathers were poor did not become rich in America? Then where could we go?

"Cheer up!" barked a young man with a small pack and a wine jug. "It's not like you're sheep to slaughter. *We're* here for adventure, me and my fine companion." He lofted his jug in the air and waves of talk lapped up and down the line again.

"How are you paying?" a thin man asked another who looked like a blacksmith, with his thick shoulders and burn-scarred hands.

"Italian lire. And you?"

"Bavarian marks," the thin man answered proudly.

"Make sure they don't cheat you."

"You think I'm a fool?"

I learned that I would need to change my French gold for lire and check the exchange rate on lists they were obliged to show me. I felt a whiff of pride. Who in Opi had ever used an exchange list?

As we waited, hawkers worked the line. "Sail the *Regina*. No wormy potatoes. Good meat, plenty of washrooms and fresh water. Four lire less than the *Servia* and the captain's sober."

"*Mountjoy*, fresh launched in England, steady as an oak table," cried another. "The crew's steady too. Not like some."

"Take the *Silver Star*," urged a limping boy thin as a rat tail who galloped by our line. "Big engines. You'll be in America sooner. Hot meals twice a day. Two parlors in steerage."

Prickling doubt shot through me. Was Attilio bribed to pick the *Servia*? No, surely I knew him that well. But what did he know of ships? He could have been lied to. The hawkers served the captains, but one ship might truly be better than others. And which was better, a shorter voyage, a stronger ship, or a sober captain? My mind lurched like a drunkard's. "Teresa, should we ask about the other ships?"

"Ask who? We're just cargo, whatever they say."

"But aren't we safer on the *Mountjoy* if it's new or the *Silver Star* if it's faster?"

"Signorina," snapped the thin man, "in a storm we're all in God's hands. You're in the *Servia* line now." This was true. For any other ship, I'd have to wait longer in the beating sun. At least here I knew Teresa.

I shuffled forward, pushing my bag until I reached the head of the line, or one of the two snakeheads, for Teresa was waved to one thin clerk and I was sent to a huge man whose eyes glinted from the damp moon of his face. "Well?" he demanded, snapping at a boy who darted forward with a cloth the man used to dry the ruffled folds of his neck and chin. "What are you staring at, girl? Never saw a handkerchief before? Show me your documents."

I laid them on his desk with the schoolteacher's letter. The clerk's blunt fingers left moist stains on each sheet. "A single woman in America. What are your plans?"

"It's in the letter. I'm going to marry my brother's friend in Cleveland."

"And this brother's friend has a name, perhaps?"

"Federico . . . Gallo."

"Hum. And Federico Gallo has a job?"

"Yes sir." What job? Butcher? Miner? Steelworker? His fingers drummed my letter. "He's a blacksmith," I said too loudly.

"Am I deaf, girl?"

"No sir."

An officer in a fine blue suit hung with yellow braid appeared suddenly at his side and rapped a small baton on the table edge. "Too many questions. There's hundreds in line. Signorina, can you buy a ticket?"

"Yes sir."

"Good. Take her name, age and birthplace. New York's not our problem." Red-faced, the clerk filled out a card and flicked it toward me. I gathered my documents and moved to the next table.

There a doctor with a silk cravat did not touch me, but had a shirtsleeved assistant feel my head for fever and gingerly part my hair with two spoons he then dipped in kerosene, noting that I had no lice. He made me cough and peered in my eyes. "Heart." The doctor yawned.

"Open your blouse," said the assistant. *In public?* "To here." He rapped my breastbone. When I hesitated, the doctor raised his hand to wave the next person forward.

"Wait, please," I said quickly, fingers flying at the buttons. The assistant scanned my chest and listened to my heart through a flared wooden tube.

"She's healthy, *Dottore*," he said.

The doctor stamped a number on my wrist. "That's *your* number," he warned. "If anyone copies it, you'll both be arrested. Understand?"

I nodded. "So there's no typhus on the *Servia*?"

The assistant prodded me on to the purser. "Don't bother him, girl. Everyone's healthy."

"Peasants," the doctor muttered behind me.

"How are you paying?" the purser demanded.

I set out my francs and gripped the table as he examined them. "They're French gold, sir."

"I think I know my business," the purser snapped. "You want the list?" He nodded at the exchange list, finely printed, inking his pen as I strained to read. "See? We aren't highwaymen." He wrote out a ticket and marked my wrist a second time. "If you wash it off, you pay again. Next."

"Excuse me, sir."

"What?"

"Are there separate dormitories for women?"

"Of course. Servants, feather beds and marble washstands too."

Weariness made me bold. "I just asked, sir, now that I bought a ticket."

The purser breathed a dry rasp like an angry bull, but when I didn't move, he folded his hands together and said, "Single men sleep together. You'll be with the families and other single women. Is that acceptable, signorina?"

"Yes sir."

"Good. Then move along."

At the next table I bought a straw mattress, soap for salt water and meal tickets for the lodging house where we'd sleep until the ship sailed, which would be "soon," a clerk said vaguely. Peddlers milled around us, hawking playing cards, sea-sickness herbs, crucifixes and charms, tobacco, blankets and straw hats they swore all men wore in America. Many bought without bargaining. Who would do that at home? Did they think new money would come snowing down in America? Pulling free of one peddler, I backed into a man with cuffs rolled back to show numbers on his wrist like mine but I couldn't recall his sleek red hair in the ticket line.

"They're like dogs at fresh meat," he laughed. "You're wise not to buy blankets, signorina. We'll sleep near the boilers, so heat's the devil on board, not cold. But the crew sells food on the side so they keep rations short. If you're hungry, you have to pay their prices, which go up every day. See what I got?" He showed me a sack of potatoes, onions, tea, hard cheese, biscuits, salami, dried apple and figs and a big pot of jam. "Just see Matteo over there in the red shirt. He's the only one who won't cheat you, and he'll deliver your provisions straight to the lodging house." Matteo watched us from under the brim of a wide, soft hat.

"No thank you, sir." Did he take me for a fool? I had passed scores of food carts in the city. Two weeks of provisions could not weigh more than loads I'd carried up our mountain. The red-haired man shrugged and turned away, his eye flicking back to Matteo. So they did work together.

I made my way to the lodging house, where the din was worse than any thunderstorm. Shrieking children cut through aisles between the cots and men played cards, shouting their bets. A cobbler had set up shop, his hammer ceaselessly rapping, since dozens wanted shoes repaired for America. Women called from washtubs, slapping wet clothes against rattling metal racks. Dust and sweat filled the hot air. Matrons pushed through the crowd, assigning cots, stopping fights as one family's bags bulged into another's space and shooing out peddlers who had slipped inside. Two men fought bitterly over cards.

Teresa waved to me, her thick curls tumbling out of loosened braids. "Irma, there's space over here." As I unrolled my mattress she said that for a few *centesimi* we could store our bags in a guarded room, which seemed better than watching them day and night. The guard let me step behind a screen to fold the receipt into the chamois bag between my breasts and count the money I had left. Lire that I would spend for provisions went into a pouch I tucked inside my skirt. My great-grandfather's gold pieces stayed in the bag. By the time I had threaded back to Teresa, my head was pounding.

"Lie down awhile. We have our tickets, there's nothing to do now but wait," said Teresa, calmly loosening her bodice as if there were no men around. Gabriella was sleeping, curled around a rag doll.

"I have to go buy some things," I said. "And I can't breathe here."

"At least we're not in line," Teresa sighed, peeling back blood-caked stockings. "I'll wash tomorrow. Be careful in the city." She lay down and was immediately asleep, her arms woven through Gabriella's.

Outside, afternoon sun still beat at the basalt paving, but sea breezes whipped across the port and gulls looped the blue sky. I stood in a patch of shade and then made my way to a cluster of street children by a fountain. I picked a sharp-nosed boy with wide eyes and black hair curled tight as a lamb's coat who called himself Ciro and swore he knew a merchant selling good cloth at a fair price. He set off, darting between horses and carts so quickly that I lost him. He doubled back, took me by the hand and set off through a maze of streets so narrow that the sky was a blue stick above us.

"There," he said finally, pointing to a wooden sign on which a careful hand had painted a pair of golden scissors and a bolt of blue cloth. "Franco the Dwarf." The shop was barely four paces deep, a cavern lined in fabric bolts. At the center stood a table heaped with every kind of sewing notion. No taller than the boy, Franco leaped from his bolts to greet me. "Franco the Dwarf, as you see." Stubby arms fanned his treasures. "What is your desire, signorina? I have silk, cotton, wool and linen, thread in many colors, chalk, pins, needles, buttons, thimbles and scissors. All excellent, excellent, first class for the seamstress."

I bargained for a length of Egyptian cotton that would bear dense embroidery and admired a silky fringe and deep blue satin that shone like a moonlit lake. "Touch them," Franco prompted. "Feel how fine." He brought out hanks of embroidery thread, a shimmering rainbow of violets, blues, deep greens, reds, purples, and a yellow orange as rich as poppies. "Thread like this costs more in America, signorina. You're wise to buy now." My fingers tingled, yet Ciro stood motionless at my side. Did these colors not amaze him?

Too late, I tugged at my sleeve to hide the emigrant's marks. It was then that I noticed a pair of embroidery scissors with brass handles cunningly fashioned like wings. One black screw made a tiny eye and bright steel beaks completed the stork. Catching my gaze, Franco balanced the delicate tool on his fingertips. "See? Light as a feather. You try." Yes, the scissors floated in my hand. He gave me a scrap of muslin. The sleek handles kissed my fingers and the blades moved as easily as though in curves, lines and angles, clever beaks slicing a warp line, turning a crisp angle to the woof. Even their sound was delightful, a bright snip like a sparrow's chirp. Held against light, the cut edges were as smooth as the blades themselves. "Fine English import," said Franco, "new this year."

There were no such scissors in Opi. Mine were a gift from the blacksmith after my mother died. He had stepped out of the forge as I passed with our laundry and handed them to me. "For you, Irma," he said gruffly. "In memory of her." Then he hurried back, beating his anvil loudly to cover my thanks. The blades were as thin as any master smith could make them, but so heavy that much cutting made my hand ache.

"How often must you sharpen these?" I asked Franco. Mine I honed constantly on a heavy whetting stone.

"If you keep them clean and dry, they'll hold this edge for a year." He smiled at my astonishment. "Seven lire and they're yours. Imported, remember." The stork's black eye gleamed at me. When I ran a thumb across the slender beaks they grazed my skin like a leaf edge. "They'll cost double in New York, you know."

Ciro tugged at my skirt, showing four dirty fingers. "Four lire," I offered. Franco sighed and took back the scissors. I turned away to his basting thread, aching for that light lift. Then I bargained hard again and we finally agreed on the scissors, silk thread, a pattern book and rosewood embroidery hoop, all for ten lire.

"Where are you from, signorina?" Franco asked.

"Opi in Abruzzo."

"It must be a hard place for merchants," he grumbled lightly as he wrapped my package. "You know, my cousin in California cooks and washes at a mining camp. She makes as much as the miners. Gold or no gold, they have to eat." Franco waved his stubby arms. "Here's an idea. You could work for my cousin."

I had been poor all my life but at least not a servant for a tribe of men. "Thank you, but I'm going to Cleveland," I announced, spinning out my plan: a brother waiting for me, the silk and fine linen I would work with every day. I even named Federico, the fine blacksmith waiting to marry me.

Franco stroked a bolt of English wool with his nubby fingers. "Well then, signorina, God keep you in Cleveland," he said, handing over the package. When he offered his compliments to Federico, I nearly answered, "Who?"

"Where now?" Ciro asked as we came out to the bright clatter of streets. To see Rosanna in her new home? But perhaps my visit would only draw the child back to a dark time better forgotten. "To buy food," I said. So Ciro took me to the market in Piazza Montesanto where I bought tea, cheese, dried apples, potatoes, carrots, onions, nuts and salami at good prices, surely less than Matteo's. There would be bread on board at least and even if food on the *Servia* was scant, two or even three lean weeks were nothing compared to a hunger winter at home.

Besides, I'd be doing no work, so there was no need to eat like a laborer. In the lodging house I stored the provisions, tested my new scissors and tried not to think of Opi.

For dinner they gave us cabbage stew, bread, melon and wine. Two men from Puglia played accordions while couples danced. Others played cards, drank or argued about America. Children played around the tables, their languages laced together with laughter and shouts. I sat with a circle of single women listening to songs of home. As the city grew dark behind us, many cried, their tears glittering in candlelight. A man from Calabria tugged at my arm, wanting to dance, his body damp with sweat.

"I'm married," I said, pushing him off. "I'm meeting my husband in Cleveland." How easy to be a liar far from home. I slipped back to my cot and sewed myself to sleep.

Repairs for the *Servia* dragged on. Yet we must not go wandering, the matrons warned, for boarding could begin any time. African heat closed Naples in a breathless oven. Fights sparked easily, for many had counted their coins so tightly that extra days threatened hunger at sea. Yet at night, when street vendors sold cheap wine, many bought freely. Children played and couples found dark corners that hid faces but not muffled heaves.

By day, with hundreds of travelers suffering the pressing heat, any sliver of shade went to the strongest. Grumbles and curses ran down the long tables where we took our meals. "What repairs? There's not a thing wrong with that ship," a fisherman from Bacoli announced. "The captain made a deal with the lodging house. Besides, he has our ticket money. He could pull out one night and leave us stranded."

"I saw the wood they brought on for repairs," a carpenter said. "Second-rate pine. Could be we never reach America."

"Shut up," snapped a day laborer. "I talked to the steward. He says she's stout enough. And at least we're not back home working like donkeys in other men's fields."

On the third day I found a tree-shaded scrap of wall and climbed it "like a mountain goat," Teresa said. Perched there before dawn, I watched fishermen row over the glassy bay, their voices floating to shore. A man jumped in the water and swam, not as our boys paddled like dogs in mountain lakes, but churning his arms overhead like a water wheel. Astonishing, but were all these new wonders washing Opi from my mind? Gripping the wall, I closed my eyes to piece out Zia's high brow, thin lips and wrinkles nesting her eyes.

Suddenly, shrill whistles blew and Gabriella came running, shouting, "Come down, Irma! We're going to America!"

The lodging house roared like a winter storm, the air thick with straw and wool fluff. We threw wet and dry clothes into sacks, rolled mattresses and shook the guard awake to get our baggage. Women changed shamelessly in daylight, pulling on traveling clothes. "Roll up your sleeves! Show your numbers," the matrons ordered. "Hold on to your children."

Outside the lodging house, we stood sweating as clerks checked our numbers against lists. They yanked a coughing woman out of line. "It was my sister's number," she cried. "What's the harm in that?"

"The harm is defrauding the company. You could get prison for it," a clerk snapped, herding her into a roped-off knot of old, lame and sickly travelers who had tried to sneak on the *Servia*. As the woman's husband protested, begging for the ticket money back at least, the clerk stood stone-faced. "You knew the rules," he said calmly.

"It's better this way," Teresa comforted a wailing woman torn loose from an old man. "If your father dies in steerage, they'd bury him at sea for fish to feed on. Get work in America and send him a first-class ticket. Doctors don't test the gentlefolk."

"He'll die before then," the woman sobbed.

So I would have to work hard to buy Zia a first-class ticket. What would Father Anselmo say of a land where only the young and healthy are welcome? As we culled lame sheep, perhaps America culled weaklings to make their country strong.

Gabriella tugged at our sleeves. "Let's go or we'll lose our place." Trunks and large packs were taken, receipts issued and anxious passengers assured they would see their goods in America. Sailors and clerks barked orders in many languages, one laid over the other as travelers shouted, "What? What did you say? Where do we go?" In the end we only followed the waving hands and whistles. The *Servia* loomed over us with a steep plank up to the deck. I prayed. Teresa's lips moved as well and she crossed herself for we would not touch land until America.

And then suddenly I was on the *Servia*, a rocking mountain of metal and wood. Masts rose between smokestacks wide as our church. Coiled rope, winches, pipes and levers filled the deck. How could this monster float? And how could it fit us all? Those from the lodging house packed the deck and yet passengers on shore stood three and four abreast, mounded with bundles like donkeys.

"Steerage below," a sailor shouted.

"Look there," Gabriella cried, pointing to a line of rowboats hung along the ship.

A bald sailor polishing brass called out, "If any of you children give us trouble, we set you loose in there."

"*Bastardo!*" Teresa shouted, clapping her hands over Gabriella's ears.

"Shut up, Sal," barked a younger man with a rusty beard. "Those are life boats, signora. But the child needn't worry, my *Servia's* a good solid ship. She'll take you safe to America." Gabriella clung to Teresa, shivering. My knees buckled and I grabbed a brass railing. Would we die on those tiny boats, bobbing in the ocean?

Whistles flew down from rigging where sailors hung like jeering bats: "Look at them, fresh off the field. Already scared and we're still at port!"

"Down below, go on," snapped a steward. Through cracks in the crowd I glimpsed a black hole to steerage, the ship's deep belly. A hot line of sweat rolled between my breasts. No letters home had spoken of the crossing. Not one word of that hole, storms at sea or heckling sailors.

"Go on, move," a sailor prodded. In the steep, narrow stairway, bodies pressed against my chest. Oil lamps swinging in dusty gloom showed flashes of a milling crowd, each traveler humped with bags. Standing on boxes or perched on pipes, stewards barked orders dividing us in groups: single men, families and single women. I squeezed through a narrow passage and down a second stairway as steep as a ladder.

Like sheep herded too closely in summer heat, many balked or turned against the flow. Single women who had been swept into a crowd of men fought their way back through grasping hands. A lost child was passed overhead to a woman shrieking, "Over here! Nicoló, Nicoló, come back!" In the rising heat and airless space we grew slick with sweat under layers of clothing. An old woman swayed and crumbled. I reached out, but a surge from behind bore her away. I must have briefly fainted too, for suddenly I stood in rustling grass with blue sky arched overhead and a tumbling stream. Teresa shook me.

"Dormitory A to the left," a matron shouted. Gabriella tugged me into a steamy hall of stacked berths, the spaces between them clogged with bags and travelers. Teresa must have tipped the matron, for we had places together. The berths were in pairs, bolted on the long edge and butting another pair at the head. Gabriella would sleep between us, Teresa explained, so she wouldn't fall out at night. Above us was another set of four berths, reached by a rough ladder, making eight in our block.

Exhausted, I unrolled my mattress and sat down to study my new home. The long, rough-paneled dormitory had no windows. Swinging oil lamps sent bars of pale yellow light across the room. There was a center aisle between two rows of berths, forty-eight in each row. There were ninety-six berths, then, but far more than a hundred souls, for I saw three, even four small children huddled on one mattress. It was as if the whole of Opi lived in one smoky room. Since hooks on the walls would not hold all our bags, they would be piled on the floor or our berths. The center aisle was barely four paces wide.

"Look, flying tables," said Gabriella suddenly. "How can we eat up there, Irma?" I followed her tiny finger to rude tables and benches lashed to the ceiling.

"We lower them for meals, see the ropes?" said a matron. This oddity delighted the child, but glancing at Teresa, I read her thought: apart from meals there would be no place to sit but on our beds. Small lidded boxes bolted to the floor held chamber pots in full view. Even if we emptied them quickly, the room would soon be reeking.

"Washrooms and toilets up the ladder, then left to the forward deckhouse," the matrons said, but how far that was I had no idea. I tried not to think of this or of the woman great with child settling nearby. In Opi she would be home and tended by my mother and aunts, not a spectacle for strangers.

Two women threw their bags on the berth above us and scrambled after them, chatting brightly. "Serbs," Teresa whispered. "Our church hired masons who spoke like that." The two began giggling. What was so funny here? I pulled out my pattern book to study. If I could sew in Attilio's cart, I could work at sea and have my own world like those Serbian girls.

Our dormitory was filled and yet still more travelers streamed by. This must be a thoroughfare to another dormitory deeper in the ship. As the line slowly thinned, lamplight raked the walls. A boom and shudder made us leap. Then came a grinding churn and steady pounding, louder than giant anvils.

"Boiler engines," a matron called out. "We're raising anchor."

"I'm going up," I told Teresa, frantic to see the last of the hills and the road to Opi.

"You can't," she warned.

But I had already edged past a late-arriving family, their three children clinging to posts while the parents pleaded and pulled them toward the dormitory. Someone tugged at my skirt. "Take me up too, Irma," Gabriella begged. So I let her worm ahead as we followed a faint stream of daylight and fresh salt air.

"Captain says no steerage topside," a steward warned a brace of drunks pawing at a ladder. He jostled them down a corridor, offering a good price on new wine. We hid behind a post and scrambled up the ladder.

Finally we were on deck, with wind and space around us, free of the terrible smells. Four young women pressed against a rail facing land. As they waved, pointed and compared hotels, I gathered they were maids to first-class passengers. Hoping to pass as a maid myself, I stood near them, or tried to stand, for the deck rocked like boards that children set on rocks for play. I gripped the railing and made Gabriella do the same. Fishing boats scurried from our path.

"Look," cried Gabriella, pointing out our tiny lodging house and stubs of offices behind the port. Once-huge palaces shrank steadily, squeezing broad streets to threads. I saw the fishing quarter where we had left Rosanna and roads winding through hills where Attilio might be traveling. Tolling church bells dimmed. As the great city flattened into gray-green hills, the bay cupped behind us and even Vesuvius shrank.

"Zia!" my heart called. "Don't forget me!"

"*Arrivederci* Naples!" a maid cried gaily. So she would be returning someday. The bay would open wide to her, the city pull out from the hills and church bells peal, welcoming her home.

"You're from steerage?" a rough voice demanded. It was the bald sailor. Up close, he looked older, his ruddy skin wrinkled as old linen. "You're to stay below unless the captain lets you up." The maids edged away and Gabriella gripped my hand.

"I wanted to see the last of the land," I said.

"So do all of you. You think eight hundred poor folks can be on deck and leave us space to work? Get going or they dock my pay."

"So we can't come up before America?" Gabriella asked mournfully.

"Maybe, a few at a time when the captain's willing and in good weather," he said. "Depends. If you fight down there, he don't let anyone up. And watch, it's not always single men who make the most trouble. Sometimes it's the ladies. That your little girl?" he asked suddenly.

"No, she's traveling with her mother."

"My father's in America," Gabriella said brightly. "Waiting for us."

"Huh." The sailor sniffed. "Wind picking up. Go on now, captain's coming."

As we climbed below, steerage smells and sounds rolled over us: onions and wet clothes, men playing cards and children running between beds with mothers calling after them. Through the walls came a steady rumble. "What's that?" Gabriella demanded.

"The engine that takes us to America."

"How?"

"Maybe with blades that turn like oars," I said vaguely.

"What makes the blades go around?"

"Coal heats water to make steam," said one of the card players, "in an oven as big as a church. Don't go near the engine room. It's hot as hell and cooks you up." The child's eyes widened. I pulled her along.

"Never mind him," I said, but in the next days we heard of boiler men burned by steam and leaping sparks; mechanics losing fingers, hands or whole limbs; sailors broken from falls off the rigging and mast or scoured out to sea on waves. "Just be glad you're not a sailor," a matron muttered.

For our first meal at sea, Teresa wedged us next to the Serbian girls. Their names were Gordana and Milenka, they explained in scraps of Italian. "We are sisters. Our father send us to America when we don't marry bad men he choose for us."

"They don't look like sisters," muttered Simona, a gap-toothed woman from Puglia who plowed her way into conversations and soon knew every name in our dormitory.

"One father. Two mothers. Hers die," Gordana said, pointing to Milenka.

"So you're half sisters," Teresa said briskly.

"How did you know they were bad men?" Gabriella demanded, pulling Milenka's sleeve.

"Leave her alone," said Teresa. "Eat."

The matrons ladled out a stew of onions, potatoes and bits of tough meat, careful to spread the bits evenly. The bread was good, chewy with a thick crust like Assunta's. "We have three days' worth," the matrons said when we asked for more. "After that, it's hardtack."

"Irma, let's try to watch the sea tomorrow," Gabriella whispered. But we could not go up the next day or the next. There was "a problem" on deck, the matrons explained shortly. All across the Mediterranean we stayed below. Our world was the dormitory, the steamy crowd of the washrooms, rank toilet room where we might wait an hour for a seat and tiny openings around the stairwells where crowds squeezed into shafts of fresh air. We saw nothing of the world outside but patches of gray waves through portal windows. I passed hours on my berth embroidering roses, buds tight and half open, full-blown roses and a drift of falling petals. Bent over my needle, I fixed on its soft *pluck, pluck* inside the steady drum of voices, children playing, babes crying and the ceaseless pounding of pistons.

Days passed without changing, lit by our oil lamps. Many finished their provisions and became prey to stewards who peddled cheese, dried beef, fruit, eggs, beer and wine at terrible prices. "So live on cabbage soup," they taunted those who balked. I bought nothing and ate little, for the ship's rocking churned my stomach.

Four

Storm in Steerage

A day beyond Gibraltar, shrill winds rose over the engine's fiercer pounding. "Bad storm coming," a matron warned. "Tie up your bags." The ship bucked fiercely at dinner. We clung to our trenchers and spoons until stewards suddenly ordered the tables and benches hoisted and "secured." Could they fall in a storm? Gordana and Milenka deftly lashed their bags and ours to posts, then moved from berth to berth helping the others. Even Simona stepped aside to let Milenka work.

"Everybody on their beds," the stewards ordered. "Now!" The ship dipped wildly, hurling small children off their feet. Dazed men staggered back from card games in the stairwells, groping from post to post as swinging lanterns scraped streaks of light across their faces.

Shrieks laced the howling wind, first of children and soon of women and men. Some cried the ship was witched. Many prayed. I saw men cover their heads with shawls and chant, rocking steadily. Their rocking, the rocking ship and everywhere the clicking rosaries like ravenous mice made me dizzy. I closed my eyes as matrons careened down the aisles, ordering mothers to tie small children to the posts. Private chamber pots tumbled across the room. A flying bucket caught a woman full in the face. She fainted and her husband cried for a doctor.

"He can't come," a steward shouted. I had lived through mountain storms, but in a stone house rooted in the earth with my own people near me.

"Stay on your berths!" the matrons shouted. The ship pitched, yanking a babe from his mother's arms and hurling him against a post, screaming.

Gordana and Milenka climbed down to us, announcing, "Take storm together." We passed the night with our arms linked around Gabriella, who whimpered herself to sleep. I say "night," but faint ship's bells under the screeching wind and creaking timbers were all that signaled day or night. "Holy Mother of God," I repeated gripping my rosary, too light-headed to work the beads. "Be with us now." Sickness filled me top to toe. Teresa held a bowl for my vomit until a sudden lurch tore it from her hands, soaking us all.

With each wave crashing full against the ship, I thought, *this one* breaks her, *now* sea water swallows us like the avalanche that took a village near Opi, sweeping out trees, houses, men and sheep. A bag weakly tied broke free and slid across the floor, spilling clothes, cups, a clock and Bible that skidded back and forth.

The air throbbed with retching, first here and there and then in waves across the dormitory. I gripped our galloping bed. Words rattled in my head like marbles in a cup: *Lord, I'm dying.* Then: *Lord, let me die. Let. Die.* For an instant the ship held steady, the wind dropped, then raged again after the mocking calm. I'm dead, I thought wildly, dead among strangers like my great-grandfather in Russia. This is hell. No flames, only storm without end. We were the damned, battered for our sins. Sailors' feet pounded overhead. Whistle blasts. It is finished. We sink, the ocean takes us. Now at least, the peace of death, but still we toss on mountain waves. I closed my eyes and somehow slept, tangled and gasping for air under a vast black cloak.

I dreamed a pale green light spread like oil over rocking waves. The *Servia* was broken away and I alone was left, clinging to my bed at sea. Carlo floated past, astride a piston. Laughing, he reached for me, his arm a smoky glass showing angry waves below. A mast spun by, shattering the arm to shimmers. My bed melted into waves and I floated free. A faceless shadow man appeared on a battered raft. "Here's my sail," he said, hoisting Carlo's limp and gauzy body. "Come, Irma, there's room for you."

Someone shook me and I saw Gordana's hovering face, felt a cup at my lips, woke and slept again. A night, a day, another night and day. Twice I ate rough dryness, hardtack perhaps. Someone wet my brow. I tasted warm tea and struggled to sit. Gordana and Milenka must have returned to their berths. From whispering and laughter, paper slaps and creaking wood above us I gathered they were playing the fast, complex card game that they swore only Serbs could learn. Near me Gabriella slept, arms and legs splayed out like a rag doll. Teresa worked around us, rolling soiled linens together and feeling through bags for clean clothes.

A new sound came slowly through what ship's bells told us was night—a low moaning, and then a woman's sharp grunting cries, closer and closer together. Teresa whispered. "It's Angela. She's in labor, poor creature." Voices barked for clean water and linens, needle and thread. My sewing box was not a span away, but I could not bend to reach it. Perhaps the Lord will take both mother and babe, I thought, drifting back to sleep. Minutes later, Teresa shook me awake to a shrill cry that filled the room now, triumphant and imperious: "I'm here! Attend me!"

"A healthy girl!" women shouted. Some beat their cups together. Men cheered weakly and children shouted, some excited, some confused.

"Where did she come from?" a little boy demanded. "Did the storm bring her?"

"Lord be praised!" Teresa whispered. The Serbs sang a birthing song and Teresa helped me stand. From all over the rolling room, we made our way to Angela's bed, grasping posts to keep from falling as the babe's sharp wails rose over the wind.

"I'll call her Marina," the mother said as she nursed the swaddled, red-faced babe, "because she out-cried the storm." Someone laughed, then others, until we were all holding our still aching bellies, laughing and crying in pain.

All day the storm slowly weakened. In the evening the captain himself paid his respects to Marina. He held a linen handkerchief to his nose, but removed it long enough to give Angela an amulet for the child and congratulate her on the birth. Then he clapped the handkerchief to his mouth again and made for the door, stopping to speak in angry whispers to a matron as he pointed at the room. Had we grown used to smells that made a visitor gag?

"Signor Captain, may we go on deck when the storm's over?" Gabriella called out, but he turned his squared shoulders away and did not answer.

"Those who can walk," said the matrons briskly, "help clean this pigsty." I could do little more than slowly straighten our bedclothes, but Teresa and the Serbian girls joined a score of others washing floors with salt water, sorting tangled possessions and scattering dried lavender and rosemary from a Greek woman's stores to freshen the air. As my strength crept back, I helped Gordana straighten our beds.

It was then that I learned a thief had moved in the storm. In the darkness and tossing, someone had passed among the sick and those lying in stupor, plucking a little from each. The last of my Opi gold coins were gone from the chamois pouch around my neck, leaving only the lire squirreled inside my bag.

"You felt nothing, no? So it must have been a gypsy. Only they are so light in hand," said Milenka grimly.

"Or an Albanian," Teresa insisted. "They're the sly ones."

"Greek for sure. Everyone knows how they smell out silver and gold," Simona announced. She had lost her mother's silver icon. Up and down the rows of berths, curses and cries of fury signaled others discovering their losses. The thief or thieves were surely wailing as well, as if their own treasures too had been stolen. We should all open our bags for inspection, Simona insisted, but the matrons hushed her: no thief would be fool enough to keep the stolen goods in the dormitory. "It could have been one of them," hissed Simona, pointing at the matrons. "*They* weren't sick."

"You have lire enough for the train, at least," Teresa consoled me.

"In Cleveland you make more," said Gordana.

Yes, I could make money, but no more of the Opi gold I had meant to hoard as my family's women had done for one to come whose need would be greater than mine.

"We live the storm," Milenka said loudly. "That is the good thing. We clean now." So we did, working in grim silence and resting in turns, our limbs weak from disuse. The babe Marina slept calmly, born in tempest and easy to calm. We had lost three days in the storm, a matron grumbled. Do not think of this, I told myself, and not of the gold either. Be like Marina, each day new.

At dinner we picked at our food, our bellies wary and most of us daring only hardtack and tea. The ship eased to a steady rocking. As the evening drew on and many felt stronger, talk turned to America, how jobs fell in your hand there like ripe plums from a tree. "Good land," someone swore. "Work it and it's free."

"And herds of wild horses, catch one and he's yours," a woman bubbled. Others spoke of painted canyons, forests vaster than Tuscany, black loam deep as a man is high, streets lined with factories, each with hundreds of workers, a brown river wider than a city, a former shepherd who owned a vast ranch now and paid his sisters' dowries in Sicily. The stories were like winter tales in Opi of talking bears, two-headed sheep, crafty second sons, doomed or triumphant lovers and miracles seen "long ago, in a certain dukedom." Swept up in the talk, I spoke of my own plans.

"You'll find sewing work everywhere," one man assured me. Others said no, machines made all the clothes in America.

"If you don't find work in Cleveland," suggested a woman with rippling red hair, "take the bride train to California. Fifty men for every woman; you just pick."

"What, like a horse market?" Teresa scoffed.

"Better than factory work," said others.

"Why Cleveland?" a Sicilian woman demanded. "What if your brother's not there?"

Teresa studied my face. "She's right. You could stay in New York with us."

"Yes, with my father," Gabriella added eagerly. I rubbed the grease-slick table.

"What do you know about Cleveland anyway?" the Sicilian persisted.

Nothing. Except that I had chosen it, having chosen so little in my life.

"Irma's brother's there and the man she'll marry," Teresa said dryly.

"Oh," said Gabriella, perplexed. "Then why isn't she happy?"

"It's late," Teresa announced, bustling the child to our berth. "We'll sleep well tonight. And Irma, here's my husband's address in New York. You can write to us, or come if you don't like Cleveland."

"We not think of America now," Milenka advised. "We think of calm seas." Soon we were all in our berths, the engine drone bearing us on. I woke once at a cry at the edge of the room and was drifting back to sleep as something in Gordana and Milenka's muffled murmurs caught me. A pause, then a cautious creaking in their beds, silence and a creak again. In the dim light I saw Teresa's eyes open, note mine, flicker up and close quickly. She turned away, cupping Gabriella to her body. The creaking sharpened, followed by a deep sigh, covering coughs and a sigh again. I had heard those sounds from my parents' bed, but two women together, sighing? I lay very still. A chamber pot rattled nearby and a child whimpered. The engines throbbed; I squeezed my eyes to sleep and did not mention these things in the morning.

The long, calm days stretched on. Each day, for some new cause, the captain would not let steerage up on deck. "It's not our place," the matrons said flatly when we begged them to appeal for us. "It goes hard for everyone if he's angry."

So we lived below. We scrubbed clothes in salt water that left them stiff. We took turns emptying the chamber pots, cleaning the dormitory and dodging clothes that hung in moist mazes between our berths. Hours crawled in the flickering gloom. We found a sea gait, rocking as we walked, flattening ourselves against walls and posts to let one another pass. The air was thick with sweat, kerosene, garlic, wet wool, fouled linens and our stale breath. We spoke loudly, leaning close to slip our words beneath the boiler room's steady growl, the cries of babes and children and the clamor of the sailors working just outside the thin walls of our chamber. We were always hungry, yet often could barely stomach the monotony of grease-slicked potage, beans, cabbage soup and dry bread. The ship's stores of potatoes had spoiled in the storm; rats had gnawed the dried fruit and thieves among us had found private stores of salami, cheese and nuts. Even music from the first-class quarters was a torment, too faint for pleasure and too present to ignore.

When I could, I sewed. I sat on my bunk and learned to feel the stitches even when lamplight rocked away. Combining designs from my pattern book, I made borders, medallions, and "Irma" in five scripts. Tying off a line of fringe, I dreamed I was in Opi again, sitting in our doorway with cool air brushing my face, Zia beside me, the bright beat of the blacksmith down the street and a child running past us barefoot on packed earth. I made a church in cross-stitches, one for every soul in Opi.

On the third day after the storm, I found a shaft of light by a ladder to the upper deck. A locked wooden grid kept us below, but fresh sea air poured through it. Young couples crowded the breezy shaftway, laughing and talking, some dancing in a square of space barely large enough for a ram to lie in. I wedged into a corner to finish stitching a patch of golden meadow grass rolling like waves with bluebirds flying over.

"Beautiful," said a voice close by. I looked up at the rusty-bearded sailor from the day we came aboard in Naples.

"It's just a scrap for practice."

"Practice or not, it reminds me of home. The grass blew like that in my father's fields. Could I buy it, signorina?" he asked as my crane nipped off thread ends.

"The grass could be smoother here. And it needs more birds. It's not my best."

He smiled and his eyes sparkled, full of sun and air. "No one but me would see it, I promise. If you won't sell, I'll trade for a hunk of sheep cheese. Big as this." He held out two bronzed fists.

Sheep cheese! I could almost taste the creamy tang; Gabriella cried for change from our weary meals. "We can trade," I agreed.

As the young people clapped time for the dancers, the sailor leaned in and whispered. "At the end of the second dog watch, tonight, eight bells, that grate will be open. Come on deck. The captain and all the officers are at a banquet tonight in first class. I'll bring you the cheese. Perhaps you've never seen the ocean on a clear night. It is the most beautiful sight on earth."

From far away hissing voices curled in my ear: *You know what he wants. You know what kind of woman walks at night with strange men.* Even Zia whispered: *"Remember Filomena."*

I could bring my scissors for defense, I reasoned. And if he had wanted the company of a beautiful woman, they were easily found in steerage. He spoke respectfully, did not touch me and back in Naples had comforted Gabriella for no advantage to himself. "I could bring you the cheese now if you want, signorina."

"I've never seen an ocean at night," I admitted.

"Then come. I am not—I only mean to show you something beautiful."

People might talk, but for clean night air after the stench below, forgive me, Zia, I agreed. After dinner, as Teresa finished a dress for Gabriella to wear in New York and the Serbian girls played cards on their bed, I groped along the dark corridor and steep ladder, pushed open the grate that had always been locked and came on deck, gasping.

The Milky Way sprayed overhead. Cupped over the sea edge, a half-moon spilled glimmering silver over blue-black waves. Who could imagine such endless water, a vast smoothed satin skirt, its distant hem tucked under a dome of sky? Space to walk without twisting past bodies, cots, heaped baggage and the flap of dank clothing. The quiet was delicious, with only the distant engine's gentle rumble, a waltz seeping up from the ballroom and close by, the soft paddle of waves against the ship. I felt—yes, joy despite the storm, despite loneliness and losing Opi and fears of America. As waves ruffled the moon path, I opened my mouth as I did as a child years ago on the meadows. Wind ran through me and my heart buoyed up.

"There's nothing like it, is there?" asked a quiet voice behind me. I jumped, hot with embarrassment and gripping the billowing folds of my skirt. The sailor jumped nimbly over a coiled rope. "I remember my first moonlit night at sea. Every sailor does."

"Thank you for opening the grate, sir."

"My name is Gustavo Parodi. And yours, signorina?"

"Irma Vitale. Of Opi, in Abruzzo, in the mountains. It's very small."

He nodded. "But beautiful, I'm sure. Do you miss it?"

"Not here," I said, astonished at my words. "But in steerage, yes. And you?"

"I left Genoa years ago."

"Do you miss it?"

"I have nobody there. They all died of cholera in the same week and I went to sea as a cabin boy." Gustavo leaned against the rail. Even at home, I had never spoken easily to men, not even Carlo. A sharp, curling wind nearly spun me backward. I gripped the rail, careful to avoid his hand. Remember Filomena. I looked out at the waves that buoyed the great ship like a feather.

"What are you thinking?" his voice asked, filled with wind.

"That—there are no birds here."

"No, they don't live so far out." So we lived beyond birds, like the time of Noah's flood. Gustavo pulled two cloth-wrapped packages from his shirt. "Here is your cheese and some dried figs. They're very good." In Opi no decent girl shared food with a man not her family or engaged to her, but at sea, here beyond birds, I took three figs, thrilled with their tough sweetness, warm from his shirt. I gave him the stitched square and he tucked it carefully where the cheese and figs had been.

"Thank you." His eyes washed over me, glimmering in the pale light. My neck burned. He has a wife, maybe wives. Even in Opi we had heard of sailors' ways.

"So you never go home?" I managed.

"I'm a sailor now. Storms or doldrums, I can't leave the sea."

"I thought I couldn't leave Opi." He nodded, courteously saying nothing. Dark waves rippled the sparkling moon path. "But I had no work," I said finally.

"Ah." In the way he looked steadily out to the waves, I saw that he knew there were other reasons for my leaving. But how to speak of the altar cloth and my father's hands that night? Gustavo nodded toward steerage. "A lot of them would be home now if they could, never mind all the gold in America."

A sudden splash turned our eyes to the sea, where a fish as large as a man leaped free of the waves, arched up and dove—then another fish and another following the first in leaping loops. Gustavo pointed beyond the last splash. "Look there," he said. "And—now." As if he'd drawn them from the deep, the fish arched up again, then two more together. "Dolphins," he explained. "Good omens for fair seas. The captain says we'll make New York in eight days." Eight more days in steerage under the grate that might not open again. "Look how we're sailing, straight and true." Gustavo pointed at the foamy white behind us.

"It looks like a trail plowed in the snow," I said.

He laughed. "It's so long since I've seen snow on land." Leaning on the rail, he spoke of a winter spent with an uncle in the Alps. "I suppose mountains are like the sea," he mused. "They get in your blood. My uncle wouldn't leave, even when an avalanche took his family."

"I know." I spoke of Opi's sunsets, spring flowers and bright blaze of autumn.

His smile was a warm bath. I watched the waves as he described his last trip through the terrible Straits of Magellan, up the spiny coast of South America and past the Spanish mission towns in California: San Diego, Los Angeles, Santa Barbara and Santa Cruz. San Francisco, he said, was born when gold spewed out of the mountains. Fifty years ago there was no city and now new wooden houses crept up every hill. He had been to the Sandwich Islands, flecks in the Pacific where people drank milk from coconuts and flowers draped the trees, but it was San Francisco that amazed me.

"A city made in fifty years? It took longer to build our church."

"Tell me about your church." It was so new to me, this telling. Of course we told stories in Opi, but they were all so familiar that we listened only for vagaries of each version. Gustavo asked about my family, our sheep and the seasons on the mountain, how Carlo had left for Cleveland and how I hoped to find him there. He leaned on the rail smoking his pipe as if the whole night rolled out before us. When I stopped, embarrassed that my tales must seem so poor, he shook his head. "You know, Irma, we see cities and strange lands, but week after week our whole world is right here on a ship that's smaller than your village."

We spoke of the storm. It was bad, he agreed, but not the worst by far. "She's a stout one, the *Servia*." His hand grazed mine. "I wish I could show her to you."

My chest tightened. "The captain would be angry."

Gustavo sighed. "I know. But at least come up again at night, Irma. I'll send you word and unlock the grate."

"Gustavo!" someone called. "They need you aft."

"Please come," he asked again.

"Captain's on deck!" said the rough voice.

"Thanks for the sewing," he said quickly. "I'll get word to you." He vaulted the coiled rope and joined a tangle of shadows silhouetted against the foaming wake. I stood at the rail as long as I dared. Dolphins leaped by the sea edge. Close by, a crosswind rippled the waves and a new waltz drifted up from the ballroom.

If I could be here with the waves and stars again. If Gustavo sent word and no one saw us. "*If*," my mother used to scoff at my dreams: "If we had *if* for bread." I opened the grate slowly, careful of squeaking, and slipped downstairs to the hot bath of steerage: women at the wash basin and Greeks playing cards in the stairwell screaming their bets.

Marina wailed. An Albanian boy coughed as women forced syrup down his throat. I would not dwell on these things, I would sew leaping dolphins.

But I did no sewing that night, for there was trouble by our berths. A knot of women had clustered around Gordana and Milenka, pressing them back against wet linens. Gabriella wormed toward me, sobbing. "Irma, they're cursing the Serbian girls. Mamma's at the washroom."

I told her to get Teresa and wedged myself into the angry group. Gordana and Milenka's proud faces had paled. The crowd looked at them now as townspeople looked at twisted beggars or monster children shown around markets for a few centesimi and easy sport. "What happened?" I demanded.

"Unnatural beasts," hissed Simona, "I saw them under the ladder, *talking*." She made a childish mimic of lovers' murmuring, then worked her jaw and spat a foamy glob on Gordana's breast. Milenka wiped it off.

"So what?" I demanded. "They weren't *talking* to you."

"Serbian pigs. They'll disgrace us all."

"How? You'll never see them in America."

"Irma, is not your problem," said Gordana quietly.

"They've done nothing to you," I persisted. "And they helped us all in the storm."

"Irma's right," said a new voice, Teresa shouldering into the crowd.

Simona's face darkened. She pointed to our four berths. "You're all cozy here, eh? Do you all *talk* together?" And then she spun to me. "Ha, Irma, I saw you sneak up on deck tonight. What did *that* cost you?"

"Nothing," I stammered. "It cost me nothing."

In a whip of time, Teresa stepped between us.

"Get away!" Simona snapped.

Across the room the matrons called, "Half rations for everyone if you don't back off."

Pushing Teresa aside, Simona grabbed my arm and pulled me close, her onion breath steaming my face. "I'm not getting half rations for your dirty business, not yours or your Serbian sluts."

I pushed her, the only time I ever pushed a woman. Simona fell against the next bunk, scrambled up and launched herself forward, howling. I tripped backward into a bedpost. Simona knocked me to the floor, scraping my face along the post. My cheek must have caught on a nail, tearing flesh. Gabriella shrieked. Touching my cheek, I felt the gash and yanked my hand away, red.

The matrons rushed over, dragging us apart as hunters do with dogs. "On the beds, all of you!" Men ran from card games, collecting their women, cursing the half rations, but then they saw my face and went silent.

The ship's doctor would not come. Teresa washed my cheek with the little fresh water they allowed us, then salt water that stung like fire. An older woman we called Nonna, for she was like everyone's grandmother, came with herbs, calendula and comfrey. "I could sew it closed," she said doubtfully, "but my hand shakes. You don't want my stitches." She looked at Teresa, who shook her head. "Best we can do is hold it closed until it heals. Could be hours."

"I'll hold it for hours," said Teresa quietly.

"Keep the edges right together and dab off the blood." The old woman patted my shoulder. "It's a pity, child. You were no beauty before, but now—well, you'll live. Watch for fever," she told Teresa. "I have to go. There's men sick in the next dormitory." She laughed. "Things turn strange at sea. Women fight and men cry over belly pains."

Teresa held my wound closed all night. Milenka and Gordana wiped away blood with scraps of fresh linen that other women laid wordlessly on my bed. No fever came, but when they gave me a broken bit of mirror in the morning, I saw my face pale at the length of the gash.

"Good, no pus," Nonna said when she came to inspect the wound. She sat on my bed and rambled on with news from all the decks: trysts at the ball, a theft in second class. "A sailor fell from the rigging last night. The doctor's still drunk, so I set his leg."

"Which sailor?" I whispered.

She looked at me sharply. "Which one do you know? Says he's from Genoa. Brave enough. Bit on a wood stake while I set his leg. Never made a sound and thanked me afterwards." She raised her wide hands. "They said he wasn't paying attention. The captain said he'll lash the next man that's distracted. The sailor's washing pots in the first-class galley until he's fit for deck work."

Teresa watched me thoughtfully. "Should I find him?" she whispered as Nonna bustled away, but I shook my head. No one would let Teresa in the kitchen and if she did find Gustavo and if we could meet, suppose he turned away from a scar that even moonlight couldn't hide?

The matrons reported that the captain was so furious to hear of the fight and what he called "unnatural indecencies" that no one from Dormitory A could go on deck until we reached New York. The next days brewed resentment. At meals, in the washroom and in the milling crowds around the blocked stairwells, no one spoke to Simona, Gordana or Milenka. They turned from my face and were curt with Teresa. Children squabbled in the narrow spaces between berths. Card games turned bitter. Gustavo's cheese was delicious, sharp and rich, but I had little stomach for eating and lay in bed, covering my scar.

Teresa made me come to English lessons, at least to leave my bed. A young man on his third voyage to America taught bits of English, but our accents enflamed him. "Th . . . th . . . *TH!*" he repeated, rapping his pipe against long yellow teeth. "The tongue *here*, imbecile, not on the roof of your mouth. Why waste my time with you?" he demanded of a startled child.

"It's an ugly language if people talk through their teeth," someone observed.

"If you live in New York with us, Irma, you won't need English," Gabriella said, but I practiced silently, pressing my tongue to my teeth: *the, three, think.* The next day, when Gordana and Milenka joined the lesson a clot of women moved away.

I asked Nonna for news of Gustavo. "The one with the broken leg? Still washing pots I suppose." He sent no word. Perhaps he had heard of my scar. Or our night had cost him too much. Or he had forgotten me.

"Forget him," Teresa whispered. But she had not eaten figs by moonlight and her face was not gashed.

"We dock Tuesday morning," the matron announced on a Sunday night, the sixteenth of our voyage. "Make sure you're packed." They passed out syrups for coughs, powders for lice, creams to hide rashes and drops for rheumy eyes. Even children took them willingly, for we had all heard about those who were turned away from America. Many died on the passage home.

"Fair skies to the west and calm seas. At worst, we'll have fog in the harbor," the matrons reported. Suddenly even New York seemed so present and real, a city with a foggy harbor that opened to land vast enough to swallow us like pebbles. My hands shook as I counted my few remaining coins and mended a rip in my skirt. I took out the stone from our house and tried to smell in it the must of our walls, smoky bite of our fires, damp wool of our clothes, the rosemary and lavender hung over our beds and tang of new cheese.

My face still hurt, more at night, a sharp tug beneath the skin. Even if Carlo had a friend in America, why would that friend want a woman both plain and scarred?

"We'll see Papà soon," Gabriella chanted happily. "I'll wear my new red dress. He'll pick me up and carry me on his shoulders. What about you, Irma? How will you fix your hair for America? What will you wear?"

"Don't bother her, child," Teresa said.

Gordana and Milenka silently slid off their beds. While the others prepared their bags, brushed shoes, and pulled out once again their worn maps and letters, the two somehow found fresh water to wash my hair, then brushed and combed it shining.

"Now we make knots," Gordana announced. With deft fingers, they began braiding. They finished, conferred, undid their work and began again. "We have better idea, wait," they said, gently moving my hands away. One by one, women came to watch. Gordana touched my skirt. "Look down here."

Silence fell over the group. When I tried to look up, Milenka tugged so sharply on a hank of hair that my scalp burned. Simona was standing before me holding a russet velvet ribbon. "I don't need this," she said, letting it curl in my lap. "I'm sorry about—your face."

"Is pretty color," Gordana said gruffly.

Simona nodded. "Well, I have to pack now." When she backed away, Gordana drew the ribbon from my hand.

"Look, Mamma," piped Gabriella. "They made her hair like a rose."

"Irma, it's beautiful," Teresa whispered.

They showed me the rose with mirrors, wound with Simona's ribbon. Milenka's long fingers wiped away my tears. "I know we pull tight," she said, "but at night when you sleep, it stay good."

"Doesn't she look like a fine lady?" Gabriella demanded. Teresa straightened my dress and nodded.

"No, Irma!" said Milenka and Gordana when I tried to thank them. "Is nothing what we do for you."

After dinner, matrons called all the steerage passengers into one chamber, where we stood shoulder to shoulder in the damp, thick air. A steward climbed on a table flanked by translators. As each language took its turn, we learned what would happen at New York. If we satisfied the port doctors, government clerks would help us buy train tickets to other cities. We could bathe in hot fresh water with soap and towels to dry ourselves. Many cheered, for days of salt water had crusted our skin. We would be fed by ladies of charity, given our baggage, and those leaving the city would be directed to train stations. So the city would be rid of us by nightfall, like gypsies or stray dogs.

"The city's full," the steward warned. "If you stay, you'd live worse than here." He waved his hands at the dank sea of us. "Wages are low and many have no work. Those of you from the country are better off west." As for seeing the port of New York, he warned, the *Servia*'s deck was far too small for all of us. Only a few could go up in the morning. He wished us well and curtly took his leave with translators bustling after him.

"He's lying," said Teresa. "How can a city be full?" Everyone agreed, but I was silently grateful to be headed west. I would go first to the church in Cleveland, the one on the main piazza, I had decided. If there was another church, I'd go there too. The priests would know, as

Father Anselmo knew, everyone in their parish. And if the priests didn't know, I would go to the marketplace on a feast day. Surely Carlo would be there.

Teresa, Gabriella, Milenka, Gordana and I spent our last night in line below the grate to be sure to have space on deck. We shared the last of my cheese and slept on our heaped bags. No one troubled the Serbian girls. To protect my braids, I sat braced against a post, dreaming of Ohio's mountains and towns bustling with people who spoke with tongues pressed against their teeth. When Gabriella shivered, Gordana and Milenka covered her with their skirts.

Sailors unlocked the grate before dawn and we clambered on deck in a gray fog so dense that we could barely see the ship's own railings. The *Servia* seemed to float on clouds, her mast scraping a low ceiling that hid flocks of noisy gulls. Muffled horns and bells called out from all sides. The engines lurched and died. We stopped, waited, bobbing on mist until, slowly, a faint white sun hoisted itself and wind skittered across the deck.

"Look!" cried Gabriella as the fog lifted. "Tall buildings like teeth." She was right. Jagged teeth bit the sky. So this was New York, a great wolf's open mouth.

"Irma," said a low, familiar voice beside me. It was Gustavo, leaning on a crude crutch. "I'm glad I found you," he whispered. "Here, it's not as fine as your sewing, but I hope you remember me." He tugged from his pocket a disk of polished whalebone the size of a palm. Scratched roughly into the bone was a half moon hung over waves. Out of the waves leaped three dolphins. Below them was scratched "Gustavo of Genoa."

"I'll remember you even without this," I said. "How is your leg?"

"Better already. Sailors bounce, you know."

When he looked at me curiously I turned my cut cheek away. "Your hair," he said. "It's very beautiful."

"My Serbian friends did it."

"I heard what happened." He looked at my cheek. "It's not as bad as they said." All around us, women from steerage politely turned away, pretending not to listen. "You were brave to defend them."

Heat swirled over me. "You'll stay on the *Servia*?" I managed.

"Of course. When my leg's healed, I'm on the rigging again, but Irma, may I write to you?"

"How?"

"I'll send it to General Delivery in Cleveland. We go to Liverpool next. I'll write from there."

"Yes, I'd like that."

"Gustavo!" came a shout. He touched my hand gently and then limped into the crowd. Teresa braced my shoulder and Gordana wound her arm around my waist as we steamed into port.

"He seems like a good man," Teresa whispered. "You'll find another like him." But I had not "found" Gustavo. I had only briefly known him when my face was whole. I slipped the whalebone into my bag with my stone from Opi.

They herded us into barges, fifty together, splattered by the choppy, cold water. When we stepped on land, it seemed to rock as well, to heave and dip. We fell against each other as American boys in woven caps laughed and pointed. Clerks appeared at the door of a brick palace to divide us into lines, tugging apart those bound west and those staying in New York. So I lost all my friends: Teresa and Gabriella, Gordana and Milenka. When I craned my neck to see them one last time, a clerk impatiently thumped his desk.

"*Italiana?*" he demanded. I nodded, still searching the crowd. "May I have your attention, signorina?"

"Yes sir," I managed.

"What is your business in America?" I told him of Carlo and Federico. "Proof?" he demanded. I handed him the schoolteacher's letter and my documents from Naples and Opi. "Profession? Skill, what can you do?"

"Needlework," I stammered. "Fine needlework." When I showed him my muslin with "Irma" in five scripts, he nodded and scratched words on a long ruled page.

"How much money do you have?" Did he want a bribe? I had barely enough for my train ticket. "I mean, will you be a public charge? Can you get to Cleveland?" When I nodded and held out my lire, he did not touch them, only wrote something, pinned a card on my shawl and sent me to a doctor who had me cough and breathe, show I had no rash, lift a weight over my head and do sums in my head. He spoke in English to a clerk beside him, pinned another card on my shawl and pointed me to the baths.

There I was instructed where to undress and given a number to retrieve my clothes. We were hurried through the lines with neither cruelty nor kindness, only brisk exactness, as my father moved sheep. But they made me take out my wonderful braids to check for lice. The baths were foggy with steam, a small blessing for the shame of being naked among strange women and plain again, with dull brown hair streaming down. I thought I saw Teresa and squirmed between wet bodies, calling her name, but the pockmarked face that turned to me was not hers.

"I'm sorry, signora," I stammered, covering myself with the cloth they gave us. The woman backed away and I finished quickly, my eyes streaming tears. Outside the baths, I heard, long tables of American ladies would offer clothes to women whose country dress might offend their new country or waiting husband. I stood straighter then, dried my eyes, smoothed my skirt and arranged my shawl neatly. My hair was back in its customary winding, some coiled on top and the rest hanging down. The ladies let me pass, so at least I entered America in my own clothes.

In a vast, echoing dining room, we were served a kind of minestrone, dark bread and a mug of watered beer. At my table there was not one person from the *Servia*. Had so many ships arrived that our little world was already scattered? "Good food," said an Italian. "And free. So far, America's one fine country."

In another line a tall blond clerk read my ticket and pointed to a courtyard where from the milling mass a shrill voice cried out, "Irma!" It was Gabriella, who had clambered up a lamppost and was waving wildly. "We saw Papà! He has a beautiful doll for me and flowers for Mamma." Below her was Teresa's gleaming face. "God bless you, Irma!" she called.

"I'll write!" I shouted as a blond guard plucked the child from her perch and handed her to Teresa before the crowd surged them both away and dragged me past a knot of peddlers hawking their cities. "Boston! Philadelphia, Chicago!"

"Mill work in Hartford," said a woman who plucked at my sleeve. "Sleep and eat where you work, don't pay rent."

"Iowa, rich black earth. Plant your grain, turn around and reap," another called out.

"*Treni per* Cleveland?" I asked an officer.

"Trains for Cleveland," he corrected sharply, and then told me in Italian to find Track 34. "Get on the wrong train and they'll throw you off at the first stop." He spoke in the flat, weary way of one who repeats the same words all day. "Get your provisions here. There's none on the train and it's a long ride."

"How long, sir?"

"Long."

I bought bread and cheese for more than they cost in Naples. "That's America, good pay, high prices," the peddler said, but still it was exciting to see this light, spongy foreign bread and have change in American coins. At the Cleveland track an agent helped me into the last carriage, where a trio of broad-shouldered Polish men amiably squeezed together and made room for me. My gold was gone, but Zia, look at me, safe in America with American food in my bag and American coins in my purse. Our train shuddered, lurched and rolled out of the station.

Five

CUT, SEW, WORK

We wove through a maze of tracks branching as wildly as Rosanna's first embroidery, then plunged through a tunnel and out into blazing sun. As passengers shut their windows against the racketing wheels and dusty wind, the cabin grew hot, stinking of sweat and garlic, sausage, cheese and pickles. Babies wailed and children spilled into aisles, playing loudly while the Poles beside me spoke quietly, a lulling stream of sound. Exhausted, I hugged my bag, pressing Gustavo's whalebone into my chest.

I must have slept, for when I woke we were flying through a green blur, passing houses so quickly that their edges feathered like torn silk. Whole towns seemed to be made of wood, even a squat white church. Was there no stone in this land? "Ohio?" I asked.

A Pole laughed. "Nu Jersay," he explained, pointing. In tiny stations we stopped while express trains raced by. Around noon I ate some of my bread but its airy loft did not fill the stomach as Assunta's loaves always did. To beat down hunger, I turned back to the dusty window and studied America. Father Anselmo had told us of a great civil war here that killed half a million men. Yet how could that be if every station bustled? Gentlemen in fine suits lifted glistening black hats to each other, while around them swarmed shopkeepers, farmers, day laborers, some few cripples and drunks. Women moved easily among the men, most in simple cotton prints, but every station boasted ladies in fine layered gowns under flounced parasols. Girls trailed their mothers or played in knots outside houses. Black men worked at the train stations in crisp uniforms or by the roads in tattered shirts. Two boys raced beside the train tracks, arms swirling like cartwheels. Once we slowed to a rattling crawl, keeping easy pace with two black women stepping nimbly along a footpath with wash baskets large as lambs perched on their heads. It seemed they were singing, but when I leaned toward the window to hear them, the Poles stared at my scar. I sat back quickly. The one they called Josep spoke sharply and the men turned away.

As the train lurched ahead, Josep began a long tale in a rolling voice that put me in mind of the old ones in Opi who told the best stories and thus earned the best seats by winter fires. The Poles leaned forward to listen, eyes flaring when Josep's voice deepened and passing him a bottle each time he paused. Once he paused so long that the men grew restless. When he snapped out a line in an old man's voice, they sat perplexed an instant and then burst into wild guffaws, repeating the phrase and roaring again. One even slapped my knee as if I understood. Suddenly I was laughing too and they laughed that I laughed. Josep handed me the bottle. Zia would be horrified, but I took a sip and later shared my cheese and tried their salami. The train rattled on and the men dozed off, although from time to time one would murmur Josep's line, chuckle, tap his knee and rock back to sleep.

We passed a rosary of towns clutching the tracks, low hills cloaked in forests and barns with painted disks like gypsy charms. Cattle grazed in herds as large as a nobleman might own, but there were no villas, only tidy wooden houses.

At one station the porter had us understand that we must wait at least an hour to fix the engine. When I looked longingly at this land the porter called Pennsylvania, Josep made finger signs for walking and pointed from my bag to his eye. With my last coins, crane scissors, pewter buttons, cloth and rock from Opi safe beneath my apron, perhaps I might trust my bag to Josep and take some steps outside.

A wooden sidewalk met the rails—how astonishing to walk on wood. Peddlers swarmed the station selling meat pies, salted twists of bread and beer from tin mugs on long chains tied to barrels. A woman sold curved yellow fruit she called bananas and let me smell their sweetness. When I bought one for a penny, a skipping boy mimed eating it whole and howled with laughter when I bit into the rubbery bitter skin. The peddler grabbed my banana and peeled it, pointing from the white flesh to my mouth. "Greenhorn," she called me and snapped out words that made the boy cower.

I hurried along the tracks until the laughter faded and then I tasted my first banana. Oh! What creamy flesh, sweet and melting soft as custard. I ate slowly, savoring, as a little masked and humpbacked striped cat with a fat tail waddled across my path. Nobody had warned me that in America even the animals are different.

A cherry tree's laden branches arched nearby, the crimson fruit far sweeter than our own. If only I could fill our bread bowl and tell Zia, "Take all you want, bury your hands in cherries!" When I reached for more, an ugly little flat-muzzled dog leaped from the bushes, snarling at me. A sandy-haired boy appeared beside him, snapped an order and the dog sat, his eyes pinned to me as the boy held up a cotton sack and three fingers.

At home no one would dare charge for wild fruit, but gathering cherries in my apron would stain it for Cleveland. I showed two fingers and the boy shot up the tree. He scrambled from branch to branch, both hands picking, and then landed lightly on the ground, the filled bag in his teeth. After I thanked and paid him, he tugged a tiny arrowhead from a pocket, batting his mouth and crying, "Woo, woo, Injan!" until a sudden blaring whistle made me grab my bag and run, briars tearing at my skirt. I had barely reached the wooden walkway as the last passengers boarded and the train lurched forward. "No!" I cried. "Wait!"

At that moment Josep leaned from a doorway rushing toward me, shouted and reached out a wide hand. I caught it and leaped, still gripping the cherry bag. My feet found purchase and I was safe on the landing, wind flapping my torn skirt. Josep held my arm until I caught my breath and then politely stepped away. "*Grazie,*" I said. "Grazie, grazie." He smiled and patted my shoulder.

Wedged back in my seat, I offered him cherries. He waved his square hand around our little circle. We emptied the bag quickly, licking our fingers and tossing pits out the window. After the last cherry, the Poles drifted to sleep as we rattled on, stopped for express trains and rolled again through green Pennsylvania. Careful not to expose my legs, I mended my skirt to be respectable in Cleveland.

When the Poles woke, they pushed bags together for a rough table and began a card game. A thin-faced man in a fur hat first watched intently from another bench and then eased into the game. He bet eagerly, ignoring a woman who tugged at his sleeve, batting at her hand until Josep looked sharply at him. I remembered Emilio, who married my mother's cousin and gambled her dowry away. Fur Hat

dug into his jacket and fished out a fine meerschaum pipe, which he
bet and lost. One night Emilio would have gambled his whole flock if
Carlo had not dragged him from the tavern, shouting, "Idiota, only
dice are dumber than sheep."

"Pittsburgh!" shouted the porter but outside I saw only a wool-
thick, acrid fog that Alfredo of Pescasseroli never mentioned in his
letter. Here and there, passengers herded their children together and
dragged trunks and bags down the aisle. Fur Hat and his wife hurried
after them.

"Mountains in Ohio?" I mimed to Josep. He shook his head and
swept a hand flat out from his chest. One man stamped on the wood
floor, smiling. Flat as this floor. He drew a hump in the air and
frowned: mountains are bad. Had they never looked down on fields
rippled like soft wool beneath them, seen dawn brush the far hilltops
or springtime creep up brown slopes? Don't think of the shape of the
land. Think: work, make money and see Zia again. I leaned against the
window, watching the darkness stream by until the porter passed
again, calling: "Cleveland, Cleveland." Travelers stretched and gathered bags. Zia would frown, but I let the Poles kiss me farewell. Josep
pressed his hand to his heart, his words swallowed by a shrill whistle
as I joined a swarm pushing off the train. When it lurched away, I realized I had left my food bag behind.

There seemed to be Italian in the jumble of voices on the platform,
but I could not follow them through the swirls of children and babies
passed around for kissing, men and women falling into each others'
arms, bags and trunks handed off to young men and lesser relatives
waiting at the circle's rim. Slowly the families pulled apart, still touching the new arrivals' faces, children tugged along, questions flying and
gifts pulled from jackets. Some single men were met by others with

easy cheer, as if after a short week away. Three Hungarians shouldered their bags and strode off purposefully, following a tiny hand-drawn map they held among them and suddenly I was alone.

Of course Carlo wasn't there. Even if he had reached Cleveland, how would he have known that I would come this night? How absurd to have dreamed of seeing his peaked hat, hearing the rough, familiar voice complaining that I was late, and having him take my bags and hurry me off to our new house.

The last train lights blinked away. A porter sweeping the platform glanced at me and returned to work. I gathered my bags and walked out the great iron gates of the station. Gaslight gleamed on wet brick. A stumbling shadow crossed a street, nailed shoes clicking. I leaned against a wall. What now? What had Alfredo done on his first night in Pittsburgh? Probably a cousin or friend already rooted in America had cut him from a crowd and hurried him home. Dizzy, I pressed into the wall, remembering how once while picking wild herbs I had seen a field mouse run onto a bald stone patch and freeze, flicking its little head left and right. "Go!" I had shouted, clapping my hands. "If you stay, a hawk will get you."

From deep in the station came an echoing metal clang. I gathered my bags and walked toward a wider street that would surely lead to the main piazza and church. Carlo could be out walking late at night. But I found only tavern crowds clustered under gaslights. A one-armed man waved his hook at me, clucking as if I were a Filomena.

I hurried into a net of streets with no churches, only locked shops, shabby wooden houses and squares of scrubland where rats rustled as I passed. Carlo could live in any of these streets. Or none of them. Puddles soaked my shoes and blisters grew. I saw a plant like the one whose leaves we used on open wounds, but perhaps in America this plant was poison. My arms ached from the weight of my bag. I was cold, afraid and alone, like the night my father touched me.

A church appeared, but with no welcoming Virgin statue, only an empty cross. Sinking, exhausted, on the steps and bent over my bag, I must have slept, for a policeman woke me with the crack of his stick on the stone step, making sharp words and shooing signs as if to a stray cat. Feet swollen and hunger burning my stomach, I stumbled on with no plan now but enduring the night. And then? Once I leaned against a lamppost and a passing gentleman offered a coin. I hurried away. Fog filled the streets with a soft woolen gray that muted the knife lines of buildings and bleak tattoo of my shoes. Finally I came upon a great reach of water. Had I walked back to the Atlantic? A chill breeze pried the fog apart, revealing an iron bench. I sank onto it, squeezing my bag for warmth and slowly recalling a map on the *Servia* that showed lakes on top of America, big as the Mediterranean. Impossible, I had thought then.

A gauzy moon hanging over the charcoal waters showed broken hulls of small boats, a battered pier and pebbled shore. Far away a campfire glittered. Men gathered around it might have food, but how could I know until I got too close what kind of men they were? I rinsed my bleeding feet in the waves and hurried back to the bench.

A rising wind skimmed the water, chilling my heart and empty stomach. If I died here, who would know? A stranger who found my body could only report "Italian girl, immigrant" and I would have died alone like all who left Opi. Laughter from the fire floated over me. I fumbled for my rosary beads. The Lord had brought me safe across the ocean. But Fortune is like bread loaves, my mother once said. Some people have smaller loaves than others. Mine could end here on this bench at the frayed edge of America.

I would sit until first light, I decided, and then search for food and shelter, like those who first came to our mountain. But they were together at least, that band of wanderers. Exhausted, every muscle spent, I closed my eyes and must have slept again, for when I woke, a pale rosy band had slid across the water and a hand was shaking my shoulder.

"*Italiana?*" a voice demanded. I nodded. I turned to face a woman in a thick gray jacket with a long nose and black eyes that narrowed at the scar along my cheek. By her voice she was not Italian. She studied me as men study livestock at markets, then grasped my hand, prodding my fingertips. "You come now to Cleveland?"

"Last night on the train," I said, pulling my hand back.

"And this?" she jabbed my scar.

"On the ship. I was not to blame." She waited for more, arms crossed.

"You speak English?"

"No."

"Good." Why was this good? "You want work?"

I nodded.

"What can you do?"

"I embroider."

"Show me," she snapped and studied my samples, front and back. "They're yours? The Missus will test you."

"They're mine."

"You know nobody in Cleveland?"

"My brother was coming here. I'm looking for him."

"But he didn't meet train?" I said nothing. "Listen girl, you're not the first who doesn't get met at the station. I am"—she laughed—"a Samaritan." Was she some kind of holy sister? But she wore no cross. When she leaned down to return my samples, her breath smelled of wine.

"You hungry?"

Why lie? "Yes, signora."

"Then come." She nodded when I stood and my stiff legs buckled. "You see? Lake air is very bad. Second night you die. What is your name?"

"Irma Vitale of—"

"Never mind, Irma is enough. Is a long walk, let's go." She marched a pace ahead, drawing me briskly through the waking streets, shooing rangy cats aside. Women balancing clothes bundles on their heads dogged the hurrying crowds. Barefoot, ragged children settled on steps as if they would spend the day there. Was there nobody old in this city?

"What is your name?" I asked as we stopped for a wagon loaded with coal.

"Maria," she said shortly.

"From?"

"Greece. Hurry up." If this woman had wanted to rob me, she would have done it at the lake. But if not charity, what was her interest in me? When I stumbled at a curb Maria slowed her pace a little and noted, "You eat soon if she takes you." I walked faster despite my burning feet.

"What is the work, Signora Maria?"

"Collars. We're here," she said suddenly, pulling me into the tiny entryway of a dark brick building. I leaned against a wall as the door opened slightly, some words were exchanged, the door closed again and we waited until a steel-haired woman jerked it open and peered at me through baggy pleats around her coal black eyes. "Missus Ballios," announced Maria shortly. "You call her Missus. Show your work."

The Missus examined my scripts and flowers, her lips pursed, and then turned to Maria. Words flew between them. The Missus nodded, jerked her thumb at me and snapped out clacking sounds that seemed like "Teh er dat."

Maria cleared her throat. "You eat here and sleep with the other girls. You make linen collars from six in the morning until six at night. Piecework. She pays for what you make. If you're quick and clever, you make three, maybe four dollars a week after room and board. Half day off on Sunday the first six weeks, then all day Sunday. That is generous, you understand? You don't speak English, remember. You know nobody and can't get other work."

"I can learn English."

Maria looked at me sharply. "You want sleep at the lake again and bad men find you?"

I shook my head. "No, but I thought—"

"You think about *work*, girl. No work, no food. Understand?"

"Yes." *Oh Zia, to have come so far for this.*

Maria nodded at the Missus, who pulled a cloth purse from inside her skirt and plucked out coins for Maria. "Why are you staring?" she snapped. "I get your first week's wages. Finder's fee." When the Missus spoke and jerked her thumb at me, she added, "The Missus say she runs a decent shop. Unmarried girls, good girls. If you get in the baby way, you leave. I say no problem, you're not pretty and you have that." She pointed to my scar. "But no more fights, understand?"

"I'll do good work for her."

"You must," Maria snapped, dropping the coins in a bag. After some words to the Missus she was gone.

A sturdy black woman appeared and motioned me to a long, narrow dining room. She said "sit" and pushed me firmly in a chair. Then she held up a hand, said, "wait," left and returned with bread, a mug of water, wedge of orange cheese and a bowl of green mash. Pointing, she said, "*Pea soup, bread, cheese, water*," and then had me repeat these sounds. Then she put her hand to her mouth and said, "Eat." While I ate the warm mash, she pointed to herself and announced, "Lula."

"Irma," I said. She patted my shoulder. I ate until my stomach eased. From the other room, a shrill voice repeated words I would soon understand: "Cut, sew, work."

"Eat, Irma," Lula urged. Sun poured through the tall, dusty windows, brushing a photogravure hung on the wall. A sad, ugly bearded man gazed kindly down on us, perhaps an American saint. I pointed and Lula tapped her heart. "Abraham Lincoln," she said reverently.

I whispered to my soup: "Saint Abraham, keep me safe in America and help me find Carlo."

Lula touched my shoulder. I finished my bread and she hurried me to a second narrow room, where rows of women bent over long tables, fingers flying like birds. Thread bits and cotton fluff drifted through the warm air. The Missus snapped her fingers and a cross-eyed Albanian girl who spoke Italian came to explain the work.

"These are collars for gentlemen," Bèla said, holding up linen strips. "And these for the ladies." A creamy embroidered tendril curled around the collar edge. The Missus spoke rapidly and Bèla continued: "She said they're for *fine* gentlemen and ladies. The work must be perfect." Bèla showed how to measure and cut for the two Hungarian girls who would sew the pieces on machines in another room and bring them back for finishing.

"Machines that sew?" I asked. "What do they look like?"

The Missus snapped at Bèla, who barreled on. "Black machines," she said. "Then we trim and turn, add buttons and loops, starch and iron them. If she lets you embroider, you make a little more money." The Missus touched a long, curved finger to her eye and Bèla added,

"She inspects each one. If she can't sell them," Bèla lowered her voice, "if *she says* she can't sell them, you don't get paid. And don't bloody the linen."

I understood that I must work harder than I ever worked in Opi, even in shearing season. And this was America that so many longed to reach. Should I have stayed in New York with Teresa or searched longer for Carlo last night? But where? And I could not risk the lake again.

The Missus gave me a place on a bench, patterns, thread, needles, cording and tiny shell buttons. I would soon learn that workplaces were carefully set to separate our languages. I was wedged between a Swede and a Hungarian, then came an Irish girl and next a Pole. "Cut, sew, work," the Missus snapped if girls whispered across the table. She threw away my first six collars. The next seemed perfect to me, but her fingers jabbed a curve. My next was bloodied. When the Swede nodded at my ninth, I raised a hand for the Missus. She inspected it minutely and grudgingly dropped it in my "finished" box. Tomorrow, I vowed, every one would reach the box. And I would work as fast as the Swede.

With Lula's bell, the workroom exploded in sound: a rasp of benches pulled back, one knocked over, women stretching, sighing and calling to friends. I staggered as I stood, my back, legs, neck and shoulders all knotted in pain. I had never worked so steadily, so hunched tight and pressed on both sides. Even making the altar cloth, there was always our fire to feed, water to draw, and constant small services for Zia. Simply moving my chair to catch the shifting sun gave a little rest. Now my body screamed, "Not a collar more." And the day was only half over. Bèla seized my hand and rubbed it while the Swede worked my shoulders like Assunta's dough.

"At least you finished the morning," said an Italian girl from Puglia called Elena. "Some don't. The afternoon goes faster," she assured me but I wondered how one eternity could outlast another. Lula dished out a thin stew, watered beer and yellow squares she called corn bread, rough-grained but warm and slightly sweet. I ate slowly, flexing stiff fingers. Talk filled the room in layers of languages like on the *Servia*.

Corn bead, eat, sit, collar, stew, pea soup, greenhorn, banana. My few English words were blades of grass plucked from a meadow. To learn a new language would be like mowing that meadow blade by blade. Yet sitting silently making collars, how could I learn enough to find a better job, send money to Zia, bring her here or go home myself?

"Tell us news," clamored the Italians. But I knew nothing of their cities and none of them knew Opi or had seen a man like Carlo. There was a Lucinda from Abruzzo once, but she met a button peddler. Elena made signs for a rounded belly. "He unbuttoned her and disappeared," she said. The others howled with laughter.

"What happened to Lucinda?" I asked.

Elena waved to the dusty window and the streets beyond. Saint Abraham's great sad eyes said, *"Irma, be careful."*

The afternoon crawled by, but at least more of my collars reached the box. Elena raised a finger: one more hour. At the closing bell, I staggered from the workroom, aching to my fingertips. Dinner was sparse. "*She* got her work from us today," Elena muttered.

In the evening the girls stayed at the tables in their language knots, clustered around lamps doled out by the Missus, but I had Lula take me up a dark stairway to a dormitory under the roof. I shook a snow of thread snips from my dress, found my rosary and crawled into bed, my first in two days. I prayed for Lucinda, alone with child. English voices passed in the street below, trailing streams of laughter. I pulled the blanket tight around me and vowed not to go walking with men. Terrible as this work was, I would be safe here, watched by Saint Abraham. Twisting gingerly in bed to stretch my aching muscles, I drifted into a dream of Opi, standing with Zia in our piazza, watching white-collared birds skim the valley below us.

In my third afternoon, Elena was called from her bench. She did not return to work and her cot sat empty that night. I was the fifth Italian, I discovered. The Missus disliked having too many girls who spoke the same language and I was already faster than Elena. So she was sent away and replaced by a gaunt Norwegian. For days the Italians looked at me slant-eyed. "Listen, girls, it's not Irma's fault," Bèla insisted. "Elena *was* slow and the Missus always lets the slow ones go." Gradually the others started speaking to me again or perhaps they had simply forgotten Elena.

On Sunday afternoon, my half day off, I bound my blisters with linen scraps and put on my good shoes to go walking in Cleveland. Across the street, a mother with a tiny baby came carefully down the stairs, her husband guiding her. A red-haired girl clung to his free hand, chattering brightly. When they reached the sunny street, her hair blazed like Attilio's new pots. She waved and smiled at me, calling out, "Hello, Collar Girl." How quickly names fell away in this country.

Walking in widening circles to keep from getting lost, I joined swirls of families, couples and men in bright caps. I did not see Elena or Carlo, but the city seemed endless and I walked further. Everywhere raw brick glowed and the air rattled with hammers. Ragged children tumbled from doorways. I watched women's dresses, jackets and hats, the loops of their hair, their shoes and cloth purses, the lift of their shoulders and roll of their hips in walking. The few visitors to Opi always said we might all be cousins, we looked so much alike. Not so in Cleveland. These people varied as wildly in height and hair, color and the shape of their bodies as swallows differ from herons or hawks. Surely these people could not guess a neighbor's step behind them and friends they walked with might not know their families. Yet they seemed at ease.

Two Italians sent me to what they called "Little Italy," a tight knot of streets around Woodland Avenue. There I found shops and cafés sending out sweet, familiar smells, children playing games I knew, bags of pasta and dried beans, barrels of olives and a church with an Italian priest. But no one had seen Carlo. "Working in Tripoli?" a man from Naples repeated, glancing at his friend. "And the ship owner will buy his passage to America? It might be a while before he gets here." They backed away from me, melting into a knot of card players.

I found no better jobs. Some girls did piecework from their homes, but I had no home. Shop girls must be pretty, shop owners had me understand, and not have scars. "Don't work in rich people's houses," warned a woman selling dry beans. "Servant girls get seduced by the master and then fired by the mistress. Leave that for the Irish." For a single woman speaking no English, I heard over and over, I couldn't do better in Cleveland than making collars.

A scribe from Sicily had set his table just outside a grocer's shop with paper, pens, and three ink pots neatly laid out. A short letter cost ten cents with paper and postage to Italy. My last ten cents. I had him begin: "Dearest Zia. I am in Cleveland, looking for Carlo. I am sewing for rich people and live with respectable girls in a wooden house. I eat well and am learning English. I miss you very much and pray for your health and to see you soon. Greet my father and Assunta for me and Father Anselmo." Weeks from now in Opi, this letter would be un-folded and smoothed and Father Anselmo would read it to Zia. The

scribe peered at my face. "First letter home?" he asked kindly. I nodded. "The next will be easier." He signed my name before asking if I
could do at least this much myself, swept my pennies into a pouch and
promised to mail the letter.

At dusk I found my way back to the workhouse with families
wending home. The little red-haired girl hung on her father's shoulder,
exhausted but still singing softly to herself. He held her as carefully as
my father carried his prize lambs—he never carried me. A clap of
laughter burst from the dining room and pushed those thoughts away.
The girls were playing cards. "Irma, come join us!" Bèla cried and I
did. Someone had found a game we all knew and our languages shuffled together easily all evening, first with cards and then with songs
and dancing.

Days and weeks with the Missus passed like beads on my rosary.
Every Sunday after church I asked about Carlo in the shops around
Woodland. No one had heard of him or anyone who had worked on
ships between Naples and Tripoli. I wrote to Teresa in New York,
but she never wrote back, nor did Attilio's sister Lucia. Perhaps my
letters were lost. No letter came from Zia or Gustavo. Yet in the Italian
blocks, others were finding their people. Sicilians knit themselves
together, while immigrants from Naples, Puglia and Calabria claimed
their own streets and shops. Of Opi everyone said, "Never heard of
it." When someone insisted there was no such place I felt as transpar-
ent as glass.

In our workhouse the Swedish girl Katrin's belly swelled and then
she was gone. No one spoke of her. A Greek named Irene from Delos
appeared and at first was a favorite of the Missus. But as weeks passed

Irene grew silent, refusing to play cards or sing with us in the evening, seeming to live on currants from a Greek grocer near Woodland. She nibbled the black nubs all day, eyes half closed as if each held a memory of home. She had a little etching of a white house surrounded by olive trees and perched on a cliff over a glassy blue sea, and she took to setting it in front of her as she worked, at meals and by her bed at night. Her dark eyes fixed on the scene as a starving man stares through a bakery window. Once I saw her finger tracing an arc from the house to the sea.

"Devil's breath," said Lula, making a sign to brush away evil when Irene passed by, thin and silent as a shadow. At a shop on Woodland I spied a postal card of a mountain village in Italy, but when the clerk urged, "Just a penny for a picture of home," I hurried away.

And then Irene was gone. I came back from walking in the city one Sunday to find policemen talking with the Missus. A muddy black shawl dripped from a chair. Irene had waded into Lake Erie with stones tied in her apron, I learned from Bèla. By chance the father of the red-headed girl on our street recognized Irene and ran after her, but she was dead by the time he dragged her back to shore. Her body would go in a common grave kept by the city for the poor, the nameless and criminals, in a pit with strangers like my uncle Emilio.

"I should have known," the Missus said. "Delos women! Strong as goats but crazy as bats."

Lula piled Irene's clothes in the back room, muttering, "Devil's breath." We found no address in her bags or any document bearing her name. Perhaps she took them with her to her death, but now we could not write to her family and they would never know her fate. We burned her picture of the white house and I tried to forget how her finger marked a path to the sea.

The Missus shifted the benches so Irene's workspace was gone and replaced a photogravure in the dining room of a country lake with one of fine ladies strolling through a park. CHICAGO IN SUMMER was written in fine script below.

"If my brother comes to Cleveland," I told Bèla at lunch, "we'll get an apartment and I'll find work making dresses like that."

"You really think he's coming?" she asked mildly. "I'm sorry, Irma, but wouldn't he be here by now?"

I said nothing. Perhaps she was right. For weeks now I had been beating down the suspicion that waiting was hopeless, that I would not ever turn a corner on Woodland and see Carlo or hear a merchant say, "Signorina Vitale, I met your brother in a tavern last night." That afternoon as I worked, memories of him tumbled across my mind, each one announcing that it was not in his nature to come.

Carlo had fought, often bitterly, with every man in Opi. "If your mother wasn't my wife's cousin," the tavern keeper told me once, "I would have kicked him out long ago." Then there was the night of the lentils, soon after my mother died. Carlo and my father had been arguing over the sale of two ewes at market. In a fury, Carlo knocked each of our wooden trenchers to the floor. I swept up the lentils and we ate them dusty, for that was our dinner. "Never mind Carlo," Zia had whispered to me in bed. "He's mourning your mother. That's just how he's made."

Somewhere on the road to Naples or on the sea trip to Tripoli or in a foreign tavern, Carlo could have had such a fight with nobody there to say, "Never mind Carlo, that's just how he's made." He could have fought with the stranger who had promised a job in Cleveland. On shipboard, would he bend to the ship captain's will and humbly learn a new craft? I imagined him climbing high rigging, his foot pawing air. Sparring with a deck hand, he might trip on coiled rope, fall against pipes or slide across a slick deck in heavy squall with nobody to catch and hold him. Men went overboard in storms. An angry captain could send him aloft on dangerous tasks, anxious to save a troublemaker's pay. I saw his body sink under waves.

If by some miracle Carlo had safely reached America, he might easily be distracted by tales of an easy life in another city, farms in Ohio, ranches or gold mines in California. He might have stayed in New York with other Italians. Why push on to Cleveland if he couldn't know I was waiting there? After all, I had said I would never leave Opi. Like two pebbles on a mountain, what was the chance that we would ever meet?

No, Carlo was lost to me. With this certainty came grief and waves of softer memories. Careless and quick to anger, arrogant and often gruff, still he was never unkind to me. When I was a child he had carved me a doll and made her a bed with a sheepskin blanket. He shielded me from Gabriele's torments and the other boys' teasing. He scoured the high meadows for herbs to treat our mother. At her funeral he wept with me. Despite his rough talk, he was quietly attentive to Zia, never leaving her without firewood, once buying a salve for her aching shoulder when he overheard an old woman call it miraculous. And there was the softness I saw in my brother's face at night when the day's tightness eased away in sleep.

"Are you alright, girl?" demanded Lula at dinner.

"Yes," I said with my little English, "I'm fine."

That Sunday I asked the priest at my church to say a mass for Carlo. When I could give no particulars of his death, the priest gently folded the coins back in my hand, but knelt with me to pray for my brother's wandering soul. I lit a candle, said a rosary and did not mention Carlo in my letter home. Walking slowly back to the workhouse, I understood that I must stop waiting like a sheep to be led into better pasture. I must find it myself. "I am alone," I repeated in English words plucked from Lula's rough lessons.

"You're right. Carlo won't be coming to Cleveland," I admitted to Bèla that night.

She patted my shoulder. "We're all orphans," she said. "If not, we won't be here, no?"

The next day the Missus showed us a pattern book. We crowded around as she turned the wide pages, showing ruffles and flounces, layers of deep gathers, pleats and swirls of fine fabric. "Imagine wearing that one," Bèla sighed, but I imagined the beautiful weight of silk across my legs in sewing such a gown, streams of lace between the fingers and the joy of shaping curves from lengths of cloth.

"Look at the shirts," the Missus demanded, pointing to an etching of gentlewomen strolling along the edge of Lake Michigan.

"Is that in Chicago?" I whispered to Bèla.

"Enough," the Missus said, snapping the book shut. That afternoon the Missus dangled a bribe: the best of us would make shirt fronts which paid a little more. I must get this work and save more money in the bank.

At first, like the other girls, I had kept my pay in a sock inside my cabinet. But Lula took hers to a bank where it was safe and grew more money, called "interest," and she could have it all whenever she wanted. Once, delivering collars for the Missus, we had walked past this bank. Well-dressed Negroes went in and out along with merchants, ladies, and even servant girls. On the next delivery day, Lula helped me open an account. I wish Zia could have seen the little gray book with my own name elegantly written on the front and columns inside for deposits and interest. When a squint-eyed Hungarian collar girl slipped away one day, taking half the socks in our dormitory, my money was safe.

On Tuesday and Thursday evenings now I walked to Woodland and joined a dozen women in a hot little room in the church where an American nun taught us new catechisms: "What is this?" she would say, pointing.

"This is a window," we answered.

"What are these?"

"These are shoes."

I learned to say: "I am Irma Vitale. I am Italian. I am single. I make collars." The nun had us copy these sentences, so my first whole written sentences were in English, when all I ever wrote in Italian was my name.

Soon, with these new words I could speak haltingly to Lula of Gustavo as we peeled potatoes in the yard behind the house. She spat on the dirt. "Sailors. You know what they do, girl, every chance they get on land?"

"We only talked." I showed Lula his whalebone etching. "He gave me this."

"How many times did you do this talking?"

"Two times."

"He said he'd write?"

"Yes, by General Delivery."

"You done with those potatoes?"

Had I been as much of a fool for Gustavo as I'd been for Carlo? Full summer came and no letter. Sweat dripped from our fingers, staining the collars. The red-haired girl and her baby brother played listlessly in shreds of shade. On Sunday afternoons now, I took a streetcar to Lake Erie that lay like glass under a creamy blue sky. The shimmer of willows and bright clumps of wildflowers relieved the sameness of my days: the dull pine of our worktables, the white of collars, the brown bread and bean soup. Each month I wrote to Zia, but dared not send money until she wrote back, for if letters did not reach her, how could my money arrive safely? If she sent no letter, was it because she—no, I yanked back that thought. She was alive, safe and well in Assunta's house.

At last an envelope came from Gustavo with two thin sheets of paper. On one was a drawing of the *Servia* surrounded by leaping dolphins. A man and a woman stood on the deck. The other sheet bore a sketch of a busy port under dark skies with "Liverpool" written below. On the back was a note: "Dear Irma, I think of you and your mountain. The leg heals. We go to Africa tomorrow. They say it is beautiful. I hope you are well in America. God keep you. Gustavo Parodi." The careful script of the letter was the same as his signature. So he had written it himself—or used a scribe for both.

"The pictures are nice," Lula conceded.

Ashamed of my still awkward script, I endured the scribe's bushy raised eyebrow when I explained that I was writing a sailor. I thanked Gustavo for the drawings and said that I had found work and friends, was learning English and hoped to see him again. I did not say I lived in a workhouse. I signed the letter, folded it around an embroidery of olive trees and gave the scribe Gustavo's letter with the long English address of the shipping company to copy.

"So this sailor wrote you already?" the scribe asked.

"Of course."

"Huh."

"Now don't be looking every day for a letter," warned Lula. "He'll be in Africa when yours gets to England."

"No I won't." Yet even if my ties to Gustavo were as slender as a spider's line, without Carlo or any news from Opi, Gustavo was my link to Italy.

Times were hard in Cleveland. Prices rose for linen, beans and bread. The Missus said customers wanted more embroidery, so each collar took us longer. Unbending after work, our backs made cracking pops and we spent hours at night rubbing the knots from our bodies. "You're lucky to have work," the Missus snapped. She was right: ragged women passed the dusty windows, gazing at us longingly.

Brisk autumn winds drove the heat away and brought a spectacle I never imagined: leaves turning scarlet, yellow, orange and russet, a thrilling blaze of splendor splashed against a cobalt sky, nothing like the browns of our autumns at home. But when Lula found a fuzzy worm with a dark band around his belly, she shook her head and muttered, "Trouble. Bad winter coming."

Lula was right. The cold came fast, harder and deeper with more snow than I had ever known in Opi. Erie froze hard by late November. Night winds cut the walls of our sleeping room and snow dusted the floors. Wet clothes that were hung from the rafters froze stiff by morning. Our plates and mugs were cold, our needles and scissors, even the wood of tables and benches. The Missus put small stoves in the workroom, but charged us for coal and complained that our collars were ill made and she could not sell them. Our fingers stiffened. We bled easily, stained the collars and had to wash them at night in icy water.

In early December, on the day of the Immaculate Conception, the coroner's wagon stopped at the house across the street. We watched black-caped men hurry up the stairs and return with a small, stiff bundle. "Cut, sew, work!" the Missus demanded. "It's not your family."

Yes, Lula discovered the next day, they had come for the red-haired girl. Her father had lost his job and the weakened child died of fever. I still had Assunta's five pewter buttons and brought them to the mother. "From Italy," I explained, showing their soft sheen. I had seen such buttons in a store fetching good prices. She could buy food for the baby at least, and perhaps a little coal. Weeping, she thanked me and I hurried home through the blistering wind, aching for Zia's arms around me at night, the spit of our fire and even the smell of my father's tobacco. Winter crawled on. Lula thinned our soup. The girls grew angry, demanding more bread.

"And cheese, like we used to have," Bèla snapped.

Fools, I thought, but said nothing. Didn't they see that by the next year or the next, there would be no more use for collar girls? Walking home from a delivery I had stopped at a storefront, pressing the bulb of my sock-wrapped hands against the glass to study a display of women's collars and men's shirtfronts, all machine made and costing less than ours. Yes, a few fine hand-embroidered collars rested like tiny white crowns on wooden stands, but how many of these could be sold in Cleveland? The Missus was squeezing the last dollars out of a shrinking trade.

What now? The light lift of a needle between my fingers and the slip-whisper of thread through cloth, that was the work I knew. I had walked home slowly despite the cold, stitching a new plan together. I would save money, then go west to Chicago, where rich women roamed grand parks in fine dresses.

That night in the kitchen I whispered my plan to Lula. "You know any rich women in Chicago? You can't just walk up to some fine house with your needle. Ladies got their own fancy dressmakers," she said.

"I'll find a dressmaker then."

"If you're going, don't tell no one until you've saved every penny you need," Lula warned. She jerked her finger at the dining room where waves of laughter rolled over the table as collar girls took turns miming the Missus. "Not even your friends. If you're leaving, you've got no friends. *She'll* sniff it out from them and if she thinks you crossed her, wanting something better for yourself, girl, you're out on the streets, no matter how good you sew."

Six

DEVIL'S BREATH

So I waited, driving my hands to work faster, saying nothing of my plans, a silent traitor to my friends. On the warm days in early March, gritty rivulets ran from snow piled in alleys like old rags, but at night dank cold still seeped through cracks in our dormitory walls, shivering us to sleep. Each dawn paled to a dull white sky and filmy disk of sun, nothing like Opi's winter-sunrise bands of violet, purple, rose and magenta, and azure skies of noon. Mountain winters were hungry, but at least we had colors.

"I *want* springtime!" said Marta, our new Italian girl. She stamped out crusty patches of snow as we trudged across town, burdened like donkeys with boxes of finished collars. On delivery mornings, we earned no piecework. "The Greeks and Swedes never get sent out," Marta said bitterly. It was true. The Missus played each group against the others, doling out tiny liberties and capriciously rating our work.

I had determined to leave Cleveland when I saved twenty dollars, with luck before the maple leaves unfurled. Meanwhile, the city oppressed me with the weight of my secret and the white roof of winter sky. Even Woodland Avenue was a torment as new immigrant women eyed my scar and edged away in furls of whispers.

Say nothing to *them*, Lula constantly reminded me. If Marta knew, how could she not breathe my leaving to Sara, who might pass that breath to Bèla, and from there to a Greek and the Missus? It's true. When Sigrid the German girl gave notice, the Missus found such faults with her collars that Sigrid left owing the Missus for room and board.

When girls did leave, it was rarely for better work, but because they had found husbands. A Swede quit in February when a man she met at a dance appeared one afternoon with a deed for land in Nebraska. Most girls simply stayed. "Where else can we go?" they said, as if deserving nothing better than watered soup, a mice-ridden dormitory and schemes of the Missus to trim away our pay. "It's not *so* bad here," they assured each other. "It's better than scrubbing floors and safer than mill work or factories."

"Come to the dance tonight," urged Marta, but I refused. Men had their pick of beautiful girls without scars.

"If I married," I reminded her, "the money we sent home would go to his family, not mine. I have to think of my Zia."

"Irma, the truth is, you're afraid of men," said Marta flatly.

Not Gustavo, I thought, but of the others, yes, perhaps. "It's just not my time for dancing."

"But if we go, you'll be alone here tonight."

True, but better alone than hovering at the edge of a social hall. I begged a lamp from Lula to practice the tucks and smocking, piping, matched plaids and scalloped hems in *Godey's Lady's Book*. That night I dreamed of gowns: small as a finger, I wandered ruffled hills and slipped through shimmering galleys of tucks, crossing taffeta fields

strewn with bright buttons until storm clouds of collars covered the
sky. I was first on the bench in the mornings and the last to leave.
Finished collars mounded in my box and the Missus bought them all.
"You're learning," she conceded coldly.

Late in March, a letter came from Opi. I pressed it into my hand,
smelled it, ran my fingers around the envelope edges and studied King
Umberto's face on the stamp. "Read it!" Marta demanded. I tore open
the envelope and read slowly:

Dear Irma.

The new postman brought all your letters last month, which
was a great relief. We had been so worried not to hear from
you. We have no word of Carlo but thank Our Lord that you
are well and working. Zia Carmela sends her love. She has had
fever and chest pains and a cough this winter. Your father asks
that you send money for a doctor. He and Signora Assunta are
married and Assunta is with child. The bishop praised your
altar cloth when he saw our church. The mayor had a new well
dug by his house. Old Tommaso died. Gabriele was killed
by his own sheepdogs. I must close now for the postman is
waiting. The Lord bless you in America.

Father Anselmo

Nothing else was in the envelope. What had I expected: a clump of
our earth, the smell of spring rain or the savor of our bread? I tried to
see home faces through the pale page. Did Old Tommaso have a
beard? Which of Gabriele's eyes was crossed? Were all of his dogs lame
from his beatings or only the spotted bitch? I pictured my father's

hand on Assunta's swelling belly. I thought of Zia wrapped in her shawl, sick. I must go to Chicago, make more money and send it home for medicine.

"Irma!" Marta cried. "Look what you're doing!" I smoothed out the crushed letter. "Something wrong?" she asked anxiously.

"No, I'm just happy to hear from home." I would send five dollars to Father Anselmo right away for Zia's doctor although it would cost me another week with the Missus. I looked for my scribe on Sunday, but he was gone.

"Went home to Sicily," said the fruit seller. "Try Bruno the clerk. He lost an arm in a streetcar crash, but he still writes. You'll find him in his uncle's butcher shop."

The shop smelled of blood and raw meat. At a tiny corner table, gaslight pooled in the caved cheeks of a young man whose jacket sleeve dangled on his lap. He sat motionless, bent over a thick book. "Look alive, Bruno, you've got a customer," the butcher called.

The young man sighed and closed his book. "Good day," he murmured. "Please sit down, signorina." From a neat stack, Bruno drew a single clean sheet of gentleman's paper, not the old scribe's rough pages. He set a leather-covered rod to weight the sheet, selected a pen from a wooden box, wrote the date and paused for my first sentence. In elegant script, he wrote my words: I had sent five dollars for Zia through a bank and would soon go to Chicago to find better work since Carlo had not come here and I could no longer wait for him.

The soft scratching of Bruno's pen eased out every other sound: rumbles and shouts from the street, steady thwack of the butcher's cleaver, yowl of cats and shrill laments of customers fighting over their places in line. Bruno was not like the old scribe. He wrote carefully and gently perfected my grammar. I hoped that Father Anselmo would describe to Zia his elegant writing on the clean white page. "Would you like to sign?" Bruno asked politely, offering me his pen as the old scribe never did.

"Yes, thank you." Gaslight warmed my face as I leaned over the tiny table. I drew back, turning away.

"It's only a scar," said Bruno softly. "Not like this." He picked up the empty sleeve and let it flap on the table.

"But look how beautifully you write."

"I work in a butcher shop," he said ruefully. "And out there," his eyes flicked to the churning street, "people think I'm a monster. Girls don't talk to cripples."

"I'm talking to you."

"But you're leaving, no? For Chicago." I nodded. "Then, addio, signorina." He sighed.

"Addio," I said, sliding my coins across his desk. He swept them into a drawer, folded the letter and deftly slipped it in an envelope he braced against a paperweight. When he had addressed the envelope and given it to me, his hand dropped heavily on the folded empty jacket sleeve. This was a good man, I was sure of it, like Attilio and Gustavo. And like them he would slip out of my life.

"Bruno! Customers!" the butcher called. Leaving, I dodged a beaming couple in new wool suits.

"Your best paper, scribe!" the man boomed. "For a marriage announcement."

I made my customary circle of the Italian shops around Woodland, one last futile time seeking Carlo and explaining that he could reach me at General Delivery in Chicago.

"We'll look for him," said the Genovese baker.

"Don't be a meat packer," the wife warned. "My sister caught her hand in a grinder, then the whole arm turned black and they cut it off." When I described my plan of making fine dresses, the couple glanced at each other and the wife said, "Well, good luck, signorina."

The winter had ruined my old shoes. With the cost of new ones and a better dress to look for work in Chicago, it took three more weeks to earn my leaving money. Finally, the last payday came. The Missus sat at the dining table with her great ledger and piles of coins. When she pushed my six dollars at me with her pen as if the very coins were tainted, I swept them into a pouch and said, "Missus, I'm going to Chicago to be a dressmaker." A gasp ruffled the line of collar girls.

"You're a fool, Irma!" the Missus snapped. "You think dressmakers take just anyone? You'll starve before you earn a cent. Besides," she said darkly, "girls disappear in Chicago *like that.*" She snapped her fingers, closing the ledger with a thud that filled the narrow room.

I didn't move. "If there's work, Missus, I'll find it."

The girls who spoke a little English listened avidly, as if we were one of the puppet shows in Garfield Park. Bèla's face hardened. Sara took Marta's hand and only Saint Abraham looked down kindly.

I took a long breath. "I'll need a letter of reference, Missus." Without such a letter, Lula had insisted, I'd get no decent job in Chicago.

The Missus stood up so suddenly that her chair clattered to the floor. "You leave without notice *and* want a letter? I should write that my shop wasn't fine enough for our little Italian dressmaker?"

Silence rolled across the room. "Missus, I did good work, you said so yourself." Lula stood at the kitchen door, pitcher in hand. The mantle clock hammered two ticks. Carts rumbled outside and a drunkard kicked at ash cans. I said nothing.

Finally the Missus sighed loudly, her gray curls trembling. "You will leave tomorrow before breakfast," she announced, moving so close that a fine spray misted my face, "without disturbing the *working* girls. A letter will be on the table, saying that your work was satisfactory. It will not note that you are ungrateful and abandoned one who befriended you when you were a stranger in this city."

A year ago I would have begged her pardon. Now I said only, "Thank you, Missus." She stalked out, her footsteps hammering down the hallway until the heavy door to her apartment slammed shut and a lock bolt clacked into place.

"Well," said Lula. "Anybody want gingerbread?" She had bought a bucket of beer as well, but it was a somber farewell party. The Italian girls sat near me but were wary and cool, as if I were already a stranger. The others clustered by language, eating, drinking and glancing at me.

"You kept secrets, Irma," Bèla said flatly.

"You know how the Missus sniffs out everything. Lula said if she knew I was going, she'd keep my last week's pay."

"But *why* are you going? We're like a family here. You're never alone."

"Yes, but I don't want—"

"To live in a workhouse?" Marta asked quietly, brushing gingerbread crumbs from her skirt. "You think we're not good enough?"

"No, no," I stammered.

"Irma wants *fine* sewing, for fine women," Sara announced, gulping her beer. The oiled table was a dark pool between us. "Isn't that true? You don't want to be a poor collar girl."

Her words were knives on my face. "I've been poor all my life, Sara. It's not that. Don't you see? I want to work with good wool and silk, Egyptian cotton, making pleats and gathers, lacing, smocking. Don't you—" But Sara had turned to Bèla.

"Irma, there's more gingerbread," Lula announced, but it was dry in my mouth and the beer burned.

"Perhaps you're right," said Bèla finally. "You weren't happy here and your brother didn't come. Chicago might be better. Write to us when you get there. Here, to remember me." She took one of the delicate carved wood combs from her glossy black hair and gave it to me. I had embroidered poppies on handkerchiefs for her, Sara and Marta. They thanked me politely, and we finished our gingerbread and managed to speak and even laugh a little together. They wished me well and we kissed each other.

Soon clumps of girls drifted up to the dormitory. "God keep you, Irma," some said. Others laid a hand on my arm and muttered blessings in their languages. I tried to help Lula gather dishes but she brushed me away.

"Go to bed. You'll need your sleep."

But I did not sleep that night, only lay on the cot watching hazy stars drift across a patch of attic window as voices tossed in my mind like waves in a narrow tub: *Stay, go. Chicago will be better. Worse. End in the streets. End as a collar girl. Make fine dresses. Be alone again and die with strangers.* Mice skittered across our floor. Girls sighed in sleep, snored and moaned. In the chill hour before our rising bell I dressed and crept downstairs with my traveling bag.

In the kitchen, Lula was already at the stove. "There," she whispered. "For the train." She pointed to a basket with corn bread, boiled egg, a bit of potato pie and a jar of tea. A letter from the Missus lay on the table. "And take this," she added, holding out a palm-sized photogravure of Abraham Lincoln. "So you won't be alone in Chicago."

"Thank you, Lula."

She pressed her dark, warm hand to my cheek, then pushed me away. "Run now, girl. That train don't wait. Be careful. Look alive."

"Yes, of course."

"Don't you 'yes, of course' me. Write. And send me some money from your rich ladies."

I kissed her quickly, hoisted my bags and ran down the workhouse steps with the basket bumping my side, not looking back. A thick, cool mist revived me. I had twenty dollars in the chamois bag between my breasts, my crane scissors, a rock from the house in Opi, Gustavo's carved bone, his drawings and address. When I was settled in Chicago, I would write him and he would write me back, not to General Delivery but to a boardinghouse. I would turn twenty-one that month, April 1882. Soon I could send Zia more money from Chicago and a drawing of the first fine lady's dress I had made. I would write to Lula and the collar girls and try again to reach Teresa in New York and Attilio's sister Lucia. In Chicago I might even go to dances. The maple leaves were still unfurling and I was leaving this city.

A block from the workhouse, my dreams bloomed more grandly. I would visit Opi and give a fine gift to the church: silver candlesticks or even a new baptismal font. I would bring Zia to Chicago. We would go strolling in parks carrying parasols. A doctor would fix her eyes. We would eat roast chicken, white bread and sweet cakes and have our own apartment.

I never saw the two men slip behind me. Before I could cry out, a fleshy hand stinking of cigar clamped my mouth and I was yanked into an alley. "There's two of us, see?" a voice hissed in my ear. "And we can do what we want to you, but if you keep your mouth shut we'll be gentlemen." They covered my eyes with a rag tied hard behind my head. When Bèla's comb caught in the knot, they tore it out. I heard thin wood breaking at my feet.

"Turn her around," said the other voice. I was spun to the wall, forehead pressed into wet brick. They took my bag and felt under my coat for a money bag. "Make one sound and you'll be sorry, girl. Some of you greenhorns keep money in tight places." I bit my tongue, drawing blood as a hot hand groped under my skirt and up between my legs. Another dove between my breasts, pulling out my chamois purse. "Here it is, the titty bag. Some greenies never learn."

"Hold still, girl. We just want money, not your skinny ass."

In a slit below the blindfold, I glimpsed brown boots. Blood filled my mouth. I'm disappearing in the streets, I thought. *Like that.* The Missus was right. Marta was right. I should have stayed a collar girl.

"Twenty dollars. Shit. Why bother? Got any more?"

"No," I whispered. They released me. Legs trembling, I leaned against the wall.

"What's in the basket?" one demanded.

"Lunch," said the other. "Let's see. Corn bread, boiled egg. Well, well, here's old Uncle Abe Lincoln. What a jackass!" Glass shattered beside me. "Where you from?" one demanded. I said nothing. A hand on my shoulder jerked me forward and back so hard that my head slammed brick. "I asked a civil question, girl. Where you from?"

"Italy," I whispered.

"Eye-talia." A blunt finger jabbed my scar. "Look at that. A little Eye-talian fighter. We like that, don't we, Bill?" Rage ripped through me and like Gabriele's dog I snapped, whipping my head to the side where my teeth found a wide finger.

"Bitch!" cried both voices. "Now you'll get it." My blouse was torn open.

I screamed for help but their voices smothered mine: "Shut up, bitch!"

Suddenly new voices rang in the alley, and the clatter of hob-nailed shoes running on stone. "You there. Let her go!" I was spun back. Falling, I saw the brown boots racing down the alley. When two men knelt beside me and pulled off the blindfold I saw crisp uniforms and glittering buttons. "We're police. You're safe now, miss. They're gone. Can you stand up?" Clean hands lifted me. "What happened?"

"I was robbed," I gasped. "They took my bag and money."

"Well, you looked like a traveler, miss. Thieves go for them, you know, folks carrying everything they've got. And it's not the best neighborhood."

"Look alive," Lula had said. Don't go dreaming how life could be better.

The big policeman's pale wide eyes studied my scar. "That's a nasty one. Recent too."

"I got it on the ship." The policemen folded their arms comfortably across wide chests like men at a dance. "Can't you catch them?" I asked. "It was two men with brown shoes, one called Bill. They went—" I pointed down the empty alley, seeing only then how it branched into a warren of niches, stairways and dark gaps between buildings. The police barely followed my finger.

"They're gone," said the taller one. "And you were blindfolded, right? If we got two men, could you swear it was them?" No, I admitted. "And besides, if they knew you fingered them, they'd come looking, and you wouldn't be hard to find, miss." His chin jutted at my scar.

"But I'm leaving Cleveland, so they couldn't—" I began. The leaving money was gone. And my pay from the Missus. My new dress and second pair of shoes, rosary and Lincoln picture. Embroidery samples for work, my mother's apron. The crane scissors and stone from Opi, stitched picture of Opi, Teresa's address, Gustavo's whalebone, his address and any hope of reaching him. All my treasures.

What was left? One dress with a muddy, torn skirt and—Holy Mother—my blouse torn, showing a white swell of breast. I grabbed at the edges, hot with shame. The shorter officer plucked my trampled shawl from the mud, shook it out and gave it to me, dripping black water. I pressed the clammy cold around me.

"Never mind, miss, we see everything in this work. And you're lucky, you know," the broad-shouldered one said severely, as if to a whimpering child. "It could have been worse, *would* have been worse if it wasn't for us."

"Yes, thank you, sirs."

They nodded. "We do our job. But you can't go far now, looking like that. You got a home? We'll take you if it's close."

I stared at the wet brick. The short policeman cleared his throat. Like a prisoner caught, I pointed to the workhouse. "Let's go then," the tall one said.

Flanked, I retraced the path I'd taken so proudly. Black boots rang out *idiota, idiota,* for a stupid mountain girl, not looking alive—careless and arrogant. Without my bag I was as weightless as a beggar. What dressmaker would hire me now?

The policemen spoke over my head, fast and low in another language, laughing. "Watch, miss," they said at a wide puddle. For an instant, gratitude overtook shame. *Watch, miss,* as if I were a gentlewoman unaccustomed to puddles. But the very cartwheels squealed *idiota.* Factory girls in laughing pairs swept past us. *"She's not so proud now,"* their laughing said. Even the pale disk of sun gloated at my broken dream. My feet dragged.

"Miss, we don't have all day."

I pushed on like a sheep trudging back to the fold. Where else could I go? Even if somehow I reached Chicago, suppose it was only a larger Cleveland with more thieves? Go back to Opi? How, with an empty purse? And to do what? Care for my father's babe? Work for Assunta? If I looked for a new post in Cleveland, I'd be turned away at any factory, mill or even any respectable house seeking a scullery maid. Only the streets would take me. Like Filomena's father, my friends would shred their handkerchiefs. With every step, the Missus loomed larger: the jutting chin, charcoal smears around her pale eyes, gray wire of curls and long bent fingers pawing at collars, scratching for flaws.

A block from the workhouse I saw a woman leaving it, counting coins. "What's the matter, miss?" the short police officer demanded. "Why'd you stop?"

"Nothing," I murmured. The woman strode away. It was Maria the agent who must have sold another greenhorn collar girl. The policeman's heavy knocks pounded in my ear. Make me air, I prayed. Lord, blow me away from this house.

"Hum, didn't get far, did you, girl?" said Lula. She stood in the doorway, hands on hips as if the police had brought her a filthy stray cat.

"What happened?" she asked them, as if I were a stranger.

"She was robbed. Almost got worse. Right, miss?"

Lula's black eyes swung over my torn blouse, mud-splashed dress, dripping shawl and empty hands. "Irma, didn't I say to look alive? You got devil's breath?" She flicked her fingers, chasing my bad luck away from her.

"So this is home?" the big policeman asked. I nodded slowly. "Then good day, miss." He touched the rim of his helmet with a thick finger that slid down his cheek. "Watch your step. Some of them bad 'uns come back like dogs, once they got the taste. They'll figure you live around here." With that both men turned and strolled away, boots clicking on the cobblestones.

Lula folded her arms and blocked the doorstep. In the terrible walk home, I had not once imagined this. "Lula, I was *robbed*. Two thieves took my leaving money. They took everything. They almost—"

"I see what they done. Question is, what now?" She lowered her voice. "The Missus just got herself another girl. And she's all fired angry you asked for a letter in front of the others."

"Lula, if you loan me money for a ticket and another dress, I could go to Chicago and when I get work—"

"*If* you get work. Suppose you don't? Or you do and then forget Lula? I want to leave here too, you know," she whispered.

The Missus appeared, smiling. "So, we didn't like Chicago, did we, Irma? No fine ladies?"

Even Lula stiffened. "She was robbed, Missus. Wasn't her fault."

"Come crawling back wanting my work again, I bet."

"Just for a while, Missus," I pleaded, mortified at how much like a beggar I sounded. "They took everything."

"But, Irma, I want girls who'll *stay*, who *like* this work, don't you see? Girls I can trust. And I just got a nice little grateful Serb. So don't you be wasting Lula's time. She wastes enough on her own. You go on to your fine ladies. Or out there." She waved to the street.

Tears burned my eyes. "Please, Missus."

"She *is* a good worker, Missus," said Lula finally.

A smile curled over the ragged teeth. "But the Serb has Irma's bed, remember? So *if* I take her, she'd have to sleep with you, Lula, and then where would your dusky gentleman caller sleep? You thought I didn't know about him? Didn't enter your wooly head? But that's a good idea. You can share your bed with our dressmaker."

Lula's face darkened with fury that my devil's breath had blown on her. The Missus smiled again. "Well, Irma? You may stay and work and help Lula with *her* work, since I have plenty of girls now. Maybe if you're lucky, you can make a few collars." She looked at my torn skirt and mud-black dripping shawl. "Lula can get you something from the back room." She meant the pile of dead girls' dresses. "What? Not fine enough?"

I made myself face her glinting eyes. "Missus, it's not charity I'm asking for, only a few weeks' work."

"We'll see," she said, turning away.

"White bitch witch," said Lula when she closed the door of her narrow bedroom and waved me to a chipped water basin. "How'd she know about Albert?" Lula demanded. "You told her?"

"I don't know anything, Lula. I swear. You never said anything about him."

"Hum, that's true. She has her own witch ways. Doesn't need any devil's breath Eye-talians."

"Who is Albert?"

"My man. *Was* my man," said Lula bitterly. "He's a porter on the railroad and visits me sometimes at night. Except *now* I got company."

"I'm sorry, Lula. I'll leave as fast as I can."

"You do that, girl, and don't waste time dreaming. That's what got you in this fix. And watch out. *Now* you'll see the real Missus."

I did. I worked frantically, rising early, hauling coal and water for Lula, helping her wash the breakfast dishes and then hurrying to the bench. Exhausted as I was, I forced out tiny stitches and smooth arched curves of perfect collars. The Missus faulted each one, loudly praising the new Serb's work, once giving her three of my collars to "fix," three that ended in her basket. When I protested, Marta hissed, "Quiet, you make it worse for everybody." I bit my lips and sewed, every stitch a stab.

The Missus cut up my sewing time with deliveries. "I favor the *faithful* girls," she said. "And besides, you do look like a servant these days."

"She's right," Lula said that night. "Buy yourself a decent dress if you don't want Irene's old ones."

"I can't spend my leaving money," I protested.

"Don't your people have an aid society?"

"You mean charity? My family never—"

"And how would they know what you do, way over there? If you're poor, you do what poor folks do. Go get yourself a dress."

"Thieves took my clothes," I told a blunt-faced woman at the Italian Aid Society as she silently handed me two cotton dresses and three sets of underclothes.

"Everyone has troubles," she said. "Look out the next time. It's not like home."

"I'm saving to go to Chicago," I persisted.

"Everyone's saving for something. Next?" A family from Calabria stepped to the table. Their bags had been stolen on the train from New York: their clothes, his woodworking tools and medicine for the child. I gave them twenty cents, all that I had with me.

When Albert came that night, I sat in the dining room for hours while muffled, happy groans seeped through the door cracks. I copied lines from *Godey's Lady's Book* on scraps of paper until past midnight, when Lula shook my shoulder. "So now you're writing like your fine ladies? Come to bed. Albert's gone."

"Can you write?" I asked as I undressed in the dark.

Lula snorted. "When I was young like you we had the War. And before that," she added bitterly, "the plantation."

"There wasn't a priest to teach you?"

Lula's rolling laughter filled the narrow room. "I got to tell Albert about you. A *priest* on the plantation for us? No, girl, just an over-seer, and he didn't keep no slave school. Go to sleep. Sun's coming soon."

Sleepless and stiff the next day, I worked poorly. "Is *this* how a la-dies' dressmaker sews?" the Missus demanded. "Aren't you ashamed?"

I made only three dollars that week, and barely more the next week. Day and night, resentment smoldered. The Missus robbed me constantly, refusing good collars, stealing work hours or simply taking my collars, as brazen as if I were blind. Bèla, Marta and the other girls wove a net around themselves, offended that I once scorned a place that they endured and frightened that leaving had brought down such disaster. I was *sfortuna*, bad luck, and they kept their distance. I ate little and moved like a shadow. In Lula's narrow bed, I squeezed against the damp, rough wall.

"Too bad you're not Albert," she muttered, and I wished I was any-one but myself. Chicago glimmered like the Promised Land, always further west. Weeks of misery passed.

One Tuesday the Missus left in haste before dawn, giving orders that I was to clean the gas lamps before breakfast, a dirty, tedious job. Lula hummed and sang in the kitchen, for Albert had come that night. In the hallway outside the apartment of the Missus, I brushed past her door and was astonished when it moved. Impossible—she was always so careful, even locking away our needles at night. I eased the door open, slipped into her parlor and closed the door behind me.

There were Persian carpets and silk lampshades, a fine desk with a dozen small drawers, four stuffed chairs and dark velvet curtains puddled at the floor, more wealth in this one room than in all of Opi. But it was the four boxes on the floor that drew me: collars packed for sale. I recognized my own embroidered work on top, dozens of collars, those few she paid me for, those she called faulty and those she had given away for "fixing." Below was other girls' work, but a buyer would see mine and think the rest were equal.

Rage ripped through me for my stolen collars and her mocking cruelty, pitting poor girls against each other, for our watered soup and icy rooms, for lodging me with Lula to punish us both, for the hours I worked without pay. Rage for girls cheated of their last week's pay and buyers cheated with indifferent goods. Rage for the thieves, laughing and laying their hands on my body. Rage at Cleveland, where I was alone and miserable.

Lord forgive me, Father Anselmo and Zia forgive me, I began to rob the Missus. First I took only English needles from a sewing basket, for she had so many. Then a set of fine muslin handkerchiefs and hanks of silk embroidery thread, all shoved into my apron. Anger burned hotter, wanting more. Did Gabriele of Opi burn this way the first time he beat a dog? But I had been *wronged*, my feverish mind insisted. In the desk drawers I found paper, pens and stamps: useless. One drawer would not open until my questing fingers found a tiny knob behind the letter slats. Deep inside the desk a click sounded, sharp as a snapped twig. The locked drawer sprang open, revealing stacks of dollars tied with string and a bag heavy with coins, money squeezed from us. Or perhaps (how thievery makes us think like thieves) some darker business made wealth for the Missus and she masked it by selling collars. Never mind how she got this money; it would get me to Chicago.

I took the five dollars stolen from my pay in each of four weeks, then ten more for her cruelty. I took no coins, lest she note a change in the weight of the bag. From her sewing basket, I plucked a little pair of scissors and golden thimble light as air, working quickly to outrun my conscience. As wind spins dry leaves in running circles, a chant whipped through my head: *she robbed me, thieves robbed me, I was wronged.*

Needles, thread, thimble, four handkerchiefs, little scissors and paper money weighed my apron pocket like bricks. Like a starving man who eats until he sickens, I circled the room for more, fingering porcelain teacups and heavy silver plates, china dogs as high as my knee, a porcelain shepherd boy playing a flute, velvet cushions and crystal vases. What would I do with such things? Even a pawnshop might question a poor girl with a china dog and smelling a trailing policeman. It was Chicago I wanted, not prison. Lula would wonder why I was so long at cleaning lamps and the Missus might return.

I examined the room for anything ruffled or out of place. No, she would suspect nothing until she counted her money. Take more, just one, two small things more, whispered a fevered voice. What would it matter since I was already a thief? From a bronze bowl in a corner hutch I plucked a dusty rosary of amber and coral. Since thieves had taken mine, surely I deserved this. Then for no reason but the fever of taking, I took a carved jade cat no bigger than my thumb. Opi faces gaped at me: Zia, Father Anselmo, even my father who for all his gruffness and easy anger had never robbed any man. *"Who are you?"* they demanded. *"Where is Irma?"*

"The Missus robbed me," I reminded them and faltered. I'd do penance, I'd give to the poor in Chicago. When I had money, I'd return what I took. I crept to the door, listening like a practiced thief. From the kitchen came a steady rain of *thwacks*: Lula making beaten biscuits, her small celebration when the Missus was gone. She would hear nothing from this room. I patted my apron to flatten its bulge and crept toward the dormitory stairs for my coat and few clothes.

"Irma!" Lula called out. I jumped, sweating cold, and slipped into the kitchen, standing where a laundry basin could shield my apron. Huffing, Lula stirred the thick batter, counting strokes, "nineteen, twenty," as her brown arm circled the wide wooden bowl. "Eighty more. You took your sweet time out there."

"The lamps were dirty."

"Well anyway, we need more ice. The Missus didn't leave me no money so have old McGowen put it on credit. Tell him I want it this morning or I'll lose my butter and milk." Was the Lord blessing my sin? "Did you hear me, Irma? If you do it now you'll be back for breakfast."

I swallowed. "The Missus?"

"Gone for the day. Thank you Jesus."

So it could be hours before she knew she'd been robbed. "I need my coat."

"So go get it. What you waiting for?"

To thank her for sharing a bed, even unwillingly. To wish her well with Albert and to remember her wide, dark face. To say I was not evil and not a thief, only wanting what was mine. "I'll get my coat."

"You said that. A *big* block, hear? None of them little lumps."

In the dormitory some girls were rousing, dressing, and splashing their faces with water. The Swedes stood in a tight circle, weaving intricate braids in each others' hair. Bèla, Marta and Sara still slept. If I whispered my leaving they would ask how, with what money. In some way they might betray me to Lula, who, to keep her own job, might run after me. So I said nothing as I stuffed the charity clothes into a bag hidden under my coat and slipped out the front door, listening for Lula's *thwacks* and huffing counts: "eighty-one, eighty-two, eighty-three." I would write to her from Chicago. Don't think of Chicago, I told myself. Just think of leaving without getting robbed.

No, no, not just yet. I would stop at McGowen's, for the Missus or even Lula would surely check there and perhaps then conclude that some disaster had befallen me between the iceman and the workhouse. So I ordered ice, trying to show no hurry or impatience as Mr. McGowen carefully scratched a figure in his credit book, slowly wrote out a delivery order, considered my thoughts on the weather and finally let me go. By good fortune a swirl of foundry workers was passing the door. I slipped among them so Mr. McGowen wouldn't notice that I was headed away from the workhouse.

This time I was careful and looked alive, hurrying past alleys and avoiding pairs of men. Because people sitting on a streetcar might have time to note my scar, I walked to the train station, staying in crowds. I bought food for the train from peddlers: a roll and sausage, two apples and a cone of salted peas, trying to seem easy, calm and relaxed.

At the desk for the Buffalo, Cleveland and Chicago Railway Company, I asked for a one-way third-class ticket to Chicago. "Hard money or paper?" the clerk asked. Was this a test?

"Paper," I managed.

"Let's see." When I pushed my bills across the polished counter he examined them carefully, holding each to a candle and glancing from the bill to my face. Could he feel stolen money? Was he waiting for a blurted confession? Then he would call the police, perhaps the very two who would remember where I came from and drag me back to the Missus, not a victim this time, but a thief.

"Sorry, miss, there's lots of counterfeit bills around. But these are fine. Don't worry, nobody cheated you." I forced a smile, tight as a gather in heavy cloth. "Here's your ticket. The eight oh six for Chicago leaves from Platform Three, right over there." He jabbed a stubby finger to the right. "Better hurry, you can just make it."

I flew across the station, stunned by this good fortune. "Just running to get a train," I could tell any officer. Not running away. If the porter thought it odd to go so far with only an old cloth bag, he said nothing. In the hot car, passengers beat the air with penny fans and sloughed off coats, but I kept mine on to hide my heaving chest, searching the platform for policemen in case the Missus had laid a trap for me.

The doors groaned shut. Then came a long hiss of steam and the train lurched forward. As ruffling winds stirred the air, passengers sighed and put down fans. I drew the stolen rosary from my apron pocket, my fingers so slick with sweat that I lost count of the prayers, stopped and started again. "*Thief,*" said the clattering wheels as we left the city, "*thief, thief, thief.*" Fog lay over broad plowed fields and my reflection in the window gave back not Irma but the pale face of a stranger.

"Lady," said a young boy tugging on my skirt, "you dropped your pretty beads."

Seven

MADAME HÉLÈNE

I stuffed the rosary beads in my bag while the boy regarded me, green eyes blazing under straw-stiff hair. Did he think I was soft-handed, like drunken men in taverns, reeling and spilling their beer? Would he believe it wasn't truly me who was the thief? That was Irma the collar girl. *I* was Irma Vitale who made an altar cloth and rubbed Zia's feet in the morning, the Irma that people called plain, but a good girl, always a good girl.

"Those were Catholic beads," he announced. The woman beside him pressed a clean gloved hand against his shoulder. "My mother doesn't talk much, even in Swedish. She thinks I'm bothering you. We're Lutheran." I nodded. The woman pulled a leather-bound book from her bag and set it on his lap. "I'm supposed to read this," he explained, holding out the book like a thick slice of cake. "But it's good. You know *Gulliver's Travels*?"

I shook my head. The boy's thin lips opened in a perfect pink *O*, then rippled on. "It's about a man named Gulliver who visits four lands. In the first one, everyone's tiny, like this." When he stretched apart his thumb and forefinger, the gloved hand opened his book. "Anyway," he whispered, "it's an almighty—" The mother gave a warning glance. "I mean a bully good story." I nodded. The woman carefully opened her own volume to a place marked with a single strand of thread and both began reading. The boy's eyes skimmed the close-set lines but he never touched the page. Father Anselmo used his finger to turn newspapers or proclamations from Rome. For the Bible he had a wooden pointer whose tip was a tiny ivory hand. But this American child read with eyes alone. Once I found work in Chicago, I vowed, I would learn to read like this. Then I remembered that I was a thief.

The mother's book rested on a starched white apron that skimmed the crisp pleats of a traveling dress. Her conscience must be smooth as well. I twisted thieving fingers in the coarse folds of my charity skirt. When the porter passed, I cringed. At any station where the train took on mail bags he might receive a telegram: "Young Italian female. Brown dress. Face scar. Arrest for theft." The passengers, Americans and greenhorns, all seemed light and easy as they played cards, slept, read or talked together quietly. Three men studied a map, making lists in leather notebooks. Honest men, surely.

"Are you sick, miss?" asked the soft, rolling voice of the porter.

"I'm fine, thank you." One of my first English phrases tripped off the tongue so easily.

"Look," he said, pointing out the window. "Indiana already, God's good black earth."

We were crossing farmland, flat as pressed linen, with neat white houses scattered like toys among the fields. "How was it to live on a mountain?" Attilio once asked me on the long road into Naples. It was good to be lifted up from troubles that brewed in the valleys. With the earth so flat, how easy for the swooping hand of God to destroy the evil-doer. Where could he hide? Don't think of this. Better to sew, to practice folds and tucks, smocking and hidden hem stitches. I pulled scraps from my bag and tried to work them with my stolen needle but nothing came right. Scissors from the Missus made false turns and blunt corners. Like this starched land, the muslin would not tuck. Smocking samples bunched and puckered. Cross-stitching lost its easy rhythm.

The porter's shadow crossed my work. "Learning to sew, miss?"

"Yes," I said faintly.

He smiled as I had smiled at Rosanna's first wild stitching. When he moved on, I fingered the rosary beads inside my bag but only one chant came smoothly: cut, sew, work. I lay two raw edges of cotton scrap together and whipped them closed with blanket stitching, breathing with my needle's pricks. Then I moved to chains. When they came out even, I made them smaller.

"Hey, you could sew for Lilliputians," said a happy voice. I looked up at the boy. "Those little people Gulliver met." His mother frowned and handed him a neatly packaged lunch. I took out my own food so she would not feed me out of pity. The boy peered at a tiny watch hanging from his mother's waist. "An hour more for us," he announced. I nodded, brushed crumbs from my skirt and leaned against the window, slipping into a well of sleep. When I woke, the mother and boy were gone. Afternoon sun coated their empty seats, but a tiny slip of paper hid in the folds of my skirt. "Gulliver's Travels," it said. The boy was real, then, not conjured by the strangeness of the day.

"Chicago, Chicago," the wheels rattled on. Solitary trees in the far fields cut rounded C's against a pale blue sky. Lula had given me the address of a boarding house where her cousin once worked. Mrs. Gaveston's was nothing elegant, she said, but decent and safe for single women. I could pay for a week's room and board, but then must find a job without any letter of recommendation and without selling myself to a workhouse.

"Chicago, Chicago, Illinois Central Depot," the conductor chanted. Far ahead, dark teeth of the city nipped at a hazy sky. Soon Chicago spread like a giant stain across the land. Could I find my place there? In my last Opi winter, high winds ripped a pine tree from the ground and sent it tumbling down our mountain, where it wedged against rocks and withered to sticks. Don't think of this. Think—what? That even an uprooted tree could find a scoop of welcoming earth. I clutched my bag and waited.

We reached the station at four in the afternoon. When I showed a station officer the boardinghouse address, he sketched a map on a scrap of paper, muttering as he worked, waxed mustache jumping. "It's pretty far, miss. Be careful." A thick forefinger tugging down loose skin below his eye made the gesture: watch for thieves.

I joined a stream of passengers flowing through the station. Sunlight pouring through high windows burnished lacy wrought-iron gates and spilled down the street, so rich and buoyant that the people hurrying past seemed to walk on golden air. A whoosh of wind ruffled my skirt, tugging me along. I can do this, I thought. I can find honest work. *Look alive*, another voice hissed in my mind. *Remember the first time you left the Missus, so happy and full of dreams.*

Still, the bustle and swell were thrilling. I followed wide avenues dividing palaces of brick and stone leading to blocks of wooden houses, new ones and others still gutted by a great fire ten years ago that our English teacher once described. Following my map, I turned onto a long brick street that should take me to the boardinghouse. On a quiet block a stock wagon lurched at a pothole. Its back gate flew open and a dozen spotted pigs tumbled out, shook themselves and scattered, squealing through the street.

"Forty cents each if you catch them," bawled the driver. Soon boys, men, even old women and young girls burst from doorways. Stumbling men poured through a tavern door, waving beer mugs, whooping and chasing frenzied pigs, crashing into each other, cursing and laughing. Drivers reined their horses as pigs, their hopeful captors and wildly barking dogs swept by. Two well-dressed gentlemen helped street boys flush a screeching pig from a clump of ash cans.

A little girl with long black braids and two pigs trotting docilely beside her shouted at the driver. "Give me a dollar, mister, or I make them run away. I'm very good with pigs." The driver paid and at a word from her, the pigs scampered up a ramp into the cart. "Bye pigs," she called cheerfully. "You'll be pork pie soon." I squeezed past the roiling crowd and eight blocks later found Mrs. Gaveston's boarding-house. ROOM TO LET, said a neat sign in the window.

Mrs. Gaveston opened the door. She was a tall woman with lustrous gray hair who listened with hands on hips as I introduced myself. "Harriet was a good worker," she conceded when I spoke of Lula's cousin. "But she found a sweetheart and moved to Wyoming. Are you Polish?"

"Italian," I said.

"Good. The city's filling up with Poles. What's going on in their country?" She seemed to need no answer and bustled me through a sitting room with a piano. "Strings broke," she said shortly, taking us up two steep flights to a door marked NINE and handing me a key. I fingered the smooth steel shaft. "Never had your own before?" I shook my head. "Well, no time like the present." I unlocked the door and slowly pushed it open. The room was so narrow that a man with outstretched arms could nearly touch both walls, but it had a metal bed with a flat pillow, green cloth spread and neat stack of sheets and blankets, a tiny table with wash bowl and pitcher, a rush-bottom chair, clothes pegs, gas lamp on the wall and one small window with faded gingham curtains.

"It's beautiful," I said.

"Don't know about beautiful, but decent for a working girl. You *do* have work?" When I explained that I would find a job with a dressmaker, Mrs. Gaveston folded her arms as I showed samples I made on the train. She barely glanced at them. "I never sew," she said briskly. "No patience for it. If you don't have a job, I need two weeks' room and board." That would take nearly all I had. She studied my face. "You seem like a decent sort. Not too pretty at least. My damn fool maid left this morning. She found a sweetheart too. Listen, if you clean for me an hour each morning, two more in the evening and all day Saturday, I'll charge you half rate until I find a proper maid. That's more than fair, right? You can look for work in the daytime."

So I'd be a servant, but at least not a slave as I was for the Missus. Surely I'd find a job within the week. I thanked Mrs. Gaveston, stumbling over my words. "Never mind, Irma," she said. "Come on, you can start now." I dusted the downstairs rooms, swept the floor with her new Bissell carpet sweeper and rubbed lemon oil into the woodwork.

I found no job by Saturday, but Mrs. Gaveston found Molly, a bigboned Irish maid with references who cleaned with both hands, moving so quickly that rooms seemed to shine themselves as she whirled through. With her extra time, Molly shopped, helped cook, and spaded over a patch of earth behind the boardinghouse for a kitchen garden. Mrs. Gaveston said nothing on Monday when I paid my full room and board. After buying a decent dress to look for work and streetcar fares to search more quickly, I had five dollars left. I fell asleep over my rosary, imploring the Virgin for mercy.

Signs on dressmakers' windows said, NOT HIRING. Once I saw no sign, but the owner, her mouth full of pins, pointed to a discrete NO in tailor's chalk on the doorpost. NO read other doorposts. Some dressmakers stopped me at my first words. "No foreigners," they said. One pointed to my scar. "No trouble." Yet everywhere there were women in fine dresses that no factory could have fashioned. Someone had fitted these bustles, folded narrow pleats and matched plaids. Someone had set sleeves that bloomed like clouds from tight bodices. Once I stopped a kind-faced gentlewoman stepping out of an apothecary, thinking she could tell me who made her dress, perhaps a shop I hadn't tried. But she backed away, grasping a jeweled purse to her chest. Mortified, I hurried across the street, so close to a coal wagon's horse that his sweat-slick flanks brushed me.

"Hey girl," the coal man shouted. "Look alive!"

At least in the workhouse a handful of people knew me. Here I walked for hours in crowds, invisible. A dry-goods man smoking a pipe in his doorway stared through me. "I'm *Irma*," I wanted to cry out. "Irma Vitale of Opi." The man ducked back in his shop.

There were dress shops near the train depot, Mrs. Gaveston suggested, but none were hiring. Walking in widening circles through the city I ate day-old buns and wore holes in my shoes, which I stuffed with felt that Molly gave me. I pawned the little jade cat I had stolen from the Missus for streetcar fare. When it rained, I bought an umbrella from a peddler, since no respectable dressmaker would let me come dripping into her shop. "Thirty cents? He cheated you," scoffed Molly. "But come in the kitchen and have some tea." I sank in a chair as muddy water dripped from my skirt. It was my fourteenth day in Chicago.

As Molly chopped cabbage for soup, I spoke of the Missus, the workhouse and Lula, but not how I robbed the Missus. "Funny you didn't save more, coming alone to a new city and all," said Molly briskly, her back turned from me. "Left quick or something?"

I clenched my chair. "I was tired of Cleveland."

"I see." What did she see? I helped chop to keep my hands from shaking. "Listen, Irma, what about your own kind, all those Italians around Polk Street? Don't they have ideas?"

I had asked on Polk Street. "Some Russian's hiring girls to make collars and cuffs," said an olive vendor. "Try the factories," his wife added. "There's always meat packing. And sausages."

"No," I said, "no, thank you."

"What, you're too fine?" she muttered. "Or just not hungry enough?"

It's true that factories and meat packers sprouted thick as weeds. Streams of workers crossed the city each morning. I watched women through greasy windows as they canned, sorted, stamped, stuffed and packed. In low brick buildings near the slaughterhouses they stood on slatted frames over pools of blood, stuffing sausages all day. Who was I to want better work? My feet ached from walking. Once I nearly fainted on the stairs to my room. Perhaps it was folly to come here, but where could I go now, even with train fare to leave? In New York's Lower East Side, said Molly, police pulled bodies from gutters each morning, frozen in winter, rat-bitten and robbed of their clothes. "Don't ever go east," she warned. "It only gets worse for the poor."

On my fifteenth day in the city, I lay in bed staring out my tiny window. Before Chicago, I had never slept in a room alone. How could Americans endure such solitude? In the night silence I considered my own death. And what of Zia then? If she grew sicker, if my father had his own babe to feed or a bad year for sheep, would he care for her if I could send no money, if I was gone? Sinking into despair, I conjured the year before my mother took sick, when sleet blew all day at shearing time. Wet, matted wool dulled our blades. My father and Carlo stopped constantly to hone them. We fell hours behind. My mother and I washed wool until our hands were raw and bleeding, stiff with cold. "We can't finish by morning, it's impossible," Carlo protested.

"That's when the wool buyer comes," my father snapped.

"Keep working," my mother repeated. "Just keep working. We need wool to live."

This was *my* shearing time. I must not stop. I needed a job to live. I decided to look for sewing work one more morning and then go to the sausage factory. I'd stand over blood twelve hours a day but at least have work. At the bakery where I bought my stale bun for lunch, two Italian women suggested Hyde Park, where rich people lived.

I walked across the city as an early fog thickened into rain. There were no dressmakers hiring in the ten blocks around Hyde Park, only chalk-marked NOs on doorposts. When the rain stopped I wandered into the park past two old soldiers in ragged jackets. One was drawing old battle lines in mud with his crutch. The other begged from gentlemen hurrying by.

"You have Union pensions," one man chided.

"They're not enough to feed a dog," the crippled soldier called back.

I found an empty bench and sat, too late remembering my skirt. It would be wet and clammy now. But who would notice if every door said NO? Sausage makers wouldn't care: their workers' skirts were soaked in blood.

A quick patter on the brick walkway announced a fine lady coming. Despite myself, I studied her dress from a distance: fine tuckwork on the bodice and matched plaids in a ruffled skirt, tumbling waterfalls of lace at the throat. I knew the pattern from *Godey's*, but the dressmaker had made a wider skirt that brushed park benches as the lady sidestepped puddles. Light-headed, I nibbled my bun as the dress came closer. Egyptian cotton with a satin waistband. Crinoline petticoats swished under the soldiers' drone. Then a loud *rip*. The lady wailed and tugged at her skirt, caught on a bench nail. Faster than thought or prudence, I crossed the space between us and knelt beside her on the wet pavement.

"What are you doing?" she shrieked, yanking loose a wider gash of ruffle until it sagged toward the muddy brick in a gaping mouth. "Here!" she fumbled in her purse. "Go away."

My English crumbled. "I fix," I said, beating the air gently to calm her. "I am a sew girl."

"A *what*?" She looked around wildly. The crippled soldier started toward me.

I gestured threading, sewing, cutting and held up my bag, pulling out samples. "Don't move, lady. You hurt the beautiful dress. I fix it." This was child's English, I knew, but at least the lady ceased pulling, horrified by the size of the tear, so wide now that the skirt would drag in the mud if she took another step. "You mean fix it here? Now?"

"Yes, yes, but be still, please." I carefully worked the fabric free and draped it over my knee to examine the gash more closely. "Idiota," Carlo would say. "Suppose you can't fix it?" But Zia would answer: *"Irma, do your best. Or else make sausages."*

Sweat slicked my brow, for the rip was terrible and near the front. Pulling raw edges together would make the plaid lines waver and then every eye would see the repair. The rip must be patched. In Opi, we basted scraps over holes without hope of hiding the repair. But this one must be invisible. I examined the hem: six fingers deep, a rich woman's hem. I could replace the gashed cloth with a patch darned into place, then tack down the cut-out hem.

"How long will it take?" the lady demanded.

"A little bit." I must do better work than ever in my life, and faster too.

"You may sit, ma'am," the soldier offered, pointing his crutch to the ragged army jacket he had laid on the wet bench. The lady nodded and she and I shuffled toward the bench, the skirt held like a train between us. When she gave the soldier a coin, he bowed gallantly. "Lieutenant Rafferty, Army of the Potomac, at your service."

The other soldier disappeared into the brush and returned lugging a stone he set by the bench. "And a stool for you, miss," he said. "Nearly dry."

I thanked him, prepared a needle and began. My hands, at least, were clean. The soldiers hovered, stinking of tobacco and sweat-stained cloth, until the lady coughed and they drew back. Bored and fretful, she asked idly about their wounds and battles. They spoke of a place called Gettysburg and another, Vicksburg. I barely listened, seeing only plaid lines, my needle and the lift and fall of ruffles. The lady sighed. I worked faster. Such fine fabric, and so wondrous much of it. How delicious to touch this softness every day and shape it into gowns.

"Almost done, girl?"

Almost—just two edges of the patch to finish, the needle barely nipping the warp threads, blending into the greens and reds. I held my breath. Yes, the patch matched perfectly: plaid lines skimmed across the seam. The Virgin had blessed my fingers.

"Well God damn if that don't just fix the flint," exclaimed Rafferty, bending over the skirt, his breath warm on my ear. "Begging your pardon, ma'am, but you can't hardly see what she done."

The lady studied the patched skirt and neatly tacked hem. "It will suffice, I'm sure. Here, girl, and I thank you." She extracted a half dollar from her purse and held it out to me with as pretty a gesture as a queen might make.

I scrambled to my feet. "I need a job, ma'am. Can you speak for me to your dressmaker?"

The outstretched arm slowly lowered. "You want *me* to find you work? I took a risk, you understand, letting you do this. And fifty cents is more than generous for a patch, don't you agree?"

"Yes, ma'am, but I need—"

"Here." She fished in her purse again, reached for my hand, planted another quarter in it and stood. "There, that's far more than my dressmaker would ask." She turned on the heels of fine polished shoes and hurried off, leaving me with coins in one hand and a threaded needle in the other, staring at the disappearing plaid.

"Can't blame the lady," said Rafferty's rough voice behind me. "It ain't her funeral if we don't have work."

"They're always wanting girls at the factories," said the other soldier. "You're cheaper than men." The brick pathway curved away, swallowing the skirt's last billow. The needle pricked my finger. Only that pain was real, that and the sinking certainty that tomorrow I would be packing sausages. Numbed and cut, my fingers would lose their skill. As mist rises from the valleys and thins into air, my dreams were fading. If the machines mauled me, who would ever know I had been Irma Vitale of Opi, so skilled with her needle?

Suddenly I was splashing through puddles, water filling my shoes, calling out: "Please, ma'am, stop!"

"I *paid* you," the lady called over her shoulder, hurrying faster, heels clipping brick. "Stop chasing me!"

I circled in front, blocking her path like a sheepdog. "Please," I panted. "I am looking for work two weeks. I embroider beautiful flowers. I do smocking and tucks. Could you speak to your dressmaker? Could you show her my work?" Rafferty was hobbling towards us.

The lady stepped back, eyes wide in terror. "You're together? I knew it! Get away from me, both of you!" She turned on Rafferty. "My husband's on the Pension Board. You come one step closer and you won't get a penny for the rest of your life."

"Nobody's wanting to rob you, ma'am," soothed Rafferty. "I swear I don't know this lassie, but didn't you say she fixed that frock good?"

"I paid her. Besides, you heard her talk. She's a foreigner."

"And where's the crime in that? So were all of us, one time or another. I came from Ireland before Mr. Lincoln's War." Rafferty studied her face boldly. "And begging pardon, ma'am, you have the fine look of the Irish about you, if I'm not far mistaken."

Her mouth softened. "My people were from County Cork," she admitted finally.

"I knew it!" he cried. "None so handsome as the women of Cork. Nor so charitable, I've heard."

Her eyes slid down my limp hair, damp dress and worn shoes and then up to the threaded needle in my hand. When I sighed she seemed startled, as if a photogravure had come to life. "You have worked—in this country?" she asked.

"Yes, in Cleveland I made collars. But I want to make fine dresses like yours." Although Zia once said that one must never point to gentlewomen, I pointed to her dress. "See how the plaid matches, and the tucks here and here, piping on the seams and how the ruffles fall like water?" She looked down at the dress as if seeing it new and lightly touched a gather. When Rafferty cleared his throat, she waved him silent.

"I trust you're honest, clean, sober." I nodded. She looked at my face, frowning at the scar. "No running after sweethearts."

"I have no sweetheart. I work hard, I send money home."

"Well, my dressmaker *is* nearby," she said finally. "Madame Hèléne. I don't suppose you speak French?"

I shook my head.

"She just needs to work for the Frenchy, not talk to her," Rafferty said, so close that his crutch brushed the swaying hem.

"Sir, I believe I can speak for myself." The lady turned to me. "Your name?"

"Irma Vitale."

"Very well, Irma. I'll introduce you to Madame Hèléne. Only that, you understand."

"Yes, ma'am."

"My name is Mrs. Clayburn. And now, if you'll permit me, gentlemen."

Rafferty stepped back and saluted. "Good luck, Irma. Do us proud—us *immigrants*. And ma'am," he added, "a small token of gratitude for a soldier would be much appreciated." Frowning, Mrs. Clayburn drew two quarters from a beaded purse. Rafferty saluted. "We shall toast the Union and your good health." He called to his friend and they set out across the soggy grass toward a tavern at the edge of the park.

"Come along then, Irma," Mrs. Clayburn said impatiently. So I rode in my first carriage. She did not speak as we rode and I studied her dress in the silence. "Stop here," she called crisply. The driver jerked his horses to a halt and helped her from the carriage, letting me scramble down behind her.

We were in front of a small store with MME. HÉLÉNE, DRESS-MAKER freshly painted on a hanging sign. I had been here before and seen the tiny doorpost NO. Now I stepped inside. Sunlight splashed the clean-swept floor. A slight woman with wide violet eyes and thick honey hair neatly pinned with tortoise combs hurried to greet us.

While Mrs. Clayburn explained what I had done, the dressmaker's gaze dropped to the skirt. When her brow knit slightly, joy flushed my heart. Had she not seen the mend? Don't smile, I warned myself. Do not offend her.

Dropping quickly to my knees, I found the patch and carefully lifted the fabric, explaining in Italian where I had taken the patch, what stitches I used and how I lined the patch along the plaid. Madame Héléne knelt by me, smelling of lavender. White hands studied the patch as she asked questions in French that I answered in Italian, our languages feathering together. She ran a forefinger lightly over the rich folds. I knew what she meant: a fine English weave.

"Ahem," said a voice above us. "I really must go."

"Pardon," said Madame, coming lightly to her feet. "We try—" she glanced at me.

"Irma Vitale," I said.

"We try Irma Vitale today. Then we see. Yes?"

My heart bloomed. "Yes, Madame. *Oui.* Grazie." Turning to thank Mrs. Clayburn, I wiped my eyes.

"Goodness gracious, girl, collect yourself. It's only a day's work, nothing to cry over. Just try to make the best of it." She spoke briefly to Madame and was gone in a swish of plaid. When the door closed, Madame Hèléne waved me toward an oaken chair with a high curved back and seat cushion. Not even Opi's mayor had cushioned chairs. She held out a starched linen smock and I put it on, scarcely breathing.

Eight

THE GREEN DRESS

"Simone!" called Madame Hélène. A slight, round-shouldered girl some few years younger than I scuttled into the room, her bird-bright eyes peeking over an armload of gold and crimson satin strips which she set before me as one would lay out a treasure, patted them with a housemaid's rosy chapped hand and silently stepped away.

With fluttering fingers and rapid French, Madame Hélène showed how the strips must be pinned and basted together. Simone would sew them on the machine and Madame would finish the seams, trimming one raw edge close, then tucking and stitching the other edge around it. Did I understand, she asked? Yes, I understood my task and something new about the very rich: even the seams of their clothing were finer than ours.

Simone returned with a thimble and a pair of scissors, not crane scissors like my stolen treasures, but as light and finely made as mine. Then she led me past neat arrays of tools adorning the shop: long-bladed shears for cutting bolts of cloth, each on its peg, baskets of tailor's chalk, boxes of hooks and eyes, plump cushions stuck with pins, a set of pressing irons by a gleaming stove, big wool-wrapped egg shapes that served, I would learn, for pressing out curves, spools of thread on spindles like bright colored teeth and lengths of velvet ribbon. One long shelf was filled with button boxes: mother-of-pearl, coral, pewter, whalebone, brass, leather and polished wood. Madame Hélène followed my dazzled eyes and seemed pleased, but when a bell over the door rang and a gentlewoman entered the shop, Madame tapped her lips, pointed to my chair and turned away from me.

So I must be as silent, serviceable and unremarkable as the oak platform that the stout, grim woman mounted to have a mourning gown hemmed. As Madame soundlessly marked the lusterless black bombazine, the widow's eyes brushed past me and flitted away. If someone asked her later, "Who else works at the shop?" she would not remember.

The sharp sting of a pinprick and bright bead of blood on my fingertip returned me to my task. Gentlewomen might ignore me, but at least I had my place at this table. Gradually the clop of horses, peddlers' calls, shouting boys and clatter of carriages faded behind the pluck of our needles and I saw nothing but strips of satin and thought only of stitches. After the skirt panels, I was given a hem to finish. An aged gray cat lumbered across the room to curl up on a sheet of sunlight by the front window. Here was the peace of Opi.

My work was constantly inspected. Narrowed eyes meant "Do this part again." A forefinger brushed across stitching meant "This can stay." There was little praise, but none of the humiliation that spiked each day at the workhouse. Customers swept in and out for fittings, barely glancing at me, but Simone silently filled my water cup and in mid-afternoon brought a thick slice of crusty bread on a china plate. I prayed that this workday would last forever, but the cat's sun spot slowly melted away and dark thread grew hard to see. I bent closer to my work. If Madame Hélène paid me now, her message would be clear: don't come back tomorrow.

When the wall clock chimed half past six, Simone tapped my shoulder and announced, "It's time to clean." As she collected fabric scraps for the rag man, I swept the shop, my hands so slick with sweat that twice the broom fell clattering to the floor. Simone cleared her throat and Madame Hélène looked up. Her mouth sprouting pins, she chalked 8 on the table, then pointed from the clock to me and raised her eyebrows in a question. Yes, I said happily, I would be here at 8 A.M. I floated back to the boardinghouse.

"So you have a job? How much does it pay? Did you even ask?" Molly demanded. I hadn't. Molly shook her head. "Well, come on, there's veal stew for dinner. It's just you and me and Mrs. Gaveston. The other boarders work nights this week." After dinner, when Mrs. Gaveston had gone to her rooms, Molly bustled me into the kitchen. "Now that you're set, I'll tell you my plan. I wasn't wanting you to feel bad," she announced, washing dishes so quickly they seemed to fly into the drying racks. "I'm saving every cent from old Gaveston. By September I'll be making loans to greenhorns."

"How?" Even if Molly was white and thus paid more than Lula; even if Mrs. Gaveston was less stingy than the Missus, how could a servant girl save enough to make loans?

"Not big loans like the banks, but lots of little ones, a dollar, two dollars. I charge interest and collect on payday. Bit by bit, the business grows. Besides," Molly added vaguely, "I can do other services for Gaveston." She showed me a calendar written on and erased until the paper was as soft as cotton. "Here I'm saving," she flipped through the summer weeks, each with black figures scrawled in, sums for every month. "Here in September, I'm making loans." She pointed to numbers in boxes, percentages added and sums slowly growing. "Clever, no?"

"Yes, clever."

"Immigrants need furniture; most don't bring more than their clothes from the Old Country," Molly continued eagerly. She would pay Mrs. Gaveston to let her store old beds, tables and chairs in the basement and rent them out to families until they bought their own. "There's money *everywhere*, Irma," insisted Molly, her chapped hands waving over the parlor as if coins lay on the rag carpet, under end tables, inside the broken piano or stuffed behind worn horsehair cushions.

"What's *your* plan, Irma?" Molly demanded. I tried to explain the marvelous intricacy of a gentlewoman's gown: invisible seams and pleats straight as knife edges, smocking and gathers and ruffles falling like water. "What else?" Sending money to Opi was the other part of my plan, as was Zia being healed enough to visit me and stroll by the lake as sunset colors lit the water. If an American doctor could not heal her eyes, I would at least paint my new country for her with words. "And?" Molly persisted. And the plan of me in Opi with Father Anselmo admiring a stained-glass window that my dollars had bought for the church. I did not mention the plan of watching dolphins again with a sailor under a star-swept sky.

Molly sighed. "Irma, you're such a peasant. Listen, if you help me get loans from Italians I'll give you a percentage. In three years you could have a shop. Sooner if we're partners."

Closing my eyes, I saw ladies sweeping past a painted sign: IRMA OF OPI, FINE DRESSMAKING. "Good morning, Signora Irma," they would say. Girls, *my* girls, would be working quietly as customers turned the pages of *Godey's Lady's Book*. "Could you make this?" they would ask and I would say yes, of course. We would consider velvets, silks, Swiss muslin, gossamer satin or piqué, choose bodices and bustle lines, the puff of sleeves, the curve of skirts, the depth of cuffs or the precise fall of a skirt draped over crinoline. I sighed. "I can't have a shop yet, Molly. There's too much I don't know."

"So you could help me. Go to the Italian Aid Society and ask who needs money. It's easy." For her perhaps. Not me. "You have some secret beau then, someone to work for you?" she asked, lifting a dark brow.

"How?" When I pointed at my scar, she snorted.

"You think *that* puts men off? Dress up and get some property behind your name and they'll come drooling after you, believe me, Irma Vitale, hordes of men."

"But—"

"Shush." Molly tapped my head. "Think it over tonight." But instead of drooling men I dreamed of green flowered and pleated fields, crossing velvet meadows swelling like bodices and wandering through valleys of tiny waists that bulged into bustles.

Saturday afternoon a neat stack of coins sat at my place. I paid Mrs. Gaveston and took the rest to an Italian bank near Polk Street. In time, Madame promised, when my pleats and piping came better, the stack would be higher. When I offered to embroider bodices with tendrils and flowers, she agreed, but had me understand that to turn flat cloth into a dress that made plain women captivating, to see a skirt billow as we had imagined it, *that* was the great skill, the thrilling victory. When we unfurled a fresh bolt of fabric across our cutting table, she skimmed her palm along the weave, eyes sparkling and a flush running up her neck. "*Imagine*, Irma," she breathed. "What we make of this."

I sewed constantly, by day for Madame and in the evenings embroidered handkerchiefs, table runners and antimacassars that Molly
sold for me or I bartered with Mrs. Gaveston to prune my room and
board. I thought of Gustavo, but could not write him without the address stolen in Cleveland, so I had only my dream of the night we
talked.

Yet a peaceful calm curled through me that summer. I had work, a
place to live and if there was nobody to share my free Sundays while
Molly tended her "plans," there were parks and markets to stroll
through, a lake even grander than Erie, puppet shows, concerts and
the friendly nods of immigrant families in the blocks around our
boardinghouse.

At noon each day, Simone set a table in the back room with bread
and cheese, sometimes bean potage, boiled and salted radishes, potatoes or onions cooked to a silky brown. We spoke of the day's dresses,
our French, Italian and English words woven into patterns that we all
understood. One afternoon so rainy that fine women did not go out in
carriages, Madame Hélène spoke of her life. She was setting a puffed
sleeve as wide as a mutton leg for an opera gown. Flounces for the
skirt flowed over my knees in falls of rosy satin. In a map of Europe
that Father Anselmo once showed us, France was precisely that shade,
a proud block edging the smooth Atlantic blue. "Where did you live
before?" I asked.

Madame Hélène frowned at the sleeve, describing Alsace: a foggy
place where men dug coal and women sorted rivers of black rock.
Children crawled on their hands and knees through mine shafts,
hitched like ponies to little wagons piled with coal.

"Hitched like ponies?" I repeated. Surely the truth had tangled in
our languages.

"Children," she insisted, holding out her hand to show how small: four or five years old. She bent over the sleeve, rocking.

"You worked in mines too?" I asked, when the rocking ceased.

"No, for the owner's wife. First to clean and then to sew." She bit off a thread.

"Why did you leave Alsace, Madame?"

"Too much death," she said bitterly. As she trimmed the seam, a curl of satin snaked across her lap. Coal veins often collapsed, killing harnessed children. Men dragged the little bodies out, handed them to weeping women and were immediately sent back down again. Explosions killed miners deep in the earth and women were crushed when sorting bins tipped. Many died in bed, coughing blood. Pellagra ravaged villages.

Father Anselmo had told us how pellagra makes the skin scale and bleed. The stricken grow listless, weak and confused. Sunlight pains their eyes. Many turn delirious. Children starve when parents can't work. Malaria curses both rich and poor, but pellagra eats only the poor.

"How did you leave?"

An uncle in Chicago sent money for his son's passage, not knowing the boy had died in the mines. So Hélène went to America in his stead. Dumb with grief, the uncle helped her start a shop and then drifted north to Canada, where he hunted, trapped, and sometimes sent her furs. So he was the source of the fox, wolf and sable pelts she kept in a cedar chest. Ladies paid well for them, chiding Madame Hélène that she might easily be a furrier, but lately no furs had arrived. Perhaps the uncle was dead.

Madame Hélène never sent money to France. All her people were dead or in America. Four baby cousins died in the village the week she left, laid in shallow graves hacked from frozen earth. "More gathers at the bustle, Irma," she said and then her mouth closed tight as a stitched seam.

Simone bent over her machine; its steady click-click filled the shop. Fixing the bustle, I imagined death bells in Hélène's village and babes stiff in blankets. My needle stopped. Madame's shop made no baptismal gowns, I realized with a start, not once since I had come, although we often made children's clothes. Even Mrs. Richards, the banker's wife and our best customer, was refused.

"I'm sorry," Madame Hélène had told her. "There is no time."

"Surely, you could manage. Just white satin with a little lace down the front. The girl could do it." She pointed at me. Madame shook her head. "But I pay well and always on time." This was true. Mrs. Richards wasn't like some, who regularly "forgot" to get money from their husbands. "Fifteen dollars," Mrs. Richards offered. "That's extravagant." It *was* extravagant for a yard of cloth and bits of lace. "So I must go to another dressmaker for this?" the lady taunted.

"Yes, you must," Madame agreed.

The ivory brow furrowed. "You'll lose business with this stubbornness."

"Perhaps."

Now I understood Madame, but who could explain to Mrs. Richards so many tiny bodies buried in their baptismal gowns? Could she hear the thuds of frozen earth? Hélène had eight brothers and sisters, Simone once told me, all dead before she left. Three in one spring. Watching Madame work, I thought of the old widows in Opi, whose black shawls seemed to grow into their flesh and were buried with the women to warm them in their graves. Madame wore her sorrow thus.

Madame Hélène turned to Simone and said, "Enough of these sad things. Get the rag bag. Jacob is coming today."

Jacob the rag collector was a lame, whistling peddler who made the rounds of dress shops with a bulging pack on his back and bright rags stitched to his jacket in a fluttering rainbow. When roving boys snatched away a tatter, Jacob took his loss mildly. "Simone, perhaps you have a bit of something for my arm here?" he would ask. "It seems the ravens plucked me." On Hélène's orders, Simone often slipped longer lengths of cloth into the bag, which Jacob sold to a man he called the Ragmaster. "You are righteous women," he often said. "May the God of Israel bless you." On rainy days when we had no customers, he sometimes sorted his scraps in a corner of our shop. "Blue for the Greeks, red for the Poles, green for the Slovaks," he'd chant. "I know my chickens." He brought us little gifts: flowers twisted from bright bits of paper, prune pastries his sisters made or odd pebbles he found in his travels. When he appeared with a bag of mother-of-pearl buttons he'd gleaned in trade, Madame paid him well, even adding two velvet ribbons for his sisters.

Hélène was as generous with me as she was with Jacob. She paid nine, then ten dollars a week. With the money I sent home, Father Anselmo took Zia Carmela to a doctor who had studied in Naples. Her fever passed, he wrote, but still she coughed and spent days huddled in a chair by the bakery oven, sometimes speaking of me as if I were still in Opi.

"Sending money home is *not* a plan," scolded Molly one evening as I embroidered and she laboriously worked her accounts. "You should be saving for a shop. Women need property. *That's* how we survive." Her calendar, beloved as a Bible, was dark with numbers marked in pencil, erased, added, circled and boxed. She made her first loans in September.

*   *   *

The telegram from Opi came in early December. I felt it through the boardinghouse door as I stamped snow from my boots. I heard it in the yowl of an alley cat and the brush of Molly's broom that ceased as I entered the foyer. The envelope glimmered in the dim hall light on a side table that Mrs. Gaveston had covered with my embroidered linen runner, loathsome now with too-bright roses and a fat bluebird. Molly leaned her broom against the wall. "Maybe it's good news from your father," she offered. "Aren't they expecting a baby?"

"We don't send telegrams for babies," I said, my voice flat as paper.

"Irma, if you want—"

"I'll read it." The gold-brown paper seemed too frail to bear dark news. Perhaps my money *had* changed them. "Western Union," I read slowly, then the date, my address and the message: "My dear Irma, Zia Carmela died peacefully last week, speaking of you. We used your money for the funeral. I will leave Opi soon to serve a church in Calabria. God keep you. Father Anselmo."

"Sit down," said a far voice. "I'll make tea." Soon a hot cup was wedged in my hands. "Not to be cruel, but wasn't she coughing for months? Old folks don't live long once that starts. Not in Ireland at least." Tea pooled in my mouth and I made myself swallow. "Irma!" A strong hand shook my shoulder. "You're scaring me, girl."

Every day since leaving Opi I had pictured Zia in her chair, coughing perhaps, but always there, waiting for me. I imagined Father Anselmo hurrying through the sanctuary to greet me, sandals clicking on the stone floor. Now the long cord linking my soul to home was fraying over the rough Atlantic. When the parlor clock tolled, I found a damp cloth wound through my fingers.

"There's cabbage and boiled beef," said an anxious voice behind me. "Come eat at least."

But I climbed the narrow stairs to my room and lay in bed weeping for Zia, the spare hardness of her life and her loneliness and long sickness. I wept for myself, seeing her empty chair if I ever returned. "If you leave Opi you will die with strangers," my mother had warned a thousand times, but she might have added: "And those you love and leave behind will be dead to you. Someone else will close their eyes."

I lay very still in the dark room, imagining women helping Assunta wash Zia's body and put on her one good dress. With my money there would have been choirboys and wax candles, perhaps a good coffin. A fall breeze ruffled the curtains, curling through the narrow room. What of *my* soul if I died in America? Madame Hélène was not a believer and Molly would not waste money on the dead. I decided to buy funeral insurance from the Sicilian agent on Polk Street.

In the weeks after my Zia died, a dank cold settled over the city. Coal dust hung in the air, close as a cloak when I trudged to the shop and back again. Only work distracted me from billowing doubts. Why had I come to America? That I might live? For whose sake? Not for my people, all dead, disappeared or making new families without me. Not to earn passage home, I was slowly concluding, for who would truly welcome me there? In my father's house a new babe would more than fill the space that once was mine. In Opi I rarely questioned my life. One does not ask "why" in a hunger year, only: "What will I eat tomorrow?" My ancestors who climbed our mountain never asked why. But alone in Chicago, a steady "why?" oppressed me.

"You *could* marry, you know, and have your own family," Molly insisted. "Wouldn't your aunt have said so? You're thinking too much. Come dancing with me."

I couldn't. *Cut, sew, work*—the words filled my dark valley like iron bells, tolling me to sleep, rousing me in the morning and sounding beneath the clatter of carts as I hurried to the shop. Even pigeons on snowy roofs cooed *cut, sew, work.*

Sewing machines only made rich women greedy for more finery: pleats, ruffles, flounces, dips, gathers and close fittings even in their day dresses. Much of this was handwork. New patterns came from Europe, New York and Boston. Our customers wanted them all, and before their neighbors. Madame Hélène made curt condolences when I told her Zia died, but she had seen too many die, and this was a sick old woman. My long mourning perplexed her.

Even Simone was puzzled. "Is it better now, the sadness?" she asked often.

"Yes," I always said, "better." But she and Madame exchanged glances.

"Come, Irma, try this on," Madame said late in February. "Mrs. Straub wants to surprise her daughter, who is exactly your size." I was handed a fine moss-green merino wool walking dress enriched with velvet ribbons. While Simone buttoned me in back, I stood stunned behind our dressing screen. Such lush softness had never touched my skin.

"Come, we mark the hem," Madame called briskly.

When I walked, the dress caressed my legs with a whispering sigh. "When did you cut and piece it?" I asked.

"Sunday," said Madame briefly, her mouth full of pins. "Up." I mounted our hemming block.

"Look at the color," Simone ventured. "Like the beautiful soft green of your eyes." No one had ever exclaimed over my eyes. "And see how it shows off the little waist?" Tucks and velvet bands ran down the bodice, accentuating the tightening line. My own gray work smocks hung straight, masking my breasts. "And see, the new cuirass look," Simone continued. "How it suits you." Perhaps it did, the long waist dipping to points front and back, then easing out to the hips with a deep swan curve. Rich young women sought this line; it was far too binding for working girls.

"Oh, Irma," Simone said, "You look like a gentlewoman." How would it be to walk down the street in such a dress, to see myself mirrored in windows, to hear that rustle and feel the muslin underskirt against my skin?

Madame finished the hem and ran her fingers over my chest and breasts, across my back, around the waist, feeling where the bodice might be loose and making tiny marks with tailor's chalk. At any other hand I would have cringed, but her careful touch was all for the dress and how perfect it must be for Mrs. Straub's daughter.

Jacob's familiar whistle sounded at the door. When Simone opened it, he stepped back, for a fine propriety ruled him, and he never intruded on fittings. "Don't worry, it's only Irma," Simone said, pulling him in by the tatters of his sleeve.

Jacob entered cautiously, studying me intently. "Irma? Such a princess! Oh, Madame Hélène," he said mournfully, "she'll never marry me now." For it had been his habit to gravely propose to Simone or to me on each visit, offering bouquets of daisies or bright feathers he found in his walks. "Alas, I'm an old man," he would conclude with a sigh, "an old, *hungry* man." Then Madame, in fond exasperation, would have Simone bring him thick ends of bread and cheese, an apple and slices of pickle. I hadn't worked at the shop long before noting that Simone bought extra food for Jacob. Pulling a stool close to the stove where we heated our pressing irons, he would nibble his bread and speak of the Russian Jews and Poles flooding his neighborhood, their trials and sometimes joys.

"Do they need loans? Furniture?" Molly asked when I brought home these stories. "Ask." But I never did.

That day of the green dress Jacob simply sat, regarding me as Madame Hélène turned her white hand and I turned with it as she studied the fit. "Irma," said Jacob, carefully, wrapping the cheese and pickle in a clean rag, "you must not hide behind that scar. I have seen how you turn your face when any speak to you, even Simone and the good Madame. But you must not do this. That scar may be God's special sign. And see how beautiful you are in this fine dress?"

"She was unlucky," scoffed Madame. "Who needs a god who makes scars?" She marked the hem with pins where we would add the tiny lead weights that held down ladies' gowns against immodest Chicago winds. When I slipped behind our screen to shed the dress, it seemed I was shedding my own skin. The hem must be finished today, Madame ordered crisply, and the bodice shaped with the tiny tucks at the chalk marks. Jacob left in a flutter of rags, and silence settled over the shop.

Finishing the dress left barely time for lunch and none for the bread Simone brought in mid-afternoon. Yet the wool moved so easily under my fingers, folding, curving, stretching and shaping itself to my needs. This once I was sorry for my speed, for soon the fine green would be boxed and delivered. I felt poor and shabby in my drab gray smock. Even old Jacob had seen me with new eyes.

The clock struck seven. I looked up and saw Madame Hélène and Simone standing together, smiling. How odd, I thought: Madame smiling. She took the long dress box from Simone and handed it to me. "The address?" I asked, for she always wrote it in chalk that I brushed off before delivery.

"Is yours, Irma," said Madame.

I touched the box, incredulous. "For me, this beautiful dress?"

"Yes, so you feel beautiful and not so sad," said Madame briskly. I scrambled to my feet, stammering thanks, but she raised a finger to stop me. "You are a good worker. My ladies like you. Now go home with your dress, Irma, go. I do not like the little scenes. *Merci* is enough. Enjoy your dress. Be pretty."

"Yours?" breathed Molly when I opened the box at the boarding-house. "You could sell that dress for forty dollars, then loan out those forty and earn, let's see," she scribbled furiously, then looked up, curious, as if she had never seen my face before. "You know, that green *does* suit you. It makes your eyes sparkle." She threw down her stub of pencil. "Irma, you deserve something pretty. Listen, wear it on Sunday. I have to go meet some Poles. I'll wear my good blue and we'll have a promenade."

Intoxicated by the green dress, I agreed. It was strangely warm that Sunday despite the season, with a soft breeze that scurried around my skirt, as if spring were peeking through the winter. We went west toward the new neighborhoods, my green swaying against Molly's peacock blue. We had both washed our hair on Saturday night, brushed and bound it with pretty combs. I relished the delicious ripple of the lamb-soft green, its soft press on my chest, warm wrap of the waist and billowing waves of the skirt as I walked.

We came to a street lined with taverns. "The curse of whiskey," Molly muttered. "Instead of drinking themselves to death, they could be buying houses."

"With your loans?" I suggested.

Molly laughed and wove her arm through mine. "Come on, Irma, there's no harm in a bit of show." Men leaning against tavern doorways turned their heads like cats watching birds. Their eyes raked my body, tightening the bodice and burning my skin. Molly laughed, white teeth showing. Is this what other women felt, that every street was a stage, every watching eye hotly eager and all of this a happy game? Walking was never like this in Opi. Because I was plain and not beautiful like the baker's daughters? Because my clothes were shabby? Now in this marvelous dress I was equal to the baker's daughters, at least for men lounging by taverns. Yet when their whistles nipped my ears, the dress felt thin as voile and I crowded Molly on the sidewalk.

"Really, Irma, sometimes you're such a nun," she whispered, shaking herself free. "It's fun, no, to play with men a little? Keep your chin up. They won't do a thing if you walk fast. It's like playing with kittens. You dangle a bit in their faces and then snatch it away. Come on, it's a beautiful day and they're just admiring the scenery. Relax."

I tried. My dress was modest enough and decently covered, I reminded myself. Madame had been mindful of this. So as we walked on with Molly still laughing at me, I did relax. The dress helped, with its swish and softness, the glint of sunlight on ruffles, the gentle tightness at my waist and our sculpted shadows moving over brick. If Zia could see how eyes followed *me*, Irma Vitale of Opi, yes, she would be happy. I held my head up proudly despite my scar, my too-high nose and common brown hair.

Molly's pace quickened. She grasped my hand. "Never mind the men. Look at all these houses, new families coming every day, Jews in these blocks, and Poles further on. A few years ago all this was fields. Look over there, three boardinghouses in a row. Gaveston should buy one." Now we were walking past families whose men watched us cautiously, mindful of their wives. Girls held out their hands to feel our dresses brushing by. "Little grubbers!" Molly groused cheerfully, waving aside girls with dirty hands, but this was a game too, as we twisted and swerved to keep our skirts free of the giggling gauntlet. "You there!" Molly ordered a girl whose face was smeared with jam, "Scat!" I gave one child a penny. What a country, to be in this dress on this beautiful day with a friend on the streets in Chicago and money in my purse to scatter.

"Come on now," Molly urged, "we're not there yet, the Poles are a few blocks on." We turned left and right as Molly muttered her directions until she stopped, triumphant, and pointed: "There! Look!"

A swarm of men were laying brick while little girls played with rag dolls, boys mixed mortar and women poured beer for the men. "See," Molly announced with a flourish. "It cost me a deal of trouble, but I found out they're building a church and they'll need chairs, you see? I know where there's a warehouse full of them and a man with a cart." Molly located a translator and began a long debate between those who wanted to build their own pews and others who liked the ease of Molly's proposal.

"Father Michal must decide," the translator finally announced.

"Can you go get him, Irma?" Molly pleaded. "They say he's with a new family a few blocks away, blessing their flat or something."

"Let's go together if it's so close."

"Please, Irma. If I stay, I'm sure I can make some loans. It's safe; there's no taverns around here, just houses."

This much was true, and not to be called a nun again, I agreed to fetch the priest. It wasn't far, the translator assured me, just a few blocks east, a narrow house, number seventeen, with blue curtains. Red curtains, one of the women must have insisted, for the translator shrugged. "Red or blue. The important thing is finding Father Michal."

I set off through streets the translator had described, not the way I had come with Molly, but soon this new quarter defied the easy name of "blocks." In tangled lanes and alleys no one spoke English or Italian or had heard of a Father Michal. There were wide houses with blue or red curtains and narrow ones with no curtains, just dark glinting windows. Some had no numbers. Certainly there was no seventeen. My green dress grew heavy and tight. Perhaps Father Michal had left that house and gone to another. Perhaps the matter of chairs was already settled. I would go back to Molly, I decided. If the priest was still needed, the translator could find him. I had been gone a long time and perhaps she was waiting for me.

Turning west to shorten my path, I followed a street that ended at a dank wooden shop whose crude hanging sign showed a cow head circled by sausages. Buckets outside brimmed with clotted blood and chunks of fat and gristle. Rangy dogs fought for scraps. Gagging from the stench, I hurried toward a doorstep where two women sat talking: "Church, Polish church?" I asked desperately, then tried Italian: "*Chiesa?*" A word circled back from Cleveland. "*Kirke?*" They seemed distrustful. What was a lady doing in this quarter, accosting them? Boys playing stickball stared frankly at my breasts. One made a crude gesture, another snorted. I looked frantically around. When had the sun dropped below treetops and dusty haze begun filling the streets?

"Miss, are you lost? May I help you?" asked a genteel voice so close behind me that I jumped. "Don't worry. I'm a policeman." He was tall, with thick sandy hair and wide mustache, broad-shouldered in a chesterfield coat, striped trousers and buffed oxford shoes, a gentleman. So why call himself a policeman? I stepped warily away.

"We have our days off too, you know. But for a lady in distress," he touched his brown derby hat, "we of the brotherhood are always on duty." He stepped closer, putting a large hand on my arm. "This is no place for a lady like yourself." He shouted roughly at the boys and they scampered away. "Greenhorns," he muttered. "Have to put them in their place. Now where are you headed, miss?"

I stepped back, for his breath smelled of beer, yet it must be true that policemen had days off. I was surely lost and only a nun or peasant would distrust *every* man. Besides, Molly would be waiting and anxious. I described the block where I left her with men working in shirtsleeves. "Yes, the Polish church. It's not far," he assured me, "but let's go this way, away from the stench." My guide never gave his name, but acted the gentleman, taking my arm at every curb. When he asked where I lived and I said in a boardinghouse, pale blue eyes scanned the fineness of my dress.

"A gift from the dressmaker I work for," I admitted. Idiota, I realized, the instant the words left my mouth and his eyes met mine boldly. Idiota, I had laid myself bare.

"Ah, so, we're a dressmaker's assistant then? A working girl?" His hand tightened on my arm. With a husky ruffle in his voice he said, "Come, your church is right this way." This was no policeman, I knew then. Flushed with the heat of panic, I looked around wildly for someone to call, to run to.

"Street's pretty empty," he said.

True, but far better to be lost, to pound on any door, run down any street, hide in alleys all night, if only to be far from him. "I'll go on myself, sir, since it's close," I said, trying to speak evenly, eyes averted, as we did at home to snarling dogs. In the instant that a faroff whistle distracted him, I wrenched my arm free but he lunged and caught me.

"I wouldn't, miss. Greenhorn thieves would rob you for that gown." He grasped a fold of my skirt. "Fine clothes like this are worth a pretty penny." He swerved me around a corner toward a row of charred, abandoned houses I surely hadn't passed before.

"Let me go!" I shouted more loudly, jerking back until a streetlamp blocked me. He had both arms now and I was trapped. Wolf eyes glittered in the dusk.

"Whoa, not so fast. 'Cause here's *my* church, girl, made for me expressly by the Great Chicago Fire." He laughed roughly, nodding at a charred house with yawning door and broken windows. A rat scurried out and the great hands squeezed more tightly.

"Let me go!" I shouted again, kicking, yanking, calling, "Help! *Aiuto!*"

"You shut up, girl!" he hissed, hot breath in my ear. "Nobody hears you. Or if they do, they'll want a turn themselves. After I've had mine." A fleshy hand clapped over my mouth and I was dragged through the doorway. "You shouldn't be dressing like your betters, girl. Not in this part of the city. Not with all these Jews around acting so holy. They're rats like the rest of you greenies."

He dragged me over broken glass that crunched under my scrabbling feet. I bit his hand. He slapped my face. "Italian bitch. Can tell by your voice. Coming to our country, stealing our jobs, breeding bastards." With each word I was shoved harder against the charred, shaking wall. With a shriek I tore loose. He caught and slammed my body back against the wall, then ripped a ruffle from my dress. "Good for something," he muttered, tying it in a gag. "There. A bridle for this filly bitch," he panted. "Now whoa there, Missy, while I mount you. Just don't make me use my whip." He yanked a thick belt from its loops and sliced it through the air. The heavy buckle clanged on a charred beam. "Want it on your face, bitch?" he demanded. "Or here?" He pushed my breast. Panting harder now, he fumbled at his trousers, broad chest pinning me to the wall, the hard lump of his pocket watch drilling my ribs. I heaved for breath. When I tried to scream, the gag took my words. "Excited, hey, filly? Well, here comes your stallion, your big *American* stallion. Damn this skirt." A rip like lightning tearing the sky. I kicked. I tore one hand free and hammered his face, once, twice, wild with frantic strength.

"I said hold still, girl!" A sudden flash of metal and a keen blade pressed my neck. Like my father's sheep-butchering knife. *Oh Jesus, Mary, Mother of God.* "Lost, girl? I'll show you lost. Here's lost. Like it? Do you like it, girl?" Bloomers ripped. Legs knocked apart, throat seared from screaming, but no sound, only my roaring heart. And then an iron bolt thrust inside me, a sharp tearing and his grunting heaves. Blood ran down my legs. *Lord Jesus take me.* I slumped.

"Damn you bitch, stand up till I'm finished or I'll cut the other cheek!" Again. Again, harder, deeper, his body pounding mine, grunting uh-uh until he stepped back so suddenly that I crumbled like cloth on the glass-strewn floor.

He stared down at me, lips curled. "Now *that's* a good greenhorn. I'm counting to a hundred, girl. You make a single sound before that, you move *one* muscle and I'll come back and cut your throat. You'll die here with rats before anybody finds you. Understand?"

I nodded and he backed away, calmly cleaned himself with a handkerchief, buttoned his striped trousers, replaced the wide belt, noted the time on his pocket watch, righted his hat and then he was gone, glass crunching beneath his shoes. I pulled off the gag and counted slowly into the darkness: *Uno, due, tre . . . Zia, it's better you died before this. Uno, due, tre . . .* Then came blackness and from this blackness, thoughts spinning against me like slow knives. So *this* was the end of my long path out of Opi? The Lord had brought me *here*, to this pit of glass and darkness, this humiliation and pain? Broken, used. My father touched me, only that. The thieves in Cleveland robbed my purse. And yet I had pressed on: *fool, fool, idiota*. So vain in my green dress, taunting men until one of them reared against me. My mother was wrong. To die with strangers is no great thing. My great-grandfather on a Russian field had died a hero, a slow sleep in the snow. "Death finds us where it will," said Father Anselmo.

Yet I lived. Wasn't this far worse, shame among strangers? How could I return to Molly and Madame or any decent life? Better what Irene did, to walk into dark water, her apron filled with rocks. Lord forgive me, I felt on the ground for a wedge of glass and raised it to my throat. I'd make my own dark lake for drowning, my own sleep in the snow, blood mixed with cinders. Who of my people would be lessened by my death? Zia was gone, Carlo lost or gone. My father had Assunta and a coming babe. Who here would mourn me? Molly, Madame and Simone, for a little while, perhaps. The Lord had no use for me, perhaps even despised me for my vanity.

Just a push, a little push against the neck, here where the vein pulsed. This time no Teresa would hold the wound closed. A little more blood, just a little more.

Uno. I said a Paternoster for my soul. *Due.* Who would blame me if I pressed? *Tre.* I took a breath, then stopped, shaking, squeezing my eyes shut against that wide mocking face, curled lips, striped trousers puddled at his feet, the tiny eyes of rats, waiting.

Oh Lord, can't you save me? My hand shook. After the rats, in time someone would find me, even here in the great, indifferent city. And then? When the woodcutter's daughter hanged herself in Opi, Father Anselmo could not bury her in sacred soil. Violated and shamed, yet her soul would wander, eternally homeless. And what of Irene, rotting in a pit with strangers?

I do not know how long I sat thus, gripping the glass against my neck until from far in the darkness beyond the house came, first indistinct and then more strongly, a familiar whistled song, lilting and light, a mockery from my old life. The shard fell, clattering on wood.

"Jacob! Jacob!" A cry rang out so wild and howling, it could not be mine. Again, "Jacob!" and then an old man's panting and heavy feet on wooden stairs, glass crackling.

"Irma? Is it you? What are you doing here?" Jacob knelt in the darkness. "What happened?" His fingers must have reached my torn skirt. "What have they done?" Rough hands held me close, a soft rag wiped my burning cheeks. "Praise the God of Israel for guiding my steps here. Shh, now shh." He rocked me as I sobbed, murmuring, "May he who did this evil be devoured by wild beasts, dashed against rocks, drowned in dark waters. Oh my dear child. There now, there now." With deft hands, he plucked glass from my skirt. "My sisters will care for you," he went on soothingly, pulling cloth lengths from his bag to wrap me. "Can you walk a little? It's not far, very close." When we stepped into the faint gaslight, he saw my bloody skirt and quavered. "That beast! May God—never mind, Irma, come, come home to my sisters." He led me through the streets, keeping to shadows until we reached a narrow brick tenement. "There now, my dear. You are safe with us."

Nine

INFALLIBLE CURE, NUMBER TWO

The pale faces of Jacob's sisters hovered over me, two hazy moons in the smoky kerosene light. I still smelled burned wood. When Jacob paced behind us in stocking feet on the rag rug, I heard the crunch of broken glass. A mound of striped cloth in the corner heaved. Striped curtains fluttered like *his* striped trousers. I tried to twist away, but at every side hands pressed me down.

"Irma, be still," said Jacob patiently. "My sisters help you." Two women hovered like tall crows with flapping black shawls, chattering, cooing, stroking, unpinning my hair. An avalanche of weakness crushed me. Jacob pointed to a bed.

"No bed, no bed!" I gripped the chair. Heavy footsteps sounded on the stairway and a man's voice growled beyond the wall. I shuddered.

"It's just Mr. Rosenberg, our neighbor. The door's locked, don't worry." The sisters wrapped a blanket around me and Jacob said,

"Irma, I'll get a policeman. Can you describe the man?" He crossed to the door, pants legs hinged like scissors cutting the room.

"No, no!" I shouted. Who could know a real policeman? A false one might fool Jacob, break in and do *that* again, even to his sisters. "Don't go!"

"But the police can look for that man, that vile beast," Jacob explained patiently. Yiddish flew over my head. I understood only "police" and the sisters' voices trampling his down.

Jacob knelt by me. "I'm sorry, Irma, that was just my *mishigas*, my craziness. Sarah will make a special bath so you are clean again and purified." The smaller sister hurried to the kitchen. A metal thud hit the floor: a wash basin. I would be unwrapped and wet in this shaking cold? Couldn't they hear my bones rattle? Didn't they know I wanted only dryness and heat now, and to never have my body touched?

"There now, go with Freyda." The tall one pulled me up before I could protest and walked me in the tiny kitchen, stiff as the doll in Mrs. Gaveston's parlor, left by a daughter who died young. Propped in a corner, trapped, I watched the two sisters fill the tub, adding herbs and pouring in vinegar and turpentine. A piercing tang filled the air.

"Why?" I demanded in English and Italian, but they only smiled and pulled a curtain to close off the little room.

"Gud," said Freyda, pointing at the tub. They circled me, voices high, shawls fluttering, peeling clothes from my body until I was utterly plucked, then maneuvered to the tub and made to step inside. Look how they fold, these doll legs. My eyes burned.

"What are these?" I asked, scooping dried buds and twigs from the pale foam, but they said only "gud" and washed me with sponges, at least not with hands. Softening, I looked up and saw Freyda, tall and stern, fluttering rag wings, holding a glass rod with rubber bulb tip pointed between my legs. Not there—not there. "No!" I screamed. "Take the rod away."

"Shh!" they soothed. "Shh! Shh!" Now from under the floor came thuds shaking the room and a man's angry voice, then thuds again like a broomstick pounding. Sarah's little hand clapped my mouth. Freyda spoke urgently to her brother.

"Irma!" Jacob called from behind a curtain dividing the rooms. "Stop your *tumul*, please, or the landlord comes. My sister say if you use the rod, perhaps no seed grows in you."

Horror shot through me. I hadn't thought of this, *his* seed rooting like a sapling feeding on a fallen tree, eating me out, a rotten stump? So, yes, wash out the seed, but not with a rod, I begged Jacob. "Tell them, please, not with a rod."

The sisters' voices rushed at Jacob. The toes of his worn boots shuffled below the curtain. His voice came softly as the pounding stopped. "Listen to me, Irma. My sisters know how it is for you. They know. Cossacks came to our village in Poland. You have heard how the Cossacks hate the Jews? They came with guns and long sabers and forced all the young girls and wives into the forest. Freyda and Sarah too. It was winter, with snow. You understand me?"

"Yes," I whispered. Sarah sponged my back, making sheets of pungent warmth.

"They send the women back one by one, their clothes ripped and bloody. Some fell in snow. We ran across the field and carried them home. The old women washed them. Sarah, the youngest and most beautiful, the soldiers keep longest. When finally they rode away, we searched the woods and found her curled under leaves, without clothes. She was three days not speaking. Even now, she is afraid outside. Always afraid. But at least no seed grew in her or in Freyda. Only one girl made a Cossack baby, blond like them. Her father took it to the woods and left it there for wolves. So you see, Irma, my sisters know. Let them help you. And be quiet, please, or the landlord sends us away. Will you let them?"

I nodded. Freyda pried open my hand and worked the bulb inside. I closed my eyes so tightly that my whole face ached. Overhead their voices rippled like water on pebbles as I squeezed the bulb, thinking: water on pebbles, wash his seed away. "Gud, Irma. Gud," said Freyda and then other words to Jacob. "They say more, Irma, deeper. And wash yourself well against the pox." At last Freyda took the rod and let me stand. I was dried and wrapped in a robe, but the cold crept back as if it lived in my body now. Sarah emptied the tub. Freya stirred cabbage in a pot. Food? Eating? Bile filled my throat.

A table was set. "Eat," said Jacob. "You must eat." They set out bread and cabbage, but the cabbage smelled of wet ash to me. Better to be empty, far better. Freyda touched my arm and I lifted the fork, heavy as an iron fire tong. The moon faces beamed. Salty steam rose from the plates, a hand brushed mine again and I was crying, tears splashed on cabbage. Voices swept the table and then my plate was gone and another blanket wrapped around me. Good, no one sees my body, no part of it, none.

A muffled voice said, "We make you a bed, my dear." In the other room the three bustled, shawls fluttering, rolling out a thin mattress, but I wanted only to curl in the rag nest.

"I'll sleep here," I pointed and before they could answer I had curled in the rags, face to the wall, wrapped against voices lapping at my back.

"So then good night, Irma," said Jacob, and the sisters repeated, "Gut nytte, Irma." Slowly voices dimmed to what must have been prayers. Then came rattles from the kitchen and the rustle of clothes. A coal stove banked. Tightly curled, I warmed at last. Jacob's snoring soon rolled in from the kitchen. Near me the sisters murmured.

In the darkness, I saw myself in a green dress splashed with sun. Then green slumped in a charred house. Was that another Irma? Blessed Virgin, who was I now? I stared into darkness sharp with turpentine and cabbage, searching for Her mild eyes and veiled head. Instead I found *his* eyes, glinting. Grunts, uh-uh, belt buckle clanging, crunch of glass. Covering my face with hot hands, I smelled vinegar again. Think of warm water, sliding sponge and splashes.

But weren't there other splashes years ago? In Opi we slept in shuttered darkness and in those black nights before my mother sickened, I sometimes woke to bed ropes creaking, my father's groans, uh-uh, her stifled gasps and then a furtive splashing never explained. Was she trying to wash out seeds that couldn't grow in hunger years? Even as I pressed my hands to my face, breathing vinegar, another memory came rushing back. Once the midwife appeared at our door when my mother's belly was still flat. When I asked why she came, no one answered. Carlo and I, still small, were sent to gather wild asparagus from the far fields. We returned with stringy bouquets to find our mother pale in bed, Zia bent over her and my father staring at the fire.

Yes, now I remembered, always after the groaning at night came splashing. To wash away his seed? But not always enough, if the midwife came. Why did he torment my mother, knowing the cost? And why did she accede, even invite this risk if all it gave her was groaning? Why? My chest ached for breath, as if a great hand pressed my heart.

Moonlight caught a folded shawl, white as my altar cloth whose beauty provoked my father. Inside my blanket I swam in guilty sweat. Was it women's skill that called down men's assaults? Our vanity and pride? Somewhere in the city was another woman pressed against a wall, hot breath in her face, enduring thrusts brought on by a dress of mine?

No, no, remember the Cossacks who rode into the village. Evil, sheer evil. They crossed the plains to ravage peasant girls in rags. "May he who did this be devoured by wild beasts," Jacob had said. I mouthed in the darkness: "Lord curse him, send the wild beasts upon him. Tear his flesh." But what of *me*, a greenhorn who lured my own Cossack out of the gnarled Chicago streets?

Looking out the black mouth of the window, I shrank at the thought of daybreak. Had I been wrong, a coward, not to press harder on the glass against my neck? How could I leave this room when evil men lurked everywhere outside? A moment's daydreams called out thieves in Cleveland. Sarah murmured in her sleep. Who could question why she shunned the streets, she who hid naked and bleeding under leaves in an earthen hollow? How to face Madame or Molly tomorrow, sit at Mrs. Gaveston's table or go to my church on Polk Street? How to pray to Our Lord again?

I closed my eyes and in the darkness the pale face of the child Rosanna appeared. How had she endured, when death entered her house like a prowling beast, seizing one and then the next in her family until all were dead of malaria? Yet she endured. She learned to sew on scraps and went, seemingly gladly, to the fisherman's house. But Rosanna was innocent, unspoiled, and I . . . Zia's fog-soft voice fanned my ear. "*Sleep, Irma,*" she whispered. "*You're Irma of Opi still. Irma of Opi, Irma, Irma.*" Wrung dry, I sank into tumbling sleep.

In the deep gray before dawn, the sisters moved like shadows, dressing and folding bedclothes. When I sat up, Jacob protested. "Stay and rest today. I'll tell Madame that you're sick."

"No, don't, she'll ask why." I must endure this day and last night must be my secret, damped like coals in the evening. Speaking of it would only fan new flames.

Jacob chewed his lip. "Well then, eat breakfast with us at least."

Freyda rustled in a corner, producing a modest tan dress she quietly set at my side, and then drew Jacob into the kitchen. I put it on and joined them. Jacob was sorting rags while Sarah stitched beads on a blue velvet evening bag. In her scrap bag I spied bits of my work from Madame's: a length of rose satin, scarlet silk from an opera gown, yellow organdy of a bride's trousseau we had just completed, a widow's black bombazine, and just below it, moss green wool. *My* green. I turned away.

"Look, Irma," said Jacob. "Your fine dress is here and not so badly ripped. It can be fixed." When he held it up, the torn skirt gaped at the waist like a leering mouth. Green engulfed the room.

"Please, you keep it."

"But you were so beautiful, like a princess. It could be fixed and sold for a good price if you don't want to wear it," he persisted until Freyda tugged the fluttering edge of his sleeve, glancing at me. "Is it my mishigas again? I'm sorry, Irma, but you are too generous."

"You helped me. Give it to your sisters or use the cloth for purses."

He put the green away. "Thank you, Irma, but it is nothing what we did. We are all strangers in this city, here to help each other. Sarah, come eat with our guest."

Sarah blinked at his English, but sat at the table. Freyda served strong coffee, dark bread, jam, boiled potatoes, hard-boiled eggs and balls of pickled fish. They would eat sparely at night for the wealth of this breakfast. I nibbled at an egg that tasted of wood and took a bit of potato. "Very good," I told Jacob. "Tell them it's delicious."

Eat, Freyda must have said, rolling another fish ball on my plate. They ate solemnly, glancing at me until a street vendor's cry brought Jacob scrambling to his feet. "That's the ice man. We must go." He hustled me out the door before I could thank the sisters.

Morning sun dazzled my eyes. "What will people think?" said Jacob in his gentle, jesting voice. "Me walking with a lovely Gentile."

"Jacob, I'm not—"

"You are," he insisted, "a lovely Gentile."

What would people think? They would think I was no virgin. Somehow they would see that I was spoiled. They would read it in my face and walk. The blade sharpener chanting, "Razors, blades, knives to grind," knew, and the brewer rolling kegs of beer off his cart knew as well. I snapped my head away and saw a news boy smirking.

The sweet-potato lady by her charcoal brazier sang: "Yeddy go, sweet potatoes-O!" Was she thinking, seeing me: "One of *those* women?"

A bricklayer mixing mortar looked up, licking dusty lips.

A baker resting against a doorpost idly squeezed a bit of dough, soft as a woman's flesh.

Even the old French silhouette cutter who used to nod at me when I passed bent over his work, scissors flashing.

Messenger boys in tattered shirts, clerks in round black hats all must be thinking: "*He* had her. Why not me?" In a knot of men by the bank, I saw striped trousers flash.

"Stop!" Jacob yanked my arm backward as a fire engine roared past, legs of the great white horses churning, spotted dogs racing beside them. Only then did I hear the brass bell clang. "Be careful, Irma!" Jacob mopped his creased brow. "Suppose you are hurt? What I tell my sisters? Even afraid, you must be careful."

"How did—?"

"How I know you are afraid? I feel it." He pulled back his sleeve, revealing a fresh bruise circling the thin wrist.

"Jacob, I'm so sorry."

"It is nothing. But Irma," he said earnestly. "You cannot let that man's evil live here or here," Jacob lightly touched his head and heart. "That is the way you become the crazy one, the mishigas. You must forget."

"How? I could see him again. He could—"

Jacob shook his head. "Chicago is too big. You will never see him. Or if you do, you run another way. The Cossacks did not return. Even they had shame." How could I believe this when every man's smile mocked me and every jacket hid a belt? Jacob sighed. "Look, we are almost to your shop. Who is that by the lamppost, calling you?"

Heart pounding, I looked where Jacob pointed and saw Molly waving wildly. Molly! I hadn't once thought of her. She darted across the street, dodging a coal cart. When the driver cursed, she didn't hurl back her customary hot retorts but grabbed my arms and shook me. "Irma, what happened? I looked, we all looked for you everywhere. I waited and waited with the Poles. What happened?"

How could I explain? And why? To make her suffer more for me? "I got lost," I said finally. "Jacob our ragman found me. I told you about him. I stayed with him and his sisters."

Molly flicked her head to Jacob, then whirled back on me. "Do you know how long a night can last, waiting? You could have sent a messenger boy."

"Molly, I'm sorry."

Her shoulders fell and she dropped her arms. "No, it was my fault. I shouldn't have sent you off alone." Limp as a weary child, nothing like the old Molly with calendars and plans, she leaned against the lamppost. Suddenly her eyes widened and she pointed at my dress. "Where's the green?" Her voice shrilled as she turned on Jacob. "What happened to her? Where is the dress?"

"I tore it on—a fence. So I borrowed this from his sister." I tried to look away, but Molly held me. That I rarely lie is only habit, for it was useless in Opi where every neighbor knows your family, all you have and everything you do each day. So I only said, "I can't talk about it."

She dropped her hands. "But you will later? Tonight, when we're alone?" When I said nothing, she stepped away, shoulders sagging.

"Molly, I'm sorry. Madame is waiting."

She stared at me. "You're different. You've changed. And it's my fault."

"Miss," said Jacob suddenly, "Irma must work. You'll walk a bit with me?" When Molly opened her mouth to protest, I kissed her, swearing to be home that evening.

"Take the streetcar tonight," she said. "Here, use this." She pressed a coin into my hand as Jacob led her away. He would not tell my secret. And I would cut, sew, work and think of nothing else that day. Mother of God, help me do this.

In the shop, Madame was curious about Freyda's tan dress. "A strange cut," she commented. "But the fullness here is good?"

"It's comfortable," I managed.

"For girls with the small breast," she persisted, "we could try. With more gathers at the waist perhaps, and finer cloth, of course, we could show off the line." When I opened my mouth, nothing came from the dryness inside. Fortunately, a steady stream of customers carried us through the morning. Work, I told myself. Hear only the steady whirl of Simone's machine and the whining senator's wife. Remember only stitches. But when I pricked a finger and dabbed the blood with cotton, a new fear rushed in: my monthly flow, suppose the washing didn't wash the seed away? Pins dropped from my mouth.

"What is it?" Madame demanded. We were draping muslin on a dress model to try a new design.

"Nothing," I said hastily. "Only, that I see more tailored jackets on the street."

"True," she said. "Always more." She pulled her little notebook from a pocket and sketched busily. "You have worn the green dress?" she asked, thank the Lord not looking up at me. From behind the dress model I said yes, I had worn it. "And it was noticed?" A page turned. Her pencil roughed another jacket.

"Yes, Madame. It was noticed."

"Good. Is good a woman is noticed." The whirl of the sewing machine did not cease, but I felt Simone's great soft eyes on me. She never again spoke of the green dress.

Late that afternoon Mrs. Maxwell came for a fitting with her customary peppermint candies, complaining that her stomach was swollen from dyspepsia and she could not lace her corset tight. "Help," she begged Madame.

Who would help me if my flow didn't come? I bent over an intricate panel of shirring, trying to be as invisible in the shop as I once was.

"We will cut the neck lower," said Madame. "You agree, Irma?" I nodded. "A man does not notice flesh at the waist if there's more skin above it." Mrs. Maxwell laughed loudly. I made myself smile. Behind her machine, Simone giggled politely as Madame chalked a lower neckline on the bodice. "We add some fine French lace here," Madame added. "Costly, but it draws the eye." Mrs. Maxwell praised us all and went away.

At last the clock released me, but wedged in a crowded streetcar, I could not cease thinking of Filomena. When we were children, how fast her bare feet skimmed over the meadows and tumbled boulders, faster even than Carlo's. I remembered the lustrous stream of her black hair and a nose so big that boys called her Hawkface. When my uncle dragged her to a Naples convent, the family gained a benediction and one less hungry child. Never pious, Filomena must have hated the cloistered, ordered days, the lack of sun and space for running. Perhaps she looked for city work, but merchants shunned a rough-hewn mountain girl, and fine houses wanted comely servants. In the end only the street would take her. Near the boardinghouse, church bells called out: Filomena, Filomena, Filomena. Were they calling out her death?

Once, in Cleveland on the way back from the market, Lula and I had passed a prostitute slumped in a doorway. Lula fished a coin from her purse and a potato from our bag. I gaped at the bruised face, ragged shawl and gray teeth gnawing the raw potato. "Four years is all a body lasts in that life," Lula whispered as she hurried me away. "If the pox or drink don't get her, if some man don't beat or cut her bad enough to die, and if she don't die of getting her womb cut up too often or poisoned, she'll hang herself with her own bedsheets. If she's got any." It had been, I counted quickly, six years since Filomena left Opi. I stopped in a church to light a candle that might help ease her soul through purgatory.

At the boardinghouse, I went to my room after dinner, so weary I could barely mount the stairs. When her evening work was done, Molly knocked on my door, bringing a plate of oatcakes and a little glass. She sat on my bed, her long, freckled face taut with worry. "Irma, I won't ask what happened to you last night, but I swear on my mother's grave, I wish it had happened to me. I shouldn't have sent you alone."

"Molly, you meant no harm."

"Have a dram of whiskey." I drank to oblige her and nibbled an oatcake as she spoke of her country, her brothers who went to sea and cousins gone to serve in English houses. When she left to dim the gaslights and bank the coal fires, I crawled into bed, praying the sisters' herbs had cleansed me.

Don't think of yesterday. Dream the old dream, I told myself. My own shop. On the wall a photogravure of Opi, tinted with the greens, blues and tender browns. I would surround myself with women and never think of—what happened. But the smell of charred wood wormed through the window. I put lavender oil on my pillow, but still the smell remained.

Always before, my blood had come regularly, but that month it did not come. I put linen strips in my underclothes each morning and in the evening they were clean. At church after lighting another candle for Filomena, I lit one for my blood. Worry can make a woman late, I once heard Molly tell a friend, but how to stop this worry? Hurrying through the streets, keeping wide of clots of men, taverns or police, scanning for that thick sandy hair, wide mustache and striped trousers, I constantly thought of blood. By the time the full moon shone like a great white plate over the city, I knew I was with child.

And now? My mind churned. When I could no longer hide a growing belly, what would Madame's customers say, knowing I was single? She could never keep me if they complained. Would even Mrs. Gaveston keep me, she who constantly intoned, "*I* have a reputation to think of"? Even if a big belly could be hid, what if I died after childbirth, as so many women did? What became of orphaned bastard babes? Collar girls had whispered of newborns quenched in their birthing cloths for a merciful quick death.

How often did Father Paolo bid families to be fruitful, to welcome the gift of each child? But the church did not help families feed and clothe these children, poor women whispered after mass, and many used what means they had to block another birth. How could a single working girl keep a child? And where? Not at the boardinghouse and surely not at the shop, for Madame disliked "little screamers." Our customers wanted no babes underfoot. Hire a wet nurse? I could pay only the poorest with many mouths to suckle. Many died of neglect in such hands, crawled too close to hot stoves or went unaccountably "lost." If by some miracle my child survived, how could I look into its eyes and not see *him* or hear in its laughter that sneer when he bridled me? Wouldn't I feel in a child's warm touch the crush of *his* hand on my breast? Lord forgive me, but I could not keep this child.

I sought out a drugstore near Vernon Park in the blocks called Little Italy. Waiting for the crowded shop to empty, I gripped a polished wooden counter, thinking how to phrase my problem. When the last clutch of customers pressed out the door, a squat, round-headed druggist shuffled to my side.

"*Buon giorno, signorina,*" he said politely and must have sensed my unease, for he spoke of the weather, inquired where I came from and exclaimed over the extraordinary coincidence that he himself was from Isernia, quite near to Opi. A cousin's flocks grazed the hills south of ours. He glanced at my white hand gripping the counter.

"You are wanting female pills perhaps, signorina, for some internal obstruction?"

"Yes," I said gratefully, "for an—obstruction."

"And you wish to be restored, to have this obstacle removed?"

"Yes."

He nodded. "There is a simple preparation. If you'll excuse me." He scuttled into a back room and returned with two small boxes. "Made by a fine house in New York, absolutely safe for the most delicate constitution. We have Dr. Bronson's Infallible Cure, Number One, two dollars the box and also Dr. Bronson's Infallible Cure, Number Two, four degrees stronger, for obstinate cases of obstruction. Five dollars the box. Take two each day for three days." The boxes looked up at me like eyes. Five dollars. A week's room and board.

"Perhaps you are wondering which to buy?"

I nodded.

"It is your choice entirely. Both are very fine. However, if Number One does not remove the obstruction, you must purchase Number Two, which would be, of course, seven dollars in total."

I cleared my throat. "And if Number Two does not remove it?"

The druggist's round eyes flicked toward the closed door. "Then you will return to my shop and I will recommend an excellent woman, very skilled in female matters, who will remove this obstruction by other means."

My dry mouth barely framed the words: "An *abortista*?"

He nodded. "I'm sorry, signorina, that is the only way. But," he said, patting my shoulder, "for good luck, we won't speak of this yet. Take these pills and I hope, for your sake, not to meet again."

"Grazie, I will take the Number Two," I whispered, setting five crumpled dollars on the counter. When a pair of women bustled into the store, he turned his back to them, shielding me as I slipped Dr. Bronson's Infallible Cure in my bag.

I took the pills but nothing happened. On the fourth night, Molly stopped me by the water closet. "You are worried about something?" she asked, glancing at the door and dropping her voice. "Something female?" I nodded. "There are pills, Irma."

"I know."

Molly drew me further from the boarders' rooms and whispered: "There is a woman who helps girls in trouble. She costs only ten dollars." I looked away. "You don't want to talk of this?"

"No."

"But if you need her, ask me."

Mr. Roane, the new boarder, passed us in the hall. "Molly, come look at the tablecloth I embroidered," I said, leading her to my room. The violets and pansies scattered across blond linen were lovely, Molly agreed. She could easily sell it to the coal dealer's wife for seven dollars. Good. I might need these dollars for an abortista.

The pills brought vomiting, stabbing pains in the belly and loosened bowels but no release of my obstruction. Three days later, I returned to the druggist. Again he waited for the store to empty before asking quietly: "The Infallibles, Signorina?" I shook my head. "I'm sorry," he said, "but it is good you came now. Signora D'Angelo is here." I froze. I would have the abortion now? The druggist patted my shoulder. "Today you only talk to her," he said amiably. "Come." He led me to a room behind the shop where a tall, wiry-haired woman of perhaps forty measured powders on a gleaming brass scale. When he introduced me, she nodded, still working.

"Thank you, Vittorio. Signorina Irma, you may sit."

The druggist left us, closing the door quietly behind him. When Signora D'Angelo finished, she bid me follow her out a back stairway, across a narrow alley and into her own immaculate flat, where a bright room held a long scrubbed oak table and bookshelves filled the walls.

All these books were hers? I didn't ask for fear she'd think me a peasant.

"Now Irma, why do you believe that you're pregnant?" Her manner was calm, listening as Zia did, hands folded in her lap as if nothing on earth could shock or disturb her. In the end I told her everything: the charred house, the man, his belt and thrusts. She nodded, asking how long ago I was attacked and how late I was in bleeding.

"There is no morning sickness," I offered. "Could this mean there is no—obstruction?"

"That you're not pregnant?" prompted Signora D'Angelo. "Irma, use the word. Not using it changes nothing. Let me examine you." Before I could protest that country doctors barely touched a woman, she had me lift my skirt, pull down my bloomers and lie flat on the table. "I'm feeling for the pregnancy," she explained, pressing gently on my belly. "Breathe deeply. Don't tighten. You are from Abruzzo? Where?" I told her. "Ah, Opi. Now I must feel inside. What is your work now?" Her touch was careful, but waves of heat washed over me to be touched again *there*. "What stitches do you use?" she persisted. Clenching my fists, I spoke of running, whip, blind, blanket, cross and feather stitches. "Really? How do you sew a feather?" she interrupted. I told her. "Definitely pregnant," she announced. "You may dress now."

"You are sure?"

Her back to me as she washed her hands, she said firmly, "It is my business to be sure. And *you* are sure you cannot have this child?"

"Yes."

"You know there are orphanages?"

"Yes, but I could not hide this—pregnancy and still work."

"And if you cannot work, you cannot live. Correct?" I nodded. She dried her hands. "So then, Irma, you must have an abortion. Not this evening, but a Sunday morning, so you can rest afterwards. Now I'll make us some chamomile tea."

Abortion. The full truth of this word flooded over me. The signora returned with a tea tray and sat down at the long table with me. "Listen, Irma. For weeks you have thought of nothing else but of whether you were pregnant and how to keep this baby. But you cannot."

"No."

"So you must have an abortion," she said gently. "Irma, your body has been abused. So you come here and I will restore it. Where is the sin? There is no other way for working girls. And therefore you want to know the cost?"

"Yes," I murmured.

"It is twenty-three dollars."

After Dr. Bronson's Pills and the costs of Zia's funeral, I had only the dollars Molly would bring me for the tablecloth, and only if she found a buyer. After room and board, I'd have five dollars left from next week's pay. Signora D'Angelo set a teapot between us, two cups and two saucers, five things. Twenty-three dollars. "There are those who work for less," she said. Yes, Molly's woman asked for ten. "But I follow the practices of Dr. Lister and the great Mrs. Nightingale. Everything that touches your body will be clean. I have lost no one to puerperal fever and I have done this—wait." She opened a small ledger. "Five hundred and sixty-five times. I work quickly, so you will not be long in pain. Afterwards, I don't turn you on the street, bleeding, like some do."

"There is pain?"

"When the cervix is disturbed, there is cramping and therefore pain. If you wish, you may have an opium sponge. Bite down and relief comes quickly. You can return to work on Monday and no one will know. If you have trouble or discomfort, I will care for you and when you choose to bear a child, you may do so easily, for there will be no damage to the uterus. For this I ask twenty-three dollars before we begin."

Of course she wanted payment first. How many women promise to pay, have their abortions and never return? "If I come, what will you do? I mean, how do you make an abortion?"

She cocked her head, studying me afresh. "Most girls don't want to know."

"I do."

"We use these tools." She uncovered a tray of gleaming instruments. "Would you like to hear names?" I nodded. She pointed to a device the size of a hand and shaped like a crane's beak. "This is the speculum, to see into the vaginal passage. And here," she pointed to a finely made clamp, "is the tenaculum to open the cervix. And here," she said proudly, "from Germany, a dilator designed by the great Dr. Hegar. You may visit a hundred abortionists and not find these implements. Inside the uterus I use Dr. Sim's curette." She touched a delicate triangular steel ring on a slim silver stem with a polished ebony handle.

"To scrape?" I ventured.

"Yes, to scrape out the pregnancy quickly without puncturing the uterus." Late-afternoon sun caught the keen edges, but I could not look away. Nothing made in Opi was so delicate and precise. Signora D'Angelo draped a starched linen cloth over the tools again. "Irma, I'm not a doctor, but I study the same texts and buy the same tools. When great doctors speak at Chicago Medical School, I go to hear them. I read their books." She refilled my teacup. "You know how some women try to end their pregnancies? Punches, blows, kicks to the belly, hard riding on horseback. Last month a Sicilian girl threw herself down a stairway to dislodge a babe. She broke her neck and died. Some wild herbs may contract the uterus," the signora admitted. "There's foxglove, hellebore, mistletoe, aloe. But if the voiding is not complete, dead tissue stays in the womb and rots. Or the woman is poisoned, for what kills a fetus may kill the mother too. Some use electric shocks to the cervix, because we are so modern now," she added bitterly, "we in 1883. Others open the uterus with sharp tools and even if there is no infection and the woman does not bleed to death, the uterus is scarred and the woman becomes sterile. Should I stop?"

I shook my head. In that bright, ordered space, I could hear these horrors without flinching. I had pulled lambs from bellowing ewes. Once in butchering, my father found a uterus with a lamb half formed inside and threw it to a lunging dog. So I was not as shocked as a city girl might be. Yet amazement wound inside my horror: so many women had used such desperate means.

"Irma, I know dozens of abortistas. Some can't write their own names, but still have great skill for simple cases. Yet if an infection begins or too much blood is lost, if a woman's anatomy is unusual, they can have difficulties. The patient suffers." She took my hand. "When I watched my sister die of puerperal fever, I swore that no woman I touched would come to this. Irma, you will be safe."

I glanced toward her tray and thought how deftly my crane scissors worked in the hand. I thought of Father Anselmo's hands holding mine as if they were fine and precious things. This woman's hands were skilled, blessed perhaps. I must only find the money. "This Sunday, Signora?"

She nodded. "If you wait too long, not even the greatest London doctor can help. Be here by seven in the morning. Eat well Saturday night, but nothing after that." A bell rang twice. "Vittorio needs me." She darted off and I let myself out the door.

On the street outside her house a giddy swarm of children flocked around a Sicilian vendor selling shaved ice drizzled with bright fruit syrups. A young couple strolled by with a tiny, bright-faced girl in a starched pinafore skipping between them. When the father bought a cup of ice and knelt to feed the child, her rippling laugh wove them in a tender circle of delight. I froze.

"Would you like some lemon *granita*, signorina?" the Sicilian asked politely, waving toward his cart.

"No!" I said, so loudly that both parents turned to stare at me. I hurried away, tears burning my eyes. Outside Signora D'Angelo's bright, ordered room I felt like a sinner and unclean, one of *those* women who killed their own children.

Ten

A CLEAN OAK TABLE

Trying not to think of fruit ice or families, I hurried through the Italian streets and out into the American section. FINE WIGS. WE BUY HAIR, read a sign across the street. The wigmaker examined my hair, had me sit on a stool in bright light while he checked for lice, weighed it in his pudgy hands and shrugged. "Clean enough," he said, "but a very plain brown, dearie, with no undertones at all. Frankly, who'd *choose* it for a wig? I could make a chignon, perhaps a few braids or some filler for a pompadour." He dropped my hair and waved me toward a mirror behind the door. The gilded glass on his counter must have been for customers, not sellers. "Listen, dearie," he called out as I quickly pinned up my hair again, "you seem like a nice girl and nobody comes here for no reason. I can give you six dollars, say seven, since it's clean, but I'd need most of it." He showed me how I would be sheared, a hand's-length from the scalp, like a boy. How could I explain myself to Madame Hélène? I thanked him and left.

The streets filled with women crowned with blonde, auburn, lustrous black or chestnut hair. An old woman swept past me under a sleek gray pompadour. Only one head with my brown passed, a galloping messenger boy in torn knickers.

Fifteen dollars rose like a mountain between me and Sunday. Jacob's sisters must have cut my green dress into a dozen purses by now. I owned nothing else to sell. If I asked for pay in advance from Madame, she would surely wonder why. I couldn't look her in the face and lie and yet how could I say, "For an abortion, Madame"? In the long walk home, I discovered no better plan than to borrow from Molly and put myself on her calendar.

After dinner I asked for a loan of fifteen dollars. Molly set down the pot she was scrubbing and leaned over the wash basin, her back to me and wide shoulders hunched. "So the pills didn't work?"

"No."

She turned, her eyes rimmed red. "Wait here." She hurried out of the kitchen and returned with a heavy knotted sock. "Here," she said, pressing it into my hands. "I haven't sold the tablecloth yet, but the Poles paid for their chairs today."

"Thank you, Molly. You'll have it back in one month." I fished a card from my apron with my figuring: so much from my pay each week, so much for embroideries, so much for interest. Molly jerked open the stove door and jammed my card into the smoldering coals.

"I'd do *that* to the bastard who hurt you," she said fiercely. "I'm no saint, Irma, you know that. I'm a money lender. But I haven't slept in weeks after what I think happened to you that night. Please, this money is a gift. Don't return it."

"Molly, you don't have to do this."

"Yes, I do. And now put the sock away before Old Gaveston raises your rent." I slipped the sock in my apron and Molly returned to her pots. "So," she said over the clatter. "You're not using my ten-dollar woman."

"No."

"Then it's a real doctor you've got?"

"She works for a druggist and uses doctors' tools and goes to doctors' lectures."

Molly laughed. *"Doctors' tools.* Good for you, Irma. When is it?"

"This Sunday."

"We'll go together."

"Thank you, Molly, but no."

She looked back at me, curls wet with steam pressed against her cheeks. "Irma, was everyone in your village like you? So alone?" In steam rising from the washtub, I saw Opi's people, shoulders bunched together in a tight herd. Even my family looked curiously back at me. Was I alone now because I left Opi or because I had lived apart even when I passed my people daily in the narrow streets?

A wet hand touched my shoulder. "Irma, you go by yourself if that's what you want. I'll be here when you come back. But take a bit of whiskey with me now at least." So we tarried in the kitchen. The next morning I sent a messenger boy to Signora D'Angelo with a note that I would come on Sunday, in four more days.

With the sewing machine's steady whirl and a press of ladies demanding summer gowns and garden dresses, I fixed on the problem of a railroad-owner's wife who wanted a riding habit for a grand hotel in the Sierra Mountains of California. With Madame's help I had combined a tailored bodice with ruffled peplum below the waist and pleated skirt hiding pantaloon legs so a woman could be respectable while walking and yet still ride astride like a man.

When the dress was done, Madame ran her little fingers over the crisp pleats, smiling at the plaid lines that met precisely at the seams as if the skirt were molded of a single hoop of wool. Madame herself modeled the habit for our customer. Standing, walking or sitting, the pantaloons were invisible, but when she mounted a chair, spreading her legs wide, the customer was ecstatic. That was Saturday.

I woke early on Sunday and slipped out of the boardinghouse. High winds tugging at my skirt came from every side, twisting and turning me at each street corner. "Don't go, don't go," they seemed to say, but I pressed forward, my belly hot and heavy.

In her office, dressed in a clean cotton smock, Signora D'Angelo pointed to a tray where I should leave the money. She did not count it. The room, which had seemed clean enough before, was spotless now. The oak table gleamed. Snowy linen covered the implement tray. Signora D'Angelo led me to a desk and carefully opened a book. "This is *The Midwife's Practical Directory*, by Dr. Thomas Hersey," she explained. "Do you want to see it?"

"Yes, thank you." The signora turned to a plate called *Female Reproductive Organs*. Astonishing, as if a woman's skin had turned to glass. She explained the intricate drawing, pointing out tubes and folds, receptacles and channels. Here was the cervix that Dr. Hegar's dilator would open and here an egg growing against the uterine wall, here the blood-rich lining which the curette would scrape away. My stomach cramped.

"It is seven thirty," Signora D'Angelo said quietly, pointing to a clock. "By eight, we'll be finished. First, drink some willow-bark tea to relax." I sipped the bitter, pungent brew. "Now undress behind the screen and wrap yourself in this sheet."

I did, returning like a ghost in the room, bare feet padding weightless across the floor. She helped me on the table and gently leaned me back.

"Will"—I coughed—"will you explain what you're doing?"

She smiled. "Yes, of course. I've cleaned the instruments and covered them with cloth. I'm drawing the tray table close by." The tray rattled slightly. "Now bend your knees. Good, and now spread them. Wider please. Good. The speculum is cold. There will be a click as I insert it." I heard the click. She went on calmly announcing each step as if her fingers linked our bodies, sensing my thoughts. "You are afraid, but you are very safe. You'll feel some cramping now, growing stronger." Waves of pain rolled across my belly. Sweat washed my face. Pain, pain, a stairway of pain. I clenched my teeth and gripped the table edge. "Do you want the opium sponge, Irma? It's ready."

"No," I gasped. "Just talk to me."

"Everything is going well. We're beginning the curettage. Steady, steady. Breathe deeply. Remember the illustration, the lining we must remove?" A blaze of cramps smeared her words but their steady flow made a grappling line that hauled me through each minute, even as the room hazed with tears.

"Excellent, Irma, we're almost done. You're very brave. Now you'll feel some blood flow. That is the uterus emptying." A warm stream gushed between my legs. "Don't worry, it's cleaning you. Now I'm removing the curette through the cervix. Four, three, two, one, and it's out. Releasing the dilator. The tenaculum . . . the speculum. The cramps will be easing now." And so they did, as a pounding rain slowly slackens. Just as I began shivering, she laid a blanket over me. "Rest now," said a distant voice, "you are tired." As chills slowly passed, I heard her cleaning instruments. She brought a basin and towel, helped me wash myself and deftly rolled away the bloodied sheets. "They'll be boiled tonight," she said. "Soiled linen spreads infection. Mrs. Nightingale said a hospital can be judged by its laundry."

The clock showed eight as she helped me into a freshly made bed. I was safe and clean. Washed free of *him*. "Chamomile tea to help you sleep," she said, pressing a cup into my hand. I slept until noon and woke to a plate of pasta and lentils by my bed, comforting tastes of home. I ate slowly and dressed myself.

Signora D'Angelo was writing at her desk. "I describe each procedure in my journal afterwards," she explained. "There's always more to learn."

I nodded. How does one take leave of an abortionist? "Thank you for—the procedure. And the pasta," I said awkwardly. "I'll get the streetcar now." The night before, Molly had given me the fare, saying, "Come home like a lady."

The signora shook her head. "It's better to walk afterwards, even slowly. Take off your corset and carry it. They're evil inventions. A crime against women." She closed her book. "Suppose I come too? I try to walk an hour each day. We'll rest when you like."

On the slow way back, the signora spoke of her childhood outside Milan, her parents who died of pellagra, her sister who died of childbed fever and how the great doctors laughed when she tried to enroll in medical school. "So I apprenticed with a midwife. When I delivered a healthy son to a countess who had suffered years of stillbirths and miscarriages, she gave me a fine gold brooch. I sold it to come to America. Shall we rest a little?" We found a bench.

When we set out again, she spoke of Chicago. Between her hours of work for Vittorio, abortions and midwifery, she read and studied medicine.

"Who do you treat?" I asked.

"Those who need me," she said simply. "Irma, you've seen where the poor and the immigrants live. Huts built of wood scraps, some left from the Great Fire. Whole tenements using one toilet. Foul water, rat bites, blazing heat in the summer, ice in the water buckets all winter. Crowded like stable animals and more coming every day. Coloreds from the South, poor whites, Jews, Poles, Slovaks, Hungarians and Swedes—more crowded and filthy than any village at home." She was speaking so intently that an American couple separated to let us pass.

It's true that I knew these places in Chicago and before that in Cleveland, but my boardinghouse was in a "respectable" neighborhood, as Mrs. Gaveston tirelessly repeated, and the streets around the dress shop were elegant. Lately I had begun skirting the poor districts and not just to avoid *him*. I simply didn't care to see them.

"Irma, I run a clinic at my house on Friday evenings," Signora D'Angelo continued. "The poor pay what they can. If they're afraid of hospitals or can't afford doctors, they come to me. Vittorio says that one person can't heal all Chicago, but I do what I can." She took my arm. "Irma, you must be clever with your hands if you do fine dressmaking." We stood in the shade of a maple tree. Her eyes glittered. "Will you help me at the clinic? Vittorio does sometimes, but his wife doesn't like him 'giving his time away,' as she calls it. Perhaps you could come just to the end of this month, three Fridays. If you agree, the abortion was free."

"But I know nothing about medicine. I'm not a nurse. I'm just a—"

"Just a curious, intelligent young woman and I believe a compassionate one as well. You could help with the washing and bandaging. Can you write?"

"Not fast or well, but I'm learning in English class." We were near the boardinghouse.

"So you could keep my record book. At home, if wolves attacked your sheep, if they were hurt in some way, what did you do? Let them bleed to death?"

"We cared for them, but they were *sheep*."

"Well? There are people in pain. You nursed your mother, you told me, and helped your aunt."

"But that was my family."

"Yes, that's true and these are other families. Come this Friday, just come and watch. Could you think about it, at least?" I said I would. She reminded me to rest that night, to drink warm liquids and not wear a corset for the week. Then she took her leave and walked swiftly down the street until her wiry hair, wide shoulders and the straight line of her back were hidden by a liveryman leading a string of horses to the stables around the corner.

Molly brought a cup of broth to my room. "Agnes, the maid next door, went to the ten-dollar woman last week," she whispered. "She lost blood and fainted in front of her mistress, who asked questions of course. Agnes told her everything, the little fool. Now she'll lose her post and have no references. I worried all day for you."

"It went well, Molly. She was very careful. And she walked me home."

"There was pain?"

"Some." I looked away.

"You don't want to talk about it?"

"No. Tell me about your calendar."

As I sipped the broth, Molly described a loan to Swiss brothers who spoke five languages between them and would sell kitchen goods to immigrants. She rolled on and I ceased listening, breathing in the cool late-afternoon breeze until I felt empty as a shell. "You're tired. Rest before dinner," said a distant voice.

"Yes, I'll come down later," I answered, but the door had already closed. In the silent room my cramps pulsed like waves: pain and release. Tools floated in the darkness: curette, dilator, speculum. I imagined the signora's office on Friday evenings filled with immigrants, parents and children and those whose families were far away. I imagined the cries, like wolf-torn sheep. I did not come down for dinner but lay in bed that evening and into the night, thinking of my family and what they would say if they knew what I had done and why.

The cramps had dulled by morning, but at work Simone and Madame agreed that I looked pale, and Jacob hovered over a dress I was smocking for a banker's young daughter. "You are well, my dear?" he asked. "Always you say 'yes, yes,' but still—"

"I'm well, Jacob. And your sisters?"

"Well also and send their greetings. They're selling their work on State Street near the great Marshall Field's store. Look, Madame, how fine." He pulled from his jacket a black velvet purse enriched with fringe and purple beading. Madame held it near and far, tugged the beads to see how strongly they were sewn and examined the seams, fringe and cording.

"Could they make these to match our gowns?" she asked. As the bargaining commenced, Jacob's eyes flicked constantly across the room. When a cramp bent me over the smocking, his brow furrowed.

"I'll supply the fabric and beads, remember," Madame pressed.

I slipped into the kitchen and leaned against the wall, breathing hard. Jacob's voice rose in the shop. "Ah, but the cost of their *skill*, Madame, the magic in their fingers." Their voices faded as I squeezed my eyes shut, remembering the stringy sheaths of muscles casing the uterus in Dr. Hersey's drawing. These muscles must be contracting, that was the cause. Contract and release. Contract and release. The pain will pass. There, there, it's passing.

"Irma," said a low voice beside me. "Freyda and Sarah are worried. The washing wasn't enough?" I shook my head and Jacob touched my arm, sleeve tatters fluttering like fingers. "Ah, Irma, you poor child. Someone helped you?" I nodded. "Someone skilled?"

"Yes, very skilled."

Madame called out a question and we hurried back into the bright shop. "Our customers will love these purses, Madame," I announced. "His sisters could make plain ones as well, for the day dresses."

"Perhaps," said Madame thoughtfully. "If we have a good price. Let me consider."

"Sarah's apple cake. I nearly forgot!" Jacob cried, pulling a paper-wrapped package from his jacket. "Three pieces, one for each." But he whispered to me, "We pray for you, dear child." Then he was gone, slipping out the back way as our doorbell jangled in a gentlewoman.

That evening Molly handed me an envelope left by a messenger boy. Signora D'Angelo trusted I was well and hoped to see me that Friday evening.

"What is it?" Molly demanded. "An admirer?"

"The woman who—helped me—has a charity clinic. She wants me to help on Friday."

"What? You're a dressmaker. Besides, there's diseases. Irma, don't do it."

"She'll pay me. You can have your money back."

Molly's back straightened. "I said it was a gift. And what do you want with a clinic?"

What *did* I want with a clinic? I asked myself that night in bed. Why go back to a place that would call up the pain *he* caused me? It could be blackmail, Molly had hinted darkly: "The woman needs a free assistant and you don't help her, she'll tell Madame or Mrs. Gaveston why you came to her." No, surely not that. Yet why did Signora D'Angelo want *me*? Why not one of the healing sisters, a nurse or even a servant girl she could train? "Chicago has charity hospitals," Molly reminded me. "Crowded, yes, and maybe dirty, but better than nothing."

I wondered, finishing the tedious pearl beading of a wedding dress that week, if perhaps *I* needed Signora D'Angelo. Her ordered, book-filled flat called me. Perhaps I could be useful there. She might want something particular for herself or her tools, a storage bag for the dilator, a smock with certain pockets. Something not a wedding dress or riding suit for rich, indolent wives.

So that Friday evening I hurried after work to Signora D'Angelo's flat with my sewing basket, a pack of needles fresh from Jacob and some muslin scraps. Turning onto her street, I stopped, astonished. Sick and wounded filled the steps and spilled into the walk: a mother with a howling, spotted baby; a man whose head was roughly bandaged; a mother shepherding three sniffling children with rheumy eyes; and an old woman tied in a chair carried by two young men. A baker coughed fresh blood on a flour-strewn apron. My steps slowed. "Everyone here is for the Signora D'Angelo?" I asked two Italians, then realized, embarrassed, that one of them was the Sicilian granita vendor whom I had rebuffed so rudely.

He pointed to the blood-stained baker. "You're after him. Wait your turn."

Howling burst from the house. Children whimpered, tugging at their mother's skirt. "I'm not sick," I explained to the vendor. "Signora D'Angelo wanted me to come."

"To help?" he asked. When I nodded warily, he seized my shoulder and began propelling me through the crowd. "Aside, step aside. You!" he barked to the men with the old woman, "Move that chair! The signorina's here to help." He pushed me through the door. The flat's ordered calm was gone. Coughing, wheezing, and children's whimpers filled the air. I breathed blood, vomit, babes' fouled diapers and the tang of alcohol. Patients leaned against bookshelves, filled chairs and slumped on the floor. A ruddy boy moved deftly through the crowd, emptying pots of spittle and vomit and shoving rags at coughers.

"Cover your mouths!" he ordered. "Use the pots for spitting. Clean rags here." He pointed to a basket heaped with scraps of white cotton. "And dirties over there." He waved at the stove, where soapy water boiled in a great tub. I backed to the door, gasping for fresh air.

"Ah, Irma, there you are!" cried Signora D'Angelo. "Come here." I plucked my way across the room. She was cleaning a small Polish girl's chest, horrible with weeping pus, crusted blood and dirt. "Sit," she said. I pulled up a stool, looking past the child. "Vittorio's wife, Claudia, 'needs' him to help visit her sister. Listerine, over there." I handed her the bottle. "One would think," she muttered, moistening a square of gauze, "that a grown woman could visit her own sister without a husband's help."

"So many people, Signora. How do they know about you?"

"From friends, neighbors." She flicked her eyes to a young man jabbering at a wall between fits of coughing. "Johan over there won't go to a hospital. He's afraid they'll send him to an asylum. He's probably right. Enrico, more gauze," she called out to the ruddy boy who lofted a roll across the room.

Scrambling to my feet, I caught it. "Fold a square and wet it with Listerine," Signora D'Angelo said. "Then clean the wound. Dab like this. Don't rub. Good. Start here." I opened my mouth to protest, but she pointed to the worst patch of the ravaged little chest and I began. She stepped back, watching me work and gesturing when I should change gauze squares or clean more deeply. "What these people pay doesn't cover everything, of course. The rest I make from abortions, midwifery and work in the pharmacy. Don't press too hard where it's raw. For gentlewomen, abortions cost forty dollars, sometimes fifty. When rich men have me 'take care' of their mistresses or housemaids discretely, they pay more. At births, if they want me days ahead and make me sleep in the servants' rooms, they pay."

"Like the English bandit Robin Hood," announced Enrico.

"Empty the spittle pots," she told him sharply, "if you've nothing to do but watch. Now, Irma, look at this chest. The infection started as measles, but the child scratched herself raw. Now the rash is infected. Look at this arm. Impetigo. We have to teach the mother how to treat it. So we'll need someone who speaks Polish."

"Signora, I'm—"

"A dressmaker, I know. But you're here. And before you go, *if* you go, cut the child's nails close, and find us a translator."

A howling pierced the room as a drunken butcher stumbled in, fresh blood streaming from his arm onto an apron already stained from work. The crowd erupted as he pushed through the line, dribbling a dark red stream behind him.

Signora D'Angelo sighed. "Not again, Antonio."

"Cutting and drinking," said the man cheerfully. "Big one for you this time." When he thrust out his right arm, a cut opened like a wide mouth. I gasped. "Oh I've got more, signorina," he said. "Look." He brandished his left arm, latticed in scars.

"If you drank *after* work," said the signora, unspooling a length of catgut, "you'd cut yourself less. And I'd have more time for the others."

"True, I'll do that. I'm done working for today. Stitch me up and I'll go straight to the tavern. What about her?" he demanded, nodding at my sewing basket. "She could do it."

"No," I protested. "I never—"

"You've sewn sheep," she reminded me. "And this one's tough as a ram. You can't hurt him."

"That's for sure," Antonio agreed, settling himself on a stool. Then as calmly as Madame showed me stitches, Signora D'Angelo explained how to tie off each suture, demonstrating on a bit of gauze. I'd need ten stitches, she estimated. She examined the wound. "Rinse it well with alcohol but I doubt we'll get infection here."

"That's right," crowed Antonio. "Never had one. Good sharp cleaver."

Ignoring him, the signora handed me a curved threaded needle and pair of steel scissors. "When you cut the ends, leave enough to pull out the sutures next week. I'm not wasting my opium on him, he's drunk enough. Irma, you'll be fine, just work as fast as you can. There's others waiting."

"But—" She was gone. The needle shook.

"It's just sewing and knots, miss. I'd do it myself, but it's my right arm, see?" Antonio said, his speech starting to slur.

"Be quiet," Signora D'Angelo called across the room. "Let her work."

"You got cut too," said Antonio, "there on the cheek." I nodded. He rocked forward. "No stitch marks though."

"Someone kept it closed for me."

"Must have been a friend. Don't mind me. Won't be my first. But you *can* sew?"

"I'm a dressmaker."

"So I'm the lucky man," mumbled Antonio, leaning back. "Sew me up." Like sheep, I reminded myself. No different, really. I made the sutures and slowly unclenched my hand from the needle. "Good job," he said, swinging his head to look down his arm. "See, nothin' to it, like fixing a shirt."

Standing by my shoulder, the signora agreed. "Very even. Good knots. Bring her some wine," she told Enrico. "And have someone walk this fool to the tavern."

For the next hour I took notes for the record book, changed dressings and held babies while their mothers were examined. Wine had eased my shaking and I felt almost easy when the signora moved to a moaning man who held a hand pressed between his thighs. "Irma, you go talk to her," she said, pointing to a gaunt and glassy-eyed woman slumped in a chair.

A young boy standing by her gripped my arm. "What can I do?" he wailed. "My mother's always like this and my father says he'll leave if she can't be a proper wife. See." When the boy shook the woman's shoulder, her head flopped and wobbled. Her eyes opened but if she saw us she gave no sign.

"Irma!" came a cry from across the room. "Come!" Heart pounding, I hurried back to the signora and the moaning man. "Roberto, show Irma your hand." Blackness stretched out from the thumb, and the skin was swollen bronze-black and dry as paper, leaking a foul-smelling ooze. I stepped back.

"Why did you wait so long?" she demanded. "You should have seen a doctor days ago." He shook his head, muttering. She leaned toward him, listening intently through the cries and talk that clogged the room.

"You're afraid he'd cut off your thumb? You're right, he would have, any doctor would have—to save your hand. By tomorrow they'll take the whole arm. *If* you live that long." She knelt by his side. "Listen to me, Roberto. This blackness is called gangrene. The blood is poisoned now. That poison will spread up your arm and into your heart and kill you by morning. Look." When she touched his blackened skin with a square of clean linen, it splintered and cracked. "The hand can't be saved. Any doctor will tell you that."

"Take it off then," said a woman's voice behind us. "Roberto, our sons can work, I can work. You'll learn another trade. Don't die of stubbornness and leave us alone. It's *you* we love, not your hand."

Signora D'Angelo's eyes fixed on Roberto. "You can go to a hospital. Talk to a doctor, but do it today."

"No," he whispered. "My brother died in a hospital. You do it. Here."

"You're sure?"

"Yes."

"Well then, we'll be quick." She ordered the table scrubbed, a saw and scissors boiled, opium sponge prepared, a cautering rod heated, Roberto's shirt removed and his arm scrubbed down to the blackened hand. She had Enrico find four strong men to hold him. When I backed away in the milling crowd, she pulled me gently toward the table. "Irma, the stump must be sewn after I cut. There's catgut here. I'll show you the stitch."

"Signora, please. It's not like—the other."

"No, it's not like Antonio. Roberto will die if you we don't help him now."

"Will you give him this?" the wife asked, unfastening a slender crucifix from her neck. "Put it in his—other hand."

"Irma, please," the signora whispered, stepping closer. "If he leaves, he'll go home. Have you seen a man die of tetanus? It's an agony, believe me. Will you sew him?"

"Yes, I'll sew him."

"Good, thank you." I helped Roberto onto the table, gave him the crucifix, and when the signora produced an opium-soaked sponge, I wedged it between his chattering teeth and had the men holding him leave space for the signora to cut.

"Can you write?" I asked Roberto. He nodded, eyes wide in a whitened face slick with sweat. I described Bruno the one-armed clerk in Cleveland who scribed for Italians. Roberto's eyes bore into me. When I began to explain what was happening, that a razor was being readied, perhaps to shave the arm, he shook his head so hard that it thudded against the table.

"Don't talk. Just pray," the wife whispered in my ear. I recited every prayer I knew, leaning close to block his view. So I did not see the amputation, but heard it: the wife's prayers rising over Roberto's mounting howls, the grunts of the four men holding him, the saw's steady rasp and finally a dull thud of the hand in a basin. "Almost done," the signora murmured, calling for the cautering rod. Roberto howled, a wolf shriek in the clamorous room, and then fell utterly silent.

"Irma, has he fainted?" she demanded, not looking up.

"Yes."

"Good. Now, have someone else hold his head while you scrub your hands and then come here. Here's how I want it sewn." She calmly explained how to trim the dangling tendon, where the stitches must go, how deep and wide to make them. "You understand?"

I nodded, my chest pounding with prayer. *Lord help me.* I breathed deeply and punctured the skin. Cut, sew, work. "Good," the signora said, bending over me. "Fast as you can before he comes to." She moved away to the gaunt woman. "When you're done," she called back, "I'll show you how to bandage the stump."

It was past midnight when the last patient had been seen. The gaunt woman, Harriet, was moving slowly through the room, helping Enrico clean. Two husky men—Salvatore the granita vendor and his friend—were ordered to deliver me to the boardinghouse. "Take care," the signora warned. "Make sure she's safe, you understand?" They did as she ordered, and each Friday night all the rest of that spring and summer, they or other men she appointed—Germans, Slovaks, Greeks, Poles or Finns—walked me home after my work at the clinic.

Eleven

SOFIA

I remember that Chicago summer as a long hurry through steaming streets, sweat-soaked linens pasted to my skin. Even the once-fresh breezes off Lake Michigan were like the hot, moist panting of a heaving beast. Pressed under a close white sky, the air grew spongy. Clydesdales strained at their harnesses. Flanks foaming, heads down, they plowed the streets dragging water barrels, beer kegs and huge blocks of ice. Rains brought sucking mud but no relief.

"Still we must be clean and fresh for our ladies," Madame Hélène insisted. So twice weekly in Mrs. Gaveston's kitchen I pumped water, scrubbed my garments, and hung them out to dry. The next evening I did ironing, stoking a coal fire to heat and reheat the flatirons. Sweat rolled down my face and arms as I mopped myself with kitchen rags, careful not to stain the crisp calico. Fine ladies wanted no reminder of the city's milling crowds, prairie dust and mucky streets or the heady stew of smells from packed streetcars and immigrant markets where I bought healing roots and herbs. Certainly they did not want to imagine the stifling tenements of those who used Signora D'Angelo's clinic.

"It's *our* clinic, Irma," she began insisting. "And please call me Sofia. I hardly pay you; at least we should be friends."

I was as much Sofia's shadow as her friend that summer, following her with books and bandages, flying up narrow stairways with her, towed by anxious, ragged children who watched for our coming.

"My father coughed blood all night. He can't work and we're so hungry."

"My baby shakes all over. What's wrong with him?"

"My aunt talks crazy. She scares me."

"The Polish kid fell down the stairs and now his leg sticks out like this."

"My mother's bleeding *there*. Please come quick!"

I tried to be as calm with the sick as Sofia was, to not hold back from the smells of their bodies or wretched homes. I watched her coax smiles from a dying man and stood with her in tiny kitchens as she took a young mother's hand and said, "Keep the baby comfortable. There's nothing more we can do." Strong young men wept in her arms and anxious children spoke their fears.

When a woman lost her unborn twins in a torrent of blood, I helped Sofia clean the wizened gray bodies for the funeral her faith required, but then sank on the stairs as we left the flat. "I can't do this, Sofia. I'll make bandages, I'll clean tools, but I can't watch so many children die."

"You cared for sheep," Sofia reminded me. "You've seen them die." Yes, all my life I had seen lambs born dead, sheep slaughtered or torn open by wolves. I had helped nurse their many troubles: bluetongue, rabies, swayback, sore mouth, rickets and worms of every kind, but in a family of shepherds, you can't weep over each dead lamb. There was no call for cruelty and I never hated them as Carlo did, but neither did I see myself in their glassy black eyes. Nothing prepared me for women who seized our hands and cried, "Help him! Make him well again!"

There were joys, of course, and cures that seemed miraculous. Two men carried in their friend, flushed and clawing at his chest. "Pounding—hammer," he gasped. Sofia forced the man's mouth open, dosed him with a tiny pill and I watched dumbfounded as the hand unclenched, the breathing eased and the man slowly stood upright. "It's gone!" he whispered, his eyes darting about the room as if hunting out the pain lurking in a corner. He tried to kiss Sofia's hand but she stepped back to her desk and wrote a prescription.

"I just gave you digitalis, a medicine for angina pectoris. It can't fix the heart, but it stops these attacks for a while. Vittorio can sell you a bottle." The man nodded and took the slip of paper, but still he stared at Sofia as if she had cast out demons.

An Irish couple brought their small son, who had suddenly changed from a bright, active, happy child to a sullen little stranger. Sofia examined Rory as he solved a wooden puzzle, wolfed down a slice of bread and caught a ball she threw him. "Smart enough," she muttered, "good appetite and reflexes." She peered in his ears, then stepped back and had me look. "Irma, what do you see?"

"Wax."

"Hum. Bring two men to hold the child," she said and added in Italian: "If you have a choice, don't use the parents. They never hold tight enough." In fact, it took three adults to wrestle a howling, biting Rory to the table and hold him steady as Sofia used a tiny pair of tweezers and one of my needles to pry a dried pea from each of his ears.

"He *is* a good boy," Sofia told the mother, handing her the peas. "He just couldn't hear you."

"How did you know?" I demanded when they left. "How did you *see*?"

"The wax was bulged. You'll learn what to look for," Sofia said. At least I could wash and bandage wounds as well as she did, wrapping the gauze tight and smooth, copying her as I had copied Madame Hélène's pleats and gathers. I clipped my fingernails as closely as she did and rolled my sleeves above the elbows like a peasant girl. I even hemmed my skirts, although Mrs. Gaveston raised an arched eyebrow when she glimpsed the knob of my ankle and Molly caught me in the hall to ask, "Irma, do you want *that* to happen again?"

No, of course not. But carrying bandages and books up tenement steps left no free hand to gracefully lift a skirt. And yes, if I ever needed to outrun a man, shorter skirts would help. Work filled my days and mind that summer, dulling the memories of *his* belt falling on shards of glass, the thrusts and shame, his striped pants leaving the charred house, and the hot rush of blood when Sofia's tools opened me up and I was emptied of a life I could not bear. Work, I must constantly work. When laughter gushed from the open windows of dance halls, it was not calling me.

"Why not?" Molly demanded. "Because of—what happened?"

Partly, but also because I was plain and scarred, with heavy feet for dancing. Only old men had ever cared for me: a priest, a tin peddler and a ragman.

"What about that sailor?" coaxed Molly. "He wasn't old."

Yes, I thought of Gustavo on the *Servia*, especially at night as shadows drifting across my ceiling became waves rippling over an indigo sea or faint cracks in the plaster bent into lines in the drawing he once sent me. "I don't have his address," I reminded Molly, "and he doesn't have mine. Besides, he's a sailor. He could be anywhere. With anyone."

"That's for sure," Molly agreed readily, "but at least he was one young man pleased to be passing time with you. You could find another. It's a big city."

But I had little time for searching. My week was pieced in services. Monday to Saturday, I worked for Madame, starting early to profit from the cooler mornings. On Monday evenings Sofia and I made tenement calls. Fridays after work we held the clinic. Late nights after washing or ironing, I memorized lists of symptoms and cures. Tuesday and Thursday evenings I studied English in a cramped community hall on the North Side, where we read aloud from newspapers as blue-eyed Miss McGuire cajoled away our foreign accents.

"*Wind*," she repeated earnestly. "Hold *wrists* to your mouths. *Wind, wonder, where. W's whisper* on the *wrist*. Repeat and then write all the 'w' words that you know."

On Sundays, on streetcars, in any slice of time, I made embroideries for Molly to sell. The hollow of Wednesday night was soon filled. At the corner grocery with Molly, I watched two sisters fresh from Calabria struggle to buy flour, salt and sugar, pointing and miming for the stolid grocer who folded his arms across a doughy chest and told me he was sick and tired of helping greenhorns all day. When I translated for them and checked their change, the women kissed me. How long since I had been held like this, my cheeks softened with kisses?

"What are they, some kind of cousins?" Molly whispered.

"Teach us English," the women begged. "At least enough for stores." I protested that I was learning English myself, that I had never taught and had no books. "Please, Signorina."

"Why not?" asked Molly, who had fished the word "Inglese" from our talk. "You speak pretty well for a foreigner. But charge them something. *Somebody* should pay you, since the doctor lady barely does. Didn't you say you had to send some money back to Cleveland?"

Yes, I had told her that, but not why—that the money I had stolen from the workhouse Missus had begun to gnaw at me. In confession at Church of the Assumption, I had recounted my story to Father Paolo, how the Missus robbed us and tried to turn Lula against me. "Stealing from a saint or stealing from a sinner is stealing just the same, is it not?" he intoned.

"Yes, Father."

"Suppose Lula was blamed for your theft? That would go hard for a Negro."

I had never thought of how I might have hurt Lula, my first American friend. "But I can't pay it all back now."

"You could start, my child."

So each Wednesday night a dozen men and women crowded into a kitchen that the Calabrese girls shared with their aunt. Each student gravely counted out ten cents for the lesson. The bolder ones fingered my dress. Women touched my braids, tried my shoes and leaned close to stare at my mouth when I spoke. They called out sentences in Italian and asked, "How do you Americans say this?" *You Americans.*

"I've only been here two years," I reminded them.

"Yes, but you're different already, you're not like us," a girl from Bari insisted.

"How? Tell me. *How* am I different?"

The girl shook her head as if the truth were too obvious for debate. Croatian, Polish and Russian neighbors soon discovered these Wednesdays. Someone found a larger room, where more crowded in, bringing stools or leaning against walls. They mimed their skills and tools and I fed them words: *carpenter, bricklayer, butcher, cook, barkeeper, laborer, hammer, anvil, oven, shovel*. A bearded Armenian yanked a gleaming knife from his boot, flashed it in the air and showed with a flourish how neatly it cleaved a hair from his head. I had him stow the weapon and repeat, "I am a skilled metalworker."

Soon I could mail five dollars to Cleveland with a letter my English teacher corrected, my first in English. The Missus sent a curt reply: she had always thought me ungrateful and liable to betray any trust. However, she accepted this first repayment and expected the next installments "with all due speed." Lula, she wrote bitterly, "married that darky soon after you left." So Lula was gone and safe, I could happily tell Father Paolo, and I would repay my debt before September.

"Listen, Irma," said Molly. "Let's do something fun at least once this summer."

"You should," said Sofia.

So on the Fourth of July, when even Madame Hélène closed her shop, I went with Molly to a grand celebration by Lake Michigan with bands and speeches, a stilt walker called Uncle Sam, ice cream and balloons. Children flew like bright birds across the lawn chasing hoops. German peddlers sold boiled sausages in long buns and fireworks burst over the lake: red, white and blue sparkles drifted into the dark water.

"Beautiful, isn't it?" shouted Molly. "Nothing like this at home." Yes, beautiful, like the night on deck of the *Servia*, a blue-black sky stitched with stars.

In the long, slow walk back to the boardinghouse, savoring our ice cream, Molly asked what drew me to dressmaking. "I can sew, of course," said Molly. "Every girl learns that. But why do you love it?" I tried to explain how fabric will bend and stretch to take the shape we willed it, how thread can paint pictures. I described the magic when suddenly bodice joins sleeves, the skirt is attached and a gown appears. But the truth was that my old joy had begun to drain away.

Our best clients, the Cooley and Glessners women—"railroad queens," we called them—wanted private fittings at home. I was sent to kneel on thick Persian carpets to mark hems, watch them pose before silver-edged mirrors and sit with them on damask couches to study fabric samples that I drew from Madame's carpet bag.

"Tell me about the houses," Molly pleaded, and I tried, but the sitting rooms flowed together, alike in shimmer and gleam and in the sighing indecision of ladies comparing samples of satin or Chinese silk for yet another summer garden party.

"I don't *know*. What do *you* think, Irma?" they asked in bleating whines. When Mrs. Cooley hugged me, so delighted with her daughter's wedding gown that she forgot her place and mine, French cologne lingered on my smock. The streetcar conductor scanned me, doubtless wondering how a shop girl could smell so much of money.

"One of those fancy dresses costs more than our farm rent in Galway," an Irish maid said bitterly as she walked me out to the service door. "Think about that!"

I did. I thought more and more of money in those months. By late July, Madame Hélène was sending me to wholesale houses to choose fabrics, facings, buttons and bindings, for my English was better and I drove harder bargains than she did. In the same warehouses, chiseling time from these services, I bought cheap bolt ends of gauze to cut into bandages. In a tiny shop near Mercy Hospital, I found suture thread and surgeon's needles. I begged Jacob for odd lengths of cloth we used for arm slings and bindings. "A little profit you'll permit me?" he lamented.

"I'm sorry, Jacob, but Sofia must—"

"I know. You and she must be healing the whole South Side."

I harried Molly to find us a space for a larger clinic, but when I told her how little Sofia could pay in rent, she laughed. "You're crazy, both of you."

Sofia shrugged. "Someone has to help. When it rains, people waiting outside get wet. We need translators, chairs, supplies. I can't pay for everything with abortions and midwifery."

It seemed that I sat down only for sewing that summer. I learned to eat while walking, stopping at street vendors to buy food no one in Opi ate or imagined: apple dumplings, fried potato slices, doughy pretzels, salted peanuts in paper cones, taffy from penny candy stores, ginger snaps, corn still on the cob and St. Louis hot dogs. "*What happened to you?*" Zia Carmela would have demanded. "*Only animals eat standing up.*"

Perhaps my students were right. I *was* becoming American, but change came quickly in those years in Chicago. The land itself was changing: the city was squeezing up around the lake and pressing out into the rich black fields to the south. Day and night, immigrants poured out of the train station and lake ports. The city ground away our foreignness as we milled past one another in shops, parks and the clattering streets. In their first months, it was easy to pick out Swedes, Irish, Italians, Germans, Slovenians, Hungarians, Bulgarians and Russian Jews who clustered around Maxwell Street. But in the tenements, factory blocks and work crews swarming around the new buildings that sprouted everywhere, Old Country ways melted like fruit ice in summer.

The home songs remained. Hurrying through the streets, I heard strips of song in a dozen tongues, refrains torn to shreds by harness bells, street calls and steady rain of hammering. Under our breaths, we sang in dialect from our villages, dredging old wells of memory, but we sang alone. When Mrs. Gaveston hired a Sicilian carpenter, I understood nothing of his sweet, haunting lament and he had never heard my Opi songs.

Once that summer I saw two men catch each other's tunes across a crowded streetcar. They were Bulgarian, someone said, as they pushed toward each other, heedless as lovers. "From my village—Brazigovo!" one of them shouted to us all in English as they beat each other on the back, weeping and scrambling off at the next stop, arm in arm. Women on the streetcar smoothed the folds of their skirts and men tugged at leather hand straps. Where were *our* people from *our* villages who knew *our* songs?

A letter came to me that summer saying that Assunta and my father had a baby girl they named Luisa. I sent a little money and asked for a photograph of the child. Yet even these photographs from home locked us helplessly in the past. If I ever saw Luisa, she would be long past her baby looks. So often at the boardinghouse I watched Mr. Janek, the telegraph clerk, fondle a photograph of his infant son back home until the tiny black eyes were worn to a gray smudge. Mr. Janek boasted that he would bring his wife and son to America, not in steerage, but *second class.* Not only that: by the time they came, he would have a house with a bathroom and yard of his own where his wife could grow roses. By then, I feared, the boy might be half grown.

Yet, week by week, more of my waking thoughts turned to the clinic and my house calls with Sofia. Even now, I remember the first babe I birthed on my own that summer, the first *grand mal* seizure I witnessed and a beautiful little Russian girl carried in limp by frantic parents. The heart raced and when Sofia pinched the child's pale skin it pleated like an old woman's.

"Dehydration," she announced. "Probably from cholera, it's bad in the Russian quarters, I hear. Irma, find a translator. She'll need twenty-five laudanum drops every four hours, and as much sugar water as she'll take. They must boil all the water she drinks and wash their own hands constantly." The parents listened carefully to the translator, nodding and repeating her words.

Two weeks later, the child burst into our clinic, rosy and gleaming with two mushroom-shaped cakes, one for Sofia and one for me.

"Could your Sofia cure pellagra?" Madame Hélène asked wistfully as I shared my cake with her and Simone at lunch the next day.

"No. She says the poor suffer the most, but not everywhere or in every season. We don't know where it comes from or why. There's so much we don't know: how to cure paralysis or blindness or weak hearts, how to stop consumption or cancer. Why some babies are born perfect and some are not."

"Better not to worry about what you can't know," Simone announced, plucking cake crumbs from her apron.

"I know how to make a dress a lady asks for," said Madame. "What I *don't* know is if she'll still like it at the fitting. What do you think, Irma? Will Mrs. Cooley like the russet? Irma, are you listening?"

"Excuse me, Madame. Which?"

"The russet walking dress with lined jacket. Will she like it? Remember the gray damask ball gown? She had us change the sleeves three times."

"She'll like the russet," I said quickly. "Perhaps with ivory buttons."

"Ivory? Hum. Where to get the best ones?" From Jacob, Simone thought. Madame said no, better Alfonso the Portuguese who had them straight from Africa. But I was thinking of how Sofia had given quinine to a Negro man with malarial chills who had come from New Orleans. We stood with his wife and son, dripping with sweat in the stifling room as the sick man moaned for blankets, shivering so hard that his cot rattled on the wooden floor and his teeth chattered like tiny hammers.

"Will they break?" the son asked anxiously. I tried to force a length of cloth into the man's mouth, but he batted my hand away.

"Never mind the teeth. Give him this," Sofia told the wife, handing her a small bottle of quinine. "But it's all I have. You'll have to buy more." Quinine costs, she told me bitterly as we walked to the next patient, and so the poor with malaria would keep on dying. If there had been quinine in the village I had passed with Attilio, little Rosanna would not have watched her family die.

"Irma!" said Madame. "I asked if you'll get buttons from the Portuguese."

"Yes, Madame. Certainly."

I went on Monday and bargained a good price. That evening I was working with Sofia, making calls in a shabby street north of Maxwell, when a brightly dressed, slightly hunchbacked young woman stopped us on a stairwell.

"My husband—" she began. The women snickered. *"My husband,"* she insisted, "he shakes and says he don't see straight."

"Because he's corned, Daisy, what's new about that? He's corned blind," a voice called out.

"Jake's *not* drunk," Daisy insisted. "He ain't been out of the flat in three days. He drinks water all the time and still he says he's dying of thirst. I'm so scared, lady. He's never been like this."

Sofia set down her bag and leaned back against the banister. "His breath?" she asked calmly. "Is it the same as before?" The women hanging on the stairways protested: one called us to her child's wracking cough; a woman complained of a gnawing burn in the stomach. A carpenter's wrist was broken; another's limp was worse; there was a woman half starved from morning sickness and a baby that would not grow.

"His breath's *always* the same," said a lanky woman leaning over the railing. "Always stinks of whiskey."

"I told you, Jake's *not* drunk," shouted Daisy. Her dark-rimmed eyes scanned the crowd up and down the stairwell. "He stopped all that. He took the Temperance Pledge last month." She turned to Sofia. "His breath *is* changed. It smells like medicine something strange."

"Let's go, Irma," said Sofia. With the women calling angrily after us, we followed Daisy up the dank stairway to a one-room flat on the fifth floor.

"Thank you, thank you, lady. He's not so bad like they say." Daisy pushed open a battered door and cried, "Jake, here's the doctor lady."

A tall man lay splayed facedown on a narrow cot, twitching, his face turned from us. Red splotches covered his arms and the skin on his back seemed loose, as if the flesh was melting away. Sweaty curls of sandy hair plastered his head like a wet lamb's wool. A filthy cup bobbed in a water bucket on the floor.

Sofia stepped close to the man and gently took his wrist, feeling for pulse. "Has he lost weight recently?"

"Yes, he don't eat, just drinks and drinks and excuse me, ma'am, pisses all the time. Then he stopped going to work. He said he's afraid of these stairs. He don't look it now, but he was a big, strong man before he started melting away."

"Does he have pains anywhere?"

"No, not that he said. First I thought it was just laziness, but this morning he was got up to piss and just fell, right there on the floor. Like a baby, weak as a baby. I put him to bed and he's gone worse and worse since then."

"Why didn't you get a doctor?"

"He wouldn't let me. He said it wasn't worth it. Then I heard a boy shouting that the Eye-talian doctor lady was coming and with Jake sleeping I figured I'd fetch you even if he yells at me again. But he's not yelling no more. He just lays there twitching, just melting away." She sobbed into her sleeve.

"Daisy, do you have anything sweet here, honey or sugar, penny candy?"

She looked up. "No, but I got some porridge and potatoes. Isn't there medicine to fix him? I can pay. I got a little money"—she hesitated—"last night."

"Right now, he needs sugar. See if the neighbors have some, or go to the corner store." With a desperate glance back at the cot, Daisy took her shawl and fled. Waves of nickering laughter followed the clatter of her shoes down the stairs.

"It's bad," Sofia whispered wearily. "Irma, can you bring me a chair?"

There was one in the corner of the cluttered room heaped with clothes. I made space on a table stacked with crusted plates and sprouting potatoes and began moving the clothes there: cotton drawers and a chemise, a crushed bonnet and fringed shawl, a man's vest and chesterfield coat. My outstretched hands froze over a pair of striped trousers, brown derby hat, and slung across them, a wide leather belt. The chesterfield, the sandy hair. The heavy belt buckle clanging on a charred floor. Pain. Blood. The glass shard in my hand. When I lay on the scrubbed oak table.

"And, Irma, look at the chamber pot," Sofia called. "We need to check his urine." The cot creaked. Sofia must be turning him over. I glanced at a chipped bowl pushed half under the foot of the bed but not at the man, at *him*.

"The bowl's empty," I said, my voice as dry as wood.

My hand closed around the belt until it dug into my palms. How many girls had he dragged into that house, his den? Rage filled my body top to toe, a flame of rage. I was strong. I could do it. If I was alone in the room for an instant, couldn't I press that belt down on his neck, sick as he was, or better, bridle him? Couldn't I stand over his cot and scream into the clammy white face: "Remember me! Remember what you did to me, your filly bitch!"

I looked over my shoulder. The man lay on his back now, brushy mustache pointing up, ragged on the shrunken face. Sofia was shaking the bony shoulders, calling, "Jake!" Can you hear me?" The man groaned, eyes closed. If he opened them, they would be pale blue, gleaming hot in the dingy room.

Sofia was leaning close to him. *Get back!* I wanted to cry out. *Don't touch him.* I should leave, I knew, just leave the room, this building, this street, but my feet would not move.

"Irma, can you bring the chair?" Sofia asked impatiently. "And come smell his breath. Like alcohol but more fruity. His urine would taste sweet too, come." But I stood at the table, eyes nailed to the lank body. Then I closed my eyes. Sofia's breath was heavy then, I remember, and his was uneven. The room filled with heaving air. She sighed and began: "It's diabetes mellitus that caused the thirst and the wasting as well. I'm sure of it. The urine test was described by Thomas

Willis in the 1600s," her teaching voice was saying. "It's a sure sign of diabetic shock, which leads—Irma?"

"Sofia, I'm sorry. I can't stay."

She sighed. "I know. There's someone sick in every flat. They all want—"

"I mean that's the man who raped me. This is his belt. And those are his trousers behind me. He called me his—" My voice collapsed.

Sofia looked between us. "You're sure it's him?" I nodded. Then she saw the belt taut in my hands. Her eyes widened. "Irma, put that down. Drop it."

"He had a knife. He said he'd cut my throat if I made a sound. He said—" In two steps she had closed the distance between us, blocking my view of the man. "Please, drop the belt. Let it go." Perhaps I dropped it, for the clasp rang on the floor with a sickening jolt through my body. "Irma," she said quietly, taking my empty hands. "If you say that it's him I believe you. And I can imagine—it's my work to imagine the pain that he caused you. But would it help, really, to hurt him now? Would that undo anything?" I closed my eyes.

"I don't know," I whispered.

"Irma, open your eyes and look at him." The large hands had flopped toward the floor. Spittle ran from his mouth. He seemed to have shrunken, even in these last minutes. "For those who believe in judgment, he has been judged, he's dying. Can you bring me that chair at least?"

How could she speak so calmly? But I walked to the table, picked up the chair and carried it to the bedside, stepping over the fallen belt. My legs were stiff as sticks.

"Thank you," she said, sinking into the chair. "Irma, I'm not a priest. I don't ask that you forgive what he did, certainly not excuse it, but *the man* must be attended. That's why we're here. It's our work now." She turned to me, taking my hot hand in her cool white ones. "Listen. Pulling a pea from a child's ear, that was easy. And for the rest, you study anatomy and symptoms, you learn treatments. It gets easier, you get more sure. Even amputations get easier. It's all here," she touched her head. "But doing this," she pointed to the twitching man, "tending someone who did wrong, and to you, that's the hard part. It may be too hard."

I stared at a bit of trampled ribbon on the worn wooden floor.

"I know that he raped you and probably others as well. I also know that sugar may revive him a little, but soon he'll be in coma." Sofia touched the long, naked feet. So clean. Had Daisy washed them? "They're cool already. Irma, believe me, *this* is not the man who hurt you. This is a dying man. But you're right, perhaps he deserves it."

I forced myself to watch the heaving, bony chest. So many times I had wished on him the pain and mortal fear he caused me, at least bitter remorse and shame for what he'd done. The pale eyes opened and closed. The body heaved. What were his thoughts now, in the hour of his death?

The calm voice continued. "Irma, will you stay at least until Daisy returns? Then I can tend the others."

"Yes," I whispered, "I'll stay."

"Good then." Sofia stood up slowly, pressed my shoulder. "Have her give him the sugar. I'll be back." She left us together, closing the door quietly behind her. Terrible breathing filled the room. A rat gnawed inside a wall and the bony blond head turned briefly toward the sound. I stared out the window into the gathering dusk until Daisy came panting in with a sack of penny candy.

"See if he'll take one," I told her. My voice seemed flat and strange.

The eyes flicked open and glazed blue fixed on me for an instant and then drifted off. The eyes closed again and the heavy head flopped toward Daisy. She pressed a cherry candy between dry lips. "Here, Jake. It'll make you better, the lady doctor says so."

"Huh," he muttered. A long pause and then again, "Huh." The wet red drop crested, peaked and fell on the thin pillow. The head lurched toward me and a word puffed out: "Who?"

"She came with the doctor. Rest now, Jake. You'll feel better soon." The eyes closed and the face sagged as if these few sounds had wasted him. He seemed smaller now. Daisy turned to me. "I'll straighten up a bit, miss. I'm sorry, but with him sick, I let things go." She took the belt from the floor, laid it carefully across the chesterfield and righted a penny print of dairymaids on the wall.

"Never mind that now, Daisy. You just sit with him." I took a dingy washcloth from its nail and rinsed it in the water bucket. "Here, wipe his brow with this." The breath came wet and rasping, paused and rasped again. The blotches were fading, leaving the long arms tinged with gray. I walked up to the dust-caked window that looked over ruffled domes of sycamores, silhouetted now against the sky. Behind me I heard Daisy's steady "There, there now, Jake" and the slosh of her rag in water. I longed for Sofia's light step to release me from this room with its stink of sickness and wide hands too close to mine, but the thin plank door barely muffled the other tenants shouting that their case was worse, far worse than their neighbors' and Sofia must see them next.

"Miss?" Daisy whispered. "He's sleeping now. I want you to know that it's true what they say about us out there, how Jake sends me to the streets for work. I'm not a lady like you. Jake wasn't always decent. He'd pick fights, drink too much and stay out late, but he always came back to me. We had our good times," she insisted. "You believe me, don't you?"

"Yes, I believe you." Would she believe that her Jake dragged girls into empty houses, gagged and raped them? How could she, and still sit by his bed?

She wiped the wide forehead gently, then the gaunt face and neck. "He was such a handsome man. All the girls looked at him when we went walking. They were jealous, you know?" I said nothing, which she took for assent. "Nobody but Jake ever paid me any mind. Because I'm a hunchback. See?" She lifted the shawl to show a bulge between the shoulders, high as a hand.

"A little, yes." There would be constant pain, Sofia had once commented when a barkeeper showed us such a hump. No spine can be so bent and not have pain. I found an empty wooden crate and sat beside Daisy. She studied my face.

"You have a scar, miss," she said.

"Yes. From the ship coming over."

She nodded. "So you know. Most men won't want a girl that's not perfect when there's plenty that are. So the ones that do want us usually aren't so perfect either. Maybe not on the outside, but on the inside, see, so girls like us make them feel better. Anyway, that's what I think."

My cheek burned. What was Gustavo's imperfection, then, that had him seek me out?

"Look at Jake!" Daisy cried. I followed her finger and yes, in this little time his flesh had changed again. It was grayish now, with a faint blue tinge around the mouth. Daisy smoothed the slick blond curls. "He won't be getting better, will he?"

"No, Daisy, he won't."

"And it won't be long now?"

"No, not long."

"At least he's not hurting, is he?"

I looked at the slack jaw. "No, I don't think so."

"I'm not calling any preacher man. Jake didn't hold with any kind of God talk." She sat straighter. "It's true what they said," she jutted her chin towards the stairwell. "We aren't married." Her voice rose. "But we were going to, soon. And he was going to get a job from a friend with the police in Indiana. He always wanted to be a copper, the kind on horseback. Jake loved horses."

Now whoa there while I mount you, filly bitch. I gripped the crate.

Daisy looked over in alarm. "Miss, what's wrong? You want some water?" She pointed to the water bucket and dirty bobbing cup. "Fresh from the well this morning." I shook my head, although my throat felt dry as ash.

The dying man's face smoothed as the white hands curled upward like a sleeping child's. Think of him this way, only this way. "Where is his family, Daisy?" I managed.

She shook her head. "Jake never talked about them." As twilight came, mothers up and down the street began calling their children home. "I come from a farm near Perth Amboy in New Jersey. We kept dairy cows. And you, miss, where are you from?"

"A little town in Italy called Opi. We kept sheep."

She smiled. "Was it nice there?"

"I liked it."

"I liked Perth Amboy too, but—I had to leave." She stroked the waxy brow. "Miss, do you think Jake can hear me, if I talk real close in his ear?"

"I think so, Daisy."

"Well then, can I say good-bye? He was good to me mostly, whatever they say, and I tried to take care of him like a wife. Do you mind?"

I stood up. "No, I don't mind." At the door I asked, "Will you go to Indiana—afterwards?"

She looked around the shabby flat. "Maybe. I got no reason to stay here. Thank you for asking, and for trying to help Jake and thank the doctor lady too. God bless both of you." I held out my hand, but then hugged her, stretching my arms around the ridged back.

Sofia met me in the stairway. She looked tired and let me carry her bag. "Gone?" she asked, nodding at the door.

"Not yet." It was full dark on the hushed street.

"Was he conscious?"

"Once, for a minute."

"Did he know you?"

"I don't think so."

"Just as well. Irma, I know it was hard. But you stayed and I'm proud of you. Very proud." She slipped her arm in mine and leaned slightly against me as we walked a block in silence. A warm breeze ruffled our skirts. We talked of the night's cases, a new anatomy book and a clinic like hers that had just opened in San Francisco, the Pacific Dispensary. She wanted to show me a letter from its director. I listened vaguely, still hearing Daisy's voice and Jake's rasping breath. Yet the long walk was peaceful and the pain in my chest released a little, like a tight corset loosened. At her door, I gave Sofia her bag. "Jake did do one good thing," she said. "He brought you to me and I'm grateful for that." She laid a cool hand along my cheek. "Buona notte, Irma."

"Buona notte, Sofia." I roused Enrico and he walked me home in the muggy night.

Twelve

MR. JOHN MUIR

That Friday, Vittorio met me at Sofia's door. "She won't be here this evening. She's with her sister," he said, staring over my shoulder at boys kicking a rag bag up and down the street.

"What sister?" I demanded. "She only had the one who died in childbirth."

"A half sister then. Let's get ready. We'll be running the clinic ourselves this time."

"How? Vittorio, that's impossible. Sofia checks all our work, even bandaging."

"We'll do it ourselves," he repeated, and then more warmly: "Besides, Irma, you know more than you think. For catarrh with coughing, what do we give?"

"Iodide of potassium, but—"

"For diarrhea?"

"Salts and castor oil."

"If it persists?"

"Laudanum."

"There, you see?" Vittorio said, hurrying me back to the office. "Serious cases we'll send to the hospital. Where they should all go anyway," he muttered. He kept his back to me as he dealt out instruments, powders, pills, ointments and bandages. I scrubbed the examining table and set out chairs. To every question and objection, Vittorio stolidly insisted: "Sofia wanted this."

But nothing made sense, neither Vittorio's brusque firmness nor Sofia's sudden absence. She had never spoken of a half sister and said nothing on Monday of a guest on Friday. Even if this half sister had come, couldn't she help at the clinic, or watch at least?

At least it began as an easy night. A mother brought two children with head lice. I hurried her out the door with instructions to rinse their hair with kerosene, wrap their heads in cloth and comb out the lice at night. We had a wracking chorus of coughers, whom I dosed as usual. Dyspepsia we treated with subnitrate of bismuth. Following Sofia's notes, I gave the bricklayer with rheumatism a tincture of aconite. For babes limp and listless from diarrhea, I used our familiar cures. But we could think of no relief for a young Irish sausage stuffer whose right arm had suddenly become paralyzed, nor for a Serbian boy rolled in a knot who howled when we tried to straighten his legs. There was an Irishman who twitched uncontrollably and an old woman who insisted that something heavy was growing in her belly. We sent those last four to the hospital and I began to clean the room.

"Will Sofia be here tomorrow?" I asked, but Vittorio had gone to answer a light knock at the door.

He came back muttering in Italian: "It's some hunchbacked American for you. Be as quick as you can and tell me when she's gone." He waved Daisy impatiently into the office.

She was clean and modestly dressed, hair brushed smooth and face unpainted. The calico dress bulged at the ridge of her hump, but she walked in proudly and set two silver dollars on the table. "For the house call," she said.

Vittorio recorded her payment and left us. Daisy sat down, hands folded neatly as a schoolgirl, but looked around curiously. "Where's the doctor lady?"

"She couldn't come tonight."

Daisy nodded. "Jake didn't last long after you left."

"I'm sorry."

She nodded. "Well, at least he died easy, and maybe he heard what I told him. Anyway, I stopped the clock and covered the mirror, you know, so the spirit don't see itself. And then I sent for the doctors' men."

I started. "What doctors' men?"

Daisy's brown eyes widened. "You don't know about them, miss? The ones who buy bodies from poor folk, so doctors can cut them up to see what we look like inside. They said that because Jake wasn't old or gunshot or consumptive and since he was, you know, fresh, they'd give me twenty dollars silver. They were dressed all respectable, like regular undertakers with a good black cloth to cover him, so the neighbors wouldn't talk. They took him out feet first, like for any funeral. You don't have doctors' men in your country, miss?" I shook my head. "Well, funerals cost here, you know, and like I said, Jake didn't hold with churches or wasting good money on dead folks. He would have done the same if it was me that went first."

I nodded, stunned. So in America the dead might be stripped naked, sliced, pulled apart and talked over? In Opi, we buried even drunkards and thieves. No one probed their bowels or peeled back the ribs. But what a fool I'd been not to trace the fine drawings in Sofia's books back to bodies of the poor acquired by "doctors' men." How else could we learn? Still, to have strangers cut open your chest, releasing the soul. *"What* soul?" Molly would ask. "It's better than he deserves."

"Miss," Daisy was saying. "I want you to have this." She set a man's pocket watch on the table. I remembered it pressed against me. "It keeps good time, but you can sell it if you want. See, real gold plate. Feel how heavy."

I didn't touch it. "Daisy, you paid for the visit. And you might want that to—to remember him."

"No, miss, you heard how the others talked, but you treated me right. And I don't need money now. With what the doctors' men gave me, I'll be fine. I'm not going to Indiana. My cousins in Michigan have a dairy farm. I used to like making cheese at home so I telegraphed and they said to come. I'm tired of city people anyhow, staring at my hump and calling me names." She pushed the watch away. "I don't need one of those now anyway. On a farm you just follow the cows. Well, miss, I have to pack. I'm leaving on the morning train." She stood up.

I walked Daisy to the door and came back to finish cleaning, leaving the watch untouched. Vittorio returned and cleared his throat. "Irma," he began.

"Yes?" I was wiping tongue depressors with cotton soaked in alcohol, my back to him. "There's a watch on the table," I said. "Will you give it to Enrico?"

"It's from the hunchback?" Vittorio asked, his voice high and strained.

"From Daisy, yes." When I turned and saw his face, a depressor clattered from my hand. "What's wrong? It's about Sofia. What happened?"

"Her pains came back this morning and this time they didn't pass."

"What?" Silence. "Vittorio, *what* pains?"

"She didn't tell you she had angina pectoris?" I shook my head. "She took digitalis, but as you know, it doesn't cure the heart."

"Angina," I repeated. Angina pectoris, from Latin: a strangling in the chest. Sofia strangled? Not possible, no. "She's in a hospital then? Which one? I want to see her." I groped for my bag and hat.

"Irma, it's too late. She's gone."

"What?"

"I'm sorry, Irma, but Sofia died this afternoon, just a little before you came."

I sank in the chair. Death never came like this in my life, without warning, as a swooping hawk plucks a mouse from the grass. How could Sofia be dead if here were her tools, her chair, her books, her tongue depressor, her stethoscope? I squeezed the rubber tube. "Monday she was fine," I insisted. "We walked to the South Side and climbed five floors. She told me about the Pacific Dispensary. She wanted to show me a letter." There: I couldn't have invented this fact. "She wasn't sick. Just tired."

Vittorio took my hand. So she *was* dead. Breathing hurt, as if my own heart were strangled. "Enrico could have come to the shop for me."

He shook his head. "She didn't want that. She was so proud of you on Monday, whatever it was that you did, and she wanted that night to be how you remembered her, not how she was today."

Cold ran up my legs. "*How* was she today?"

Vittorio pressed his palm into the scrubbed table. "I was in the shop and she was working here, mixing compounds, and about ten this morning, Enrico shouted for me. I ran back and found her on the floor holding her arm. Her face was white." Cats screamed outside in the alley. My fingers closed around her stethoscope. "I knew it was bad this time. Claudia and I brought her to bed. The first attack passed, then another came and she asked for a priest and had me get this from her desk." Vittorio took a neatly folded page from his jacket pocket, opened and read it: "To Irma Vitale, my stethoscope, record book, whatever medical texts she chooses and the proceeds of this week. The remainder of my instruments may be given to Mercy Hospital." He showed me her accounts ledger and my eyes crawled down the neat lists: the dilator was paid for and our last shipment of clamps. Tuesday she had done a breech birth and on Wednesday an abortion, both in fine houses on Lake Shore. Vittorio handed me *The Midwife's Practical Directory.* "There's seventy-five dollars inside for you." I closed the book.

Memories of Sofia rushed over me like a battering wave: my abortion, our walking home afterward talking about the clinic, Sofia teaching me how to stitch skin and bandage wounds. Sofia listening to the sick with her head slightly cocked, and how on the hottest nights she would run, *run* upstairs after a frightened child whose father had collapsed in the kitchen.

"When did you know she was sick?" I asked.

"This spring, just before you first came here. I was bringing her a bottle of carbolic and saw her slumped over. She didn't say anything, but the next day when I asked if we needed more digitalis she said yes. She was so sly. We'd be talking, she'd cough, put a handkerchief to her face and you never saw her take a pill. In May she stopped hiding it from me and I made her see a doctor at Mercy Hospital. He said there was nothing to do. We can set a broken arm, but you can't go into the heart and fix it. I know how you cared for her. And she knew as well. You were like a daughter to her, that was one of the last things she said."

Tears poured down my face. Vittorio pushed a length of bandage gauze across the table and sat patiently as I held it to my face and wept for Sofia, for my mother and Zia Carmela, for all who cared for me and now were gone. "Why didn't she tell me she was sick?" I stammered. "I could have—"

"Done what, Irma?" He took my hand. "I told you, there's no cure. Digitalis doesn't work forever. The first time I met you, when you came for a restorative, something told me you were sent here for Sofia. And you helped her heal more people. That's all she wanted."

No, it was she who helped me, who made from my worn cloth a new Irma. And what of the children watching for us from windows, the men who carried their comrades in from work, the parents who thrust babes in our arms and the women who needed us? "Who'll run the clinic now, Vittorio?" I demanded, my voice shrill in the little room.

Vittorio excused himself and came back with two glasses of wine. "Drink, Irma, and listen to me. You know we can't take her place. I helped her when I could, but I'm just a druggist. I don't have a mission, like Sofia did. I have a wife and rent to pay. You're a very clever girl, but you're—"

"A dressmaker."

"Yes. Exactly. So the sick must go to the hospitals."

"But the hospitals are crowded and filthy. They don't want immigrants. They don't have interpreters. They don't explain anything." I stopped. Vittorio was calmly drinking his wine.

"Irma, if the sick go to the hospitals and fill the beds, if the priests and the rabbis and the pastors and the newspapers cry out, things will change. Slowly, but they will. You know we can't heal the city. You saw how hard Sofia worked and it cost her health. We did a fine thing. I was proud to be part of it and you should be too. We helped many people. But the clinic is finished now. My cousin and his family are coming from Genoa to live with us. I have to help them."

I slumped in the chair. With Sofia gone and the sick untended, my dream of a shop for fine ladies seemed a hollow, foolish thing. I felt hollow myself, as if I'd rattle when I walked.

Vittorio filled my glass again. "When Enrico brings you Sofia's papers, read them. Perhaps there's an answer there. Not for Chicago, but for you." Just then Claudia appeared. "Finished?" he asked.

"Yes. She's in the purple. Angelina helped."

So they had washed and dressed her as Opi women had washed and dressed my mother. This much was a comfort. The doctors' men would not take Sofia. I explained what Daisy had said, how the poor sold their bodies for cutting. Claudia's face darkened. "There's *nothing* Protestants won't do for money."

"Never mind that," said Vittorio. "Sofia will have a proper funeral."

"You'll see, half of Chicago will come tomorrow. And half of *them*," Claudia added bitterly, "never paid her. But when they come, they see how we care for our dead."

"Where is she?" I interrupted.

"We'll show you."

I sent Enrico to tell Molly what happened so she wouldn't worry when I didn't come home, for I would sit with Sofia all night. Vittorio and Claudia brought me to the parlor where she was laid out. Her hands crossed over her failed heart were so still. Of course. And yet— *so* pale and *so* still, with her wiry curls smoothed as they never were in life. Rouge brightened her long cheeks. Alive, she had worn no rouge. They had dressed her in a dark purple silk, elegant and severe. Touching her side, I felt a whalebone corset. Didn't they know she hated corsets? Who in a corset could run upstairs, lift children onto tables or work for hours in a steaming room?

Claudia whispered. "Doesn't she look like a gentlewoman?" I nodded. "She was good to the poor, but there *is* a limit, you know." Claudia brought me a chair and pillow, a shawl and a stool for my feet, but in her clucking care I read that if Sofia had lived, Claudia would soon enough have pried Vittorio from the clinic and kept him close at home. She brought me some chamomile tea and a little plate of biscotti and left us alone.

It was a timeless night, for the mantel clock had been stopped, the windows and mirror draped and candles lit the room. I stared at my empty hands. Sofia, what is their work now? Cloth yielded to these hands and thread followed them meekly. My work pleased women and charmed men. "These hands are a gift," Father Anselmo had once said. And the wise shape their lives according to their gifts. So why not keep sewing for gentlewomen? It was an honest, respectable craft. Molly was right: I *could* have my own shop one day. Chicago was growing and everywhere there were pockets of rich women. Soon I would be as skilled as Madame, and there was work enough for many fine dressmakers. I stared at my hands and Sofia's until dawn edged through the curtains and Claudia brought me bread and coffee.

News of Sofia's death had spread quickly across the neighborhoods. Many had seen the notice on Vittorio's door. Others heard through the air, it seemed. Mourners squeezed more chairs into the narrow room, bringing flowers, gifts or food, according to their customs. Plates and glasses were handed to me and taken away. Families filed past the body. Some touched her face, her hands, heart or clothing, murmuring prayers in their languages. Jacob came with his sisters, for Sofia had visited them when measles tore through the tenements.

A thin young woman came alone and whispered that her name was Martha. I remember hearing of her case: Martha has ceased eating, nearly herself starving to death after an uncle raped her. She swallowed poison. Sofia saved her, found her a job and a room in a new part of the city and made her come weekly to be weighed. "Look at me!" Martha said proudly. "You can't see my bones no more." She leaned close to add, "There's a young man what wants to marry me. I'm going to night school too, and learning bookkeeping."

"Signora D'Angelo would be pleased," I said.

When wealthy women came alone and filed silently past the body, I suspected that they had sought out Sofia for abortions. Late in the morning, Mrs. Clayburn slipped into the hot, close room and laid a gloved hand on Sofia's. When she looked up and saw me, she blinked. "Aren't you—?"

"Irma Vitale. You introduced me to Madame Hélène."

"Ah yes, the girl in the park, with those soldiers. But—"

"I worked at night with Signora D'Angelo. I was her assistant."

"Ah yes, you Italians, always sticking together." When I said nothing, she turned away.

In mid-afternoon the undertaker came with Sofia's coffin, for it was a hot day and we could wait no longer. Vittorio, Claudia and I lifted her in, but as the undertaker's men moved to close the lid I turned away, unable to watch that sharp-edge shadow once again cross a dear, familiar face. When they took out their hammers, I left the room. No blacksmith beating on his anvil is as loud as the pounding in of coffin nails: that sound cracks air.

We followed her carriage to church, where Father Paolo gave the mass, but I remember none of it, only my own prayer: Lord, wash away these last five days. Take me back to Monday when we walked together and I believed that Sofia was well.

"Irma, come back for the funeral meal," Claudia and Vittorio urged afterward, but I could not bear to see that house again. "Then here, Enrico," said Vittorio, giving the boy some coins. "Make sure Irma gets home safely and stop checking that watch."

Mrs. Gaveston offered condolences and Molly brought tea to my room. In the next days, boarders bowed politely in the hallways or took my hand in the dining room. Many had gone or had friends who had gone to the clinic. Somehow I worked the next days, bent over cloth and driving my needle as if it would stitch out a new path for my life. Grief was a wearying weight I carried to the shop and home, barely speaking to Molly and trudging upstairs to my room. Each night the steps seemed steeper, like the rocky path to Opi.

On the fourth day after the funeral, Molly announced that Enrico had brought something for me. On my bed sat a wooden box with Sofia's papers. There were letters from medical schools politely saying she could not be admitted because she was not an American citizen or because she had no high-school diploma or because she was a woman. There were descriptions of instruments, sutures and clamps, announcements of lectures at the Chicago Medical College, copies of the *Boston Medical and Surgical Journal*, and her own lecture notes, carefully ordered.

I found a fat bundle of correspondence from the Pacific Dispensary for Women and Children in San Francisco. In our last walk, Sofia had spoken of their care for the poor. Letters from the dispensary thanked Sofia for her mortality and morbidity lists, midwifery notes and descriptions of troubling cases. I remembered some of them: poor healing of stumps after amputation; repeated miscarriage in the first trimester; blue babies, rickets, arthritis in children, intestinal obstructions, sudden seizures and strange cases of nerve damage in meat packers.

The final page in the bundle was an announcement that the dispensary had opened a two-year nursing school, the first one west of the Rocky Mountains. Inquiries were to be directed to Dr. Martha Bucknell. A woman doctor? My fingers traced her name and then stopped. In the corner of the page, in Sofia's small, angled letters was written: "Irma?" A warm wind puffed through the open window, ruffling my hair, the linen of my chemise and the page in my hand. I looked around the little room, suddenly so familiar, a narrow, safe nest. Was this Sofia's idea, that I leave Chicago, go west and throw in my lot with strangers once again? The thought was fearful.

And yet—to be in a school, to learn and learn and know the human body as I now knew thread and cloth—the longing rose up against fear like a rock against waves. And wouldn't this work be enough for life, to heal the sick and ease those in pain? Sofia did not go to dances, I wagered. She did not stand against walls and watch young men's eyes scan the stock and never, not once, come walking toward her. She simply worked.

Near midnight, I felt my way down to Mrs. Gaveston's sitting room, where she kept stacks of *Harper's New Monthly Magazine* and *Scribner's Monthly*. I put them all on an end table, lit the gaslight and pored through articles on Indian tribes of the West, geysers, mountains full of silver and the Continental Divide. I read of San Francisco's new cable cars and mansions. Mr. John Muir described Lake Tahoe, redwood forests that were old before Rome was new, canyons, glaciers, deserts and petrified forests. San Francisco had a fine seaport, one writer noted, "where ships call from the world's great cities." My heart shook. Gustavo had been to San Francisco and might come again. South of the city, one writer said, hills rolled down the coast covered in sweet grass, where sheep and cattle grazed all year.

Gradually, as I read, Chicago seemed like a shell that I had split and outgrown. I did not sleep that night, but curled on the horsehair settee with the magazines until Molly came to start her morning chores.

Thirteen

FURRY CHICKEN

Studying me, Molly's reddened hands cupped her hips. Head cocked, she listened to my plans. I held up my own hands, spotted with needle pricks. "Molly, I have to do more with these than make fancy dresses."

"Fine. Do what you want. But you don't have to cross the country just to go to nursing school. There's Mercy Hospital right here in Chicago. They admit women."

I fanned the California pictures across the settee. "Look—it's like Abruzzo. See these beautiful hills in San Francisco!"

"Ah now, hills *in* a city, how very grand. And why do we want to be walking *up* to a dry goods store. You see something special there?"

"Yes. You can look down on the land rolling all around you, houses, churches, parks, the bay and the ocean, shadows moving, mists in the morning . . ." I trailed off as Molly sighed.

"You mean fog? Plenty of that here." Molly picked up the letter announcing the dispensary's nursing school. "Candidates must have good character," she read. "You have that. But what about this?" her finger jabbed the page. "A high-school diploma? You have one of those?"

"No, but I can read English. I can study Sofia's books."

Molly put down the letter. "You're just wanting to leave Chicago, aren't you, Irma? Because of what happened that night?"

Silence settled over us. Yes, San Francisco was far from all I longed to forget. But I was also weary of the flat earth, the heat of summer and hard press of winter cold. The etchings in *Scribner's* made me yearn for the loop and roll of land. I wanted to break free of the squeeze of buildings and streets running endlessly out to horizons. Carlo would laugh, but I even missed sheep. Chicago had squirrels and rats, crows, pigeons, rangy dogs and alley cats. Backyard pens in the new neighborhoods often held pigs, and chickens squawked in rough coops behind many houses. Mules and horses clogged the streets with their whinnies and snorts, but where was the comforting calm of sheep?

Molly's hands took my shoulders. "Irma, you could be safe in Chicago. You don't have to go to bad neighborhoods. That man who hurt you is gone. The clinic's finished. So you could come dancing with me on Friday nights, meet a good lad *and* learn nursing. Isn't that better than moving all the time, always being a stranger?"

It's true. In Opi my life was cradled in a net, knit to every soul around me. A new net was just forming in Chicago. Could I rip it again and hope to make another?

"Enough about moving," said Molly, pointing to the ceiling that shook with Mrs. Gaveston's heavy tread in the room above us. "*Herself* has arisen. You'd think a body with a little money could put down carpets and not make that racket in the morning. Yes, Your Highness, the hired girl is busy. Come on, Irma." In the kitchen she set me to grinding coffee as she put out plates, sliced a loaf into perfectly even slices and tossed out the crumbs for birds. "And now tell me, why should they take a foreign dressmaker with no high-school diploma in this San Francisco nursing school?" she asked. And then: "Grind more coffee. The boarders drink it like water."

"Madame Hélène can write me a recommendation."

"Sure she could. But that just proves you're a good dressmaker." Molly poured oatmeal into a pot of boiling water. Waves of shame washed over me as I watched her work. She had been a good and faithful friend. So many evenings we shared stories of home. I had sat on my bed as she playacted her bargaining with immigrants or mimicked Mrs. Gaveston's ways until my sides ached with laughter. I remembered the night of the charred house, when she waited and worried for me. "I'm sorry, Molly. I've just been thinking of myself."

"And just who else *should* you be thinking of? It's a free country. Go where you want. Take care of your sick people." She stirred the oatmeal hard, her wooden spoon knocking the heavy pot. "San Francisco's a new city. Newer than Chicago. Could be you'll like that." Molly wheeled around, oatmeal spoon in the air. "But the Lord knows I'll be missing you when you're gone, Irma Vitale."

I wrapped my arms around her broad shoulders. "I'll miss you too, Molly. I'll miss you so much."

"We've been good friends, haven't we?"

I nodded.

Molly stepped back to the stove. "Oatmeal's sticking." She stirred furiously. "Shouldn't you write to this Dr. Bucknell first, make sure she'll take you and *then* go? Suppose it costs? Don't you want to know how much? And why the sudden rush?"

True, all true. But what of Sofia brushing off Vittorio's steady urgings to rest between patients, to close the clinic earlier or tell patients to come back next week. "They're sick *now*," she would insist. "They need help *now*."

Molly studied my face. "I see. So you're going soon."

"Yes, as soon as I can."

"Well, put out the bread and ring the bell. It's feeding time."

Madame Hélène was setting a billowing muttonchop sleeve into a close-fitted bodice when I told her of my plan. She pulled pins from her mouth and pushed them into a cushion. "Irma, why do you go west? The women—everyone cares for you *here*. We need you." In the next room, the whirl of Simone's machine stopped. Even the old cat looked up as I described the dispensary, the new nursing school and the hills of San Francisco.

Madame Hélène nodded. "This flatness here, like a floor, is hard for me too. But why is sewing *people* better than making fine dresses that you do so well? *Every* day, all day seeing the sick, cripples, children dying, it's like the Old Country, no? Everything hopeless and sad. If you want to see mountains, take a little vacation. Then come back and we do the spring season together, the new styles from Paris. We go to New York perhaps, and see the great shops."

I wavered, as if a strong wind pushed against me. I had worked so hard, sewing enough skirt lengths to cover Opi. Yes, of course I would miss the surge of pleasure and pride when a customer asked for *me*, thanked *me* and reported how many suitors had noticed her daughter in a gown I made. And yet . . . Sofia's hands gently pressing a woman's belly or my own hands lifting a wailing child to our examining stool, knowing we could help.

Madame Hélène sighed. "So, you go west. But before you go, can you finish the trousseau for the long-waist girl at least—the senator's daughter? And the two evening gowns for the stockyard woman with too-wide shoulders, Mrs. Will."

"Willis," Simone called from the other room.

I promised. Madame yanked a needle from her cushion. "And how do I find a new Irma to help me?"

"Perhaps there's a girl looking for work now, walking through the city like I was, asking everywhere for work. You could put a notice on the door."

"Ah. A notice on the door for everyone to see?" In the way Madame Hélène tightened her lips I knew there would be no more said that morning of my going. When we gathered for our noon meal, she cleared her throat. "I have decided. First, Irma, you will teach Simone all you can while you are here. You will work extra hours with her. I pay you for this. I will put a notice *in the newspaper* for a girl to do machine sewing and decent French cooking. Not on the door. So I find a girl who reads at least. Simone, you will learn from Irma?"

"Yes, Madame!" said Simone gleefully.

"Irma, you will teach her everything?"

"I'll try, Madame."

"And second, we will have a dinner together before you go away. We will invite Jacob and his sisters and your friends if you like."

"Thank you, Madame."

She waved me silent. "You are a good dressmaker. The ladies like you. The shop is peaceful. We make money at last. And now you leave me. Such is the life. But we will eat together first, good French food."

Late summer cooled quickly into autumn. An Irish friend of Molly's would teach my English classes. I delivered Sofia's instruments to

Mercy Hospital and worked with Simone to finish the trousseau and velvet gowns. She learned quickly, having been secretly practicing on scraps of fabric and studying pictures as I once did. "Teach this to me," she would say avidly, pointing out a skirt's bias swirl or curving pleat on a tight bodice. "And the little buttonholes, how do I make them so perfect and round?"

A parade of young women answered our notice in the *Chicago Daily Tribune*. "Irish, Polish, German, Greek, American," Hélène muttered. "I want *French* food, or at least Italian." Finally a slight, caramel-skinned girl from Haiti appeared who spoke a kind of French. She called herself Lune and would not say how she had come to live in Chicago or anything of her family, but her seams were straight as shot arrows and she could take apart, clean, oil and reassemble the sewing machine as if it were a child's toy. The thick soups she called gumbo were French enough for Hélène and delicious. The old cat adored her and the customers were charmed by the waft of her songs over the whirl of the sewing machine.

The night before I left, we had our dinner. We closed early, drew the curtains and moved our cutting table to the middle of the shop. Vittorio and Claudia brought wine and I arranged flowers from the Maxwell Street market. Freyda, Sarah and Jacob brought challah, a golden braided bread. Molly came with candied nuts, a thick wedge of cheddar cheese and crystal glasses secretly borrowed from Mrs. Gaveston. Lune made a gumbo, Simone baked a flaky onion tart and Hélène had spent hours simmering a *choucroute* of potatoes, cabbage and goose, the traditional going-away meal in her village. "To give strength for the voyage," she explained. "So you carry away the taste of home." For dessert Simone produced a dense chocolate pudding called mousse. "It is the fashion in Paris," she boasted. I had never eaten anything so delicious, so dark, sweet and soft in the mouth, like a melting cloud.

We ate and ate, sharing stories of home and America. Then came the gifts. I had embroidered handkerchiefs for the women and bought pipes for Jacob and Vittorio. Claudia presented an ample carpetbag for traveling "like real Americans use." Jacob's sisters gave me one of their pieced purses. Hélène pushed a small, cloth-wrapped package across the table. "Simone told me you were robbed in Cleveland," she said. "So we find these for you, from England." It was a pair of crane-head scissors with golden handles, a bright enamel eye and even finer blades than those of my stolen pair.

"Why does she cry over scissors?" Lune demanded.

"They are beautiful, thank you," I whispered.

"Yes, certainly," Hélène agreed. "So you must not forget your sewing and you must not forget us."

"I could never forget—"

Hélène made her shooing-away wave. "And you will not to be robbed again out West with the cow-boys?"

"I'll be careful."

"If you come back, Irma, there will be space in my shop for you, always." Hélène got up abruptly and hurried to the kitchen. The water pump rattled and she returned wiping her eyes.

"And *this* is my present," Molly announced, slapping her calendar on the table. "Irma, look at November." I looked. All the numbers were erased. Curious, I turned to Molly's beaming face. "I'm going with you to San Francisco. No, listen first. They say it's full of single people looking for boardinghouses. I have a plan. We get work in a house right away: you help me clean and we have a place to live for no money. Then I find a rich widow to invest with me. By next year I should have my own house. This way at least you'll know one person in San Francisco when you go. Well, do you like my plan?"

To travel with a friend, to enter a strange city and not be alone? I gulped back my tears. "Yes, Molly, I like it very much."

Molly's old bustle returned. "Now Irma, you're going third class?"

"Yes, I have to." Second class cost eighty dollars—too much. Third class meant renting bed boards to sleep on at night and sitting all day on hard benches, but I would bear this for a week to save money for San Francisco.

"If we come back to visit," Molly vowed, "we're coming *first class*." Everyone laughed, including me, seeing myself in a Pullman car with velvet settees and Persian carpets, eating from China plates and sleeping on fine linen sheets at night. I'd have a picture made and sent to Opi, where people would pass it around, astonished.

"Now Simone," Molly was saying, "where are those dusters? Look, everyone, the first clothes I ever had of a French seamstress," she boasted. Simone fetched two gray linen dusters.

Hélène sniffed. "Very plain."

"Of course," said Molly. "They'll protect our clothes from coal dust. See, no ruffles or pleats, so they're easy to shake clean."

"I designed them myself," said Simone, blushing.

We raised our glasses to the dusters and each other. Such a warm net I had finally woven around me, a net about to be ripped. When I noticed Simone and Hélène debating the waistline of a new gown for Mrs. Willis, I looked away, embarrassed at a flush of envy. As Opi had closed behind me when I left, Hélène and Simone would go on working in this room, creating dresses I would never see. Their heads touched as they folded and refolded a bit of linen to test how the dress might drape.

A hand pressed my arm. "You will find good friends in San Francisco, my dear," Jacob whispered. "And other work to do. *Your* work."

"But no friends like these."

"That is true, none like these. And we will have no one like our Irma, but I carry you here always." He touched his heart, patting the somber black coat that Freyda said he wore on holidays and feast days. "And for *tonight*, we celebrate together." We finished the wine and mousse and sang songs from our old countries until the church bells rang midnight.

"I don't come to the station, Irma," Hélène announced suddenly. "I have had enough sadness in good-byes, but you do *well* in San Francisco, *mon amie*, you promise? And write to us. Now go home, it's late and I must think how to tell the ladies they have lost their Irma."

"Yes, we have to go," Molly announced, pulling me to the door. "The train leaves early. But don't worry, this time leaving will be different."

The next morning *was* different. I had my fine carpetbag, not an immigrant bundle. Vittorio hired a cart to take our baggage to the Central Depot, and a noisy clump of well-wishers crowded around us: Jacob, Freyda and Sarah, Molly's friends, some of my English students, Vittorio and Claudia, Simone and Lune. There were kisses and hugs, packages of sweets tucked into our baskets and addresses pushed into our hands.

"*Zay gesunt*, go in good health, my dear," Jacob said, coming close to whisper, "and remember, there *are* good men in the world." Then he handed me off to Sarah and Freyda, who warned me against strangers.

Molly called a porter to stow a trunk of linens, which she heard fetched high prices in San Francisco. We each had a clump of tickets: passage with the Chicago and North Western line to the Pacific

Transfer station in Council Bluffs, Iowa, then tickets on the Union Pacific to Omaha, and finally the Pacific line to San Francisco. We had our dusters and two dresses for the trip, underclothes, books, soap, food for the first day, my sewing box and a neat package from Vittorio with medicines for travelers' ills: sick headaches, nausea, sore throats, coal coughs, and all manner of digestive problems.

The shrieking train whistle and bustling conductor hurried us onto the train. Below our window, handkerchiefs fluttered like doves. "Good-bye, good-bye, au revoir, zay gesunt, arrivederci!" My last view of the Chicago Depot was hazy with tears.

"Six days," said Molly, busily sorting our bags. "I'll learn book-keeping and you'll study medicine. Not like those bumpkins who stare out the window or play cards all the time." I did study my book of child and infant maladies. But the window drew me relentlessly.

"You'll wear out that nose," Molly warned, "pressed to the glass like that."

But I couldn't stop, and even paid boys at the stations to wash the coal dust from my window. We roared across prairies at forty miles an hour through green-gold seas of grass. Children tumbled from sod houses to wave us by. Years ago, a traveler said, there were buffalo herds as large as lakes here, horizon to horizon, moving like thunder. Flocks of passenger pigeons once passed for hours. No matter, the golden light was enough now; hawks rose into a cobalt sky and crimson tipped the shocks of trees. I saw Indians in fringed leather with rain-straight black hair. Storm clouds bloomed over wheat fields, mounded high as mountains. Lightning laced the sky. No one had ever told me that America was so grand. If Carlo and my father were here, these sights would amaze even them.

Inside the train, hours crawled by in weary sameness. A foul "convenience" bucket at the end of each car was barely shielded by a curtain. Ceaseless card games sometimes crumbled into fights and once a wooden bench was ripped out of the floor. When we finished the food we had brought, there was only the station cafés' unvarying fare: thin, tough gray beefsteaks, weak beer, rubbery boiled eggs and potatoes fried in rancid oil. We wolfed these meals in minutes lest the train pull out without us. Twice we had to leave before the food we paid for had arrived.

"They'll sell it again to some poor fool," said a burly Irishman. "Don't you know? The stationmasters make deals with the engineer and sell the same meal three times over, then feed it to the dogs." Two days west of Chicago, chicken stew appeared on the menu. "Hah," he scoffed. "That's 'furry chicken.' The greenhorns always fall for it."

"Meaning?" Molly demanded.

"Meaning, watch the prairies." That afternoon we saw herds of sharp-nosed, puppy-fat little beasties pushing up through earthy knobs to sit on their haunches as we passed. "Prairie dogs," the traveler explained haughtily. "There's your 'chicken stew.'"

Molly stared him down. "Could be your people would have been glad for any kind of stew when potatoes failed in Ireland. Am I right, lad?" She smiled in her wide-mouthed way and thrust out a hand. "No harm meant. My friends call me Molly, if you want to know."

The man looked her up and down and smiled. "Mine call me Tom and you're right, Molly. It was grass they were eating back home in the Great Hunger and songs they lived on when there was nothing else."

"Well, then," I suggested, "shall we try the chicken stew?" We ate it at the next station. The meat was fresh, at least. Molly and Tom, splicing their stories together, determined that their fathers could have sailed on the same ship out of Ireland.

The first days passed despite the stifling afternoons, shivering sleepless nights and the growing stench in our carriage. A young woman's labor started early and the porter helped me cordon off a birthing space. I made a little nest of clean cloths and rags that Molly collected from the passengers and coached the mother's breathing as Sofia had taught me. The babe was born just west of Omaha, a rosy black-haired baby girl the giddy parents named Mary Irma. The father lined a soapbox with a buffalo blanket he bought at the next station and Tom sang lullabies to her in Gaelic—"God's own mother tongue," he insisted.

Finally, the mountains! They rose from the plains in Colorado, rank on rank of peaks, enough to hold a thousand Opis with high meadows to feed a world of sheep. I never tired of watching sunlight splash the rock faces or clouds skim over hanging lakes. Our tracks cut through forests and topped bridges that seemed flimsy as spider webs. We entered the Wasatch Mountains under a crescent moon hung over a jagged range cut into the blue-black sky. A silver waterfall poured over a dark cliff that seemed to melt into the night, as if water tumbled from the moon. I shook Molly awake.

"Look! Did you ever see anything so beautiful?"

"A beautiful dream I *was* having," she groaned, "about *not* being on trains. If these mountains are so wonderful, sew them, why don't you?" I tried that, moving to a car near the back of the train where those who could not sleep passed the night reading or playing cards by kerosene lamps.

I was stitching a varicolored mountain range on a length of linen as a storm roared in from the north. A lid of thick clouds closed over the train. Driving rain poured down, turning icy. Lightning blazed across the valley and porters whispered anxiously to each other. They had cause, said one traveler, for we had entered the "killer miles," deadly for the men who had laid these tracks and for those who ran trains over them.

We stopped in a mining town, where a brakeman was sent up to fix the coupling on a coal car. Perhaps the engineer didn't hear his cry or see his lamp swinging in the driving rain. Perhaps the brakes didn't hold. In any case, the train jerked forward and released, crushing the brakeman and then flinging him down the icy embankment.

They carried him howling into the caboose. I raced back, following his cries. They had laid him on a narrow cot that was quickly soaked with blood. Torn pants revealed a mass of gushing blood. "God damn engineers. We're cheaper than dirt to them," spat one of the men. "It's me—Hank," he said to the injured man. "We're here with you, Bill. We're not going nowhere."

"Let me see him," I said. Bill's right leg was crushed and left arm twisted out at the elbow. The side of his face was a pulp of pebbles and ice. I looked in his eyes as Sofia had taught me. The pupils were dilated and his pulse weak. Bruises covered the chest, but I dared not touch him, for perhaps an organ had been pierced. The day before, at a station diner, I'd heard passengers ask advice of a kind-faced man called Dr. Windham, who traveled first class. I asked the porter to fetch him.

"I'm sure he's sleeping, miss. He might be angry."

"Ask anyway."

I carefully cut away Bill's pants leg, but didn't touch the white bone or shredded flesh. I could clean his face at least. "Do you have any bandages? Sheets?" I asked the men.

"Sheets? They don't give us none," Hank spat again.

"Rags then, as clean as you can."

Bill opened his eyes. "My leg. What happened?" His voice rose. "Somebody! Why can't I feel it?"

"There was an accident, Bill," said a gentle voice behind me. "I'm Dr. Windham. Let me take a look at you. Give this man some whiskey," he told Hank. "If you've got any."

"Don't have sheets, but we sure got whiskey. Hold on a minute, Bill."

Bill watched avidly as Hank found a bottle, filled a cup and lifted his head to drink. In this lull, Dr. Windham set down a tooled leather case and stepped toward the cot, keeping his fine kid boots clear of the widening pool of blood.

"Doc, don't cut my leg off."

"There now, son, nobody's cutting. You rest easy, I'll give you something for the pain." The doctor opened a vial of morphine and prepared a needle, speaking slowly as he injected. "Breathe in and out for me now, Bill. Good, very good."

"Don't leave me," Bill muttered.

"We're here," Hank repeated. "We're all here."

"You won't amputate, sir?" I ventured, when Bill's eyes closed and his head fell heavily to one side. "Because if there's an infection and gangrene—"

"You're a doctor, young lady, or a nurse?"

"No, but I worked in a clinic back in Chicago."

"Miss—?"

"Vitale."

He pulled me clear of the men closing around Bill's cot. "Miss Vitale, the best London hospital couldn't save that man and for sure we can't save him on a moving train with the tools in this bag. I was a surgeon for the Union army at Antietam, Gettysburg and Chickamauga. After four hundred seventy-three amputations you come to know who'll

survive and who won't. There is doubtless cranial bleeding. You saw
the abdominal bruising?"

"Yes sir. I was afraid of—"

"Internal injuries? Certainly. They will be massive." He slipped between the men around Bill's cot, put his stethoscope to the heaving
chest and came back to me. "Water in the lungs already, possibly pre-
existing pneumonia. Many of these men have it, working in all weath-
ers, breathing that coal dust. The heart's badly weakened. He won't
last the night."

As Bill's shivers deepened to convulsions, the men tucked their
blankets and jackets around him until only his head was visible under
the mound.

"Weight on the chest—" I began, but Dr. Windham raised his
hand.

"Let them be," he whispered. "This is all the funeral he'll have."

"Fine brakeman," said one of the men.

"Flyin' Bill."

"That blizzard in seventy-two, crossing the Divide, you saved us all."

"God be with ye, Bill."

The men brought us stools and we sat by the bed as the men made
their quiet ministrations. Dr. Windham described his battlefield surgeries and I told him about Sofia's clinic and my hopes to study at the
dispensary. When Bill moaned, Hank brought a flask and lifted his
sweat-soaked head to help him drink. I tucked my stitched mountains
in his whitening hand.

Bill died near dawn. When the cloth dropped to the floor, Hank
asked me for it. "Mountains and trains kill us like that," he said, snapping his fingers, "but us brothers on the Pacific line, where else we

gonna go?" They wrapped Bill in the rain slicker that shrouded so many railroad men. Nobody knew his family. "The crew at the next station will bury him along the tracks," Hank explained. "Close enough to hear our whistle blow."

When he walked me back to Molly, the card games paused. "Hard, was it?" Molly asked. I nodded. A porter brought me breakfast from the first-class dining room with Dr. Windham's compliments, but I couldn't eat and gave the tray to Molly.

"It's strange. You can see patients all day," Sofia once said. "The sick, the wounded, children you know will die. You think you're strong, that you can do your best with each case and then go on to the next. Then one case comes along, no different from the next and you don't know why, but it's just so hard." This time, Sofia would have been wrong. There *was* something different about Bill. In the flickering dark, his bristled hair, deep eyes and long nose had slowly become Carlo's. Careless, cocky and quick to anger as he was, who would have covered Carlo with blankets when his luck ran out or passed a flask to ease his dying?

"Hard as all that?" Molly asked. "A lot of blood?"

"He reminded me of my brother."

"Ah," she said and set the dinner tray aside.

Later that morning Dr. Windham sent back a letter of recommendation for the Pacific Dispensary. Molly folded it carefully in my book while I stared out the window into the rainy dark above the Rocky Mountains.

Fourteen

IN THE DISPENSARY

The storm weakened and snow patches shrank as we neared Sacramento. After days of fried steak and old potatoes, we dove into the apples, oranges, and huge purple grapes that farmers sold at the stations, ravenous for the color, sweetness and juicy crispness of fresh foods. "California!" cried Molly, lofting a gleaming orange. "Where gold grows on trees." If only Zia could have seen this land.

We reached San Francisco on a clear bright day in November 1883. Flecks of foam sprinkled the blue bay and soft hills surrounded us like waves of green velvet. The city's gaudy bustle thrilled us both, but *Scribner's* hadn't mentioned the dizzying prices out on America's rim. The rich reaped boundless profits from mining, timber, hides and shipping. But how did the poor live here? In the hulks of rotting ships moored in the bay, men and even women rented berths for the night. The Italian blocks of North Beach were clogged with newcomers from Genoa and Calabria. We found no boardinghouses that were hiring and not even any decent rooms to rent.

I suggested we spend our first night on the ships, but Molly refused: "I didn't come so far to sleep with drunks and sailors." We rested on Market Street, sharing a loaf of soured bread that the baker swore was the finest in the world and in any case was all he had. "We only need *one room*," Molly repeated. "One room in a decent boarding-house where I can work and do my business and the landlady won't notice that I'm buying her out. That shouldn't be hard to find, if it wasn't for these hills," she said, panting. "I hope you're liking them, Irma Vitale," she said, grasping my arm on a steep ascent. "Because they can go to the devil for all of me."

At last we found a boardinghouse near Van Ness Avenue, roughly made and still unpainted. Room and board cost twice what I paid in Chicago, but the Irish widow who owned it needed a girl to cook and clean, and agreed that if I helped in the evenings, she'd charge me two dollars less each week. By the third day Mrs. Sullivan wondered aloud how she had survived without Molly's skillful economies and two-handed cleaning. She even paid me to make new curtains for the par-lor, but refused Molly's suggestion to buy the adjoining house and expand the dining room to serve more men. "If the lady's got no gumption, why not stay home in Donegal?" Molly grumbled.

Yet by the end of the first week she had gained one more conces-sion: Mrs. Sullivan let Molly rent space to store furniture she could sell to newcomers. The linens Molly brought from Chicago fetched such high prices that they nearly paid her passage west. "Now I start saving for a boardinghouse," she said, buying a fresh calendar for her San Francisco plan.

My own plan proved more difficult. The morning after we came to San Francisco, I put on a clean, pressed dress. With letters from Vittorio and Doctor Windham and Sofia's record book under my arm,

I walked to the Pacific Dispensary on Taylor Street, confident I could present these letters, ask to enroll and certainly be admitted. I would fit as easily into the school as a sleeve sets into a well-cut bodice.

"May I speak with Dr. Bucknell?" I asked a servant who answered my knock, the first Chinaman I had ever seen. Gravely astonished that I had no appointment, he left me in an antechamber thick with potted palms and ferns and glided away on felt-soled slippers. He had offered no chair, so I stood, straining to unravel words wafting from a nearby classroom. I caught only "sepsis" and then "thrombosis" before clicking heels announced an elegant woman in a starched shirtwaist dress fastened with a line of brass buttons as small as nails. A sleek gray pompadour perched on her head.

"I am Mrs. Robbins," she announced. "Dr. Bucknell's assistant. The doctor is in Denver, but you may tell me your business with the dispensary."

"My name is Irma Vitale. I've come to study nursing. I have—"

"Unfortunately, young lady, courses have already begun. You might apply for the next term. You have a high-school diploma, I presume."

"No, madam, but I can read English."

A thin eyebrow arched up. "Perhaps, then, you might have read our requirements and saved yourself the journey."

"I thought—"

"Ah, but a good nurse does not 'think,' she knows."

I had not felt so much a greenhorn since begging Mrs. Clayburn for work. "Here are two letters of recommendation and our clinic record book," I persisted.

"In *Italian*," Mrs. Robbins observed curtly, glancing at Sofia's fine script. I reminded her of Sofia's correspondence with Dr. Bucknell.

"What other work can you do, miss?" she asked, her voice just barely edged with kindness.

"Fine dressmaking and embroidery."

"Excellent. There is a great need for your kind in the city. You could go to high school in the evenings and get a diploma."

"When may I speak with Dr. Bucknell?"

"Perhaps next week, or the week after," said Mrs. Robbins. "And now if you'll excuse me, Miss Vitale, my students require me." She turned crisply and clicked away, the gray pompadour disappearing behind a high palm.

I went to the dispensary the next week and the next, but still Dr. Bucknell had not returned. On my third visit, Mrs. Robbins offered me a job scrubbing tables, washing bandages and tools, sweeping and cooking: servants' work. But I would be carefully observed and perhaps judged worthy to enter the school "at some later date" without a high-school diploma. "Given your persistence, we *may* stretch a point," she conceded. Yes, I told her, I would take the job.

On Market Street I bought a small notebook that fit in my apron pocket, two Dixon lead pencils and a small penknife to sharpen them. That way, I explained to Molly, I could copy every word on the blackboards before washing them, bits of lessons overheard, the names of tools and labeled bones of a skeleton dangling in the classroom. I bought a dictionary on Market Street and began translating Sofia's records into English. When Dr. Bucknell returned, I would be ready.

Despite the long hours of those days, there were pleasures in San Francisco. On weekends Molly and I explored the city, drinking its beauty in gulps: the grand new houses on Nob Hill, gardens brimming with vivid bougainvillea, bright winter sunlight twinkling on late roses and elegant Spaniards on horseback. South and east of the city, fruit trees and vineyards fingered through the hills. We watched fog lift over the blue basin of San Francisco Bay, revealing lush green islands and took streetcars out to the wild ocean edge, which reminded Molly of Ireland but brought back the *Servia* for me. Gustavo's face rose over the waves, I heard his voice in the steady breeze and felt the cool slickness of the whalebone he carved for me.

"There are plenty of sailors here," Molly scoffed, "and you know where *they* go." Yes, I had seen them hurrying off their ships and streaming into taverns, brothels, opium dens and gambling halls in the squalid blocks along the bay called the Barbary Coast. They caused little enough trouble in the rest of the city, she reminded me. "Everything they want is in Barbary. And supposing his ship did just happen to dock in San Francisco? What then, Irma? Would he even remember you?"

The next day, at the dispensary, folding strips of gauze into bandages for hours, I imagined Gustavo coming down the gangplank, dropping his sea bag and blinking in the sun. He would know me, even in my American clothes with a new-fashioned fringe of curls on my forehead. "Irma!" he would say. "How well you look. Why didn't you answer my letter?" And I would explain that thieves had stolen my envelope with his address. "Never mind," he would say, "let's walk in the city." And we would wander through Nob, Telegraph and Russian Hills and gaze across the windy strait at the rolling green of the Marin Headlands. I would smell the salt on his sea coat and we would walk at night by the water. He would be nothing like a Barbary sailor.

I decided to go to the port and see if, by wild chance, the *Servia* ever docked in San Francisco. Early the next morning, the port resounded with fishermen's shouts, the banging of boats returning with the morning catch, seagulls cawing and barefoot boys clamoring for work.

Italian women from North Beach swarmed the wharf, seeking broken crabs or scraps of fish to fashion into a poor man's stew they called *cioppino*.

I found the harbormaster in a tiny office cramped with charts, maps and logbooks heaped in nets hung from the wall. A telegraph receiver commanded one clear island of space on his desk. He was a big man with a peg leg and shaggy mustache that mimed the tilt of his body.

He looked me up and down before answering my query. "The *Servia*," he repeated, scratching his bristling hair. "The *Servia*, the *Servia*, yes, she docks here every year or so. Just sent word from Buenos Aires." His eyes swept the office as if he might spy out news in the jungled heaps of paper. "You're expecting a shipment?" His quizzical look said I was hardly a fine enough lady to be ordering goods by ship.

"I'm expecting—someone."

"Ah, a sweetheart?" That strange American term: *sweetheart*. My sweet heart. Carlo would laugh and even Zia would ask if Americans ate each other's hearts.

"A friend," I said stiffly.

"Well then, let's see when your *friend* might be coming." He fished a logbook from the swinging net, discarded it for another, and ran his finger along closely written lines. "Telegraph transcripts," he announced, shoving a pipe through brushy lips. "Some wire ahead, some don't, some change course, like this one," he jabbed a line, "headed here, then lit out to Australia. You've heard much about Australia, miss?" I shook my head impatiently. "Got those queer kangaroos, big as mules and jump like rabbits. Birds taller than a man. You have to wonder about their rats, no?"

"The *Servia*, sir."

"I'm getting there, yes: the *Servia* out of New York, docked in Rio de Janeiro, then Buenos Aires, left three months ago to round the Cape of Good Hope, call in San Francisco and out to the Sandwich Islands."

"When will she be here?"

"Ah, that we don't know. Like I say, some ships change course. If sailors jump ship in Rio, the captain has to hire new ones. If the ship is damaged rounding the Cape, and a lot of them are, there's repairs that take time. They may have to wait for supplies. I could keep an ear out for news, if you know what I mean." I set a quarter on his desk. He didn't move and I added another. Then he swept both into his pocket. "Fine, then, miss, come back in a fortnight. I may know something more about your—friend."

I walked to the dispensary, heart thudding with joy, until Molly's warning voice seeped into my head like smoke. Suppose Gustavo didn't remember me? How many times had he stood on decks with peasant girls? Suppose on land he was indeed only another sailor, hungry for whores and rum? By lucky chance the next two weeks left little time for supposing.

Dr. Bucknell returned unexpectedly, greeted me kindly as I cleaned the laboratory and listened to grudging good reports of my work from Mrs. Robbins. The next day the doctor called me to her office, where a file of Sofia's letters sat on her desk. "An excellent clinician. Largely self-taught but fine instincts. You were her assistant? Tell me about that." I described our clinic and house visits, our infection controls and record keeping. Dr. Bucknell listened thoughtfully.

"So, you have an excellent start. With Mrs. Robbins's good report, I believe we can make an exception and have you enroll next year without a high-school diploma. Please, sit down and have some tea," she said kindly, but I didn't sit.

"Dr. Bucknell, I would like to enroll *now*. I believe I am prepared." I took a breath. "The bones of the cranium are the ethmoid, frontal, occipital, two parietals, sphenoid and two temporals. The axial skeleton is formed by the vertebral column of twenty-six bones and—"

Dr. Bucknell set down her teacup. "I see, an oral examination. Well then, let us proceed. The spine?" I named the bones of the spine, the pelvis and legs and described the primary digestive organs and structure of the heart. She had me fold a sling for a broken arm and give the symptoms for malaria. I explained why babies might be born blue and how to effect a dilation of the uterus. Nails dug my hand as I described Dr. Sim's curette, but I relaxed when she asked about care of the stump after an amputation.

Dr. Bucknell returned to her tea. "My compliments, Miss Vitale. It seems we must find someone else to clean for us. I will tell Mrs. Robbins to expect you in the morning for lessons. Welcome to the Pacific Dispensary."

I flew home to tell Molly. We celebrated that night in a tavern with separate rooms for ladies. In the morning I dove into my lessons, drunk with all I was learning.

Fifteen

THE STRAITS

Rains swept in from the Pacific that season, storm after storm. I splashed to school in men's boots. The morning of the second week, thinking the harbormaster might have news of the *Servia*, I went to the port at dawn. The rain had paused to a misty drizzle and fishing boats returning brought a chorus of famished gulls. The harbormaster shouted over their cries. "The *Servia*? Yes, miss, I do have news. Come inside."

Yes, like a simple fact. Gustavo might be coming. *Some* sailors must be good men, the same on land as they were at sea. The harbormaster shuffled papers, pulled at his mustache and cleared his throat. Another fishing boat docked and the gulls cawed wildly. "You have news of the *Servia*, sir?"

"Yes I do. Unfortunately, miss, she was lost in an ice storm off the Straits of Magellan, down at the hook of South America. It's a devil's own passage even in summer. A cargo ship out of Liverpool saw her go down." His words tossed like gulls in my head.

"Saw her go down?"

"Sank, miss, destroyed. The cargo captain tried to approach but was driven back by high seas. He reported no survivors."

"Weren't there lifeboats?"

"She went too fast. Sometimes it's like that, miss. No time at all."

"But the *Servia* was a stout ship. Crossing from Naples we were three days in a storm."

"Begging your pardon, but that was the *North* Atlantic. These waves," he peered at the closely written report, "were sixty feet high. Yonder there, you see the *Rosa Marie?* That's twice her mainmast." I followed the line of his finger and gasped. "Any man thrown free would freeze in those waters or be pounded to death in one 'Our Father.' I'm sorry, miss. So it *was* your sweetheart on board?"

I didn't answer, only thanked the harbormaster and left. No, Gustavo was not my sweetheart, hardly even a friend, only a hope, a sweetening of the heart, a dream dashed in rough waters. When Zia Carmela died, no one thought it strange to mourn her. But my past with Gustavo was as thin as voile, fragile as the drawings he sent me that I had so briefly. Mourning such a dream would surely be daft, as Americans said, but still I felt chill, despite the rising sun, shorn as a sheep in the springtime. I walked aimlessly in the port, passing sailors with their sea bags and a man meeting his family, just arrived on a passenger ship from the East Coast. The children leaped and chattered, bursting with stories of their sea adventures, the parents walking slowly together, arms entwined. How easily death could snatch one of these, even in their youth and strength, and how great their grief would be. Better to move alone and bear the chill. I made my way to the dispensary.

"Bad news from home?" Dr. Bucknell asked kindly at the start of our lesson.

How to explain the loss of what was never mine? "No," I lied, "only a bit of indisposition."

"Miss Miller, would you get some subnitrate of bismuth for Miss Vitale?" she asked Susanna, a round-faced young woman from Texas. Properly dosed, I took a seat behind a larger girl, where I might be less observed and tended.

We began the next lesson: washing and feeding the bedridden patient. Bent over my notebook, I imagined howling winds in the Straits of Magellan. Did Gustavo see that last wave arc over the *Servia's* mast? Did he stare into the wild ocean's mouth as Jonah gaped at the swallowing whale? Still limping, could he find purchase on ice-caked decks?

"Miss Vitale! We were speaking of bedsores." Startled back to the room, I described how in Opi we sometimes put sheepskins under the very old to cheat the sores a little longer.

"An excellent folk practice," commended Dr. Bucknell. "And now Miss McClaren—"

Hard as it was to lose Sofia, I had touched her still body and cool face and heard the mourners' thanks and remembrances. If I ever went to Opi and spoke of Carlo, others I knew would remember him too. "Yes," they might say, "remember how he went after that wolf? Remember his last fight with Gabriele at the tavern?" Someone might have seen him gathering wild herbs for our mother. My Carlo was Opi's Carlo and if he was lost to me, he was lost to us all. Who could mourn Gustavo with me now? He was like a polished stone held in my pocket for so long that he seemed familiar. But what did I truly know of him? What little he shared of his life might have been just a story. Even the whalebone he might not have carved himself. Was he, as Molly often said, only my excuse to avoid risking stares or indifference at dances, my stubborn proof that the few good men were far away at sea?

The lesson over, I hurried away before Dr. Bucknell could ask about my indisposition and walked home dodging muddy water thrown up by wagons barreling through puddled streets. The collar girl's litany hissed in my ears: *cut, sew, work.* What was left for me now? *Read, study, nurse the sick.* When the road heaved up, I bent into the driving rain, thinking of those who first climbed to Opi and claimed it as their own.

"Did the harbormaster know anything?" Molly asked after dinner.

"The *Servia* was lost in the Straits of Magellan."

Molly stopped her washing. "Perhaps he was on another ship."

"Perhaps." But I couldn't spend my life at the port waiting for ships. I would work, simply work as Sofia had done. Healing and the company of healers would be sufficient for my life. Sufficient and good, I repeated, drawing my blankets up against the cold wet of the night. It would be days before I slept in my bed again.

Sixteen

An Obstruction

In the morning, while Mrs. Robbins continued our anatomy drills, Dr. Bucknell called me to translate for a patient doubled over in her office. "She's Italian, we know that much," said Dr. Bucknell. "The complexion is sallow, as you see, the pulse elevated and she manifests considerable abdominal pain."

I drew my chair close to the young woman, who seemed to be my age and wore the plain cotton dress of a factory girl. She said her name was Francesca De Santis and she worked at Mr. Levi's factory on Battery Street, sewing pockets onto the trousers that people called blue jeans. Her accent rippled through me and I nearly wept for joy. She was from Abruzzo and seemed freshly in America, still bearing the smell of our earth and savor of our bread.

"Family here?" Dr. Bucknell had me ask.

"No one now," Francesca said. "I came last month to join my sister, but she had already died of pneumonia."

When I gave my condolence and said that I was alone in America too, she leaned closer, as if tasting my words. "How long have you been in this country, Francesca?" I asked.

"Who are you?" she whispered.

"Irma Vitale of Opi. I am a student here."

"Opi?" she breathed. "So close. I'm from Scanno."

Scanno! "On a clear day we see your village."

"And we see Opi." Buttons of sweat crowded her brow as she stretched a pale hand toward mine. I grasped it.

"When you're better, Francesca, we'll talk about home. We'll—"

Dr. Bucknell coughed lightly. "Symptoms?"

"Francesca, the doctor asks where it hurts you."

She pointed to her belly below the navel, but the finger wavered. "There. But it moves, like a snake, hot."

I translated for Dr. Bucknell, whose pen scratched over a blast of laughter from the street below us. "So the pain shifts locus. See if the tongue is coated." It was. "Ask what treatment she has had so far."

"I tried mustard water to bring vomiting and then a man at the factory said I should swallow bullets."

"Bullets?" I gasped. "*Lead bullets?*"

"Yes, he said the weight would push out an obstruction. I took them and walked home, but then I must have fainted. Someone brought me here."

Dr. Bucknell threw down her pen when I translated. "Idiots! Pure idiots! Never mind, let's get her to bed. We'll try to treat without operating." Yes, Sofia always said that to open the belly makes a gaping door to infection.

Francesca tugged me closer. "Irma," she whispered, "there's blood when I pass water."

I translated for Dr. Bucknell, whose muttered "huh" shot a wave of terror across the pale face. Sofia had never shown the slightest jolt at any patient's story. Now Francesca gripped me with desperate strength. "Will I die? Will I see Scanno again? I promised Mamma I'd come back."

"We'll take care of you. You'll see Scanno again."

Francesca closed her eyes.

I whispered to Dr. Bucknell. "We can help her, can't we? She'll live?"

"Be careful of promises, Miss Vitale," said Dr. Bucknell. "We'll do our best."

With Susanna I helped Francesca into a linen shift and had her eat a little broth. We applied poultices to the abdomen and dosed her with calomel, sodium bicarbonate and pepsin. We gave morphine for pain and woke her to pass urine streaked with bloody ribbons. The lead bullets never emerged. I brushed her hair and sang an Opi song, but with each passing hour she drifted further into a private world of pain.

In the morning Dr. Bucknell called the students to Francesca's bed, explained the symptoms and had them prod the belly to feel its heat and tightness. "There is an obstruction and massive infection," she explained in the next room. "Possibly in the appendix."

"What is the treatment?" Susanna asked.

"Generally, opium to ease the patient into death. However we can try, at least, to drain off the worst of the infection. She's young and her body may expel the rest. I have summoned Mr. Benjamin."

A plump, dapper young man soon presented himself with a gauze-topped jar of leeches moving languidly in the clouded water. "The very finest specimens, imported from France," Mr. Benjamin boasted. "My last of this shipment and exquisitely famished. Each one is fifty cents." He examined Francesca, sounded and smelled her. "She may require ten," he warned.

"Then apply ten, sir," said Dr. Bucknell. "And quickly, please."

Mr. Benjamin reached in the jar and pulled out a leech, which he laid on Francesca's belly, holding gently until its head burrowed into the taut skin. He attached another and another until she was draped with pulsing black ribbons. "They will eat for an hour," he said and produced a slim book of poetry that he proceeded to read as his charges swelled to thick fingers. Francesca murmured but did not wake. When the leeches ceased to pulse, he plucked them off easily and dropped them into a wooden box. He would empty them in our cesspit, Dr. Bucknell explained. High-quality leech masters used fresh beasts for each patient. "They have done their job well," Mr. Benjamin said.

In fact there was some flattening of the belly and the skin did seem to soften. Francesca awoke and asked for water in a voice that was nearly her own. "Rest now," Dr. Bucknell told us. "We may need you later." I put a chair by Francesca's bed and finally closed my eyes.

By midnight, Francesca's moaning cut me from sleep. The tiny wounds were spitting pus and the dark, swollen belly was ghastly. I sent Susanna racing for Dr. Bucknell, who examined Francesca and then stepped sadly back. "Too much infection," she sighed. "If it continues, she will die."

"More leeches?" I suggested.

"No, they've done all they can. I have just read an account by Dr. Morton of Philadelphia of a grocer with similar symptoms. He too, attempted a cure with leeches. When they did not suffice, he opened the abdomen, cleaned it of pus, tied off and removed the appendix. The next patient treated thus did not survive, but the grocer was utterly cured. We must operate. It is our only chance for this girl. Try to get her consent."

I woke Francesca and explained what the doctor had said. "No," she gasped. "My father died from cutting. I saw him." She clenched my smock. "Get Mamma. Oh Irma, it hurts so much."

"Francesca, please let us try. The doctor is very skilled."

A wave of pain convulsed her. "Make it stop, Irma! Make—stop."

"Let us operate." The wild hands flailed. "Francesca, it's your only chance."

She found my arm again and gripped it. "You'll stay with me, Irma?"

"Yes, I'll be right here, but please let the doctor operate."

She nodded and closed her eyes, still gripping my hand.

"Miss Vitale?"

"She consents."

Dr. Bucknell studied the account from Philadelphia again as Susanna and I sterilized tools, prepared the operating table and washed Francesca's belly. Other students filed into the room and pressed against the walls, hands over their mouths.

"Phew, worse than a cesspit," one of them whispered.

"Miss Miller," said Dr. Bucknell severely, "there is no cause to dwell on the obvious."

Francesca's lips moved in prayer. After she crossed herself I took her hand as Dr. Bucknell brought the glass tube of the ether chamber to her mouth and had her breathe deeply. When a pinprick brought no response, Dr. Bucknell poised a scalpel over the taut belly. "We'll begin," she said, "and proceed as quickly as possible."

The cut gaped open, a terrible mouth. Foul streams of corruption drained into basins that Susanna handed to students who hurried them away. How could such corruption be within a body and that body live? "The bullets," Dr. Bucknell muttered, dropping three into a basin where they rattled like cherry pits. In the pulsing red mass, she found the appendix, tied it off with silk thread, then removed it neatly and closed the aperture with tiny stitches.

"Warm water," she ordered, and Susanna brought a beaker. "Gauze." She mopped the oozing blood and then folded back the skin. "Miss Vitale, you may finish," said Dr. Bucknell, and directed my first abdominal suture. When I had tied off the last stitch, she stepped away from the table and Susanna removed her blood-splattered jacket. "Now all we can do is to keep her comfortable. Give morphine for pain. We are in the hands of the Almighty."

At first Francesca slept quietly. Her heart pumped more strongly, her breathing slowed and the fever declined. "These are good signs. I'll record our procedures and then rest awhile," said Dr. Bucknell. "Wake me if I'm needed."

I sat by Francesca, holding her hand. "You'll see Scanno," I whispered. "You'll see your mother." I convinced myself that she was better, that with her quickening breath she was surely fighting infection. When she shivered, I laid a blanket over her and then another, closed the window and stoked the coal fire.

"Irma," said Susanna when she came to relieve me, "blankets won't help now." She clamped my hand over Francesca's wrist and I felt the racing pulse.

"Her heart is pumping," I insisted frantically. "She's stronger, no?"

"Irma, step away," said Susanna gently and rang the bell for help. Someone opened the window and dampened the fire. Someone else brought whiskey and said that I must drink it. Dr. Bucknell hurried in. As if watching a dumb play, I saw Susanna leave and return with a priest, who touched Francesca's brow with holy oil, prayed and left.

Her breath came in puffs now. Blue tinged her hands and the rim of her face. Once she opened her eyes and whispered: "Mamma."

"Francesca, come back," I called wildly, but the only answer was a terrible slow gurgle deep in the throat. A cable car rattled by. There were shouts from late drinkers in the tavern, dogs barking and boys playing stickball. Somewhere in that clatter, Francesca's chest heaved and her pulse eased to nothing. I closed her eyes and stood, reeling. Dr. Bucknell drew me away. "Why?" I demanded. "We followed the procedure. We cleaned everything."

"Surgery is always a risk. Remember, the grocer lived but the next patient died. Still, it was her only chance." She wiped her brow. "Perhaps we were too late."

"She trusted me. I promised she'd go home!"

Dr. Bucknell grasped my hands. "We'll do an autopsy, Irma."

Like the doctors' men. "No. Please, no."

"With an autopsy," she continued calmly, "perhaps we'll learn why we failed. Then we will bury her decently and send a telegram to her family. You know we did our best for her."

I nodded as exhaustion overwhelmed me. At least her mother would know that Francesca had not died among strangers. I made my way home in a cloud of doubt. In Madame's shop we could imagine and sketch a gown, a riding habit, then cut and create it exactly as we imagined. Women were always happy with our work. Cutting into Francesca, we had made her suffer more and uselessly.

"You were unlucky this time, but you helped so many," Molly insisted.

"I promised she'd go home. I promised!"

"Perhaps she did. Perhaps she sees it now."

That night I watched stars slowly pass, praying that Francesca's soul had found its way to Scanno.

Seventeen

BURNING WAVES

In the days after Francesca's funeral, treatments and pieces of anatomy that I knew as well as embroidery stitches flew out of my mind, leaving me mute in lessons and flooded with doubt. Perched at the rim of America, where could I go, what could I do if my nursing dream failed? Meanwhile, in the foul ships moored at the Barbary Coast, men began complaining of abdominal pains, headache and malaise. Newspapers blamed the men's chronic drunkenness but Dr. Bucknell feared typhoid fever. "If you can't concentrate on lessons, Miss Vitale," she said, "you can work in the clinic." Until we knew the certain cause of this sickness, there would be no operations, no cutting or bloodletting, she explained, just keeping the men clean and comfortable in cool, airy darkness. Endlessly sponging the brows of fevered, delirious old miners and vagabonds brought a peculiar rest and calm. If the disease was typhoid, at least the men would not die of a cure I had forced upon them.

On the fourth day I was called to stitch up a carpenter's arm. "Miss Miller could do it," I told Dr. Bucknell.

"It's deep, with risk of infection," she said, "and your antisepsis is better. I'd sew him myself but they're bringing more men from the ships. Suture the carpenter and try to reassure him. He's convinced he'll lose the arm."

Heat lapped over me. "I'm afraid. I promised Francesca and she—"

Dr. Bucknell set her hands on my shoulders. "Just clean the wound well. It's laceration without complications. You know the treatment as well as I. Your Sofia, what would she say?"

"To follow Mr. Lister's measures and sew the carpenter cleanly."

"Well then, do that." She gave me a handkerchief to dry my face. "He's in the waiting room—the red-haired one, but he says that he's Greek."

Rags binding the carpenter's arm were soaked with blood. He was broad shouldered, with wide brown eyes that watched anxiously as I exposed the wound. "You're the Italian?" he asked in English. "The best for sewing, the doctor said."

"Yes, I'm 'the Italian.' I used to be a dressmaker."

The taut face relaxed a little. "A dressmaker? That's good."

The gash ran down most of the length of his arm. I shifted my body to block his view. "What is your name?" I asked over my shoulder.

"Niko Pappas, from the island of Kos, in Greece. And yours?" He peeked around me at the wound. "It's bad, no? Very deep."

"My name is Irma Vitale. It's deep, but clean at least. How did this happen? Sit back, please, and tell me."

"My partner and I were working on Sacramento Street. The scaffolding collapsed and I fell through a window." Niko grasped my arm with his free hand. "There was a German on our crew with a smaller cut than this. They stitched him up and at first he was fine, but then the arm turned black and he lost it. Miss Vitale, carpentry is my work."

Be careful of promises. "I'll do my best, Niko. I promise you that. Shall we close the wound?" When he nodded, red curls bounced on the moist forehead. "If you like, I'll explain what I'm doing."

"Yes, please." He brushed back his hair.

"I'm scrubbing my hands and arms with lye soap." I scrubbed them red. "Now I set fresh linen on the table. The suturing thread will touch no unclean surface. Now the needle is sterilized. Do you want someone to hold your arm?" He shook his head. "Then I'll strap it down, swab the skin with extract of cocoa leaves to dull the pain and plan the stitches . . . Shall we begin?"

"Yes. Tell me about your home," he said, turning toward the window and gripping the chair with his free hand. I described Opi, how small our village was and in what a forgotten corner of Abruzzo. I spoke of our sheep, our wine and cheese, the little piazza around our church and the view from our mountain at sunset.

The hand on the chair released. The coca was working. "Kos is also very small, with a small name, but it too is very beautiful."

"Tell me about Kos."

I bent over the arm as he described whitewashed houses perched by a blue sea, the fragrance of lemon groves and ripe figs and everywhere the dusty green of olive trees. Our *neighbors'* olive trees," he added sharply, turning from the window to me. "Where did you learn dressmaking?"

"In Chicago."

"And your dresses were beautiful?"

"The customers thought so." The stitching was half done. "It will scar. I'm sorry."

"That doesn't matter if the arm is good. Dresses have seams, no? And wood joins to wood in a seam, no?"

"I never thought of that."

"America is a grand country for wood, you know." I nodded, bent over my work. "Have you walked in redwood forests, across on the ferry to Marin and up the coast?"

"No, not yet."

Dr. Bucknell walked quietly into the room as Niko described misty groves of trees born before Christ, wide as a house and higher than any cathedral. Twelve men could stand on a cut tree and the fresh wood was a deep burnished red.

"Like your hair?" I asked without thinking.

He smiled broadly. "Perhaps yes. And yours is like oak."

"Nearly finished. Three, two, one." I snipped the last thread. No line of my stitching in skin had ever been finer.

"Excellent work," pronounced Dr. Bucknell. "Have him return next week to remove the sutures."

"Could Miss Vitale do it?" Niko asked.

The steady gaze of the wide brown eyes was too pressing and warm. "The others need practice," I reminded Dr. Bucknell.

"That's true," she agreed hurriedly, for Mrs. Robbins was calling her. I bandaged the arm, explained how often to change the dressings, and gave him fresh gauze. When he struggled to put on his jacket, I helped but quickly stepped away.

"Your face is red," Susanna whispered when I passed her in the hallway. "What's wrong?"

"Nothing."

"What happened at the dispensary?" Molly asked that evening.

"Nothing. It was an ordinary day."

"Well, it wasn't ordinary here. Mrs. Sullivan and I are buying the house next door. I found an Italian bank that will loan us money. You don't have to be rich. There was a Greek carpenter ahead of me."

"What was he like?"

Molly glanced at me sharply. "Looked like an ordinary Greek: big, loud, with black hair. Why do you ask?"

"No reason."

"Well then," she said eagerly, "I'll show you the plans." For the rest of the evening, I held my pounding head as Molly explained how she and Mrs. Sullivan would have the two houses connected, enlarging the dining room and thus doubling the number of boarders they could feed from one kitchen. Once the loan was repaid, Molly would be ready to buy her own boardinghouse. When I left her at midnight, she was filling a new calendar with tiny numbers. The stairs to my room seemed as steep as a mountain path. I was too tired for undressing and slept in my clothes with a wet cloth over my brow to ease the pain.

Our patients were worse the next day with more coming nearly every hour. Now even the newspapers spoke of typhoid fever. We washed patients and changed sheets, wearing masks against the foul smell of excrement that looked precisely as Dr. Bucknell termed it: "pea soup diarrhea." During the Crimean War, she reminded us, Florence Nightingale reduced typhoid mortality to 50 percent with improved sanitation. Students were put to boiling sheets, washing chamber pots and even boiling the drinking water. I scanned the rows of moaning men. Which half would die? I held my head. "Miss Vitale," said Dr. Bucknell. "You're exhausted. First Francesca and now these cases. Go home. You need rest. Sisters from the convent on Powell Street are coming to help us."

"But there's work—"

"There's always work. Go home."

Susanna brought my coat and I stepped into the soothing foggy cool of the street, but once I was free of the patients with their constant cries for help, my strength drained away. I walked a few blocks until weariness overwhelmed me and I climbed on the first passing cable car. Afternoon shifts had just ended and jostling sweaty men crowded the car, some already smelling of whiskey and beer. "What happened, dearie?" one asked, his ruddy face pushed toward mine, a blunt finger tracing his cheek. "Cut yourself shaving?" Laughter poured from every mouth. Open as it was, the car breathed heat. Head pounding, I leaned out into the cool.

"Miss Vitale!" cried a voice and I was reined back, strong hands grasping my arms. "Give the lady a seat, you oafs." There was a shuffle and I sank into an open slot between looming shoulders. "It's me, Niko Pappas," said a voice above me. "You stitched my arm, remember? Do you live on Geary Street? Can I take you home?"

"Geary?" I repeated dully. "This is the Geary line?"

"You wanted another one?" The red-topped face came closer, blocking the cool as two arms, one bandaged, corralled me in the rattling car. "Are you lost, miss?" *Are you lost? May I help you?*

"Get back! Don't touch me! You're no policeman!" I shouted. Voices ceased around us and the wide brow furrowed.

"I'm a carpenter. I told you."

But this too could be a lie. The car was slowing for a stop. With a shove I pushed free of the grasping arms and jumped onto the street. The car rattled away with a tear of voice thrown back: "Miss Vitale, wait!" As fog wrapped the car I saw a dark figure leap from it.

"Van Ness?" I demanded of a passing woman and followed the point of her gloved finger, running block after block, then leaning, gasping, against the boardinghouse door. I remember my key rattling in the hole, my feet catching the threshold, the parlor swirling, a little sleep and then Molly's face over mine, angry.

"What's wrong with you? Two decent women were scared out of their wits by you crashing in like that, jabbering away. Now they'll never board here, ever. A man talks to you on a cable car, offers to bring you home and you lose your mind?" She leaned closer, rough hands grasping mine. "Irma, you have to stop being such a peasant."

"I'm sorry, Molly. I lost you—tenants—" The work of speech was too much. I sank back in the horsehair settee and closed my eyes against hot hammers. A hand pressed my forehead.

"Why, you're sick, lass, you're burning up and here I'm railing at you! It's bed you need, come."

Molly must have sent for Dr. Bucknell, for later I heard her voice in the darkened room, then Mrs. Sullivan's: "If it's typhoid, she must go to the dispensary."

And Molly: "With all the sailors and riffraff? I can do for her right here, good as any doctor."

My eyes closed to Dr. Bucknell's voice, her words floating across the bed: "no space in the dispensary . . . too sick to move."

So I could die far from home, like Francesca. "With the best of care, half will die," Dr. Bucknell had said. *Half will die.* The words spun in my head. Feverish and exhausted, I struggled to dodge them.

A scuffle of voices, a door closed and footsteps clattered away as Dr. Bucknell spoke of clean and dark, quinine, purges, calomel, Madeira, pea soup and opium. I slept, woke, and then was neither asleep nor awake, but swirling on burning waves, sliding down flaming walls that frayed into fingers grasping at me. Then I was hollow, purged, cold wet cloths draping my skin. Strong hands, a flash of dry white, the crisp comfort of ironed sheets and then tossed on burning waves again.

"She has to be bled," Mrs. Sullivan was saying. "Feel the pulse, it's too strong."

A man's voice protested in a voice I almost knew.

"Are you a doctor?"

"No."

"A relative of Miss Vitale?"

"Nobody's bleeding nobody," a third voice said sharply, surely Molly's. There was a scuffle of words, heavy footsteps clicking away and then there were two in the room, Molly and a dark, tall shadow moving at her direction. Darkness brought fever, always higher. "Step fever with fever, evening onset," I vaguely remembered from lessons, until words themselves boiled away and every kindly figure faded. Others took their place: my father pulling me to the looking glass as I tried to pull away, caught in an altar cloth, twisted in lace and tangled in fringe. I struggled to beat free. Now hands wrestled me still, like a sheep for shearing. My bed that was soft turned hard as brick, wet and cold. Thieves fell upon me, plucking. Blank faces laughed. Then the stink of wet ash and Jake, the false policeman, pushing, pulling, thrusting, grunting, hissing, "Working girl, greenhorn, filly bitch."

"No!" I screamed. "Let me go." A spoon forced between my teeth brought the sweet tang of opium. At first the faceless crowd still hovered, pointing at my scar, snarling, then slowly it melted into mist, leaving me as thin as a stick stretched on bobbing sea grass. Jacob floated by with Attilio, smiling and waving as I eased away to sleep.

Days and nights passed. Voices came, hands moved and washed me. Slowly the pain in the gut retreated. Once a hard nut was pushed between my lips and a deep voice whispered, "Irma, swallow this."

Molly's voice flared in the room, "What's that, you crazy Greek?"

"Olive pit. It's good for the stomach." Two voices, rising, falling and then fading away, laughing.

That day or the next I began taking broth, then bits of bread in broth. "The fever's stepping down," said Molly. "You had us worried, me and the lad."

"What lad?"

"Sh, sh now, sleep." Dr. Bucknell came, took my pulse and temperature and said the curtains might be opened in the morning. "It's late May, Irma," she said. "The poppies are blooming. You've been sick more than a month." I struggled to sit. "No, not yet, perhaps tomorrow. Look." When she held up my arm I gasped, for it was as thin as a rake and as pale as milk. "You've had good nurses, but now you must eat, get strong again and come back to us."

The next day I did sit, propped on pillows, and fed myself a little barley soup. When I tried my voice it creaked like an old tool long unused, but it was good to see a smile cross Molly's ruddy face. "There's my peasant girl again. Go on, another bit of broth." She sat back and crossed her arms. "So, Irma, that night in Chicago when you didn't come back, you were raped in a burned-out house by a man named Jake who claimed he was a copper. *That's* what you wouldn't say all these months?"

The spoon fell from my fumbling fingers. "How do you know?"

"Because you told us or as much as did, when you were out of your head. I'm your friend, lass. There was no call for such secrets."

"Told *us*?"

"Me and Niko the carpenter. He got this address from your friend Susanna and came every night after work. Don't worry, I had him out of the room when I cleaned you."

"So he knows?" Shame washed over me like fever coming back.

"He's a good man, Irma, not a child. A bit of life won't scare him off."

"What did he say?"

"What any decent soul would say: that the man who hurt you was a beast, that *any* man who hurts a woman is a beast."

"But why would Niko do so much for me? I only stitched his arm. And after the cable car, he must have thought I was crazy."

Molly laughed. "And who's to blame him if he did? So you must have stitched him well. Anyway, he kept coming and kept asking questions."

"About me? And you told him?"

"Of course." She held up a warning finger. "So next time, lass, don't get sick and delirious. He has some drat foolish Greek notions about curing folks, but since you're too weak to go running off again, you'll see him this evening and decide for yourself what sort of man he is." She helped me into a fresh nightshirt. "And listen to me, Irma, there's no call to talk about what he already knows, about that house in Chicago, I mean. Just be easy, like he's one of the lads from your village."

"I never talked to them."

"Right, no talking to lads in Opi. Well then, like he's your old rag-man, Jacob—or that sailor friend from the ship. Get under the sheets. We don't want you catching cold now."

"But Daisy said—"

"Who?" Molly demanded.

I explained who Daisy was and what she said—that no good, decent man would want a woman with humps or scars if he had his pick of those without. So a man who did would have some flaw himself.

"So your Daisy said that, did she? Well, I'm not smart like you and your Dr. Bucknell, but I know some things. First, every decent man knows there's far worse a girl can have besides humps and scars and some of that bad can be inside her. Second, if you're wanting a man that's perfect, you'd better be a holy sister married to Our Lord. But if you're wanting to see who's a good man and who's a beast, well you can use your eyes and ears and find that out yourself."

"Perhaps."

"You and your 'perhaps.' Go to sleep now." I slept and woke and washed myself in the morning and took my first steps since the sickness.

Eighteen

ALESSANDRO'S BREAD

Niko came that evening with lemons. He cut and squeezed them into a cup and had me drink the juice although Molly rolled her eyes. He showed me his arm. The cut was healing well. "Miss Miller took out the stitches," he said, "but lemon juice helped the healing. My partner Carl was jealous when he heard that a fine dressmaker had sewn me." Niko's smile was as warm and wide as sunrise. He touched his cheek. "Molly said you were hurt on the ship."

His voice was so calm and the question so frank that I told him as I had told no one else of the Serbian girls, the shouts and accusations, how I was pushed, fell and torn on the face, and how Teresa held the jagged edges together all night long.

"So the scar came of friendship, then. You can wear it proudly."

My face flushed hot and I turned to the window. Gaslights glimmered from the street. "Do you like San Francisco?" I asked.

"The hills remind me of home."

I spoke of Cleveland and Chicago and how their flatness seemed so foreign. He nodded. "As if the hand of God could wipe you off the earth?" Yes, exactly so.

Molly brought us tea and worked quietly on her calendar. I asked Niko how he came to America.

He stared out the window. "Did your family have olive trees, Irma?"

"Everyone in Opi had at least a few, except for the goat boy and the beggars."

"Yes, exactly, the beggars. My father gambled away our olive trees one by one. For a time, when the French vineyards were failing, we had a market for our wine, but when the French got new grape stock, they wanted their own, of course. My father left us and my older brothers went to sea and sent money home to our mother. There was no work in Kos except day labor in our neighbors' orchards. I couldn't stay. You understand, Irma, loving a place where you can't stay?"

I nodded and in her corner Molly bit her lip and nodded too.

"An uncle with a merchant ship hired me to help his carpenter."

"Why did you come to America?"

"I was curious about the trees. The old carpenter talked about American forests full of cherry, maple, and every kind of oak, ash and beech. I wanted to see them. So I saved money for a ship to New York, where I learned English and apprenticed myself to a German cabinet-maker, a good man, a very good man. He wanted to see the redwoods, so we took the train to California last summer."

"Did he like them?"

Niko's hand followed the wood grain of my night table. "Ernst died on the train in Iowa. I kissed his two eyes and took him to an undertaker who let me build the coffin. After the funeral I kept going west. So now I'm here."

"Do you miss Kos?"

"Everyone's gone. My father sold our fields. There's nothing in Kos for me now. Perhaps it's like that for you in Opi?"

"Perhaps, yes. But still—"

"Yes, I know—still. I miss our honey flavored with wild thyme. I miss the wind and the sound of our windmills. There are sandy beaches in the north of our island where I swam with my brothers, and an old Roman mosaic of Europa being carried over the sea on a bull. I miss the taste of our food and the sound of my people talking, the songs from our village. Is it like that for you?"

"Yes." I told him of Francesca, who had come from so close to Opi but died before we could talk of home.

Molly put down her calendar. "It's late, Niko," she said. "And Irma has to sleep."

Niko left, promising to return, and Molly helped me bind my hair for sleeping. I grasped her hand. "Thank you, Molly. You did so much for me when I was sick."

"Well, yes, there *was* a lot to do, and not all of it pretty. I'd never do it for a stranger. But you'd do the same for me, no, even if you weren't a nurse?"

"Of course."

"So then," she said briskly, "we won't talk about it. Sleep and get well and go back to your dispensary. You know, we've got nineteen boarders now and more coming from the Levi factory."

"That's good, that's very good," I said, half asleep already.

Three days later I was well enough to go to the dispensary. The students, Dr. Bucknell and even Mrs. Robbins welcomed me back. All the typhoid cases had died or recovered and we had a quiet week of study. Niko came every evening and walked me home. As I grew stronger we took longer and longer routes, at first avoiding the hills and then seeking them out. My appetite returned and once we stopped at a North Beach trattoria where a cook from Genoa brought us deep bowls of cioppino. Niko described his mother's fish stews and her soups made with greens he gathered from the fields. We had bread and it was good, but not like our bread from home. I spoke of Assunta, the tang of her dough and the warmth of her loaves in winter. I described how Zia Carmela and I had pushed my father to court her. "I was making an altar cloth," I began. Then memories of my father stopped my mouth.

In the silence, Niko took a lemon from his pocket. "When I was a boy," he said casually, "we used to cut lemons in quarters like this, close our eyes and try to taste the sweetness inside the sour. Here, Irma, you try." He put a lemon quarter in my hand. "Close your eyes." I sucked and found the curl of sweetness, like the first layer of spring warmth inside the chill of a late winter day. He sat quietly stacking lemon peels and then easing our talk to my work in the dispensary and the furniture he dreamed of making.

When the trattoria closed, we walked a long time through the quiet streets up Nob Hill and then Pacific Heights, watching moonlight graze the city as we shared stories. He told me of the tree, in whose shade Hippocrates taught, that now was so big that fifty men could not girdle it with their outstretched arms.

"Fifty men?" I repeated.

He smiled. "Well, fifty small men."

Molly pulled open the boardinghouse door as I fumbled for my key. "You're late, I was worried," she fussed, until she caught sight of Niko's red hair gleaming in the gaslight. "Ah, I see. It's midnight, you know, Irma."

"We had dinner and then we were—talking about Hippocrates."

"Were you now? And such a valuable subject *that* was. There's a dance at my church next Saturday night," she called to Niko. "Instead of keeping her out in the night air, you two might come along with me."

We did go with Molly and managed a waltz, but when we tried to follow the caller for a contra dance, my feet tangled with Niko's. I stumbled and as he caught me, his lips brushed my scar. "Shall we wait for a waltz?" he asked.

"Yes," I said, and we stood outside in the warm night, arms entwined, barely speaking. Back at the boardinghouse, Molly watched me slowly brush out my hair and observed: "You enjoyed the dance, didn't you, Irma? Was I right to have you come?"

"Yes, Molly," I admitted. "You were right."

Everything was right. Spring eased into a summer of soaring blue skies. The hills sparkled with wildflowers. I often helped Dr. Bucknell with her surgeries and studied for a diploma from an American high school. Zia Carmela would have been proud. Niko found work with a fine cabinetmaker from Boston. I floated in those days, filled with bright air.

Early in July, Niko met me at the dispensary after classes. "Come with me to North Beach," he said, "I have something to show you." We wound past peddlers on Columbus Avenue and then turned onto Union. "Now close your eyes and smell," he ordered as he led me past what was surely a poultry shop, then a fishmonger's and next a café. "Almost," he said, "here on the left," he said, and now I knew we had entered a bakery.

"Welcome. Please sit down, Signorina Irma Vitale of Opi. We have been waiting for you," said a warm voice in my own Abruzzo dialect.

My eyes flew open. A stocky, wide-mouthed baker stood before me, beaming.

"This is Alessandro Mancini," said Niko proudly. "I had him make your bread." Alessandro put a loaf in my hands, round and warm. Yes, here was the same satisfying weight of the loaf and gentle crackle of crust. I wiped my eyes and broke off a piece, filling my hand.

"Taste it, Irma," urged Alessandro. I did, slowly savoring the spongy warm tang, rich with the salty sweetness of home. I closed my eyes again, remembering our table, my mother's thick lentil soup and the slice of bread she put at my place. "When bread is fresh like this," she used to say, "and you close your eyes, you can taste the sun on the grain that made it."

"This Greek of yours wanted it warm when he brought you," the baker was saying. "I make bread as my father did; even my oven's exactly the same."

"It's good, Alessandro. It's so good."

Niko took my hand. "Shall we go now, Irma? You can take the loaf."

We walked out to the bay and sat watching the waves in a cradling wedge of rock, our hands laced together, as close as if there were no seam between us. As the first bands of violet streaked the hills, Niko took my other hand and asked, "Irma, should we go back again for more of Alessandro's bread?"

"Yes."

"Should we go often? And go walking and even to dances sometimes?"

"Yes," I said, "we should do that."

"For the rest of our lives, Irma?" He laid his hand on my face.

"Yes," I whispered, "for the rest of our lives."

"Perhaps, then, we should be married."

"Yes, Niko, we should do that."

We kissed. It was the bright sweetness of lemons, the warmth of fresh bread and the comfort of home after a long voyage. As the first stars glimmered over the bay, joy filled my chest, more joy than seemed possible in this world.

We were married four months later in the parlor of Molly's new boardinghouse. It was a bright clear day in the fall of 1884. Hélène, Simone and Lune sent a damask wedding dress. "Come visit us soon in Chicago," they wrote, "and show us your Greek." Jacob and his sisters sent ribbons for my hair and a fine velvet vest for Niko. From Vittorio and Claudia came a pair of crystal goblets. Assunta and my father sent a letter wishing us joy and a cameo brooch that had been my mother's. Alessandro baked the sweet lemon wedding cake and trays of rich biscotti. With Molly's Irish friends, Niko's Greeks, all our boarders and students from the dispensary, dozens of raised glasses toasted our joy.

Nineteen

L'AMERICANA

Six years later, the lemon trees we had planted behind our house south of the city brimmed with fruit and we had packed our first olives in brine. I was sitting outside with our daughter Sofia in late spring when Molly arrived in her carriage.

"Aunt Molly, hurry!" the child called out. "Mamma's telling about my great-great grandfather's boots in the snow."

"Again?" Molly sniffed, settling herself in a chair I brought out from the house. "Why bother the poor child with Old Country tales? They're nearly as bad as Niko's crazy goddess yarns. Here's something better for my favorite four-year-old, brand new from the East Coast. Come here, Sofia, but mind my new dress. Lovely, isn't it, Irma?" she demanded, brushing the rich violet folds.

"Are the seams—?"

"Never mind the inside, Irma. Nobody's a dressmaker here."

"It's lovely," I agreed, feeling the lush taffeta. "The cut suits you."

"It does. Now Sofia, pay attention." The child watched avidly as Molly pulled a pack of delicately painted cards marked "The Glories of Ireland" from her tapestry bag, followed by a brass-and-pasteboard contraption. "*This* is a stereopticon," she announced triumphantly. "You pick a card and put it in the holder. Like this one, the Bantry Gardens. Now look through the viewer here and slide the holder back and forth until you see one picture."

"Two pictures, two . . . one!" Sofia cried, her head pressed into the viewer. "Look, Mamma, you can almost touch the flowers! It's so beautiful!"

"Of course," said Molly primly. "It's God's own country." For the next hour, as Sofia busily studied and sorted the Ireland views, Molly described her latest plan: that I set up my doctor's office in a building she would buy near our house on Potrero Hill. When I reminded her that I still had another year at the university medical school, Molly only laughed, called me a peasant, and barreled ahead with her calendar.

The afternoon was shading into gold when Niko came home from his shop and joined us under the lemon tree. As Sofia eagerly showed off the new toy, he gave me an envelope, just arrived and pasted with Italian stamps. My eyes flew to Niko's; it was early for another Opi letter. Assunta wrote to us twice a year. At Christmastime she had not added her customary line on my father's good health. He was often tired lately, she said instead, and they had to hire a village boy for the shearing. I fingered the envelope, weighed and turned it over in my hands.

"It's not a telegram," Niko observed, "so there could be good news."

"Open it, Mamma," Sofia prompted eagerly, "and read it to me."

I slit the envelope with Niko's penknife, unfolded the thin, faintly crackling paper and scanned the few lines. My hands shook.

"Sofia, let's take a walk," I heard Molly say quietly. "You can show me the sheep. Just don't let them dirty my new dress. Then I'll make you some proper tea." We watched Sofia skitter away, red-brown curls swirling, as Molly followed, lifting her skirt over the high grass.

"What does Assunta say?" Niko asked.

"That my father has great pain in the chest like a weight," I translated. "He gasps for breath and barely eats." I fingered the paper edge.

Niko sat beside me. "What does the doctor say?"

"He wouldn't see a doctor. He wouldn't have told Assunta of the pain until it was very great and she wouldn't have written until the end was very near."

"In Kos it's the same," he said quietly. Yes, last year the letter describing his mother's sickness had come the same day as the telegram announcing her death. Niko took my hand. "But you could go back for a visit if you want, Irma. We can afford it. A Nob Hill banker just paid for a grand redwood staircase. The shop is busier all the time. If you take an express train to New York and a steamship to Italy, in two weeks you could be there." Two weeks! How astonishing to retrace the long journey so easily. "You won't have classes again until September," he reminded me, "and I can keep Sofia; she's happy here in the summer."

This was true. Sofia loved playing in our orchard, feeding the sheep and watching Niko in his shop, where he had built a little house for the family of dolls that required her constant care. Molly would take her on carriage rides, to parks and concerts, ice-cream parlors and toy stores. She would be well cared for. I brushed flecks of sawdust from Niko's ruddy arm. I would miss my husband and daughter so much—a single day without them would be hard to bear. As if I had spoken, Niko took my hands in his. "We'll be here, Irma, waiting for you, we'll be like the olive trees. If you need to go to Opi, go."

But would my going truly help my father? The "weight" in his chest was likely a tumor and beyond all cure. I could bring him morphine for the pain and attend his deathbed as I had done for my mother, as I could not do for Zia Carmela. Perhaps in lucid hours he might even tell stories of the years when he was young. He might say that he was proud of me. In the end I could close his eyes like any dutiful daughter. But Assunta had written the letter weeks ago, and weeks ago he was barely eating. He was slightly built for all his strength, and sickness would have wasted him to bone. Any doctor could tell me what I already knew: that I had little hope to see my father living, even if I left that day. Assunta was faithfully there, so he would be lovingly attended. Death would find him in his own bed, perhaps peaceful at last.

Still, how would it feel to be home again? I could walk the streets of Opi that I knew so well, hear once again the familiar accents of my own name, watch fog lift over our valley, smell the pines under a star-sprayed sky and visit Zia's grave. Assunta would be glad to see me; I could meet my half sister Luisa and bring her presents from America. But who else would truly greet me? The mayor's wife had died and her daughter gone to live with cousins. Perhaps others from our village were already in America. For the cost of second-class passage home I could send Luisa to school in Pescasseroli with a coat and leather shoes like any city girl.

If I went to Opi now, the cut and cloth of my dress, the twist of my hair, even my way of walking might set me apart. Everyone would be polite, for I had once been one of them. But still the men would watch me askance, and even women would keep a wary eye on "L'Americana," who could not know Opi's new tapestry of births, marriages, deaths, joys and sorrows, and who might even play the grand signora with them. In the church piazza where we gathered in long summer evenings, those who once knew every movement of my day would ask how long I would stay in Opi, and any answer I could give—a week, a month, a season—would only betray what I had become, a stranger passing through their lives.

And yet if I did not go to Opi, as surely it was useless to go, how could I endure the inevitable telegram announcing my father's death? I buried my face in my hands.

"Come with me, Irma," said Niko. "Let's walk a little." So we went, as we often did at twilight, to a rocky ledge looking over San Francisco Bay and sat close together watching blue melt to violet above the darkening waves, that brief cut of water before the land that rolled east to the great ocean. We would never return to Kos or to Opi, for they held no more place for us, and yet they were home, woven deep in our flesh.

Acknowledgments

I am grateful to many people for the creation of this book. Barbara Dewey, dean of the University of Tennessee Library, granted me the post of Writer in Residence, providing time, research materials and writing space. Robert Stewart published "Threads on the Mountain," the short story that became the novel's first chapter in *New Letters*. Giuseppe Trautteur's warm response to that tale set in a region he knows so intimately afforded the confidence to continue. As the novel grew, I shared chapters with members of the Knoxville Writers Guild fiction group and constantly profited from the perceptions of Carole Borges, Jackson Culpepper, Bob Cumming, Maria de la Orden, Julie Gautreau, David Joyner, Cathy Kodra, Bonny Millard, Alan Sims and Don Williams. Andrew Rasenen's unerring editor's eye caught issues large and small, presenting each critique with graceful precision as well as helping with the accuracy of the San Francisco scenes. Shannon Burke, writer and friend, gave calming perspective on the publishing process, and Roz Andrews provided expert copyediting for no more recompense than a pasta dinner.

Any work of historical fiction has a manic thirst for information.

Naturally, this book draws on a wide range of print and digital sources. A few people were invaluable. First, Karen Schoenewaldt for her historian's view of the immigration process, research suggestions, careful readings for historical accuracy and at every stage being a marvelous sister. Karmen Crowther of the University of Tennessee Library guided me to a horde of data on nineteenth-century wages and prices in the United States and Italy. The Knoxville Center for Reproductive Health and Safe Haven Center provided insight on the trauma of sexual assault. Dr. Paul Barrette offered background on the Alsace region. For gracious unfolding of Greek culture and Web site magic, I thank JoAnn and Yiannis Pantanizopoulos.

Agent Courtney Miller-Callihan of Sanford J. Greenburger Associates was simply perfect in every ramification of that role. I owe much of the final shaping of the novel to her sympathetic, knowing eye. Editor Amanda Bergeron and the entire staff at HarperCollins steered the project with enthusiasm, deft skill and buoyant energy.

Maurizio Conti

About the Author

PAMELA SCHOENEWALDT lived for ten years in a small town outside Naples, Italy. Her short stories have appeared in literary magazines in England, France, Italy, and the United States. She taught writing for the University of Maryland–European Division and the University of Tennessee, and now lives in Knoxville, Tennessee, with her husband, Maurizio Conti, a medical physicist, and their dog, Jesse, a philosopher.

THE HISTORY BEHIND THE STORY

CREATING IRMA

The inspiration for *When We Were Strangers* began with the realization that I am an exceptionally lazy cross-country skier. When we lived near Naples, Italy (1990–2000), dear friends, Ezio and Anamaria Catanzariti, invited us to come skiing with them in Abruzzo. We would rent a house in the tiny mountain town of Opi, which the Catanzaritis were sure we'd love for its magnificent vistas, the courtesy of the people, and quiet, mountain-hugging streets, a welcome change from the constant clang of Naples. I had concerns about the skiing element, but the rest sounded wonderful. We reached Opi at night, shrouded in somber darkness. The landlord unlocked a tiny, spotless house, lit the wood stove, assured us that anything we could possibly need was in Opi stores (all owned by people directly or intricately related to him), admonished us to keep the wood bin filled, wished us good night and disappeared into the silent street.

In the clear winter morning, the slightly larger valley town of Pescasseroli still lazed in shadows. Only a few kilometers below, it seemed another world from our airy perch. In the next few hours, I made the melancholy discovery that cross-country skiing in Abruzzo involved exhausting climbs and what for me were terrifying descents. That afternoon, while Ezio, Anamaria, and my husband, Maurizio, planned yet more adventurous routes, I made the generous offer to go back to Opi, get more firewood and do the shopping for our dinner.

Thus began a satisfying routine. After a few desultory hours on the slopes, I returned alone to Opi, making the rounds of baker, vegetable and fruit dealer, cheese seller, wine store, butcher and other diminutive shops which, in fact, had all we needed of non-foodstuffs. Everyone was helpful, even kind, but polite inquiries about where I was from and what I did there seemed to invite no lengthy response: Naples was as far away and insignificant as America—or Pescasseroli. *This* place, this tiny clutch of houses on the ramping spine of Abruzzo, was all that really needed to be known.

I sat in the dim, very cold church, wrote a little in the sunny, equally cold piazza, and walked the few hundred meters to the sudden edge of inhabitation, where footpaths and sheep trails began. A small child could circle Opi without tiring. Like most mountain regions of Italy, Opi has suffered a steady depopulation since the end of the nineteenth century: poverty, cold, and the utter lack of opportunity for young people were too much to bear. Looking more closely at the narrow stone houses, I began to notice keystones with dates in the 1890s. What spark of wealth made its way up this mountain to spur a building boom? Ah, of course, money from American relatives. What was their story? How many ever saw the houses their money had built? What had these emigrants felt, walking down the steep, rutted path from Opi to Pescasseroli and on to an America?

In the next days, my musing slowly coalesced on a single imagined figure: a young woman, neither pretty nor wealthy. Street-level windows in Opi invariably featured starched white cotton half curtains in cutwork or lace. Was she a needleworker? Yes, precisely so. I named her Irma after an older woman from Abruzzo I knew. My Irma would have been as intricately bound to every Opi family as our landlord, and yet I always imagined her alone on the piazza, standing against the sunset at the edge of town, hurrying back from the bakery on a frosty morning, warm bread held close to the chest, or disappearing into one of the smaller stone houses whose door was rough planks nailed to a wooden Z. Surely Irma loved Opi, knowing no other world. Like our landlord she must have assumed that it held whatever a person could want. Then I imagined her walking down the main street in Opi with every branching path blocked, leaving only a narrow road down the mountain. At that time I had no idea what, precisely, blocked each option for staying, but I knew that she left and left alone, and I believed this uneducated, inexperienced young woman with a slim packet of worldly skills did somehow endure her leaving.

Once back in Naples, other writing projects drew me from Opi and Irma but I kept my notes. For years she was quietly there, wrapped in a cape at the edge of Opi, silhouetted against a blue-purple sky. Finally I began to do research on needlework, emigration and conditions in Abruzzo in the 1880s. But for a fundamental quality of Irma—her being a stranger in America—I used my own experience of a decade lived in Italy. I was happily married, had a job I liked and was fluent enough in Italian to be earning some money from translating. My neighbor swore she felt closer to me than to her own sister. Yet I overheard her speaking of me as "L'Americana" as if I had no name. Once when she was lamenting some particularly onerous housekeeping chore, I said I didn't do *that*. "Oh Pamela," she scoffed, "what *you* do doesn't count. You're not from here. You might as well be an extraterrestrial." So there I was, her sister, and yet, fundamentally E.T., a stranger, no matter how long I stayed.

Apart from the millions forced from home unwillingly by economic, natural, or man-made disasters, many of us pass some of our lives as strangers. To go to college, to change jobs, to move, even to change life circumstances, can put us in a new world in which no past skills are relevant. We feel labeled and unknown. Ironically, as in the immigrant communities that Irma knew, the company of other strangers is not altogether a solace. Nostalgia for *our* home, *our* food, *our* people can separate us from others with other longings. Yet, as Irma discovers, there is much to be learned from being strangers together.

When I went back to creating Irma's journey in earnest, first as a short story that ends as she leaves Opi, and then as a novel, I felt an astonishing closeness to her, a sureness of how she would feel, what choices she might make and what options she would refuse. Not that the writing was easy or quick or that I didn't endlessly revise, but there was always Irma, leading me on with her quick, light walk, leaving Opi and then pressing west after a constantly shifting dream until she finally attains a new home and new company of cherished strangers in the California hills.

—Pamela Schoenewaldt

ON WRITING *WHEN WE WERE STRANGERS*

Q: When We Were Strangers explores Irma's journey from Italy to America—from girl to woman—and on a wider scale examines the human condition and the common threads that unite us all. How did you keep all these elements in play?

I knew from the first that Irma would begin in fairly self-absorbed innocence, become traumatized in Chicago and that out of that trauma, that very dark place, she would find a guide back to the light, to a resurrection of the self that would be more other-directed. I had lived in San Francisco before moving to Italy and liked the idea of Irma's voyage ending there, but also the westward journey worked for me. While writing the early chapters I chanced to see an oil by Corot in the Brooklyn Museum: *Young Woman of Albano*. It was painted about ten years before Irma leaves Opi. The woman's downward gaze, her self-possession, and the curve of her hand on her bodice spoke to me of Irma. I bought a postcard of the painting and kept it propped above my computer, imagining a scar on her face, just out of view. I also had a postcard of trunks piled up at Ellis Island. These two images—Irma and her baggage—marked for me the specificity of her character, and it does seem to be true that specificity, if deeply felt, can be a path to expressing our commonality.

In the same way, I think that a metaphor like "the journey" can be pointless and flat if the particular quality of *a* journey is not articulated. As noted elsewhere, I spent a good deal of time researching and imagining Irma's physical world—and the details of that world that would imprint themselves on her. I also worked hard to create real characters around her, people with journeys and stories of their own. That practice prepared the way for one of the most difficult scenes, when Irma confronts the humanity of Jake. It would be so much easier for her to objectify and abuse him as he has objectified and abused her. That meant, of course, that he can't be just "the rapist," but has to be someone with a past, with things he likes and dislikes and people who have other experiences of him. So Irma's encounters with the human condition have to be grounded in her experience of others *as* human, not Italian, Greek, Irish, American, etc., but people on a journey, as she is, as we are.

Q: You've said you became very close to Irma as you wrote her story. Did this make describing some of the more difficult or traumatic aspects harder to put on the page?

Yes, for sure, and I don't see any way around that pain of identification. You have to imagine a scene very graphically to write about it, press your face into it and feel what the characters would feel. Perhaps there are other ways to write but I don't know them. To pick a milder example, I'm fairly claustrophobic, so describing life in the hold of the *Servia* was uncomfortable; the storm at sea was worse. Irma's trauma in the ruins of the Chicago fire was so hard to write that I had to do it many times, each time forcing myself back to that house, observing more, listening more closely, using more senses. I even felt guilty for "letting" Irma go there, for not warning her. A character can feel like your child whom you want to protect, not only from the outside world but also from any weakness in herself. But fiction writing is not about being a hyper-protective parent, and members of my writing group warned me more than once against creating a chronicle of Saint Irma. She did things she wasn't proud of—like stealing from the Missus— and I had to let that happen, just as the rape had to happen. It was part of who she was, the situation she was in, her complex of choices and the journey that was hers to take.

Q: You don't shy away from exploring difficult issues. Irma's decision to have an abortion was a major event in her journey and could draw criticism from some readers. What would this choice have meant in the context of her time—particularly for someone with her religious upbringing?

Irma's decision is difficult and she struggles unsuccessfully to find an alternative. Clearly the church did not condone her choice, but in the nineteenth century, abortion wasn't the public policy issue it is today. The frequency of abortions varied through the century, but generally, control of fertility was a woman's concern. Perhaps Victorian reticence added to the silence. In Irma's time, abortionists were rarely prosecuted except in cases of willful harm. In many ways these weren't "the good old days." Without effective contraceptives, it wasn't uncommon for a sexually active woman at any social level to have multiple abortions in her childbearing years, as well as resorting to home treatments ranging from useless and bizarre to deadly. State-funded welfare systems were decades away and many orphanages warehoused children for "adoption" into servitude. Childbirth was so dangerous that termination of unplanned pregnancies often seemed preferable to risking death and leaving one's children motherless. Dangerous concoctions, like Dr. Bronson's Infallible Cure, were sold openly in magazines to "restore regularity" or "remove obstructions." Readers interested in this subject may want to read Janet Brodie's excellent study, *Contraception and Abortion in Nineteenth-Century America*. However, this is all sociological background. Like the decision to leave Opi, Irma does not make her choice lightly or without pain. As a writer, all I could do was to present as clearly as possible her situation and the wholeness of her person and hope that readers see Irma's course as consistent with who and where she is.

Q: Considerable research went into the careful detailing of everything from Irma's passage to medical knowledge of the time period. How did you approach this task?

I was fortunate to have begun my research when I was Writer in Residence at the University of Tennessee Libraries. My sister holds a doctorate in immigration history and she led me to classic works like Philip Taylor's *The Distant Magnet: European Emigration to the United*

States. I read a good deal in English and Italian on the economic situation in Southern Italy at that time. The Special Report of the Chief of the Bureau of Statistics produced in the 1880s gives a wealth of information on costs of consumer goods and wages (as well as recondite data, like the contribution of human hair to the GNP of various European countries and a U.S. importer's evaluation of the "moral fiber" of Venetian glassblowers. I couldn't work in this last factoid, but readers will be relieved to know that their fiber was excellent.). For background on ranges of reaction to sexual abuse I interviewed professionals in a rape crisis center and a women's clinic. Having lived in southern Italy for ten years helped, of course. I visited Opi several times, lived in a small town with some of Opi's insularity, and studied Italian at a school near Piazza Montesanto in Naples, where Irma was so overwhelmed by the exuberant chaos of that city.

Q: When We Were Strangers *grew out of a short story. Can you describe that initial project and what made you return to it?*

I published a short story in *New Letters* called "Threads on the Mountain," which is the basis of this novel's first chapter and ends with Irma leaving Opi. I always liked the story and after a difficult and unsatisfying experience with another fiction project, I began wondering what happened to Irma after she left Opi. The arc of the novel, her journey across America and metamorphosis from needleworker to medical worker, came to me in one piece and a few years ago I started to research and then write. The short story genre demands a very quick establishment of place and character, which was helpful when I began the novel, since Irma's character was so clearly in my mind: her strengths, her standards, her fears and native wit. Zia Carmela had a larger role in the short story and since we would be leaving her behind in the novel, I had to reduce that role, which was hard, since I had grown very fond of her. I suppose that's one of the costs of writing a journey-based novel like *When We Were Strangers*: there were so many characters that I grew fond of and curious about. Yet, like Irma, I had to leave them behind. Assunta, Attilio, Teresa, the Serbian girls, Lula, even the Missus, Jacob and his sisters—what happened to all of them?

Q: Some authors say they end up taking direction from their characters rather than the reverse. As you were writing did any characters or plot lines take on a life of their own?

Entrepreneurial Molly had a way of muscling herself into the plot and making herself indispensible in the same way that she managed more and more of Mrs. Gaveston's boardinghouse. I really hadn't imagined anyone like her when I started the Chicago section. Then she appeared, at first just to take away Irma's house-cleaning income, and then to become Irma's guide and prod. I think that many of Irma's sensibilities and values were truly opaque to Molly, but she is a good and loyal friend and essential to Irma's personal journey. At first I assumed that she would stay in Chicago while Irma went to San Francisco, but Molly thought otherwise and as you see, she came along and is there to the end, the "aunt" to Irma's child.

Q: Your characters are all so colorful, each with a story of his or her own. Were any inspired by people you've met or known?

There is an Italian expression, "boh," which translates to something like "darned if I know." Pieces of people come flying by, stick together with some mysterious glue, and a character takes shape. I wish that I understood the process better, but I can detect some sources for a few character qualities. Back to Molly, I think her calendars and constant writing, erasing, and refiguring in little squares remind me of my mother, who planned everything, even designed houses on tiny note-pads, as if paper were the rarest of commodities. The Missus was a bit like my first boss, a horrid woman who managed a rare books collec-tion. I had fantasies of infecting it with insects that ate old medical texts. Mostly, though, some detail of research would spark an image, or from the name itself a face would bloom. I'd write a paragraph or so about the person and then in subsequent passes over a passage or chapter, more and more qualities of that character would emerge, rather like a developing photograph. For example, I knew from the first that Madame Hélène, while generous and honest (unlike the Missus), was also emotionally repressed. But why? I saw her coming from Alsace, which was a coal-mining area in the nineteenth century. Thinking of life in the old mining towns near where I live now, in east Tennessee, I imagined her having seen far too many babies and young children die to want a family herself or even make one more baptismal gown that might become a shroud.

Q: Irma's female relatives saved and hid what would have been a small fortune for them—never touching it, even during years of hun-ger. Did you draw inspiration for these women, and the many others Irma meets along the way, from anyone in your own life?

My great-grandmother came to Iowa from Germany when she was sixteen to marry her brother's friend (just as Irma tells the immigra-tion officer she is doing). She told us of coming alone by train from

New York to Iowa, not speaking a word of English. A boy at a train station sold bananas and found it hilarious to watch foreigners try to eat the skin, so that's the origin of Irma's banana adventure. Her brother's friend was, by all accounts, a bitter, miserly man, but my great-grandmother learned English and found joy in farming and in her children. My grandfather was her favorite, but when he wanted to buy a small farm in Texas, she gave him money that she had somehow saved and secretly hidden from her husband. Like Zia Carmela sending Irma to America, it must have been so painful to watch him go.

Q: On a separate note, we've heard that you and your husband make a mean limoncello, any helpful hints for any of us would-be liqueur makers?

Well, since our utter fantasy is to fund a villa near my husband's city of Ancona on the Adriatic through limoncello production, I can only say that our recipe calls on the magic of seven (seven lemons, etc.) and requires large, unsprayed green lemons and straight grain alcohol. On vacation in the Caribbean, we once found the big green lemons and substituted strong rum. That was *not* a breakthrough limoncello. Stick with the straight stuff.

DISCUSSION QUESTIONS

1. Irma's practical skills and world knowledge seem so limited, even compared to those of her brother, Carlo. What abilities and traits help her navigate the difficult passages from Opi to Naples and then west?

2. Irma's mother devoutly believes that "If you leave Opi, you will die with strangers." How does this assertion shape Irma's experience and how does she ultimately refine it in a way that allows her to move forward in her journey? How does this family assertion compare to others you may have encountered?

3. Opi, real and remembered, is a powerful force for Irma's self-image and worldview. How does her conception of Opi change through the novel?

4. Unlike many fictional heroines, Irma has little interest in a romantic union. Why not, and what must change for her to have a satisfying intimate relationship?

5. At various times in her journey, Irma makes choices that she herself feels are at odds with the Irma Vitale that she "really is." Is she accurate in this assessment?

6. Irma Vitale is surrounded by immigrants as she makes her passage west. What various ways of relating to the "Old Country" are represented by these other immigrants, her "fellow strangers"?

7. Sofia gives Irma the option to leave Jake and Daisy's flat. Yet Irma stays. How does this choice reflect her changing sense of self since first encountering Jake?

8. Irma's profession evolves from needleworker to dressmaker and finally, surgeon. What inner changes parallel this evolution?

9. Today, as in Irma's time, many people live far from their birthplace for a variety of reasons. What pressures, challenges and supports seem universal about her experience?